My Name is

GAUHAR JAAN

Bangalore based historian, Vikram Sampath is the author of three acclaimed books: *Splendours of Royal Mysore: the Untold Story of the Wodeyars, My Name Is Gauhar Jaan: The Life and Times of a Musician* and *Voice of the Veena: S Balachander - A Biography*. Vikram was awarded the Sahitya Akademi's first Yuva Puraskar and the ARSC International Award for Excellence in Historical research in New York for his book on Gauhar Jaan. The book has also been adapted to theatre as a play "Gauhar" directed by Lillette Dubey.

Vikram was among the 4 writers and artists to be selected by former Honourable President of India Shri Pranab Mukherjee as a Writer-in-Residence, to stay at the Rashtrapati Bhawan in 2015.

With a PhD in history and music from the University of Queensland, Australia, he has been a Fellow at the Wissenschaftskolleg, Berlin; is an Aspen Global Leadership Programme Fellow, and an alumnus of the Australia-India Youth Dialogue. Vikram is also part of several Government Committees, has established the Archive of Indian Music, India's first digital sound archive for vintage recordings and is the Founder Director of the Bangalore Literature Festival.

Praise for *'My Name is Gauhar Jaan!'*

'Reading the book has opened a whole new world for me … Unquestionably Gauhar Jaan was a remarkable woman personality … what comes out of the book is the image of a very strong and vibrant personality … I commend Vikram for this fabulous job … I admire his skills as a researcher and his passion for the subject.'
—Shri M. Hamid Ansari, Honourable Vice President of India.

'The work done by Vikram is truly commendable and plugs a major gap in the history of Indian music. He has taken great pains to reconstruct the life of this famous singer from my home-town of Banaras.'
—Padmabhushan Girija Devi, eminent Hindustani vocalist
and Thumri singer.

'Vikram Sampath has produced a finely researched book on a forgotten artiste of huge talent, and in the process, given a lucid idea about the socio-cultural hence political values of the time … Sampath's book is scholarly, strong on musical, sociological and historical detail: It is written with respect and love. By the time one puts down the book, the heart is wrenched while the mind is rewarded.'

—*The Indian Express*

'In his compelling and admirably well-researched narrative, Vikram Sampath recreates the glory, the musical magic, the mercurial life and the painful last days of Gauhar Jaan. Given the amount one has to rely on anecdotal history, it is not easy to write a book about a musician of the past. Most books end up being hagiographies written by an acolyte or a boring series of facts. This one manages to navigate through the life of the artiste and also give glimpses into a very important time of cultural change — with respect to women, to musicians and to a cultural period when music was liberated from the confines of the kotha into the more democratic, accessible space of gramophone records. Sampath has done his research well.'
—*Times of India* review by Namita Devidayal, author of the 'Music
Room'

'With a heady mix of drama, romance and tragedy, hers is a story that makes for an epic telling… What makes the book significant are the appendices-a definite contribution to musical documentation.'

—*India Today*

My Name is

GAUHAR JAAN

LIFE AND TIMES OF A MUSICIAN

VIKRAM SAMPATH

RUPA

Published by
Rupa Publications India Pvt. Ltd 2012
7/16, Ansari Road, Daryaganj
New Delhi 110002

Sales centres:

Allahabad Bengaluru Chennai
Hyderabad Jaipur Kathmandu
Kolkata Mumbai

First published in hardcover in 2010

ISBN: 978-81-291-2058-8

Fourth impression 2023

10 9 8 7 6 5 4

The moral right of the author has been asserted.

Typeset by Mindways Design, New Delhi

Printed in India

For my loving parents, the pillars of my strength, without whom I wouldn't be what I am today!

Contents

Section 1: The Making of A Diva

Section 2: The Glory Years

Bakshega har gunaah woh isyaan sha aar ka; Behad hai reham bandon pe parvardigaar ka.
Tar daamani se apni nahin gham mujhe zara; Behar-e-karam hai josh pe aamarzagaar ka.
Hai khiffathe gunaah se meezaan mili hui; Palla giraan na hoga mere aitbaar ka.
Dekha jise woh shaagile gufoor hai; Nagma yahi chaman mein suna hai hazaar ka.
Malka hai jiske vird-e-zabaan naam-e-kibriya; Sadma na hoga usko lahad ke fishaar ka.

—BADI MALKA JAAN, *MAKHZAN-E-ULFAT-E-MALLIKA*

Every sin of even a habitual offender like me will be forgiven; such is the infinite grace of the Protector of this Universe.

I am steeped in sin, committed all through my life, of which I am terribly ashamed. But my condition doesn't baffle me because I know that the ocean of Mercy that my Almighty is, my sins too will be washed away.

On the Day of Judgement, the odds would be placed heavily against me due to my sins; but my sincere repentance born out of disgust for my acts of omission will see me through, my faith in His mercy will not be belied.

The entire cosmos, which is a garden of His creation, sings His praise. And when the All-merciful Creator sees that all my life, despite my sins, I have always had his praise on my lips; he will pardon me for sure.

Malka has always chanted His name all her life; she is not the one who would be tortured in her grave when her acts of this world are judged!

I have gone through the author's work on Gauhar Jaan. The author has done in-depth research by means of travelling to various places to collect data on her life. This indeed is a difficult task accomplished. Reading the author's work on Gauhar Jaan gave me a lot of happiness. It is so interesting that I feel that any music lover who gets his or her hands on the book will read it through in one sitting. The author's endeavour is indeed very praiseworthy as this historical truth has been very well presented by him in the book.

As a musician, I myself wasn't aware about most of the facts that the author has presented in his book about Gauhar Jaan and her era. Although it is difficult to describe, the author has made an honest and sincere attempt to take the readers a century back to the prevailing ceremonies of her era, her private life and her musical aspect.

After having seen the author's work I feel that now artists will have no need to worry, because enthusiastic music lovers and researchers like this author will revive the legendary musicians and their era by presenting them to the world from time to time for the benefit of mankind just as the author has done in the case of Gauhar Jaan. There is no doubt that what the author has portrayed about Gauhar Jaan's era is true as I too have witnessed some aspects of the same for myself.

I would like to add a few things from my end. Whenever any artist loses his love then his or her music tends to blossom with more depth and emotions. Artists should consider such situations in their life as a blessing in disguise by God. Similarly in Gauhar Jaan's case she is still remembered for her soulful music. As a matter of fact, thumris written by Gauhar Jaan like *Kaise Yeh Dhoom Machayi ...Arrey Kanhaiya Re* as well as thumris sung by her like *Jiyaa Mein Laagi Aaan Baan* are still sung today by many across India. However, in most cases the singers aren't aware that they are singing her compositions. Now with the author's initiative the world will recognize the thumris written by Gauhar Jaan. I too realised the same on reading the author's book.

In every era there were great musicians who had their own special travel mode. Gauhar Jaan was one of them. For instance, during the 1930-40's, other than Ustad Faiyaz Khan Saheb from Baroda no other musician had a two wheeler (a taanga). As Gauhar Jaan was exceptionally great in her time she used to commute in a Victoria buggy for which she even paid a fine.

By reading this book one thing that I understand is that Gauhar Jaan was certainly blessed with beauty and great musical talent and any artist who is blessed with the two is looked upon as an artist par excellence just like Gauhar Jaan, Zohra Bai and Kesarbai Kerkar to name a few.

—Pandit Jasraj

My introduction to Gauhar Jaan came by way of my father, Ustad Haafiz Ali Khan Saheb, who was a contemporary of hers. Gauhar Jaan was a legend even in her own life time and commanded a huge amount of respect in the music circles of the time. Trained as a baiji from an early age in Varanasi, then a centre for arts and culture, she soon settled and made a name for herself in Calcutta, known for its patronage of the arts.

Gauhar Jaan came to the limelight at a very significant moment in music history, with the invention of the gramophone record. When the science of recording was first made available it was not easily accepted by the great stalwarts of music at the time, who had grave doubts about the purity and sanctity of the music if it could be reproduced note for note at any time of one's choosing. It simply went against the grain. My own father was one of this school who could never come to terms with the possibility of his music being played out of context through a recording.

Gauhar Jaan, however, had no such reservations, and recognizing the potential of the gramophone went on to become one of the most prolific recorders of that time. She particularly excelled in, and perfected the art of condensing the essence of a thumri into the three minutes that the records could play at the time. The impact on Hindustani music must be phenomenal since she would have immortalized the musical styles of the many gharanas she learnt, and passed them on to many future generations of aspiring musicians and connoisseurs.

It is indeed a pleasure to find a young, dedicated writer like Vikram Sampath to research and 'resurrect' for us, so to speak, the colourful life of one of the most successful and historically important singers of this century. It is most creditable that he researches and writes from his own heart with no motive other than to share with his readers his passion for history and music. May he go on to write many more such books for us!

—Ustad Amjad Ali Khan

What can one say about the famous musical personality Gauhar Jaan! So much has been said—so many anecdotes about her defiant nature and so many of her records convey a lot about how unique, versatile and independent minded this great artiste was.

Hence the brave effort of Shri Vikram Sampath is indeed commendable.

The book on Gauhar Jaan, written in a lucid and incisive manner, indicates the strenuous efforts, meticulous care and thorough study that Shri Vikram Sampath has made to make the book both interesting and authentic.

I am sure the book will be well-received by many music lovers with keen interest. The insight gained would add to the knowledge that we have about the great masters, especially the great women musicians of our rich cultural past.

—Pandit Arvind Parikh

THE JOURNEY

The name 'Gauhar Jaan' first caught my attention when I was sifting through the musty, yet meticulously catalogued and maintained archives of the Mysore Palace, in the course of the research of my book *Splendours of Royal Mysore: the untold story of the Wodeyars*. The name had a certain ring to it that led me to go through the box-file containing the various letter correspondences that took place between Gauhar and the authorities of the Palace in the course of her short stay in Mysore. But the project that I was handling then was a mammoth one covering close to 600 years of a State's history. I really did not have the bandwidth, nor did I feel the need, to dwell deeper into the life of this visiting woman musician who spent barely two years in Mysore. A passing reference to her seemed sufficient. But somehow, I felt I had struck on familiar terrain.

Many years later, a few months after my book was launched in 2008, I happened to visit Mysore and Ooty. With the kind introduction of Smt Urmila Devi Kotdasanghani, a member of the royal family of Mysore, I met an affable old lady in Ooty called Mrs Ratna Chatterji. In her tastefully done up house set on a hillside, Ratna ji was a perfect hostess who treated me and my friend Siddharth, who accompanied me, to a sumptuous meal. I had gone there looking for the various linkages that existed between princely Mysore and the Bengal of those times, to include in a lecture that I was to deliver in Kolkata later that month. I was told that Ratna ji was a voracious reader and had some wonderful anecdotes and memories to share on this topic. Apart from the usual references to Swami Vivekananda whose Chicago trip was financed by the Maharaja of Mysore and Sarla Debi Chaudhrani, Tagore's niece, who spent many years there, the story veered around to the other familiar character whom I had chanced upon at the palace archives – 'Gauhar Jaan.' When I quizzed Ratna ji further about Gauhar's life, she gave us a Bengali book which had a few pages dedicated to this songstress. As Siddharth sat translating excerpts from the book I was initially astonished to know that a lady who bore such a distinctively Indian and Muslim name was not even an Indian by birth. The circumstances of her life and the several highs and lows she faced in her short, yet eventful life, really captivated my attention.

On the way back, as the bus zigzagged along the steep road, negotiating the sharp hairpin bends, I had gone silent and was mulling over the story of Gauhar that I had just heard. I decided on an impulse then to set forth on a journey to unearth more details about this long-lost musician.

There was a lull in my interest for several months thereafter. I had forgotten all about the resolve to delve deeper into the life and times of Gauhar Jaan and in fact comfortably set out on another project on aspects related to the history and growth of Carnatic classical music. But astonishingly the interest was unexpectedly revived and Gauhar somehow managed to hijack my attention. The internet has several articles on her and that was the first starting point to get an idea of the template of her life. Most articles were copies of the same source article written by a gentleman called Dr. Suresh Chandvankar, the honorary secretary of the Society of Indian Records Collectors (SIRC). His name rang a bell. I had met him several years back in Mumbai when invited by renowned singer Smt Shubha Mudgal for the launch of her company Underscore Records' production of Smt Kesarbai Kerkar's antique records. I was introduced to the pleasant and mild-mannered Dr. Chandvankar there.

I wrote to him seeking more details about Gauhar and almost immediately received a reply where he very readily agreed to share whatever information he had about the legendary singer. Incidentally when anyone is asked for information about Gauhar Jaan, they almost invariably point to this one-stop shop, Dr. Chandvankar. The SIRC has been doing a commendable job in preserving and meticulous chronicling of the musical wealth of our country. Within just two days of our first communication, I received a CD with select songs of Gauhar Jaan and a power-point presentation on her life that Dr. Chandvankar had made at the Asiatic Society. The packet included some of his articles and the journals of the Society that carried information on her discography. It was an immense treasure and a wonderful way to start off on a new voyage of discovery. As the first strains of her melodious renditions emanated from my DVD player, I was benumbed at the thought that I was listening to the first Indian voice that had left its imprint on a shellac disc! The modernity of the playing device could hardly take away the antiquity of the music. This was how Gauhar Jaan first romped into my house, in style!

From then on there was no looking back. I was seized with some strange energy and enthusiasm to go deeper into piecing together the different fragments of her life. With Suresh ji's pioneering work already done on her life and times, it initially seemed that there was precious little left for me to unearth and this led to many a frustrating moment. But I was convinced that there was more to her life and was determined to find the missing links. I wanted to bring back this ghost from the past into popular, modern discourse.

I thought I began with several handicaps. First of all I wasn't familiar with Kolkata, its culture, language and customs to attempt chronicling an era in that city's history seen in the background of my protagonist's life. Despite being a student of music all my life, I was a stranger to the world of Hindustani music, having trained in Carnatic music. But thanks to several books and the guidance of friends and well-wishers I managed to eliminate my unfamiliarity on both these counts to some extent.

Documenting the arts in India is perhaps one of the most difficult tasks a researcher can undertake. There are undoubtedly several musical treatises that have survived since ancient times. But we know so little about the nature and content of early performances, and more importantly about the lives of yesteryear musicians, that their personal lives and the challenges they faced have been completely lost. The self-effacing world of artists of those times ensured that the art was always bigger than the artist and the latter seldom merited detailed documentation. This is quite a contrast to the modern times where in many cases the indulgence with copious and aggressive public relations ensures a situation quite the contrary! Music therefore seldom has a history and survives largely through anecdotal memory. Neither the raconteurs nor the spicy gossip generated go into the persona of the musician and concentrate instead on flimsy, superficial details. The blame lies as much on these early musicians too for not having documented their own struggles, the highs and lows of their careers and basically what it meant to be a musician in that era. It reflects the Indian psyche which allows music to permeate every sphere and phase of life, but considers a documentation of it as unimportant. Music is to be heard, understood and enjoyed; what is there to write about it?

Paucity of information about the lives of women musicians is a particularly serious problem for researchers. Gauhar's life was no different, as I was to find out. For someone who was a celebrity and a rage across the country, whose pictures appeared on postcards and matchboxes manufactured in Austria, who was India's first voice to be etched on the shellac disc—is today almost forgotten and unacknowledged, even by Hindustani musicians. She walks the alleys of Hindustani music and its annals as a pale shadow. She however has a few admirers—old-timers and record collectors who value her work and speak about her in her heyday in superlatives.

While in Mumbai I also met up with a host of scholars and record collectors who gave me some valuable information about Gauhar—eminent musicologist and scholar Dr. Ashok Ranade, renowned author Mr Deepak Raja, curator and music lover Mr Kushal Gopalka and his exuberant friend Mr Vikrant Ajgaonkar among others. In fact I met Mr Vikrant in a road-side hotel, next to the Goregaon railway station, and without any inhibitions he went on to demonstrate various features of Gauhar's musical style by singing them aloud—much to the amusement of the passersby!

By and large it was the same set of stories and legends that went with her name that kept getting recycled in myriad ways and it became increasingly clear that I needed to go to ground-zero of her life—Kolkata. This city had made her the success that she was and this was where she spent the most part of her life. Mr Deepak Raja guided me to one Mr Nilaksha Gupta in Kolkata. He is the owner of the famed Signet Press and a distinguished music critic and writer himself.

Our initial email correspondences went totally haywire. Mr Gupta, a fastidious gentleman, perhaps thought of me as a rookie who had just caught some fancy for this woman from the past. He advised me sternly to first read what was up on the internet and then attempt to speak to him. He was in fact totally opposed to the very idea of writing a biography of Gauhar.

'Stick to analyzing her music, what is the use of writing about her or for that matter any other musician's life?' he had snapped back. Though this was not a very encouraging remark, I persisted. Perhaps my perseverance and relentless questioning eventually changed his attitude towards the project. What emerged thereafter was a completely transformed Mr Gupta who acquiesced to my requests and assisted me with an almost missionary zeal!

He offered to locate for me rare and obscure Bengali books and translate some relevant parts of them. I called him every day to discuss the various controversies surrounding her life and to try to crack the puzzle that it was getting to be. This discussion proved to be intellectually stimulating for both of us. Finally, I decided to make a trip to Kolkata as I knew it would be worthwhile. Battling the harshest summer the city had seen in many decades, I landed in Kolkata. There was also an impending Parliamentary election, one that generally paralyzes normal life in West Bengal! But Mr Gupta had planned my itinerary with amazing meticulousness and I managed to hit upon the right sources in a very short time.

When you ask anyone who a good source for musicians of yore is, they mention two names, Dr. Suresh Chandvankar and Dr. Amlan Dasgupta of the Jadavpur University. The music archives of the University are ranked among the best in the country. The documentation and preservation of music archives has largely been possible due to the passionate and untiring efforts of Dr. Dasgupta. I had the pleasure of having lengthy discussions with him too and he directed me to another friend of his, Mr Anindya Banerjee, an eminent sarod player and student of Late Ustad Ali Akbar Khan.

Kolkata had sizzled like a frying pan that day and I had also suffered a terrible heat-stroke and dehydration in the course of my stay there. A visit to Mr Banerjee's residence was the last halt in that city before I took the flight back to Bangalore. Just when the affable and friendly Mr Banerjee opened up his treasure trove of valuable documents on Gauhar Jaan, many of which shed important and hitherto unknown information about her early life and parentage, the weather dipped all of a sudden. A sudden storm broke out and there was some violent banging of the windows. Mr Banerjee and I looked at each other perplexed. Even for someone like me with a scientific and rational bent of mind that is not generally given to believing in spirits and ghosts, the incident appeared quite eerie. More so because something similar had happened just a few days back in Mysore when I re-visited the Palace archives with the special focus now on Gauhar. Even there as I sat benumbed seeing her hand-written letter, her signature and her hospital bills, violent winds blew all of a sudden threatening to blow away the entire file!

Information just kept pouring in from unknown and unheard quarters. I just had to seek something and my wish would be the Universe's command. Visits to Delhi and Rampur too were greatly fruitful. I could never forget my visit to the house of an ageing musician who had crossed 110, Mahapara Begum, in Rampur. She is perhaps the only surviving human to have seen Gauhar Jaan in flesh and blood. Almost all of Gauhar's other contemporaries have passed on. Seated on a *charpai* amidst scores and scores of great-grandchildren and their grandchildren, Mahapara Begum is an angry old woman! The memories of a bygone era and the indifference of the present makes her bitter, but her spirit is indomitable—quite a similarity, I thought, to my protagonist. Looking at me with great suspicion initially from a face crowded with wrinkles and in a voice barely audible, Mahapara Begum recounted some fantastic tales about this lady who was a proud inhabitant of the zenana of Rampur. The ice was broken in the course of the discussion. I had endeared myself to her and departed from there with a heavy heart, taking away a host of blessings. In fact, on my polite insistence she was kind enough to sing a couple of songs in the Rampur style and I wondered what a rage she must have been in her youth, when she sang at the Palace functions.

Several contacts from Darbhanga, Patna, Lucknow, Allahabad, Banaras—towns which had played significant roles in the life of Gauhar at various stages—lent a helping hand in some form or the other. For instance, Patna's Sri Gajendra Narayan Singh, musicologist and author, was kind enough to write out an almost 20 page letter in chaste Hindi on various aspects of Gauhar's life and career based on his own research on the topic.

This goodwill extended outside India as well. Ms Gesine Bottomley, librarian at the Institute of Advanced Study in Berlin was informed of my research by my mentor and well-wisher Prof Raghavendra Gadagkar of the Indian Institute of Science, Bangalore. She located material, especially relating to the Gramophone Company and its German agent William Frederick

Gaisberg who was the one who had spotted Gauhar's talent and recorded her. The greatest surprise however came from London.

There were numerous references to a collection of poems that Gauhar's mother, Badi Malka Jaan had composed. I was told about this *dewan* (collection) by Mr Pran Nevile, an eminent scholar and author whom I had met in Delhi. Mr Nevile has authored several books on the lives of the nautch girls of India. Malka's poems, composed in classical Urdu, were published as a dewan of Urdu poetry in 1886, titled '*Makhzan-e-Ulfat-e-Mallika*' or the 'Treasure of Mallika's love' and considered among the best poems of their times. They were deeply philosophical and introspective. While scholars were aware that such a book had been published, the work itself was untraceable in India. I decided to take a chance and asked my friends in London to check if the book was available in the British Museum and Library. I was thrilled beyond words when I received a mail a couple of months later from Ms Leena Mitford, the Urdu curator of the British Library, telling me that the book was found in her collection and that she would be happy to share the same with me! By sheer coincidence, Ms Mitford was due to visit Bangalore for a conference the following week and offered to bring a copy of it with her. I froze when she handed me the envelope with the much sought-for book, although not a word of the ornate script made any sense to me. The cover-page carried a photograph of Badi Malka Jaan, with a faraway, pensive look and all I could do was gaze at the photograph after thanking Ms Mitford profusely.

It was hectic thereafter hunting for scholars to translate both the enormous amount of literature in Bengali that I had collected from Kolkata, as also this new-found Urdu treasure. Mrs Raka Chaudhuri and Mr Anirvanjyoti Chaudhuri were strangers till the day I met them at their beautifully done-up flat in Cunningham Road, Bangalore. It was an instant connect as we shared common interests in history, music and literature and over the next few weeks, they painstakingly translated each and every word of those hitherto undecipherable volumes. Without them this book wouldn't be what it is today.

Urdu was however not that easy to deal with. But ultimately it was the goodwill and assistance of my teacher from Bishop Cottons Boys' School, Dr. Iqbal Ahmed that helped me in decoding the *Makhzan*. Through several evening sessions, coupled with some delectable snacks and interesting conversations, Dr. Iqbal introduced me to the beauty of the Urdu language in general and the verses of Malka Jaan in particular. I have no words to thank him for his kindness.

But the best was yet to come. I wanted to lay my hands on the court documents at the Calcutta High Court. These were documents related to the several cases that Gauhar fought in her stormy life and they would throw valuable light on her life and lineage. While I had the gist of those documents through the Bengali books that had been translated for me, I wanted to go over the originals myself. And that was a travail in its own right. I requested my advocate friend Mr Aditya Sondhi to help locate any information that would be of use for me and bulldozed my friend Siddharth to sift through the All India Reporter volumes in the National Library of Kolkata, hoping that something would emerge. But the documents kept eluding me and I was getting thoroughly frustrated. When I was in Kolkata, Mr Nilaksha Gupta had introduced me to Mr Shankarlal Mehta, an extremely helpful and affectionate gentleman. He had given me valuable leads in Banaras. On hearing about my predicament with the court papers, Mehta Uncle directed me to his friend Mr Sanjay Khannah. Sanjay is the great grandson of Shri Damodar Das Khannah (1889-1979,) fondly referred to in music circles as Lala Babu. An illustrious businessman, Lala Babu was a great patron of the arts and several singers like Gauhar Jaan, Malka Jaan Agrewali, Siddheshwari Devi, Vidhyadhari Bai, Rasoolan Bai, Badi Moti Bai and others were regulars at the soirees in his garden house. The All Bengal Music Conference, the All India Music conference and several other conferences and musical institutions owe their existence to Lala Babu's munificence.

True to family tradition, Sanjay is equally passionate about classical music. Even today he attends the *mehfils* or concert soirees arranged in the houses of erstwhile zamindaris of Pathuriaghata Ghosh's. Somehow my eagerness and energy seemed to rub off on Sanjay as well and he became equally possessed to unearth these documents.

A Bengali book titled '*Gauhar Jaan*' by a gentleman named Chitragupta was the first book in which there were references to these court cases. But for some strange reason, the author had not mentioned the case number or any other details that could have helped my advocate friend and others to trace case documents. Sanjay decided to look for Chitragupta. He approached the publishers of the book, through whom he came to know that unfortunately the author was dead. They however gave him the telephone number of his wife, Mrs Poorbi Gupta and Sanjay decided to call on her. Mrs Gupta was naturally suspicious of this strange visitor and his unknown friend from Bangalore who were seeking the original documents on which her late husband's book was based. Thanks to Sanjay's persuasion, she was convinced of our intentions and my conversation with her over the telephone while Sanjay was there made her finally agree to part with the originals. Within two days I was thrilled to receive all the documents from the Calcutta High Court that Sanjay had painstakingly catalogued—documents which were more than 120 years old!

There was another coincidence. One day, while I was sitting with Mrs Raka Chaudhury getting the Bengali books translated, she received a call from a friend in Allahabad, Mr Isaac Ghosh. At that point we were reading the chapter which had references to Gauhar's baptism and her parents' marriage in the Allahabad Holy Trinity Church. Strangely, Mr Ghosh's father was a pastor in that same Church and he offered to help in procuring the marriage register which had the details of the wedding of Gauhar's parents in 1872!

Noted author/historian and friend Mr V Sriram sent me a photocopy of Gauhar's compositions with notations in Tamil, which were published in Madras in 1912.

Mysore, the place where I began the journey was the last halt in my research. I was now desperate to locate records of the court cases there to wind up the research. Thanks to my friend and well-wisher Mr Mohan Deshraje Urs, we got all the information and also the Death certificate from the Municipal Corporation, courtesy the good offices of his sister-in-law and corporator Mrs Vidya Urs. My friend Vinay and I battled the sporadic rains and tried to locate Gauhar's house in Mysore, Dil Kush Cottage. We also made a visit to the Muslim Cemetery, the Kabaristan Committee, to try and find her grave. Sadly, we found none.

All through this long and exciting journey, my parents have been silent witnesses to this mania, and at the same time been tremendous pillars of strength. Not many mothers would perhaps approve of this kind of obsession for a *tawaif* or courtesan on the part of their young and unmarried sons!

Of course my mother thanked her benign stars that the *tawaif* in question was a dead one!

At the end of this hazardous, exciting and sometimes frustrating roller-coaster journey, I hope I have been able to throw some light on the life and times of one of India's most colourful and feisty musicians and bring her back into people's reckoning. I am still perplexed by the circumstances that drew me into this journey and the strange energy that I was seized with right through the exercise. Coincidences, unexpected offers of help, encouragement, all seem to suggest a supernatural power that willed me into taking up the story of 'Miss Gauhar Jaan.' It has been a personally rewarding experience and I sincerely wish that the readers will, at the end of this book, say, 'What a woman! What an age!'

Vikram Sampath
Bangalore, 2009

ACKNOWLEDGEMENTS

There have been numerous people who have lent their helping hands in the writing of this book and I wish to express my deepest sense of gratitude to all of them.

I am greatly indebted to His Excellency Shri Gopalkrishna Gandhi, Governor of West Bengal and His Excellency, Shri E.S.L. Narasimhan, Governor of Chattisgarh for the valuable inputs offered by them in my quest. My sincere thanks are also due to Dr. Karan Singh, Chairperson of the ICCR, for his precious suggestions and inputs.

This book has been blessed with messages from three musical legends of our country and I am greatly indebted to all of them— legendary Hindustani vocalist Pandit Jasraj ji, Sarod maestro Ustad Amjad Ali Khan Sahab and renowned Sitarist and President of the Indian Musicological Society Pandit Arvind Parikh for having kindly consented to bless this book with their scholarly words and affectionate blessings despite their busy schedules. I am equally thankful to the people who helped me get in touch with these great artists—Smt. Subhalakshmi Khan, Ms Durga Jasraj, Mr Deepak Raja, Mr Sandeep Das, Mr Shashank Subrahmanyam, Mr Subrahmanyam, Ms Shanthala Subrahmanyam and Mr Anand Lalwani.

I am also very thankful to the following people without whom this project would not have materialized—Dr. Suresh Chandvankar, Honorary Secretary of the Society of Indian Records Collectors, Mumbai, Mr Nilaksha Gupta, Mr Anindya Banerjee, Mr Sanjay Khannah, Mr Deepak Raja, Ms Leena Mitford of British Library, London, Smt Minakshi Mishra of the Indian Council for Cultural Relations (ICCR), Prof Raghavendra Gadagkar of IISc, Bangalore, Smt. Sangeeta Kaul of DELNET, New Delhi, Princess Urmila Devi Kotdasanghani of the Mysore Royal family, Shri. Gajendra Narayan Singh of Patna and my friend Mr Siddhartha Nath.

I am also deeply indebted to the late Mr Chitragupta and his wife Mrs Poorbi Gupta. It is thanks to the tireless efforts of the late author during his lifetime that important documents related to Gauhar entered public domain for the first time. It is immensely kind of Mrs Gupta to have trusted the intentions of a stranger and parted with such valuable information.

My sincere thanks are also due to the following organizations for the help rendered at various stages of my research—the National Archives of India, New Delhi, Sangeet Natak Academy, New Delhi, the Asiatic Society in Mumbai and Kolkata, the National Centre for Performing Arts in Mumbai, ITC-Sangeet Research Academy, Kolkata, the National Library, Kolkata; Statesman Archives in Kolkata, the Divisional Archives in Mysore, British Library in London, the Institute of Advanced Study in Berlin, the Indian Institute of Science and its Centre for Contemporary Study, the Centre for Study of Culture and Society in Bangalore, the Roja Muthaiah Research Library in Chennai, the Rampur Raza Library and the NFAI, Pune.

This book would have been impossible but for the invaluable translation assistance that I received from several people. I am deeply touched by the sincere efforts put in by the following in this regard: Mrs Raka Chaudhury and Mr Anirvanjyothi Chaudhury, Dr. Iqbal Ahmed, Ms Tahera Noorani, Mr Nilaksha Gupta and my friend Siddhartha Nath.

I owe my heartfelt gratitude to a host of people in various cities for having helped me at critical stages of this work.

• **Delhi:** Mr Rantideb Maitra, Mr Pran Nevile, danseuse Smt Shovana Narayan, Hindustani vocalist Smt. Shubha Mudgal, Mr Kiran Seth of SPICMACAY, Anshuman Jain, my friend and well-wisher; renowned Tabla artist and my brother Mr Sandeep Das, Ms Saba Dewan, Smt Charu Gupta, Mr Manna Srinivasan, the roving Editor of the Shruti magazine, Dr. Lakshmi Subramaniam, Prof Rita Ganguly, Jon Barlow, Kartikeya Misra and the extremely helpful librarian at Sangeet Natak Academy Smt. Swatantra Bagra.

- **Kolkata:** Smt. Arpita Chatterjee of ITC SRA, Dr. Amlan Dasgupta of the Jadavpur University, Mr Ashim Mukherjee, Mrs Bose and Mr Sunil Kumar Debnath--all of the National Library, Dr. Amit Kumar Roy, Mr Tayeb Khan, Smt. Iti Misra, Pandit Vijay Kichloo, Dr. Bharati Ray, Shri Shankarlal Mehta and his entire family, Mrs Gargi Nath, Mr Sarkar and Mr Vishweshwaran of the Karur Vysya Bank, Prof Janaki Nair and my friend and talented Hindustani vocalist Sounak Chattopadhyay and his wonderful parents.

- **Mumbai:** Mr Kushal Gopalka, Mr Vikrant Ajgaonkar, Dr. Ashok Ranade, eminent film-maker Shri Shyam Benegal, Hindustani vocalist Dr. Prabha Atre, Ms Shivani Gupta, Ms Lata Jagtiani, Ms Archana Anand, Mr Kishore Dixit, Mr Prakash Birude, my professor Dr. Uma Narain and Smt Soma Ghosh.

- **Bangalore:** Dr. U.R.Anantamurthy, Prof Siraj Hasan of the Institute of Astrophysics, Major General (Retd.) M.K. Paul, Ms Sumana Chandrashekar of the India Foundation for the Arts, Mr H.Y. Narayandutt, Smt. Arati Rao, Mr P.R. Dasgupta of the Bangalore International Centre, Smt. Bela Misra, Mr Gurjot Singh, Prof M. Nooruddin Sayeed of the Bangalore University, Prof Vishweshwara of the Jawaharlal Nehru planetarium, Ms Amrita Dhar, my advocate friend Mr Aditya Sondhi and Ms Srivalli Velan, Mr Lawrence Liang, Ms Radhika Misra, author and friend Ms Shinie Antony, Ms M.B. Rajani, musicologist Smt Pramila Lochan, journalists Smt Deepa Ganesh and Ms Aruna Chandaraju and my dear friends Srikrishna K.R and Sheila Bajaj. Special thanks to Smt Malini Rao and Mr Prabhakar for all their assistance at several stages of the project.

- **Mysore:** Mr Mohan Deshraje Urs, Corporator Mrs Vidya Urs, Mr Gavisiddhaiya, Archivist at the Divisional Archives, Dr. J.V.Gayathri, Dr. R. Sathyanarayana and Mr Vinay Parameshwarappa.

- **Chennai:** Mr Sundar of RMRL, Mr V. Sriram and eminent scholar Shri S. Rajam.

- **Rampur:** Nawab Kazim Ali Khan, Mr Shahid Mehmood, Sahibzada Jaffer Ali Khan and his daughter Ms Sanam Ali, Dr. W F Siddiqui and the pleasant and helpful staff of Raza Library and Smt Mahapara Begum, Master Imtiaz.

- **Banaras**: Rai Ananda Krishna ji and his son Mr Nawal Krishna Sharma and Mr Krishna Kumar Rastogi of the Sri Kashi Sangeeth Samaj.
- **Lucknow**: Mr Yogesh Praveen and Smt. Meera Mathur, Registrar of the Bhatkhande Sangeeth Vidyapith.
- **Allahabad**: Mr Isaac John.
- **Darbhanga**: Prof Hetukar Jha, Dr. N.K. Singh of Darbhanga L M University History Department and Prof Dharmendra Kumar.
- **Muzaffarnagar:** Mr Amit Kumar Verma.

None of my efforts would have materialized without the unflinching support that I got from my ever-loving and encouraging parents. It requires patience and determination of another kind to see and allow one's son tread a path of obsessive indulgence! My other great sounding board and support has been my guru Dr. Jayanthi Kumaresh who gave a patient hearing to all my frustrations and motivated me on the path of this work. I in fact owe my humble regards to all my gurus and mentors in music, who have shown me the beauty of this art in various forms: Vidwan D.V.Nagaraj, Vidwan. Srivatsa D.S, Vidwan R.K. Prasanna Kumar, Vidushi Dr. Bombay Jayashri, Vidwan Akella Mallikarjuna Sharma Vidwan R. Kumaresh and Vidushi Dr. Jayanthi Kumaresh.

Thanks are due also to my editor Smt Keerti Ramachandra for her suggestions and advice while editing the manuscript.

I would like to thank Mr Pramath Kiran for helping me with the production of the CD of Gauhar's select songs that comes along with this book; as also to Mr Darshan of Product Reach Pvt. Ltd, Bangalore for bringing the CDs out in such an aesthetic manner.

I am also thankful to my publishers Rupa & Co and Mr R.K. Mehra for reposing the faith in me. A special thanks to Ms Rashmi Menon of Rupa & Co for all her support.

But my respectful tribute and obeisance is due unto my spiritual Guru, Shri Shirdi Sai Baba and the Divine Grace without which not a single letter or word could have been written.

Lutf hai kaun si kahani mein
Aap beeti kahoon ke jag beeti?

Which story would you find more pleasing?
Should I narrate the tale of the world or the one of my life?

SECTION 1

THE MAKING OF A DIVA

Mysore, August 1928

The benign presence of the picturesque Chamundi Hills, overlooking the well-planned and beautiful city of Mysore, seemed reassuring to its people. Nestled in the idyllic and serene surroundings of the Hills, *Dil Kush* Cottage was true to its name—an abode of happiness. The cottage was not a sprawling bungalow, but its appearance seemed to guarantee to its inmate everything that was required for a comfortable and even a fairly luxurious life.

A horse-driven carriage drove up the road leading to *Dil Kush*; a road that had a stunning canopy of bougainvillea bushes in full bloom. The carriage stopped right in front of the cottage. The *gandabherunda* symbol, the mythical two-headed bird that was the royal insignia of Mysore's ruling house, on the carriage implied that it carried a royal guest. It did. From the carriage emerged a stout, slightly hunched and bespectacled lady in her fifties, supported by two of her companions. One was a young woman and the other a bearded gentleman in a skull-cap. The man quickly got into action and started directing the movement of the luggage into the cottage. 'Rahman Miya! Please handle the packages carefully, they carry some fragile and precious porcelain crockery,' the old lady instructed.

The old woman looked around, thrilled by the scenic beauty around this little cottage and stood there appreciating the loveliness of the surroundings and listening to the chirping of the singing birds in the garden. Closing her eyes, she puffed out her nostrils and took a deep breath, filling herself with the fragrance of the jasmines that Mysore was so famous for. Involuntarily, she muttered a prayer, 'Allah! Make this my last destination. I cannot travel any more. I need rest, I need shelter, and I need your mercy!' With slow faltering steps she entered the house with the help of the young woman.

The inside of the cottage was already done up. Huge chandeliers hung from the ceilings, expensive carpets, large teak and rosewood chests with mirrors, exquisite paintings, delicate furniture, a writing desk and a majestic Victorian table on which stood a stately gramophone with a gleaming horn adorned the room. She suddenly realised that she had not yet read the memo that had been handed over to her, by the Palace Durbar Bakshi Mr Urs, a little while ago. She opened her purse, took out the memo and adjusted her gold-rimmed reading glasses to read it. Her gaze fixed on one of the lines which read '....*appointed a Palace musician on a pay of Rs 500/- per mensem (inclusive of salaries of her musicians and accompaniments) with effect from the 1ˢᵗ August 1928.*'

The tranquil expression on her face changed and she turned livid with rage. Throwing away the memo she snapped, 'Five hundred rupees? What do they take me for? A whore? Oh, Sheriffen! Do you know what my income used to be in my heyday?' The young woman muttered a barely audible retort accompanied by a cynical smirk. The man was too busy shifting and assembling the trunks that were part of the vast amount of baggage, to pay any attention. In fact both of them were accustomed to these swinging moods of the ageing woman to pay them any heed. Their indifference annoyed the old lady even more and she screamed, 'Ya Allah! Am I to live with these ghosts in this huge house, who don't even bother to talk to me?'

Suddenly her eyes caught the mirror and she was aghast at what she saw there. Getting closer she sat down in front of it, and looked closely at the dishevelled self staring back at her. The wrinkled face, greying hair, dark circles around blank and expressionless eyes, the streaks of grey in those curved, arched eyebrows that joined each other on a broad, fair forehead, shocked her. 'Is this really me?' She was unrecognizable even to herself. Even as she continued to examine her face, her thoughts were interrupted by a sudden thud from inside.

'You wretched fiend, what have you dropped?' she screamed and hobbled inside. In her excitement to set up things quickly, the maid had dropped a package of gramophone records that now lay scattered on the floor. The old lady's face turned red with rage. '*La Haul Vilaquwwat*! You despicable, artless woman, do you even realise what you have dropped? They are the sum total of my entire life and whatever it is worth...' Hurling a string of abuses on the hapless maid, she picked up the package and caressed them like a child. She pulled herself to the other room to check if they had been damaged in the course of her long journey to the city and this careless act of her maid. She randomly picked a record and played it on the gramophone that rested so majestically in the drawing room. As the grooves of the record moved under the needle, a young, sultry, melodious and piercing voice struggled through:

Aan baan jiya mein laagi,
Pyari Chit kyun diya, aan basi kaise phasi
Padan laagi chhab ke paiyyan, Meherban saiyyan
Tum bin mohe kal na pade, tumhare kaaran jaagi
Aan baan jiya mein laagi.

The sweet dadra in Raga Gara turned her stomach. Her eyes welled up. The fragrance and the embrace of Amrit Keshav Nayak and those heady days at the Mahalakshmi racecourse in Bombay swirled in her mind's eyes. She hugged herself in a tight embrace.

As the record drew to a close there emerged a shrill and flirtatious voice dipped in child-like mirth that proudly announced 'My name is Gauhar Jaan.'

Envy of the carefreeness of that voice and the memories of the past made her break down completely. The dam that held back her tears just burst open. Sobbing loudly and inconsolably, even as the surprised maid and steward stood frozen in their positions, she fell on her knees lamenting 'Oh! Gauhar! Oh Gauhar! What have you done to yourself?'

Khilaaf samjha sada meri sacchi baaton ko,
Rakeeb jhoot bhi bole tho aithbaar kiya.

Every true word of mine, my beloved disbelieved
But alas! The most blatant lies of the enemy were completely trusted!

—Badi Malka Jaan, Makhzan-e-ulfat-e-Mallika

꧁꧂

1

THE EARLY YEARS

Azamgarh, 1850

The township of Azamgarh on the banks of the river Tons was founded in the year 1665 by a powerful landlord named Azam Khan who was subservient to the Mughal Emperor Shahjahan. Located about 86 miles from Allahabad and about 54 miles from the holy city of Banaras, this important town at the eastern end of the United Provinces is bounded by the districts of Gorakhpur, Jaunpur and Ghazipur. The fort and the bazaar in the town had been constructed by Azam Khan's brother Azmat.

Among the numerous British residents of Azamgarh was one Hardy Hemmings, an upright and sincere officer of the Army. He lived in a palatial bungalow known as *Neelkothi*.

The early British settlers came to India spurred by the spirit of adventure and a desire for glory and riches. While the country gave them ample opportunities to satiate their adventurous zeal, their domestic and marital lives suffered. The long and tortuous journey from England to India deterred many English women from accompanying their husbands and lovers. Those who did come remained in the cities where they landed, while their husbands were posted in far-flung areas on their assignments. Moreover the original charter of the East India Company forbade women from accompanying husbands on action stations. A statistic of the 18th century underlines this gaping imbalance in sex-ratio—there were only 250 European women in Calcutta while the menfolk's tally stood at 4000. The situation was more or less the same in all other major British cantonments. Hence it was a common practice for both civilians and soldiers to take native wives and mistresses.

This led to the concept of the *bibi*—an Indian mistress, common-law wife or a long-term consort of Englishmen cutting across ranks. This worked favourably for even those Englishmen who could not afford to set up a modest establishment in India. The ones who did manage to bring their European consorts found it difficult to maintain them. While a European wife cost her husband about Rs 5000 a month, an Indian mistress' upkeep was relatively more affordable at Rs 40 per month. Thus, economics too seemed to influence this decision of keeping Indian *bibis*. These native beauties were greatly sought after by the British because of their dusky good looks, their gentle features and limbs, and because they were known to be very efficient homemakers. Besides, they were reputed for utmost fidelity to their benefactors. Thus a *bibikhana* or the lady-house in a corner of the compound, separate from the main house, became a regular and accepted feature in many a European bungalow. Interestingly these liaisons were never looked down upon by the local populace. A woman who came under the 'protection' of a British *sahib* was in fact respected by the natives. The liaison helped the *sahib* to acquaint himself with local traditions, customs, culture and languages. It was therefore a mutually beneficial relationship.

Both parties knew that impermanence was inherent in the relationship. They were mostly under an agreement which ceased when the regiment left the station to return to England. Poignant pictures have been painted by contemporary artists of *bibis* standing desolate by the shores even as the ship carrying the men who fathered their kids sailed away to a distant land. But a woman entering into such an arrangement was aware of the inevitability that would stare at her some day.

All this changed in the mid-19th century with the opening of the Suez Canal and the increasing use of steam ships. The journey to India became easier and less time-consuming and bigger ships began to ply on this route. Utilizing the opportunity, hordes of starry-eyed, young English girls scrambled to the ships that were India-bound to get to this 'dream country' in search of an eligible suitor. This phenomenon began to be known as the 'Fishing fleet' expedition and its availability made the marriage market of India an exciting dream for thousands of British girls. The news of the arrival of these vessels generated great excitement among hopeful bachelors and the possibilities that each shipload might offer were hotly discussed. Those who were free rushed to the parties organized by the captains of the ships and well-known women of the locality to welcome these beauties. These parties went on for three to four nights in a row and were the common feature of the ribaldry and merriment that followed the arrival of each fleet. All the bachelors, young and old, attended these parties to inspect the 'latest cargo' and try their luck. Every feature, every limb and mannerism of the lady would be scrutinized. The girls on their part looked around for the wealthiest and most accomplished suitor. Many a times greed would drive them into marrying a man twice or three times their age, resulting in life-long misery and suffering. Matches were made on the spot and the pastor was summoned to solemnize the union as soon as he could. Those unfortunate damsels who did not manage to find a suitor returned to England dejected and frustrated. The ships carrying them back began to be known as 'Returning empties.'

During the times of Hardy Hemmings, the 'Fishing fleets' had not yet made their entry in to India. He therefore picked up a young, gentle and petite Indian lady, Rukmani as his *bibi*. She converted to Christianity and was officially baptized as Mrs Elijah Hemmings. Rukmani ran the household with quiet efficiency and Hemmings was quite devoted to her. The two shared a sense of mutual respect and admiration. In a couple of years they were blessed with two lovely daughters. The older, who was christened Adeline Victoria Hemmings, and nick-named Biki, was born in 1857. The younger one was named Bela. The father doted on both girls.

Everything was going really well until Hardy suddenly passed away. Rukmani was devastated by his untimely demise. The temporary nature of the relationship meant that Rukmani and her daughters had no property rights and were left to fend for themselves. Rukmani was reduced to working as a daily wage labourer in a dry-ice factory in the town to support herself and her two little daughters. After having led such a cushioned and comfortable life, it was a period of intense struggle for Rukmani.

As a result of their financial condition, the girls were deprived of a formal education. But Biki was naturally bright and had a flair for poetry. She would compose small verses, almost impromptu, much to the surprise and delight of her mother and the people around her. Biki also had a sweet and melodious voice, though yet untrained.

Years rolled by and the family barely managed to sustain themselves through Rukmani's meagre earnings. One fine day, a young, handsome and gentle-mannered engineer of Armenian descent who had seen all of twenty summers, Robert William Yeoward, was appointed as the supervisor at the dry-ice factory where Rukmani worked. Rukmani's warm and motherly behaviour and her diligence at work naturally attracted his attention and soon a bond developed between the two.

One day Rukmani invited Robert to her house and introduced him to her two daughters. Victoria had inherited her father's good looks, fair-skin and sharp features and his suave charm. She was an extremely courteous and well-mannered young lady. Robert was instantly drawn to her and by the time he left the house he was infatuated enough to have thoughts of making her his wife. With much trepidation he approached Rukmani a few days later and sought her daughter's hand in marriage. Rukmani was delighted at the prospect of her daughter marrying such a well-placed and good-looking man. Victoria too had developed a secret liking for the young visitor and therefore readily consented to the wedding.

On 10 September 1872, Rev. J. Stevenson of the Holy Trinity Church at Allahabad proclaimed the twenty year old Robert William Yeoward and the fifteen-year-old Victoria Hemmings as man and wife. The marriage register at the Holy Trinity Church of Allahabad has the following details of the ceremony:

'Robert William Yeoward: 20 years old, bachelor, Son of William Henry Yeoward. Robert William Yeoward's profession: Incharge of Ice

engines Robert William Yeoward was married to Victoria Hemmings:
15 years old, daughter of Elijah Hemmings. Marriage by Bans.
Married by J Stephenson, Offs Civil Chaplain, on 10th September
1872.
Residence at time of marriage for both—Allahabad.'
(Signatures of the witnesses were largely illegible.)

Rukmani shed tears of joy as the pastor solemnized the wedding. She had
some hope that her fortunes which had been down since Hemmings' death,
would now turn and things would begin to look up. Soon after the wedding,
Robert requested Rukmani and Bela to move into his elegant mansion in
Azamgarh.

The story of Victoria and Robert was a typical fairy tale. Victoria was
deeply in love with the young man and so was he. Their love was rewarded
with a baby girl. Their bundle of joy was born on 26 June 1873 in Azamgarh.
Two years later, on 3 June 1875, she was baptized at the Allahabad Methodist
Episcopal Church as Eileen Angelina Yeoward. The cherubic little kid had
inherited the best of features of her parents. Life seemed perfect. Things
couldn't have been better.

Barely a year after Angelina's birth one Safuzzil Hussain made Robert a
lucrative job offer as senior supervisor in an indigo plantation about four miles
away from Azamgarh. The job necessitated his relocation. At first Robert was
reluctant to leave his wife and child and go so far away, but the fact that
Rukmani would be there to take care of the mother and daughter reassured
him. He promised to visit Azamgarh every fortnight and departed to take
up his new assignment. He was given a tearful farewell by Victoria.

A couple of years went by. Victoria had started getting increasingly
restive. She was lonely. Her mother was away all day at the dry-ice factory.
The pressures of motherhood and the painful separation from her beloved
caused her ample heartache. She eagerly awaited Robert's brief visits and
when he sometimes skipped coming home due to pressures at work, she
got terribly depressed. Slowly she began to take refuge in poetry that she
had a natural gift for and pour out her angst in verse. Quite providentially
for her, her neighbour Jogeshwar Bharati was a man of letters and well
versed in music. She began spending time discussing her poems with him

and soon, with Rukmani's permission started taking basic lessons in music from him as well.

The friendship with Jogeshwar and the pursuit of the arts assuaged her heart. She was more at peace with herself. The change in her behaviour was apparent to Robert. While he appreciated her coming to terms with her life's realities, he disapproved of her intimacy with Jogeswhar. On many occasions he berated her and advised her to refrain from meeting Jogeshwar so often. Victoria would faithfully comply with his instruction when he was around, but soon after Robert left, she would make her way to her neighbour's house to get over the pangs of separation and loneliness that gnawed her heart.

But unfortunately for Victoria, the rumour mills had started working overtime. Robert overheard gossip at his work-place about his wife's fidelity. This infuriated him and he quit the job and took on a new assignment. However the seed of suspicion against his wife had been sown in his mind and would not go away. He began to make sudden and unannounced visits to Azamgarh to check on Victoria.

On one such surprise visit Robert found Jogeshwar in his house in the company of his wife. Robert was enraged. A fierce argument ensued. Too incensed to think rationally, he ranted, "I should not have expected anything better from a mistress's daughter!" He declared that he could not tolerate infidelity from his wife anymore, and would therefore terminate their marriage.

The words sounded like a death-knell to Victoria. She was too stunned to say anything. She never expected that the man she loved so dearly and with all her heart would go to such extremes and that too on a matter so trivial. With a blank expression on her face she said he was free to do whatever he deemed fit. Despite Rukmani's pleas and interventions, Robert was possessed by the devil and he submitted a divorce petition on grounds of infidelity. Victoria did not contest the case and the two were legally separated in 1879, after barely seven years of marital bliss. Robert refused to even acknowledge baby Angelina as his own and with a hard heart turned Victoria, Rukmani and the baby away from his house.

With the enforcement of the divorce, the family was back to where they came from. To add to their misfortunes, the dry-ice factory where Rukmani worked closed its operations. They had no means of earning a livelihood and were reduced to penury. To lend a helping hand to her ageing mother in running the household, Victoria started taking music lessons for a couple of young girls in the locality. However this did not help much and it was a struggle to get two meals a day. Baby Angelina was terribly malnourished and when she caught a severe infection they had to rely on the local Hakim to treat the child. He had almost given up hope of the child's survival.

It was at this critical juncture that a Muslim nobleman of the town named Khurshid came into their lives. Khurshid was a man of refined tastes and was fond of Urdu poetry and the lyrical Quwwalis. He also managed to play a little bit of the Esraj himself. He had seen Victoria in one of her music classes and had realised that she had no one to fall back on. Khurshid decided to step in and support the family in its worst moment of crisis.

But it was not some philanthropic urge that led Khurshid to take on the responsibility for Victoria and her family. Victoria's stunning looks had attracted him since the time he had seen her first. He demanded sexual favours from the young woman in return for his help. Victoria was at a crossroads in her life. Her decisions had to be instantaneous, even though they would be life-changing. Her daughter was critically ill, and the only man she loved dearly had spurned her. To stand on her chastity in anticipation of the return of her husband and decline the offer of sustenance seemed meaningless. Besides they desperately needed male support. So Victoria, having very little choice, knowingly and willingly, submitted to Khurshid's designs. Outwardly, Khurshid was the total antithesis of Robert, dark, insensitive and crass. However he took complete charge of the family immediately. The little girl was given proper and timely medical care and she survived. It was a small price that Victoria had paid!

Soon the news of this liaison became the talking point for the gossip mongers of the town. The same people, who barely came to the help of the family when the little child was dying, now dared to castigate the relationship between Victoria and Khurshid in public. They faulted Victoria for her foolish behaviour which caused her to lose such a gentlemanly and noble Armenian husband like Robert. Lewd comments were made about how the daughter of an Englishman's mistress had now become a whore—first of a Hindu neighbour and then of a Muslim nobleman. The jeers and taunts soon became too difficult to bear. Khurshid decided that it was best for them to shift to the nearest big city, which was Banaras, where they could live in anonymity, far from these jibes and snide remarks.

Thus in the year 1879, Victoria, her daughter, the six-year-old Angelina, Rukmani and Khurshid left Azamgarh for good. Rukmani and Victoria had a final parting look at the town. Their memories were inextricably entwined with the town that had given them the greatest of joys and the sharpest of pains. It was now time to move on with a hope that the new city they were proceeding to would usher in a new light in their lives.

Sadme se dhadakne laga qatil ka kaleja
Dekha na gaya usase uchalna mere dil ka.

The piteous sight of my pained heart disturbed my assassin too!

—BADI MALKA JAAN, MAKHZAN-E-ULFAT-E-MALLIKA.

Ek na ek shamaa andhere mein jalaye rakhiye
Subah hone ko hai, mahaul banaye rakhiye

Keep the little flame of hope alive amidst the engulfing darkness.
This dark night too shall pass to a glorious dawn, keep up your spirits!

—TARIQ BADAYUNI

※‿‿҉✷

2

THE CITY OF LIGHT

Banaras, 1879

The magnificent town of Banaras rises from the western banks of the River Ganga at a point where the river meanders in a broad crescent sweep northwards. The river at dawn provides one of the most spectacular sights the human eye can see. As the sunlight bathes the river, its banks come to life and the temples, shrines, ashrams and pavilions that stretch along the riverside buzz with activity. Long flights of stone steps called *ghats* reach into the river and bring along them millions of devout pilgrims for whom a dip in the holy Ganga is akin to washing away the sins of many births. However a bath in the Ganga at the crack of dawn and a worship of the rising sun is a part of daily life for the residents of the city.

The locals believed that the presiding Goddess Annapurna ensures that all the inhabitants get enough to eat; the Lord of the city, Vishwanath, (another name for Shiva) promises them liberation after death. Therefore having no worries, either for the present life or the one thereafter, the devout led a happy and carefree life. The riverside cremation grounds at Harishchandra Ghat and Manikarnika Ghat are located right in the middle of the town because the people of Banaras believed that life and death are a part of the eternal cycle and dying in the holy city is considered a blessing and a sure route to salvation. For centuries the city has been attracting pilgrims, devotees, seekers, saints and teachers like the Buddha, Mahavira and Adi Shankara to its pristine surroundings. Banaras (or Varanasi or Kashi as it is called) is the luminous city, the City of eternal light.

It was this light and hope that Banaras promised that beckoned the family of Victoria to its embrace when they wanted to get away from the throes of darkness and misery in Azamgarh. Khurshid found a modest dwelling in the town for the family.

Banaras was famous for its poets and thugs, its wrestlers and priests, its sweets, the betel leaf or *paan* and many intoxicants like *bhaang*. Banaras presented a range of enchanting contrasts. The town was not only steeped in religious rituals and spiritual pursuits but was also an active commercial node in the Doab region. The brass items, the splendid filigree work of brocade textiles and the famed saris of Banaras with their exquisite embroidery patterns were legendary. Banaras also had a hoary tradition of music and dance and was equally famous for its courtesans. There are numerous anecdotes narrated even today about the exploits of the renowned courtesans of Banaras. It is said that the fee for a night of one such distinguished courtesan equalled the daily revenues of the King of Kashi! The eighth century poet from Kashmir, Damodar Gupta eulogizes these women in his long poem 'Kuttanimata' or 'Advice of the procuress.' It gives a glimpse of the Banaras of those days and speaks of the eminent position occupied by a courtesan in that society.

By the time Khurshid and his entourage came to Banaras, the town was a teeming centre for religious, commercial and musical activity. One of the first steps that Victoria took upon reaching Banaras was to forsake all the identities related to her past. She did not want another Azamgarh kind of situation in Banaras and decided to not only change her name but also convert to the religion of her benefactor Khurshid. Accordingly Victoria and her daughter Angelina converted to Islam and assumed new names. Victoria now became Malka and her daughter was named 'Gauhar' which in Persian meant the most precious jewel. Gauhar was indeed the only bright spot in the troubled life of her mother. She was affectionately called 'Gaura.'

Meanwhile, Khurshid took up a small textiles business there and exported the famed Banarasi saris to the then capital of British India, Calcutta. This helped the family lead a fairly comfortable life. In the eyes of society Khurshid and Malka were husband and wife and Gauhar their little daughter. Victoria and Angelina were long buried in the narrow lanes of Azamgarh.

Khurshid tried his best to get Malka out of her melancholy and allowed her the indulgences that gave her the maximum pleasure. He appointed Hussain Ahmed Asghar and Qadar Hussain to teach her classical Persian and hone her literary skills in the process. Hakim Banno Sahib 'Hilal' gave her lessons in Urdu. Zeenat Bibi, a famed dancer-singer of Banaras, was appointed to train Malka in classical music. She later learnt music under Kalloo Ustad and dance under Ali Baksh, a dancer from Lucknow who had migrated to Banaras looking for patronage after the British occupation of Oudh. The pursuit of music and literature served as a balm for Malka's troubled heart and she slowly emerged out of her tumultuous past in Azamgarh. Gradually Malka started becoming a well-known name in the locality and rich patrons began to seek her to listen to her poetry or her mellifluous singing.

Banaras was deeply influenced by its neighbour, the magnificent kingdom of Oudh that was established in the early decades of the 18th century. Its rulers, who hailed from the Khorasan province of Iran, were initially subservient to the Mughal Emperor in Delhi. Faizabad was their seat of power and they titled themselves as 'Nawabs'. With the death of Aurangazeb and the political disarray that the Mughal Empire slipped into thereafter, Delhi's position of eminence in the politics of the time slowly, yet steadily, waned. But 200 miles to its south-east a new centre of power, politics and culture was emerging. It was Lucknow the new capital of the Nawabs of Oudh, who broke away from their hitherto masters, the Mughals, and declared autonomy. The shifting of the centre of power from Faizabad to Lucknow in 1775 by Nawab Asaf-ud-daula (1775-1797) ensured that this hitherto sleepy provincial town of no particular distinction attained a position of pre-eminence and became one of the most strategically important cities of the North. The substantial agricultural surplus of the fertile Doab region, watered by the North Indian rivers, was no longer sent to Delhi, but to Lucknow. These developments created a new class of government officials, revenue collectors, traders and merchants who emerged as the new aristocracy. This in turn attracted a host of courtesans, artists, musicians and dancers who migrated from Delhi to Lucknow. The city became the seat of the arts and Urdu poetry, and was the veritable last word in matters of genteel sophistication.

Achievement of independence from the Mughals did not mean complete autonomy for the Nawabs of Oudh. The British had long coveted the wealth of Oudh. The East India Company's influence in the region was on the rise since the time the Nawabs broke free from the stranglehold of Delhi. They were propped as the protégés of the Company. Thus, for the Nawabs it was merely an exchange of masters. Asaf-ud-daula signed several treaties with the East India Company sanctioning territorial rights as well as military subsidies and loans. In 1775, the Banaras region was ceded to the Company as also the revenues of Ghazipur; in 1797 Allahabad and the surrounding regions were subsumed by the Company and by 1801 the Lower Doab, Gorakhpur and Rohilkhand were formally handed over by the Nawab. Thus while the powers of Oudh shrank, those of the British Resident in the region rose dramatically. By 1819, though Nawab Ghaziuddin Hyder broke away completely from the then tottering and defunct Mughal Empire, Oudh itself was on a steady trail of political decline.

Using the infamous Doctrine of Lapse, Lord Dalhousie, the Governor General of India, sought to annex Oudh completely in 1856. The then Nawab, Wajid Ali Shah was exiled to Calcutta. The year 1857 ushered in unprecedented turmoil across the country with the outbreak of the Sepoy Mutiny. In Lucknow too the revolts erupted in the cantonment, a few miles north of the river Gomati. Begum Hazrath Mahal, one of Nawab Wajid Ali Shah's wives who stayed back in Lucknow, spearheaded the movement. A bloody 140-day siege ensured large-scale casualties and mass murders on both sides. It eventually resulted in a miraculous victory for the British in 1858 and a decimation of the forces of Oudh.

With the grievous fall of Oudh, the cultural legacy of courtly Lucknow found new centres of patronage in places like Banaras and Calcutta. There was an increasing presence of the British in the Oudh region after 1858. The city of Lucknow was fully fortified and armed to prevent future mutinies and new cantonments sprang up. The soldiers in these cantonments faced pretty much the same problems as their counterparts elsewhere in the country. As mentioned earlier, the demand-supply equation between the European men and women was always skewed and as a result many soldiers resorted to either homosexuality or made their way to the brothels of leading prostitutes of the towns. This led to a near epidemic of venereal disease among British soldiers. A flabbergasted Government enacted the comprehensive Act XXII or the Cantonment Act in 1864 which required the registration and medical inspection of all practising prostitutes in British Cantonments across the country. By 1869, the Government was pleased to see a steady decline in the number of new cases of venereal disease. The problem was also partly resolved by the arrival of the 'Fishing fleet.'

The complex new world of changing political conditions was confusing for the courtesans and prostitutes, especially because it adversely impacted their profession. A courtesan in the North Indian context was called *tawaif* or *baiji*. One school of thought opines that the word 'Tawaif' has its origins in a Sanskrit word that means circumambulation of the holy sanctum sanctorum of temples by a group of entertainers and performers. Another school of thought suggests that it is the plural form of the Arabic word '*Taifa*' which means a group. Whatever the etymology of the word, it is certain that the tawaif held a position in society that was markedly different from that of the common prostitutes who were called *veshyas* or *ganikas*. In ancient Indian scriptures, a sacrificial offering to the Gods was deemed incomplete unless accompanied by the ritualistic performance of professional women singers. This exalted status was given to these women only because they were the practitioners of an ancient and divine art.

In the case of Oudh and its surrounding areas, during the regime of the Nawabs, the prosperity of Lucknow ushered in a golden era for these tawaifs. They excelled in music, dance, poetry and prose and were of immaculate refinement. Much so that it was normal practice for the aristocrats to send their young sons to tawaifs to be trained in the art of letters and courtly etiquette or *adab* as it was called in Oudh. Free from the societal constraints of family life, the tawaifs attained levels of proficiency in the art forms that few women from traditional and respectable families could even dream of achieving.

The tawaif subscribed to a strict, if unwritten code of conduct. She was usually part of a household presided over by a chief courtesan or *chaudhrayan*. This house was called a *kotha*, which typically consisted of a main performing hall in the upper storey which was lined with mirrors. Invariably there was a caged parrot in the centre of the performance room. The presence of mirrors all round the performing hall was symbolic. One was being watched all the time and was expected to behave with dignity and decorum. If there were no mirrors all around, it could be a brothel and not a *kotha* or a tawaif's salon.

The tawaif community had thirteen major groups across the country and each was headed by its own chaudhrayan. These groups were based in Lahore, Karachi, Lucknow, Patna, Muzaffarpur, Chhapra, Calcutta, Hyderabad, Dhaka, Bhopal, Karnataka, Poona and Bombay.

The Chaudhrayan was usually a woman of substantial means, owning property that included several lavish houses. A king or zamindar in those days would patronize and support the household in the style in which he wished to be entertained. The performance was called a *mujra* and could include singing or dancing or both. Mujra is a Rajasthani term meaning salute. So a mujra was performed for one who was respected. The baijis or tawaifs too were given equal respect.

There were unwritten laws of behaviour for the attendees of these performances as well. Rich patrons could enjoy themselves in an entertaining evening of music, dance and poetry even as the maids served them cold drinks or *sherbet*, *bhang*, liquor and other intoxicants in the interval between items. But no one was allowed to bring their own alcohol. A silver paandaan to serve betel leaves, betel nuts and cardamom and a tray laden with dry fruits were an integral prop of every kotha. To ensure no unhealthy competition arose among the audience, no one was allowed to offer money openly to the performing artist. After the performance was over the maids would clear the room and retrieve money left by the audience from under the mattresses. This money was divided among the tawaif, her *ustad* or teacher and the artists who accompanied her. This too was done strictly in accordance with the guidelines laid down by the chaudhrayan of that particular kotha.

The chaudhrayan for her part was also entrusted with grooming the next generation of performers. Every reputed kotha maintained its own team of skilled male musicians who were often linked to famous lineages or gharanas of musicians. The tutors generally belonged to the Dhadi or Kathak community. They seldom performed themselves but dedicated their lives to training talented students. The other male auxiliaries of the establishment like doormen, touts and pimps were often relatives of the chief courtesan and they provided the much needed male support and security. If talent was spotted in a young boy he would be trained to be an accompanist. Girls started their training in all the arts and were given a thorough grounding in classical Persian, Arabic and Urdu, from a very young age.

The community also had a rigid social hierarchy. One had to be born to a tawaif and claim a lineage to be accepted as a tawaif. Girls who were kidnapped were never inducted into the performing space of a tawaif. They were consigned to flesh trade. Thus a clear distinction between tawaifs and prostitutes was always made in society.

The standard hierarchy of the community of professional women performers was pyramidical. The tawaifs were at the top of the social structure. Among them too, the *Bai*, who only sang, was above the *Jaan*, who sang and danced. Below the tawaifs came a broad-based category of professional women called *Mirasans* who were variously named as either *Domnis* or *Dholis* or as *Kashmira*, *Gandharva* and *Kanchan*. These Mirasans were from the lower strata of society and had their own sub-classification as well. At the top were the *Kanijs* who could be broadly defined as entertainers and were followed by the *Khanagis* who included sexual favours as part of their entertainment package. The lowest strata of women were known as *Thakahi* and *Randi* who indulged in only flesh trade and had no access to the arts.

Strict rules also determined the performance repertoire of these women. For instance the Domnis and Dholis usually performed for the 'respectable' women of wealthy households during rituals and celebrations and their repertoire included traditional songs but not classical renditions. Tawaifs on the other hand sang weighty classical renditions and that too for the menfolk in sophisticated evening chamber concerts

The tawaifs or baijis took great pride in their lineage which they traced back to several generations. Some even claimed their descent from the heavenly courts of Indra and called themselves Urvashi or Gandharva. In fact the three main *gotras* or genealogical lines of the community were Gandharva,

Kinnar and Rajmani—the names themselves having their roots in ancient Sanskrit mythology. The tawaifs thus positioned themselves as purveyors of a divine art that had been recontextualized in secular courts.

Commenting on the social status of the 20th century courtesan, McMunn, a retired army officer of British India, states that:

> 'The mass of them come from the lowest of the depressed classes and untouchables and from outcast tribes…the dancers have matriarchal descent for many generations perhaps, for though all dancers are courtesans, not all courtesans are dancers. The recruiting of the dancer class comes also from one more source, the unwanted daughter. The unwanted daughter may be sold, given to, or stolen by a gipsy tribe and sold on to some duenna of dancing girls, herself retired from the craft of keeping houses of ill fame.'

This intertwining of music and dance in all performances created its own aura of seduction. Western fascination for such gatherings that were laced with exoticism, romance and prurience comes across clearly in another comment of McMunn, an eye-witness to one such performance in a kotha:

> 'From the large chamber within the darkened lattices there comes the luring throb of the little drum…Within one of the inner rooms where the velvety cushions are super-velvety, Azizun the dancer taps the floor quietly with her embroidered crimson and green shoe to supple the sinews…you can see every muscle under the soft olive skins of the bare abdomens and the transparent muslin of the dancers…ankle and bosom moving to the pipe, now in softness, now in frenzy.'

The tawaif operated in society with a range of options open to her, none of which were available for a traditional woman from 'respected families.' Women from traditional families were never allowed to pursue the arts in the public domain. But for the tawaifs the fine arts was their monopoly and those who strove to reach the pinnacle of success in the field, did manage to get there as well. Those tawaifs who wished to settle down in life had the option of an open marriage as well. However those who wanted to lead independent lives were at liberty to do so too. Prostitutes were however denied this privilege.

More often than not, the tawaifs who opted for the open-marriage route selected the wealthiest and most well established men in society. By virtue of their refined etiquette and good looks, most tawaifs were sought after anyway. Women from respectable families were seldom given an education, let alone such options. It is interesting to note that only the names of tawaifs figure among the women tax-payers of the times, proving that they were the only female property owners of those days. Thus, at a time when most women in India were illiterate, the tawaifs were accomplished in the finest of fine arts and were skilled poets, authors, musicians and dancers themselves.

By the time Malka came to Banaras, she had been exposed to some preliminary training in versification and music. So far there was no thought in her mind to become a tawaif herself. However the atmosphere of Banaras, the all-pervasive nature of music and the distinction with which tawaifs were regarded in the society there changed things for her. With the increasing public attention that she began receiving because of her accomplishments in the arts, Malka was steadily heading towards becoming a leading courtesan of the town. It is pertinent to note that given the rigid social structure of the community, outsiders would not be easily accepted into the fold. But since Malka did eventually gain recognition and acceptance as a tawaif, one may infer that Rukmani may have belonged to a tawaif community herself. Like many tawaifs who married their rich benefactors, she had married Hardy Hemmings at Azamgarh. Besides, the fact that Rukmani, who was with the family during these major changes, hardly protested her daughter's conversion or her taking to public performance bolsters the belief that she was possibly a tawaif herself. In the absence of supporting documentary evidence, however one can only conjecture about this.

Malka was christened 'Malka Jaan' after she started performing on a regular basis for the wealthy patrons of Banaras. The addition of the suffix 'Jaan' to her name suggests that she became an accepted member of the closely guarded tawaif community of the town. (Incidentally she was called *'Badi'* Malka Jaan or the elder Malka Jaan to distinguish her from three other famous Malka Jaans of her time—Agrewali Malka Jaan of Agra, Malka Jaan of Mulk Pukhraj and Chulbuliwali Malka Jaan of Chulbuli.) She soon established herself in the tawaif community of Banaras and many of the famous baijis of Banaras like Hira, Saraswati, Muniya and Vyjayanthi became close friends of hers. A friendship laced with inherent rivalry and jealousy, no doubt.

And thus it was that Victoria Hemmings, after a long and arduous journey, became Malka Jaan.

Nikal aaye dair va haram se Malka
Kare zikr Shekh va barhman kisi ka.

What does Malka have anything to do with matters of religion? Aren't those better served in the hands of the Sheikh and the Brahman?

—Badi Malka Jaan, Makhzan-e-ulfat-e-Mallika.

⁕⸎⸏⁕

3

THE LEARNING YEARS

Banaras, 1880

The city that was deemed the ultimate destination for liberation from the cycles of rebirth liberated the family of the young woman from their troubled lives in Azamgarh. At the same time it catapulted Malka into the vortex of an altogether different life. The modest dwelling Khurshid and Malka had taken up was slowly being transformed into the mirrored salon of the courtesan. Khurshid fully supported this process as his business was not doing that well any more and he desperately needed Malka Jaan's income to sustain himself.

The all-pervading spirit of Banaras was one of festivals, celebrations and hedonistic pleasure. This naturally inspired the development of the performing arts, especially music. The city throbbed with the celebration of numerous fairs and festivals throughout the year, and dance and music performances were an integral part of these events. The main patrons of the arts were the rich aristocrats of Banaras, the landed gentry and wealthy traders who largely belonged to the Agarwal community. These people were known not only for their liberal patronage of the arts but also their innumerable idiosyncrasies and public flaunting of their wealth. It was said that many of them spread sacks and sacks of *ashrafis* (gold coins) to dry on their terraces, just as they would perhaps do with *papads* during summers! This was one way of flaunting their richness and challenging their rivals to match or outdo their display of wealth.

A leading luminary of the aristocratic family of Banaras was eminent playwright Bharatendu Harishchandra (1850-1885), known as the father of modern Hindi literature. He was a great patron of music and the tawaif culture. However his association with the professional women singers of the times made him infamous during his lifetime. But it was from these associations that Bharatendu gained his insights into human life, its tragedies and ecstasies and his literature never ceased to reflect these themes.

The two main families of Banaras that perennially vied with each other in business and patronage of the arts were the Shah family and the Rai family. The Shahs were however considered to be an eccentric family and locals referred to them as the '*Jhakkad Khandan.*' The head of the household, an elderly gentleman, Babu Advaith Prasad Shah was a scholar of great repute and could speak English with the flair of a seasoned debater. But inspite of his erudition, the man had some very strange and quirky habits. He would seat himself at the edge of the terrace of his palatial house, chewing betel leaves or *paan*, and wait for a well dressed passer-by. On spotting one such unsuspecting gentleman he would spit out a stream of betel juice on his head. This uncouth behaviour would invite a host of choicest abuses at the perpetrator of this act. Shah Sahib enjoyed listening to these crude abuses and later, to compensate, would make a generous gift to the person he had just spat on!

The Rais on the other hand were more poised and dignified and carried themselves with grace. Rai Krishnadas was considered an authority on archaeology and numismatics. He was also a distinguished poet and writer in Hindi. His house was always abuzz with activity, *mushairas* and *baithak*s, at which poets and scholars displayed their talents. It was considered a privilege to be invited to Rai Sahib's mushairas or gatherings. Rai Sahib was also a great patron of music and dance and regularly arranged for mehfils or concerts of all the leading baijis of Banaras and other visiting musicians. He had three sons—Lallan, Chaggan and Krishan, each of whom was to play a significant role in Gauhar's life.

Other affluent people like Motichand and Kishori Raman were also great connoisseurs of music. The concerts that all these wealthy patrons organized would be the talk of the town for days. Their mehfils had the distinct touch of the erstwhile Mughal durbar in their pomp and grandeur. Such events were a great opportunity at one-upmanship. The families vied with each other to be labelled the better organizer. So they made sure that the most popular and talented singer graced their concert. Specialists were hired to arrange every minute detail of the concert—décor, the choicest carpets and curtains, flower pots and chirping birds that sang alongside the baiji. Tawaifs usually employed agents called taals and darogas to get them opportunities to perform at the best of venues. The soirees went on through the night in the presence of an informed and musically sensitive, aristocratic audience. The baijis would perform exquisite dances in a seated position and demonstrate various emotions through the voice, gestures and facial expressions. The common prostitutes and their pimps were allowed to stand on the sidelines and indulge in witty exchanges and clever repartees from the background. Sometimes more than one tawaif was invited to a performance and they tried to outdo each other in the performance of items like *Gajara, Jhoomar* and *Dangal*. In a *Gajara*, a duet was sung by two tawaifs who performed standing. Four or five performers danced and sang in the *Jhoomar*, while the musical repartee and war of words between two tawaifs was called the *Dangal* (also called *nok-jhonk, ladant-bhidant* and *sawal jawab*).

The famous Burhwa Mangal and Gulab Bari festivals of Banaras reflected the exuberance and vivacity that the city was so famous for. The Burhwa Mangal festival was usually celebrated on the first Tuesday after the festival of colours, Holi. The spirit of enthusiasm that Holi usually brings along with it, carried on during the Burhwa Mangal. Day-long concerts of reputed baijis marked the festivities at the houses of reputed patrons and these went on till the early hours of the following morning. Songs sung during this time were known as the *Chaiti* since the season is *Chait* or the first month of the Hindu calendar. The wearing of colourful clothes and a liberal feasting of scrumptious delicacies like rabri-malai, malpua, kulfi and puri-kachori accompanied the merriment.

It was also customary to celebrate the Burhwa Mangal festival atop boats that would be tethered on the banks of the Ganga. As the elaborate evening worship or *arati* of the river concluded, these boats would come to life with exquisite decorations, lights and delightful music. The boats were fashioned as temporary concert rooms with colourful shamianas, flower pots, curtains and lamps. There was intense competition among the aristocratic families to be identified as the best boat concert organizer of the festival.

The same verve would manifest once again during the rainy season when women sang songs, danced, feasted on delectable and mouth-watering sweets and freshly ripened mangoes. The mehfils were called *Jhoomar ka tek*, when *jhoolas* or swings were tied to trees and women would joyously sway on them in the rain, singing songs known as *kajris*. The famous intoxicating drink of Banaras called *Thandai* would be the favourite of the season. In a way, this integration between festivals and the accompanying music underlines the manner in which Indian classical music draws heavily from nature and is inspired by the changing seasons, the different hours of a day and the joys and sorrows of people.

It was in this very environment where musical prowess was so much a part of everyone's life that Malka Jaan made her name as a leading tawaif of Banaras. Baldev was her agent or Taal who brought her lucrative offers from the aristocrats of the city. Very soon her kotha was frequented by all the wealthy connoisseurs of Banaras. Her fame spread far and wide in the then United Provinces, the Uttar Pradesh of today. This led to some relics of her past life coming to look for her. One among them was her maid and companion at Azamgarh, Ashia. She guessed that the lady who was making waves in the musical world of the province was perhaps her old mistress, Victoria. Ashia was deserted by her husband and she decided to look for Victoria in Banaras. She arrived there with her little son Bhaglu, who was perhaps a few years older than Gauhar. The two women had a tearful reunion. Malka, now financially stable, offered refuge to Ashia and her son and they became her extended family.

Meanwhile little Gauhar was growing up to be a pretty girl with a broad face, curly hair and distinct Anglo-Indian features. She had inherited her mother's talent for music and poetry. Malka Jaan had noticed her daughter's innate ability and her melodious voice, so she began training her to be a singer. After she had her initial training Malka Jaan decided to put her under the tutelage of an eminent guru of Banaras. The city had no dearth of musicians, but Malka Jaan wanted the best person to train her daughter. She approached one of the stalwarts of classical music, Pandit Bechoo Mishra, who was a versatile artiste, and had mastered several genres of North Indian classical music like khayal, thumri, tappa and tarana. He played the sarangi as well. Bechoo Mishra belonged to a family of musicians. His father Pandit Buddho Mishra and younger brother Thakur Prasad were also musicians. When he heard young Gauhar's voice, he recognized the talent in her and readily agreed to teach her. He was a strict disciplinarian and ensured that Gauhar learnt her basics well. She was slowly being groomed into the art of performing. With a mother as popular as Malka Jaan, she did not need any other role models.

As Gauhar's lessons progressed, Malka felt confident enough to take her daughter along with her to a few mujras. The audience were doubly thrilled to see a pretty young girl follow the lead singer, a beautiful woman with European features, with consummate ease. The mother-daughter duo became the toast of the town. Pandit Mishra continued to train Gauhar for a long time, and it was he who moulded her musical personality.

The fortunes of the family too were changing for the better. Soon they began to be counted among the well-to-do families of Banaras. Malka Jaan bought for herself a phaeton or horse-drawn carriage and the mother and daughter would go on joy rides in the carriage. All along Khurshid remained a steadfast supporter and did all he could to ensure Malka Jaan and Gauhar were comfortable. He revelled in their successes and shared their sorrows. Ashia remained Malka's trustworthy companion. Bhaglu was increasingly pampered by Malka, whom he referred to as '*Badi Maa.*'

Just as the domestic situation was stabilizing, and things were looking up, Malka had to face a major tragedy in her life. Her mother Rukmani passed away unexpectedly. The mother's demise left a big void in Malka's life, but she had to quickly get over her sorrow and return to singing and entertaining the rich and wealthy.

At around this time there was a new centre that was beckoning all musicians, dancers and artists of the region into its open arms. This was the city of Calcutta, the capital of British India. Apart from the commercial and political pre-eminence of the city which naturally attracted arts and artists to its vicinity, it was the benign influence of the dispossessed Nawab of Oudh, Wajid Ali Shah (1822-1887) that made Calcutta an attractive destination for all artists. Wajid Ali Shah ascended the throne of Oudh in 1847 but matters of administration and kingship seldom interested him. He was completely into the arts and esoteric sciences and paid little or no attention to matters of kingship. When the British decided to strip the Nawab of his powers, he whined and whimpered but was quietly packed off to distant Calcutta. About three or four miles south of Calcutta, on the banks of the river Hoogly was a quiet quarter known as Garden Reach. The topography of the region with its raised plateau structure made the locals call it *Matiya Buruj*. There were also some fine houses, the grounds of which stretched for two to three miles along the river bank. When the deposed Nawab reached Calcutta the British gave him three houses, two for himself (called Sultan Khana and Asad Manzil) and one for his chief consort (known as Murassa Manzil). A large expanse of land was also granted to him for his personal use.

The Nawab however refused to accept the allowance allotted to him by the British and insisted on reclaiming the crown that he believed had been snatched away from him quite unjustly. The royal family however was trying its best to plead Wajid Ali Shah's case and have his kingdom restored to him. The Nawab's son, his mother and brother travelled all the way to London for this purpose. But the 1857 Sepoy Mutiny and the role played by the Begum of Oudh Hazrat Mahal in spearheading the revolt from Lucknow soured the relationship between the estranged royal family and the East India Company further. This greatly damaged the cause of Wajid Ali Shah and his hopes of reclaiming Oudh started receding by the day.

Soon after Wajid Ali Shah arrived in Calcutta a second Lucknow began emerging in its neighbourhood. The same bustle and activity, the same courtly language the same style of poetry recitation, conversation and repartee, the practice of kite-flying, cock-fighting, quail fights, opium addictions, and the observance of Shia Muslim rituals like the Muharram mourning processions, were evident here as it was in erstwhile Lucknow. The local character of

Calcutta's neighbourhood was thus gradually but definitely being subsumed by a dying Lucknow.

As it became increasingly clear to Wajid Ali Shah that the British were not going to hand over his kingdom to him, he was resigned to his fate and took to what he loved the most —fine arts. A large number of musicians, dancers, poets, painters, and artists migrated from Lucknow to Calcutta. Ustads from all over India began coming to Calcutta to seek his patronage as that was a sure way of achieving fame at a national level. The Nawab himself was a great composer of verses and musical genres like the thumri, learnt dance and maintained many artists in his court.

This pre-eminence of Calcutta as a musical hub of North India attracted artists from other provinces too. The contacts that Khurshid had in Calcutta because of his sari export business to that city, also advised him to take his family to Calcutta. After all, they said, his wife had immense talent and should try her luck in the city that mattered. Baldev, Malka Jaan's agent too told the family that their life could completely change if they established themselves in Calcutta. It would also give young Gauhar ample choice in the matter of trainers in music and dance and also opportunities to perform, he said. Finally, after much debate, consternation and anxiety, Malka Jaan decided to move to Calcutta. The death of her mother had left her totally distraught and she felt a change of scene would do them all good.

Thus, in the year 1883, after spending four long years in the city of Banaras that had protected, shielded and nourished them and their musical careers, Malka Jaan and Gauhar packed their bags once again and made their way to Calcutta.

Ek haal mein insaan ki basar ho nahin sakti
Ab rang tabeeyat ka badal jaaye tho accha.

No human being can remain in the same state forever,
After all change is the only permanent rule of the world.
That being the case, why not adapt to this new state of my life?

❧

4

A STAR IS BORN

Calcutta, 1883

After traversing a distance of nearly 425 miles, the carriage from Banaras entered the city of Calcutta. It halted at a place called Kalutola in the city's Chitpur area, in North Calcutta. Some believed Chitpur got its name from the famous Chitreshwari temple with its magnificent Nabaratna dome and its practice of human sacrifices. However others thought that the name was drawn from that of a notorious bandit, Chitey Dakat who arranged the human sacrifices carried out in the temple.

Chitpur was a veritable city within a city. Its divisions were self-descriptive and named after landmarks or occupations. For instance, Murgighata was the chicken market; Kasaitola was the locality of the butchers and Kumartoli of the potters. Kalutola was the home of the East India Company's *kaluas* or oil-pressers who supplied mustard oil and other oils to the merchants in the adjacent Barabazar area.

In a way, Chitpur was a microcosm of what Calcutta was—a city of many parts and a delightful blend of diversities. The British had divided the whole city into 'White Town,' 'Intermediate town,' and 'Black town.' The White Town consisted of the South-Central part of Calcutta with elegant houses and a small, largely British population. North Calcutta with its dense, native population formed the Black Town. The Black Town, that included Chitpur, was a sea of poor *bustees* (shanty houses) of artisans and labourers, in the midst of which stood islands of magnificent brick and stone houses or *paka baris* of wealthy Bengalis.

People of all communities, social classes, backgrounds and occupations were found in the narrow, congested lanes and by-lanes of Chitpur. Jews, Armenians and Portuguese frequented the fruit stalls of Kalutola which offered the choicest picks from the orchards of Kulu and Kashmir, Malda and Muzaffarpur. In the Tiretta Bazaar on Lower Chitpur Road, Armenians and Portuguese shopped for birds and the bazaar offered the best foodstuffs, cigars and shoes. The narrow Chitpur road was a crowded market place too where hookah pipes were entwined with silver wire and Kabuliwalas sold their famous *chappals*. The distinctive Bengali *panjika* or almanac was printed here.

Right in the centre of the bustling Chitpur was the large and imposing Nakhoda Mosque. The largely Shia-dominated area came alive during each Muharram. Lucknowi *kurtas*, *burkhas*, *zari* worked velvet caps and waistcoats were laid out for sale all through the ten days of Muharram.

If the temple and the mosque attracted pilgrims in large numbers, the courtesans' salons in adjoining Boubazaar were regular haunts for the aristocrats of the city. Chitpur was enlivened with the *adda* or animated gossip, the *jatra* shows or street-theatre and brass bands playing 'He is a jolly good fellow' at marriage receptions—activities so typical of Bengali culture and identity.

Along with this ribaldry, the area was also known for its sobriety. In total contrast to the merriment was the sophisticated and intellectual locality of Jorasanko which got its name from the two wooden or bamboo bridges that spanned a small stream at that point. Joransako was the seat of the celebrated Thakur (Tagore) family. It was also home to many other aristocratic families like that of Kaliprasanna Sinha, Krishnadas Pal, Diwan

Banarasi Ghosh and Chandramohan Chatterji. The presence of these educated elite led to the emergence of institutions like the Adi Brahmo Samaj, the Jorasanko Bharati Natya Samaj, the Kalikata Haribhakti Pradayini Sabha, the Minerva Library and the Oriental Seminary. Jorasanko thus became a cradle of Bengali Renaissance.

It was into this crowded Chitpur locality of Calcutta that the ten-year old Gauhar made her first entry into the City of Dreams. Little did she know then that the city which she and her mother had been staring at through their carriage windows with awe and amazement was to be her home for a long time and would nourish and nurture her to phenomenal professional success.

Khurshid and Malka Jaan rented an old house in Kalutola with three rooms and a narrow passage in front. Soon one of the rooms was transformed into a salon, with exquisite mirrors, chandeliers, Moradabadi vases, silver pandaans and trays of dry fruit. The fact that Malka Jaan was already an established baiji of Banaras made things easier for them. The local tawaifs as well as the wealthy connoisseurs were curious about this young and famous singer and poetess from Banaras about whom they had heard so much and who had now migrated to their city. Very soon Malka started getting invitations for concert performances at the homes of many of the babus of Calcutta.

Much like the wealthy zamindars and mahajans of Banaras, the patronage of the arts was in the hands of the babus of Calcutta who were the landed gentry. The Shobhabazar family was among the most powerful and influential aristocracies. They were slowly replaced by the Western-educated, professional, urbanized middle class, who came to be known as the *bhadralok*. The *bhadralok*, by virtue of their English education, managed to secure plum posts in the administration and were active collaborators of the British throughout the nineteenth century. This liaison with the government helped them acquire unimaginable fortunes in a short span and they became the new Babus of the city.

There were a number of diverse components that made up this new Babu culture of the nouveau rich and neo-literate *bhadralok* class. Apart from a general fondness for *adda* which ranged from idle gossip to skilled and passionate oratory and debate on all matters of contemporary interest, the Babus were also academic, literary and religious in their orientations. Although the Babus were mostly Hindus, they were deeply influenced by the Persian nawabi culture and the Mughal court. Patronage of music and dance of the baijis was an integral part of babudom. Nautch soirees became the symbols of power and influence. On festivals like Durga Puja, Holi, and Saraswati Puja or on occasions of family celebrations like marriages, and naming ceremonies, they vied with one another to invite the most reputed baiji for a performance at their mansions. Elaborate and lavish arrangements were made for these sessions and they included huge spreads of food and foreign liquor.

Malka Jaan took little Gauhar along with her to these mujras and in a very short time their fame spread all over the city. It wasn't long before Malka Jaan received an invitation from the court of the deposed Nawab of Oudh, Wajid Ali Shah. A thrilled Malka assiduously prepared for the occasion when she could showcase her talents to the Nawab. She decided to sing two of the Nawab's favourite compositions, '*Jab Chhod chale Lucknow*' and '*Babul mora naihar chooto jaay*' that evening. Upon reaching the magnificent Sultan Khana of the Nawab, Malka Jaan realised that she was to be preceded by Tahera Bibi, acknowledged as the best singer of the court. To her dismay Tahera Bibi sang the same two songs that Malka had planned to. However, Malka was undeterred. She and Gauhar stuck to their plans and sang the same compositions, but with intense emotion, since they knew the pain of displacement. Their renditions brought tears to the eyes of the beleaguered Nawab as the songs echoed the nostalgia he felt for his lost kingdom. He richly rewarded Malka and immediately appointed her as a court musician. He blessed little Gauhar and wished her an illustrious musical career.

Present in the durbar that day was Bindadin Maharaj, the son of the resident dancer of the Nawab's court. Bindadin (1836-1917) is regarded as one of the most important figures in the development of the thumri genre of Hindustani music as also the North Indian classical dance form of Kathak. He established a distinctive style that came to be known as the Lucknow Gharana. His father Durga Prasad and uncle Thakur Prasad had established themselves as dancers in Wajid Ali Shah's court. In fact the Nawab himself became a disciple of Thakur Prasad and showered many honours on the brothers including permission to sit by his side in the court. Bindadin and his brother Kalika Prasad brought about a renaissance in Kathak and raised it to a high level of sophistication. Bindadin had started learning dance from his father and uncle from the age of nine. As a young boy of 12, he had challenged the percussion wizard and ace pakhawaj player, Pandit Kudau Singh, on matters of rhythm. The dispute was settled in the court of Nawab Wajid Ali Shah who watched with astonishment the young lad's dexterity in both theoretical and practical aspects of the art. From then on there was no looking back for Bindadin Maharaj and he emerged as one of the most respected members of the Nawab's court.

The talent of the young Gauhar caught Bindadin Maharaj's attention and after their performance he approached Malka Jaan with an offer to teach the little girl. The excitement of the mother and daughter knew no bounds. Their very purpose of shifting to Calcutta was to gain recognition at the Nawab's court and at the same time expose Gauhar to more accomplished teachers. Both these goals had been achieved within a short span of coming to the city. They counted it a blessing to be trained by the veritable authority on Kathak and Thumri of the times. Thus began a journey of unbridled success for little Gauhar.

An elaborate *gandabandhan* ceremony marked Gauhar's entry into Bindadin's school. This was a customary ritual in the learning and teaching of music in North India. A teacher tied a sacred thread around the wrist of his or her student. The thread symbolized the commitment that both the teacher and the taught were making to the pursuit of the art. The student was given whole black gram (*kala channa*) and jaggery to munch after this ceremony. It was meant to convey to the pupil that proficiency in the art was not something that was easily achievable and like those dry black grams, a 'hard nut' to crack. But as a token of encouragement, the jaggery was offered signifying that the result of such rigorous *riyaz* or practice would be sweet success.

Bindadin, known to be a tough task-master, put the 11-year-old girl through an exacting routine. Since he seldom stayed in Calcutta for a long time, Gauhar had to travel to his home-town Lucknow every now and then to continue her lessons with him. Just listening to his lilting thumris and watching him dance was a huge learning experience, apart from of course the elaborate lessons in *bhava abhinaya* (display of emotions during singing and dancing) that he gave. Another little girl who later went on to become a famous singer, Zohra Bai of Agra, was also a student of Bindadin Maharaj and visited him frequently at Lucknow to learn. Bindadin's own practice sessions were legendary. He is said to have practised only one of the *gats* or rhythmic phrases, '*Thig Dha Dhig Dhig*' for about 12 hours a day, for three whole years, to gain perfection. He instilled the same discipline and passion for the art in Gauhar. And she had an instinctive ability to absorb and assimilate all his training.

Malka Jaan was keen that her daughter expanded her repertoire. So she sent Gauhar to take lessons in Bengali songs from the famous Bamacharan Bhattacharya, who was a court singer of the Maharaja of Panchakot and also a distinguished invitee at Nawab Wajid Ali Shah's court. Ramesh Chandra Das Babaji taught Gauhar the devotional Bengali Kirtans, an essential component of the Vaishnava tradition of Bengal propounded by the likes of Chaitanya Mahaprabhu. Srijanbai imparted to her the more esoteric and contemplative genre of Dhrupad-Dhamar. In those days a thorough grounding in dhrupad, one of the oldest forms of Hindustani music, was considered essential for singers of the khayal and thumri as well. In addition to this, Malka Jaan appointed Mrs De Silva to teach Gauhar English and also hum a few English tunes. She herself taught her daughter Urdu and Persian and also guided her in the art of penning verses. Soon Gauhar was able to read, write and sing in several languages like Hindustani, Bengali, English, Arabic, Persian, and Urdu and could speak English and French as well.

Thus it was that Malka Jaan secured for her daughter a complete and well-rounded education in music and literature. She knew that this was the only asset that people of her community had and honing one's skills in all aspects of the art was quintessential to their success. Gauhar's innate talent and love for music and dance, coupled with her intelligence and sharp memory, ensured that these multiple classes and teachers did not become a stressful burden for her but a joyous exercise in the assimilation of different aspects of the same art.

In the meantime Malka Jaan continued to compose verses in Urdu. Her poetry conformed to all the techniques and norms of traditional Urdu poetry and was indicative of her command over the Urdu language, thanks to the training that she had received in Banaras. However her compositions were marked with pessimism and grief and reflected the struggles of her early life. As she was a prolific writer, her friends and well-wishers advised Malka Jaan to publish a collection of her poetry, titled, *'Makhzan-e-ulfat-e-Malka'* or the 'Treasure of Malka's love'. Gauhar wrote one of the laudatory messages for the book. This collection or *Divan* was published on 22 October 1886 by Mahomed Wazeer at the Ripon Press, No 6, Ramprasad Sahas Lane, Calcutta. This established Malka as an acknowledged poetess in her own right

Mushairas or poetic gatherings were regular features among the educated elite. Eminent poets were invited to recite their compositions, usually ghazals. The popular theme of the Ghazal was unrequited love. Imageries of the flask of wine and the nightingale, the tulip and the rose, the flowing black locks of the heartless lover, the tears of blood shed by a forlorn beloved used in these ghazals go back to medieval Persia where the form is supposed to have originated. Of course ghazals were written on other themes as well. *Tarannums* were ghazals which lent themselves to tune easily and were primarily written to be set to music. While mushairas could be informal gatherings of friends the grandest ones organized in Oudh, Lucknow and Calcutta were splendid affairs and often went on through the night. They were governed by the age-old conventions on etiquette. A candle was placed in front of the poet who was to recite. It was part of the protocol for the reciting poet to protest and make excuses about his own ignorance and unease with verse. He would then be coaxed and cajoled by his fellow poets to bring out new and fresh jewels from his treasury. This is just one example of how etiquette was stretched to the point of hypocrisy in the nawabi courts.

Usually the mushaira began with the junior and humorous poets and the great masters regaled their audience later in the session. It was customary for the audience to punctuate the recitation with exaggerated '*Wah! Wah!*' and '*Subhan Allah*' to show appreciation, and egg the poet on and persuade him or her to recite more. However they were equally critical of poorly composed verses and did not hesitate to give them a royal booing!

Poetry was also a very important part of religious activity. Muharram commemorates the martyrdom of Imam Hussain of the Holy Prophet's household in the Battle of Karbala in AD 680. During the ten days of Muharram, Shia Muslims organize gatherings known as *majlis* to mourn the death of their Imam and to recount the sad story of his defeat and death. The mourning was followed by lengthy recitations by poets on the same episode. The audience would weep and wail and beat their breasts in sympathy and pain and cry out loudly '*Ya! Hussain, Ya! Hussain!*' On the tenth day people went around the streets in a procession carrying taziyas which are replicas of Hussain's tomb. The procession would be accompanied by self-flagellation and walking barefoot over live embers. The elegies known as *marsiya* in Urdu poetry were given a stylized form by the 19th century poets Mir Babar Ali Anis and Mirza Dabir. The same verses set to poignant tunes were known as *soz*. Thus music and verse became the vehicles through which joy, sorrow, unrequited love and religious identity were expressed.

When Malka Jaan was established as a musician in the court of Wajid Ali Shah, her fame spread and her fortunes turned. Within three years, that is 1886, she bought an entire building on the same Chitpur Road in Calcutta that she first lived on. The lavish three-storeyed mansion, 'No 49, Chitpur Road,' was purchased from one Haji Mohammad Karim Siraji for Rs 40,000. The three storeys were registered as separate legal holdings- 49, 49/1 and 49/2. Malka donated one portion of it to her companion Ashia and her son Bhaglu. The two decided to become Muslims in order to be more integrated with the family. Accordingly on the occasion of Id, a Maulvi was summoned and Ashia and Bhaglu were converted to Islam at the Dharamtala mosque in the city.

No 49, Chitpur Road became an important venue for mehfils and mujras, and because of the success of her book, she was sought out by eminent poets. The noted Urdu poet, Dagh Dehlvi paid a visit to Calcutta to meet his lady love '*Hajab*', and is said to have also called on Malka Jaan to express his deep admiration for her poetic excellence. Eminent poet Akbar Allahabadi was her contemporary and held her in great esteem.

As she became more successful and affluent, Malka began to donate generously and liberally to the Nakhoda and Dharamtala mosques, as well as many madarasas in the area. She also donated money for the Calcutta Improvement Trust that had been formed for the development of the city. From penury to philanthropy was indeed a long and arduous journey for Malka and she had worked hard to reach where she was. All along she had the company of Khurshid, a man who had started the journey with her, driven by lust, but had somewhere along the way developed a sense of respect and affection for her. She in turn was grateful to Khurshid for all his support. The tables had however turned. Now it was Malka who was supporting Khurshid and his flagging business.

However it was not long before Khurshid's male ego started resenting his dependence on Malka. He began distancing himself from her. Her preoccupation with the nobility further alienated him from her and made him insecure. He felt small and insignificant in the presence of Calcutta's famous baiji. Malka pleaded with him to be his original self, but the bug had bitten Khurshid. He started staying away from home for long periods at a time.

One fine morning in 1885 a police constable knocked on the doors of 49, Chitpur Road. An alarmed Malka was shocked to see a police official at her doorstep. To her horror and dismay she was told that Khurshid had been murdered the previous night and his body had been found near the ditch at Tiretta bazaar. Amidst loud wails and mourning the body was received by the inmates of 49 Chitpur Road. Malka went into an intense depression after this sudden death of her friend and benefactor. Gauhar cried bitterly at the loss of her father. She had been brought up to believe that Khurshid was her biological father. When even after days she was inconsolable, Malka told her the truth about Robert William Yeoward in a bid to bring her out of her sorrow. The sad saga of their life with him added to the young girl's trauma. All these years, she had loved and respected Khurshid as her father. To be told after his death that her father was an Armenian gentleman, who had disowned her and abandoned them when she was barely six years old, was a huge blow. It shattered Gauhar. She was gripped with an intense desire to confront this man who had fathered her and question him about his desertion of the family. But Malka pleaded ignorance about Robert's whereabouts. She truly had had no contact with him after he deserted them that day after pronouncing the cold and terse divorce statement. It took Gauhar a long time to come to terms with this stark and cruel reality of her parentage. It continued to gnaw at her heart for long.

The days went by. Gauhar was now a young girl on the brink of womanhood. Her coming of age, in 1886, when she was thirteen, was celebrated at the Chitpur house with great enthusiasm. Gauhar's close friend

Badre Munir Chaudhrayan, who was about the same age as her, joined the festivities. All the leading aristocrats of Calcutta and the celebrated baijis were invited to the celebrations. The old Raja of Khairagarh also graced the occasion. A rich and debauched man, he was a regular fixture in the kothas of many tawaifs.

The coming of age ceremony as a rite of passage had a great significance in a tawaif's life. The 'deflowering' ritual was known as *nath utarana*, *nath uthrai* or simply *nathi*, indicating that the girl was now ready for a formal initiation into the profession as a performing artist. From this moment on, the girl changed her nose ornament from a simple ring to a pearl or diamond studded pin that adult women wore. In typical tawaif households, the chaudhrayan would formally 'advertise' for a 'nath babu', the man who would undertake to pay a sizeable dowry to 'marry' the girl or offer to support her financially and provide intimate companionship. It was a kind of a contract-based union. The nath uthrai was accompanied by much gaiety, music, dance and merriment. Amelia Maciszewski argues in her essay on tawaifs *North Indian Women musicians and their words* that numerous songs sung by the tawaifs had the subtle references to the nath utharai ceremony.

She cites a chaiti, recorded by Rasoolan Bai, a renowned tawaif of Banaras,

> *Eri thaiya, mothiya hiraye gaile Ram*
> *Na koi aila na koi jaila*
> *Chor batahu gharse bahar na jaila*
> *Eri Saiya mothiya hiraye gaile Ram*

Alas, the pearls have been lost O Ram!
No one came home, no one left,
Neither did a thief break into my house
Yet I lost the pearls of my necklace O Ram!

These lyrics subtly speak of the young tawaif's pain at the loss of virginity and her helplessness in a situation she can barely comprehend or control. But whatever the age of tawaif at the time of the ceremony, it was their way of proclaiming to the world that she now had the sanction to 'settle' down with a benefactor and was equipped to provide him conjugal bliss.

The celebrations at Chitpur Road went on till the wee hours of the morning. With the music the alcohol flowed freely. Some of the guests departed half-way through the night, while others stayed on. Malka Jaan was so carried away with happiness that she drank herself to sleep.

When she startled awake at daybreak she was stunned to see her daughter Gauhar in the next room, lying in bed with the old Raja of Khairagarh. Gauhar too had been intoxicated the previous night and did not realise that she had been compromised and had become the victim of an old man's lechery. An enraged Malka Jaan shouted at the old man for taking advantage of her daughter and that too when the latter was barely conscious of what was happening to her. A shocked Gauhar woke up to hear her mother shouting and rushed out of the room looking for cover and battling her tears, even as Malka continued to berate him.

It was bad enough that the innocent Gauhar had been taken advantage of, it was a shock for her to find out she was pregnant. Malka Jaan quickly packed her off to a lady relative at Ghutiyari Sharif in Baruipur. The whole of Calcutta noticed her absence and was abuzz with questions about where the rising star had suddenly disappeared to after her thirteenth birthday. Malka was hard put to make up convincing stories to cover up the truth. Gauhar was utterly miserable at Ghutiyari Sharif. In time she prematurely delivered a still-born child. The physical and mental agony was too much to bear. When she finally returned to Calcutta, she was deeply scarred by her traumatic experience and sank into a state of melancholy.

To bring her out of her depression, Malka started taking her along to all her soirees. Initially though Gauhar hesitated to accompany her, being young and resilient she soon got back to providing vocal support to her mother. One such event, at the Darbhanga court where Malka had been invited to perform, was to be the turning point in Gauhar's professional life. Instead of going herself, Malka decided to send Gauhar there. It would be a good launch-pad for Gauhar, she thought, and her involvement in the music would bring some cheer into her life.

The principality of the Darbhanga Raj owed its origins to Mahesh Thakurji who was appointed by Emperor Akbar to be the tax collector of the Mithila region (today's Bihar state). Slowly the family consolidated itself at Darbhanga and became the largest zamindari in India. It was also touted as the best managed estate at the time of abolition of zamindari. Assuming the title of 'Maharaja', the zamindars lived regally and were great patrons of education, architecture, music and literature. By the 19th century, Darbhanga had emerged as an important seat of Hindustani classical music in the north. Their patronage to dhrupad led to the creation of a separate Darbhanga Gharana, which was propagated by the Mallicks of Darbhanga. Maharaja Lakshmeshwar Singh Bahadur (1860-1898) was a well-known philanthropist and connoisseur and an accomplished player of the sitar himself. Performing in front of such a learned connoisseur and musician, was a matter of great prestige for Gauhar.

Gauhar made the journey to Darbhanga with trepidation. All this while she had just sung along with her mother but now she was given the opportunity to emerge from her mother's protective wings. Naturally, she was nervous. The years of rigorous training under her gurus was now going to be put to the test and she had to emerge successful.

Maharaja Lakshmeswhar Singh had a large and imposing personality that commanded instant respect. He accorded a warm reception to the young artist at the sprawling Lakshmi Vilas (also called Anand Bagh) Palace. Gauhar quickly overcame her initial fears and almost with the very first strains of her youthful and mellifluous voice, Gauhar enchanted the audience. Her well honed voice and her stunning looks made her debut concert a huge success. Applauds of '*Wah! Wah!*' filled the air as she loaded the lyrics with emotions and negotiated complicated musical phrases with utmost ease. Everyone acknowledged the new star that had arrived on the firmament of Indian music and accorded her her rightful place of honour. The Maharaja expressed supreme satisfaction at her presentation and richly rewarded Gauhar. She was appointed court musician in the Darbhanga Raj from that very day. To Gauhar, her stupendous success and the rich rewards seemed like a fairy tale. Professionally she had climbed the first rung in the ladder of success but she was still fighting the demons in her personal life.

Her success at the Darbhanga concert qualified her to add a suffix to her name and be called 'Gauhar Jaan' henceforth.

Gauhar was a lovely young woman. Her good looks, fair skin, a broad forehead with arched eyebrows that converged at the centre, lustrous eyes, a graceful figure of medium height, long, black and curly hair and her magnetic personality naturally drew the audience towards her. Gauhar not only sang with great virtuosity but like her mother, she started composing songs under varied pen-names like 'Humdum' and 'Gauhar Piya.' After her success at Darbhanga she was flooded with concert opportunities from various households of Calcutta and also outside. No self-respecting mehfil was considered complete without her presence. A popular saying of those days was 'Gauhar ke bina mehfil, jaise shauhar ke bina dulhan.' (A concert without Gauhar is like a bride without her groom.)

Despite all the happiness that her professional success had brought her, Gauhar continued to be morose and introspective. She was looking for the man who would sweep her off her feet with true and unflinching love.

It was not long before he came knocking at her doors...

Ae mohabbat tere anjaam pe rona aaya
Jaane kyun aaj tere naam pe rona aaya

Oh love! It is your outcome that has made me cry
I don't know why, but today it is the very mention of your name that
has made me cry!

—SHAKEEL BADAYUNI

❧

5

THE BLOSSOMING OF LOVE

The winter of 1887 was particularly harsh for Gauhar. Her sojourn at Ghutiyari Sharif had been one of the most traumatic experiences of her life and it haunted her for many years. When she returned to the cold, misty mornings of Calcutta, it seemed to her that they echoed her state of mind. Malka made all the efforts she could to pull her out of this state of melancholy and Gauhar responded favourably by concentrating on her musical career with single-minded focus. She tried to wash away the memories of the past through her soulful tunes. The pain Gauhar had undergone was reflected in her voice and her music appealed to the listeners even more.

One evening, their new agent Yusuf, who brought them lucrative concert offers and customers for mujras, ushered in two young men. Gauhar watched from behind the curtain as they made their way to the main hall to be presented to Malka Jaan. One of them was broad shouldered, with sharp features, a high forehead, and bright twinkling eyes. The newly sprouted moustache gave away his age. In spite of his swagger and aristocratic demeanour as he addressed Malka Jaan, there was an air of nervousness about him. The other gentleman appeared to be much older and chose to remain in the background. Yusuf whispered something in Malka Jaan's ears and she immediately stood up, greeted them and exchanged pleasantries. The maid offered them drinks even as Malka Jaan requested them to make themselves comfortable. Excusing herself, Malka went in to inform Gauhar that the scion of the famed Rai family of Banaras, Rai Chaggan had come all the way to Calcutta to listen to her. He was accompanied by his friend Manohar, she said. Something about Chaggan had attracted Gauhar the minute she saw him enter the salon.

That evening Gauhar gave one of her best performances for the aristocratic guest from Banaras. The *bol-banao* thumris, that she had been trained in, were particularly suited for such intimate gatherings. As was customary, Gauhar performed seated and unfolded the beauty of the raga, using facial expressions, gestures and hand movements from dance to elaborate the theme of the composition and improvise on it. Chaggan was enchanted by this performance; Gauhar's stunning looks had him completely bewitched. He presented her a costly pearl necklace as a gift. He returned many evenings thereafter and each time was enthralled by new compositions that Gauhar presented, accompanied by her unique and characteristic performance style. Cupid had struck!

One evening Chaggan requested Malka for Gauhar's company. He was new to Calcutta and wanted to drive around the city with someone who knew the place well. Malka agreed but before they left, warned Gauhar to be alert and watchful. They drove through the city in the horse-drawn phaeton—from Chitpur to the Maidan and the Viceroy's Palace. It was Christmas time and Calcutta was decked up like a bride. The two youngsters chatted and sang as they rode along. Chaggan was a poet of sorts himself and he made up spontaneous verses praising her beauty and this flattered Gauhar no end.

When they returned after a very pleasant evening, Chaggan told Gauhar that this was his last evening in Calcutta as he had planned to return to Banaras. Tears welled up in Gauhar's eyes. She held his hand and said, 'What if I don't let you go? Will you stay back? Was I just a muse of a few days?' Chaggan immediately fell to his knees and asked her to accompany him to Banaras. 'You can live like a queen with me!' he promised. Gauhar was more than willing to accept his offer, but she needed to take her mother's permission.

Malka was furious at first when she heard this preposterous suggestion. Gauhar had built a reputation for herself and her career was just beginning to look up. To move back to Banaras and become a rich man's mistress would automatically mean the end of her musical career. And yet Malka knew that her daughter was pining for true love and if she made any attempts to hold her back forcibly, she would elope. She had seen the intensity of love in her daughter's eyes and knew that the best option for her was to let go of her daughter.

Thus in the winter of 1887, Gauhar packed her bags and left for Banaras with the man she loved. Chaggan promised to send Rs 500 as allowance to Malka in the absence of her daughter. For Gauhar, it was a nostalgic return to a city that had been her childhood home—the same ghats, the same river Ganga, and the same courtesans' salons. Chaggan had converted a horse stable into a nice, cosy dwelling for just the two of them. The cottage was surrounded by a beautiful garden. A large iron fountain, specially ordered from Sheffield, stood in the middle of the garden; beside a gazebo for Gauhar. Those were the days when Gauhar had not a care in the world. There were no performances that she had to worry about. There was just one man she waited for. She spent all day in that pretty cottage where there was no dearth of luxuries, with attendants to wait on her hand and foot and cater to her every whim. She had all the time to practise music and dance. As the evening approached, her heart would be aflutter, in anticipation of Chaggan's arrival. She would deck herself up and give in to his embrace each evening. His warm presence in those cold, winter nights of Banaras, especially with the full moon riding the sky, the carpets and bolsters strewn around in the garden where they would lie in amorous dalliance, the atmosphere heady with the scent of blooming flowers, the bubbling hookas, the sweet-smelling paans—it all seemed like a wonderful dream to Gauhar. Gauhar began to compose verses under the pen-name of '*Chaggan Piya*', the beloved of Chaggan, and some under her own name

'*Gauhar Piya.*' On his part Chaggan too composed some amateurish verses in English, like, "Where have you gone my beloved Jaan, leaving my heart asunder," to flatter his lady love.

Gauhar's melodious composition in Raga Kafi resonated on many of those moonlit nights. A song she had composed herself for the Holi festival and with the eternal love of Krishna and Radha as imagery is popular even today.

"*Kaisi yeh dhoom machayi, Kanhaiya Re*
Arrey Kanhaiya Re, Gaari humein tum deth?
Rang chidakat ho, baanh gahat ho
Deth hoon Ram Duhaai, Kaisi yeh dhoom machayi.
Dekho Shyam tore haath na aaoon
Ith lakhon karo chaturayi, Kaisi yeh dhoom machayi.
Arey Kanhaiya Re, Gaari humein tum deth?
Ith Gauhar Pyari se Nehaya laga ke dekhte ho naar parai?
Khelan laage sang naar parai, kaisi yeh dhoom machayi?

What preposterous behaviour is this Krishna?
You splash colours on me and twist my arms and in return chide me as well?
What do you take me for? For God's sake let me go, leave me alone.
Wait and watch, you won't manage to lay your hands on me despite all your hideous plans.
What preposterous behaviour is this Krishna?
You make tall claims of love for your beloved Gauhar and at the first opportunity dally with other women? What preposterous behaviour is this Krishna?

Even as Gauhar was floating in her world of dreams, back home in Calcutta Malka Jaan was facing her own set of turmoil. Her loyal friend and confidante Ashia died after a prolonged illness. Bhaglu, Ashia's son on whom Malka had showered a great deal of affection and treated as her own son, had fallen into bad company and was going wayward. He took to squandering money on his bad habits and each time he ran out of cash, he would play on Malka's sympathy as a poor orphan or make up fanciful stories and extract money from her. After Khurshid's death he had become much more daring.

On the advice of some well-wishers Malka decided to establish a small business for him and helped him start a chinaware shop. But Bhaglu was the kind for whom work was anathema and leisure was all that mattered. He neglected his business and before long he was in debt again. Once again he pleaded with Malka to bail out his sinking business.

Believing marriage to be the ultimate panacea for all evils, Malka decided to get Bhaglu married. She thought that it would instil some sense of responsibility in him. Her cook Najiba suggested one Rehana; whose father Noor Ali had a small leather business in Tiljala slum. Noor Ali was reluctant to marry his daughter into the family of a courtesan, and that too such a rich and famous one, but finally he relented. Malka Jaan celebrated the *nikah* of Bhaglu and Rehana with great pomp. She earnestly believed that this would change the boy for the better and he would take to his duties with more diligence. However, she was mistaken. Bhaglu continued on his path of self-destruction.

Meanwhile almost two years had passed since Gauhar had left for Banaras. She kept in touch with her mother regularly through letters. Chaggan too never failed to send Malka the monthly allowance that he had promised. But Malka was getting increasingly lonely and depressed. She missed Gauhar terribly. The death of Ashia and Khurshid and the thoroughly irresponsible behaviour of Bhaglu was more than she could take. She started drinking heavily to drown her sorrows. Finally she wrote to Gauhar asking her to come home to Calcutta at least for a short while.

Immediately Gauhar asked Chaggan for permission and departed for Calcutta. It was a tearful reunion for the mother and daughter. With stars in her eyes, Gauhar described the wonderful happenings in Banaras. She told her mother how much Chaggan pampered her and did his utmost to keep her happy. But Gauhar's happiness was short lived and she was rudely jolted from her reverie by a notice from the civil court of Banaras. It was a summons order based on the plea of a local businessman Makhan Lal. Gauhar was flabbergasted. She knew nothing about this man. Malka decided to accompany her to Banaras. The case turned out to be a completely contrived one. Makhan Lal had accused Gauhar of buying expensive Banarasi saris and not paying for them. He was forced to take this extreme step of sending a court notice when he heard she had fled to Calcutta.

Malka Jaan too presented herself before the Magistrate and testified that she was among the wealthiest tawaifs of Calcutta and a courtesan in the court of none other than Nawab Wajid Ali Shah. Gauhar herself was court musician of the famed Darbhanga Raj and was now the mistress of a rich zamindar of the city. Would someone coming from a background such as this cheat a petty merchant for a couple of saris, she asked.

In a statement before the Munsiff, Pandit Raj Nath Saheb, on 29 July 1889, Malka declared that her husband was Robert Yeoward and that he was still alive, that Gauhar was born to them in 1873 and that their marriage had ended ten years ago. The birth of Gauhar has been registered at the Protestant Church at Allahabad and she has been learning singing and dancing from the age of 10, Malka elaborated. She also declared that a daughter was born to Gauhar, though unfortunately still-born. Gauhar was currently the mistress of Chagganji and she did not go out to sing and dance.

In her elaborate testimony in the Court of Banaras, Malka made the following submission:

'In this Court of the Munsif at Benares (#545 of the year 1889)—Makhan Lall Vs. Gowhar Jan. Statement of the defendant Malka, a witness for the defendant on 26 June 1890 on oath under Act X of 1873 administered by Gouri Sunker, peon. Present Babu Bipin Behari Mukherjee himself. The defendant gives her name to be Malka Jan, class Tawaif, residence Mohalla, Lower Chitpore Road. Calcutta; age 32 years, occupation: that of her class. She is literate and states as follows:

I did not purchase cloth from the plaintiff. I came to Calcutta in November or December 1888. Gowhar is my daughter. She is in the keeping of Rai Chaggan ji. I have been to Benares three times since she has been kept (by him.) It is a little less than three years that she has been kept. It will not be more than two years and a half. I came for the first time to escort her when Gowhar was engaged. I stayed for 30 days on that occasion and then went back to Calcutta. After that I came here for the second time, after I received summons of this suit. This is the third time that I have come. I did never purchase cloth when I came to Benares nor had I necessity for cloth.

I came to Benares for the first time in January 1888. Whenever there is necessity for cloth, Rai Chaggan ji supplies the same to Gowhar. She has been kept by Chaggan ji on the condition that he would send me Rs 500/- to Calcutta or I would take the same myself if I come (here.) Accordingly Chaggan ji would pay whatever expenses for cloth, food (as may be required) for herself and her servant. I purchase cloth from Durbari Mull Mill in Calcutta.

Gowhar has completed her seventeenth year today. I was a Christian at first and now I am an Armenian; and when I was a Christian my name then was Adeline Victoria Hemmings. Gowhar was born when I had been a Christian; and her name was Angelina Yeoward.

There appears to be two reasons for bringing a false suit against us. The first is that Hira Tawaif was in the keeping of Rai Chaggan ji before Gowhar was kept by him; and Moti Lall used to frequent her (Hira's) place. This woman Hira said to my friend Saraswati, Malka has by causing my dismissal got her daughter kept by Rai Chaggan ji; I shall put her to disgrace. The second reason is that Chaggan ji is a minor, as one can not bring a case against him; therefore the suit has been instituted against us because Chaggan ji will not like our going to Court. In answer to question put by the pleader for the other party states I (do not) know Moti Lall and Makhan Lall. I had never ever heard their names before this suit was instituted. When I stayed here, no cloth-seller came to Chaggan ji for selling cloth nor did I ever see any one. When I came with Gowhar for the first time from Calcutta to Benares, I stopped at the Garden house in which Chaggan ji's elder brother Lallan ji is staying. In those days, Lallan ji did not live in that garden. It is not known whither he had gone to, but I stayed in that garden for twenty days. Rings which I have on my fingers are set with precious stones and I have received the same from them; I have not purchased these myself. That is why I cannot state their price. I have four rings on one hand and two on the other, in all six rings. Whenever I go out I put on these rings. I do not put them on at home and the Kangans on my hand (wrist) are made of gold and I had them made. In all I have got about two thousand rupees worth of ornaments on my hand.

Seven years ago I stayed at Benares for four years. I was in the keeping of Rai Pawan Dass for three years. He gave me permission at that time to dance and sing. When I came for the second time after the suit was filed I enquired as to the reason why this suit was filed and learnt from Saraswati then the reason for which the suit was filed. I do not remember the names of the persons from whom I made enquiries. Hira Tawaif told Saraswati (as above) during the time when Gowhar was kept by Rai Chaggan ji. I do not know if Hira carries on the profession of dancing and singing. She must assuredly be in the keeping of somebody. I have not seen Hira in the keeping of Chaggan ji. I have never been acquainted with Hira nor had I ever seen her. I have never been to the garden of Ganesh Lall. No suit was ever brought against us before this on account of Chaggan ji's debts. But people are waiting for the result of this suit. I do not know who are going to file suits. Many persons spoke to our servants. I do not know who Chaggan ji is indebted to. My marriage took place at Allahabad when I was fifteen years of age. I have a house in Calcutta worth forty thousand rupees. Before Gowhar was kept by Chaggan ji she was kept by the Raja of Kheragarh; she remained (as such) for two months. Prior to that she did not carry on the profession.

The case dragged on for close to a year and the anxiety of the outcome kept the mother and daughter on tenter hooks. Finally, after assessing the merits of the arguments of either side, the magistrate dismissed the case in favour of Gauhar.

Though she had won the case, the incident created a fear in her mind that stayed on for long. She knew that Makhan Lal was merely a pawn in someone else's hands. The intention was clearly to besmirch her reputation and possibly bring a rift between her and Chaggan. She suspected the baijis of Banaras, including Hira Bai, who were jealous of her popularity. But she wondered how she was a threat to them when she had given up performing in public ever since she came to Banaras. It then occurred to her that it could have been someone from Chaggan's family who despised her and her association with Chaggan. Malka was very worried for her daughter and stayed with her for a couple of months before leaving for Calcutta.

The case was much talked about all over the city and the love affair of a rich and handsome zamindar's son and the supposedly cunning but pretty tawaif became a hot topic of conversation. It was to pander to his lady love that Chaggan had fallen into numerous debts, the rumour mills opined. One day while Chaggan was away from town, his elder brother Lallan Rai came to Gauhar's mansion and reprimanded her for ruining his innocent brother's life and that he was willing to give whatever sum she asked for, if she promised to forget him and leave the city for good. There was a property division on the anvil and Lallan Rai was worried that his infatuated younger brother would squander his share of property on his mistress. Gauhar was too stunned to say anything. After a few moments when the import of what he had said sank in, she replied that this was an internal family matter and that he needed to discuss it with his brother. She would remain there as long as he pleased and the day he expressed his desire that she should leave, she would not think twice before packing her bags. An incensed Lallan Rai showered abuses on her and walked away.

A rattled Gauhar related the entire incident to Chaggan the night he returned. He embraced her tightly and asked her to trust him. He admitted to differences that had cropped up among the brothers on the matter of his liaison with Gauhar and the impending property division. He promised her that he would sacrifice his family for her sake if the need arose. A reassured Gauhar shed tears of joy and kissed him.

A couple of months passed this way. But soon, Gauhar noticed a change in Chaggan's behaviour. He no longer spent long hours with her. Their nocturnal unions too became rarer by the day. Gauhar was worried but had no one to share her fears and insecurities with. She wrote long letters to her mother expressing her apprehensions about this sudden change in Chaggan's attitude. Is this the ultimate and inevitable fate of all us tawaifs, was her constant refrain.

From one of the servants she learned that Chaggan's family had come up with an ingenious solution to dispense with her evil and unwanted presence. They knew that Chaggan was a man of eclectic tastes and revelled in intellectual companionship. They had therefore found a very beautiful and intelligent Punjabi Saraswat Brahmin girl who could speak fluent English and indulge in witty repartees. She was totally different from the traditional purdah-clad illiterate women of the family. The woman immediately caught Chaggan's fancy. He readily agreed to marry her and settle down. He no longer needed the company of Gauhar to entertain himself.

Gauhar was shocked by this news. She had not expected him to legally wed her and make her his wife. But she did not think he would hide such an important development from her and instead choose to stay away. When he finally did come, their meeting was a fiery one. But Chaggan was firm. He told her that she could continue to live in Banaras as before and that he would not mind maintaining her. But certainly his visits would become less frequent and might completely cease if his wife ever objected. Gauhar was heart-broken. She did not need his mercy or his money. She was a well-established singer in her own right and could look after herself well. She had given all that up for his sake and after being used and now discarded, she no longer felt it necessary to stay on in Banaras.

She packed her belongings, bid a final adieu to Chaggan, thanked him for his kindness and returned to Calcutta on 30 July 1891, battling her tears and fighting a thousand questions. Perhaps this incident convinced her about the true status of women of her profession. They were worshipped and placed on high altars by men who made numerous promises. But could be dispensed with quite easily and nobody would question their actions. The tawaif's role was merely to deck herself and entertain the next wealthy gentleman who wanted to amuse himself for a brief spell.

Malka knew that the relationship would end this way but she wanted Gauhar to learn the lessons of life the hard way instead of being preached to or advised. When Gauhar arrived in Calcutta, sobbing inconsolably, Malka just hugged her daughter tightly, without saying a word. Gauhar remained aloof and cut-off from the world for a few weeks. Malka left her alone for a while, but then forced her to get over the experience and get back to her music and performances. That, she assured her, would be her most dependable companion and the only balm for her troubled soul. Wiping her tears, Gauhar strummed her tanpura that lay unattended for so many months and the plaintive strains of Raga Bhairavi filled the room.

Mora nahak laye gavanava re
Jabse gayi mori, sudbudha lini

Betee Jaaye jobanava re
Nahak laye gavanava re

He has left me and gone and never cared to enquire about me thereafter
And here I am, pining for his return, even as my youth withers away!

Hasrath nahin hoti hai ke naala nahin hota
Jab tum nahin hote ho tho kya kya nahin hota.

It is your presence that makes my life worth living,
Without you neither hope nor pain trouble my void heart.
How can I even explain what your absence means to me?

—Badi Malka Jaan, Makhzan-e-ulfat-e-Mallika.

6

RENDEZVOUS WITH MUSIC

Seth Dhulichand was among the greatest patrons of music in Calcutta those days. Dhulichand was a wealthy Marwari businessman of the city and given his immense love for music, he invited several leading musicians from across the country to his soirees. It was considered a matter of great honour to be invited to participate in the musical gatherings at his palatial mansion. These went on through the night and involved several back-to-back performances.

There were many contemporaries of Gauhar Jaan who were making a name for themselves at that time. Malka Jaan of Agra (also called as Malka Jaan Agrewali) was one of them. Her story was similar to Gauhar's. She too was born in Azamgarh and thereafter studied under several great ustads of Agra. Later she joined the court of Nawab Wajid Ali Shah in Calcutta. She was thus a direct competitor for Gauhar. But the two enjoyed a rare bonhomie and friendship even if tinged with professional rivalry and jealousy. Both Malka and Gauhar were among the favourites of Seth Dhulichand who never failed to invite them to every soiree of his. Shyamlal Khatri was another famous patron of Calcutta whose house was perennially bustling with music and musicians. Both Dhulichand and Shyamlal, like most patrons, were themselves trained in music and even taught some of the leading musicians a composition or two that they had picked up. But the stigma attached to public performance prevented them from taking to the stage in earnest.

Malka Jaan Agrewali became popular for developing her new full-throated thumri singing style. Like Gauhar, she too had a wide repertoire that ranged from dhrupad, khayal and thumri to the so-called light and folk pieces of hori, chaiti, kajri, tappa and ghazal. Her '*Beete jat barkha ritu sajan nahin aaye*' ('The rainy season is coming to an end but my beloved hasn't returned') in Raga Desh and '*Papihara piu piu kare*' (The *papihara* bird melodiously calls, *piu piu*) in Raga Sawan were immensely popular with the audiences. Later in life, Malka Jaan Agrewali had a long and torrid love affair with the famed Ustad of the Agra Gharana, Ustad Faiyyaz Khan, who was much younger than her.

Zohra Bai of Agra (1868-1913) was another contemporary artist of great calibre. After receiving her initial training under her father Ahmed Khan, an ace sarangi player, Zohra went on to train under eminent ustads Mehboob Khan and Kale Khan of the Agra Gharana that is known for its lyrical charm and wide and rich repertoire. Her khayal renditions were counted among the best at that time and she could elaborate a raga in a structured fashion for hours.

A friend of Gauhar Jaan, right from her Banaras days, was Janki Bai of Allahabad (1880-1934). To facilitate her musical training Janki Bai's family shifted to Allahabad where she received intense training under Ustad Hassu Khan of Lucknow. Janki Bai had a curious and interesting nickname, '*Chappanchuri*'. A jealous suitor, madly in love with her, scarred her face with fifty-six slashes when she rebuffed him and thus the nickname. Like Gauhar, Janki too was adept at singing and composing verse and knew Sanskrit, Persian, Urdu and English. Janki Bai was embarrassed by her plain looks and scarred face and hence always sang from behind a curtain or veil. It is said that once when she was performing for the Maharaja of Rewa she had the curtain screening her face. But the Maharaja, on hearing her rich and glorious voice, ordered the curtain to be removed. He said it was the artist's talent and not looks that mattered.

Malka Jaan of Chilbila, Kishtobhamini of Calcutta and courtesans like Badi Maina, Husna Bai of Banaras, Wazir Jaan, Sugganbai, Mangubai were also quietly carving a niche for themselves in the world of music and dance. Of course healthy competition and rivalry existed between them, but there were always enough opportunities and patronage for them to feel insecure. In fact, there was a lot of interaction among them and they attended each other's performances without fail, both to judge how well the other sang and to incorporate those traits into their own *gayaki*. They also learnt from mistakes the other singers made. Patrons like Seth Dhulichand and Shyamlal Khatri had their favourites no doubt but they made it a point to invite all the leading musicians of the city to their musical sessions. It was a combined journey of musical experience and education where favouritism and one-upmanship evanesced.

One of the soirees that Seth Dhulichand hosted was going to be graced by the famed musician Bhaiya Ganpatrao. Ganpatrao had promised to unveil a surprise package that evening, and this announcement created a great deal of excitement and anticipation among the guests.

Ganpatrao or Bhaiya Sahib as he was popularly known heralded a new approach to Hindustani music. He was the son of Gwalior's Maharaja Jivajirao Scindia and Chandrabhaga Devi, a courtesan of the Gwalior durbar. Both Ganpat and his brother Balwant had inherited their mother's musical genius. After a while they migrated to Bhavnagar where Ganpatrao learnt the dhrupad and sitar from Ustad Bande Ali Khan. Ganpatrao then decided to go to Lucknow for some time to study thumris under the pioneer and major contributor to the genre, Ustad Sadiq Ali Khan. The thumri at that time was considered an inferior form, and looked down upon as a flippant and shallow genre in comparison to the weighty and classical dhrupad and khayal. Ganpatrao took it upon himself to bring the thumri out of the throes of ignominy. He created such a level of stylization in its rendition that it won hearts everywhere. In addition he was solely responsible for the introduction of the harmonium into classical music performances. Melodic accompaniment to vocal music was provided predominantly by the sarangi those days. The harmonium was despised as an instrument since it was considered incapable of producing subtle nuances, and was just a lifeless, stiff-reeded and un-Indian instrument. It was entirely to the credit of Bhaiya Sahib's musical genius and innovation that he moulded the harmonium to suit Indian music, so much so that it even displaced the once reigning sarangi. Despite being of royal descent, Bhaiya Sahib was a musical mendicant and travelled from court to court giving performances and training a vast body of students in both the thumri and the harmonium.

The much awaited day for his performance at Dhulichand's house finally arrived and many of the luminaries of the world of Hindustani music reached Sethji's tastefully done up soiree hall. The list of invitees included Shyamlal Khatri, Soniji of Gaya, Bashir Khan of Gwalior, Ghaffoor Khan of Punjab, Girija Shankar Chakraborthy, Ustad Badal Khan and Bahadur Khan and the female stars of those times, Gauhar Jaan, Malka Jaan of Agra, Malka Jaan of Chilbila, Kishtobhamini and others.

As she was walking in, Gauhar noticed a man with a colourful turban and long drooping moustache and guessed that he must be Bhaiya Sahib. Along with him was a shy, diffident but extremely good-looking young man with the features of a Nawab who stood right behind Bhaiya Sahib greeting everyone whom he was asked to. He was dressed in a Punjabi kurta-pyjama of the most exquisite foreign cloth and wore a beautiful 'Gaya topi' (cap) that was embroidered with golden thread.

Gauhar immediately recognized him. She had known him as 'Mauzu' in her Banaras days. The young man's family had lived in Mohalla Sheikh Saleem's Phatak and had then shifted to Mohalla Chota Tala. She recalled stories she had heard then of a good-looking young boy who was taught by his mother Begum Zebunnissa and his favourite Bhairavi thumri, *'Bajuband khul khul jaay'* was the toast of the town. So much so that the eight year old boy would be stopped by shopkeepers and requested to sing that song in return for sweets. A little crowd of fascinated passers-by would form each time he opened his mouth and sang with his melodious voice. Gauhar knew that much later Mauzu had begun training under a very noted exponent of the Banaras-ang or style of thumri singing, Guru Jagdeepji.

Gauhar heard about the same boy many years later, again at Banaras, this time at Rai Chaggan's place. Chaggan had narrated to her the anecdote of a young man who was desperate to be listed among the musicians patronized by the Rai family. Since he knew that gaining an entry into their household was a very tough task, he had decided to conceal himself in a thick bush near the outer compound wall of the Rai mansion and sing in his clear, loud and melodious voice. When the inmates heard his voice, Lallan Rai sent for him and he was immediately appointed singer of the Rai family. Gauhar remembered how they had had a hearty laugh about this when Chaggan narrated the incident to her, though she had not managed to catch a glimpse of the young man while she was there. By then it was time for her to bid farewell to Banaras. She wondered what he was doing with Bhaiya Sahib and whether his benefactors at Banaras had betrayed him as well.

The *mehfil* commenced and many of the local celebrities including Gauhar Jaan gave stellar performances.

Bhaiya Sahib then got up to speak. He introduced the young man sitting by his side as Mauzuddin, his *shagird* or student. He had met him during his visit to Banaras at a famous musical soiree arranged at the Phulanpur residence of a wealthy patron of Banaras, Raja Munshi Madanlal. Bhaiya Sahib had first seen Mauzuddin sing with Najju Khan accompanying him on the sarangi and Shyamlal and Bashir Khan on the harmonium. So enchanted was Bhaiya Sahib by the young man's brilliance that he nudged the harmonium player aside and accompanied the singer himself. Mauzuddin was lost in his world and sang with his eyes closed. Suddenly when he opened his eyes he was astonished to see the legendary Bhaiya Sahib on the harmonium. From that day he was taken as a disciple and Bhaiya Sahib treated him with utmost affection. Narrating this incident to the overawed audience, Bhaiya Sahib called upon Mauzu to take the stage.

Terribly diffident and shy by nature, Mauzuddin was overwhelmed by this laudatory prelude that Bhaiya Sahib had given. Also, the brilliance of the singers who preceded him increased his nervousness. He felt ill at ease and afraid that he would ruin the show and bring disgrace to his guru. However, his ever supportive master and friend, Bhaiya Sahib blessed the young man and told him not to be afraid and that he would accompany him that evening. With all humility Mauzuddin took his guru's blessings and started off with a khayal bandish and slowly meandered to his forte, the

Banarasi-ang Thumri. Starting with '*Piya bina nahin avat chain*' (No succour to my heart without my beloved) in Raga Behari, Mauzuddin sang with such depth of emotion that the connoisseurs and musicians were stunned. The impact of all the preceding performances was wiped out and his stood out as the only true and pure music. The audience goaded him not to stop, and he sang till the wee hours of the morning. In just one performance, Mauzuddin had conquered the musical world of Calcutta.

Reminiscing about this event, the late Prof. D.P. Mukherjee wrote:

'During our college days, the foundations of a whole new school of thumri were being laid in a room on the third floor of a house on Harrison Road. There Bhaiya Ganapatrao brought Mauzuddin Khan, an unknown singer then. Nobody knew his gharana. People used to whisper that he had no training…but then, when he would start a thumri with either Ganapatrao or Mirza Saheb on the harmonium, nothing else mattered. The best dhruvapadiyas and khayaliyas would listen to him spell-bound. In my own view, India has not produced another thumri singer like him. I have seen tears in the eyes of Gauhar Jan, Malka Jan, Shyamlal Khatri, Girija Babu and many others when Mauzuddin improvised on a simple Bhairavi…'

Gauhar did indeed cry that night not only at the brilliance of music that she had just witnessed but also at her own ignorance and for whiling her time away in wasteful pursuits and faithless lovers. Here was a music as pristine and magnificent as the ocean before which no one and nothing mattered. At the end of the concert she fell at the feet of both Bhaiya Sahib and Mauzuddin. So self-effacing was the young man that he felt distinctly uncomfortable that the most famous baiji of Calcutta was touching his feet. During the course of the previous night's performance, Mauzuddin had announced that his concluding item in Raga Paraj Bahar, '*Daal Phool Phal*' was something that he had picked up by listening to Gauhar Jaan. It was a complicated piece that involved trips to many allied and not so allied ragas. Gauhar confessed to Bhaiya Sahab and Mauzuddin that the latter had added such new dimensions to her song that she felt she no longer deserved to sing it. Gauhar never sang that piece ever again. She beseeched both Bhaiya Sahib and Mauzuddin to take her under their wings and impart some of their musical knowledge to her. They readily agreed and this began a new era in Gauhar's musical journey.

Bhaiya Sahib's approach to thumri had created, as was mentioned by Prof D P Mukherjee, a whole school of thumri singers. The list of his disciples included some of the top-most performers of the times. Apart from Mauzuddin and Gauhar Jaan, Nawab Saheb Chamman of Rampur, Nawab Hamid Hussain of Rampur, Thakur Nawab Ali of Lucknow, Seth Dhulichand, Babban Saheb of Lucknow, Sonibabu, Bashir Khan, Meer Saheb, Pandit Girija Shankar Chakrabarthy, Jangi Khan and others were among his illustrious students. The training of Bindadin Maharaj and now Bhaiya Sahib created a unique and distinct musical identity for Gauhar, especially in her renditions of thumris that she went on to become so popular for.

An important aspect of Gauhar's musical character was her open-mindedness and willingness to accept every new thought and idea related to music. She would assimilate, adapt and make it her own style. Right from her early learning days till the time she reached the pinnacle of success as a reigning Empress of Hindustani music, Gauhar was ever humble and hungry for knowledge. She would attend the concerts of every big ustad who came to Calcutta; if she found something worth emulating in their music and if she could internalize it by herself, she would gladly do it. Else she would humbly request them to take her as a disciple. Hence the list of her ustads was endless. At a time when most traditional musicians swore by the gharana system with its water-tight compartments that was so prevalent in Hindustani music, Gauhar and many other women musicians of her time, were emancipated enough in their thinking to realise that music could not be bound by such narrow, geographical and stylistical limitations and that a healthy interaction and intermixing of styles to create one's own individual style was important.

Gauhar was not at all embarrassed to ask even her contemporaries to teach her. Apart from Mauzuddin, she also learnt a little from Peara Sahab (c.1870-1945). Hailing from a family of musicians, Peara Sahab was another star musician of his times. His father had established himself at Nawab Wajid Ali Shah's court at Matia Buruj. He learnt a wide range of genres and also the light-classical ones and like Gauhar was among the most sought after and expensive artists of his times.

The well-rounded training that Gauhar sought for herself made her dominate the musical stage of the country for a long time. Abdul Halim Sharar, the famous writer from Lucknow, who witnessed a performance of Gauhar Jaan in 1896 in Calcutta, was dazzled. He recounts this performance thus:

> 'It is unlikely that anywhere else there were more perfect demonstrations of dance than the courtesans of Lucknow... At one performance I witnessed her (Gauhar Jaan's) skill in *batana* on the same theme for three full hours. All those present at the gathering, including the most expert dancers and distinguished people of Matiyaburj were spellbound. There was not even a child who was not impressed by the performance.'

Gauhar's fame spread beyond the concert stage of Calcutta and the North and reached as far as Southern India. The Maharaja of Mysore Chamarajendra Wodeyar X was a colourful man who frequently visited Calcutta to call on the Viceroy of India who lived in the city. After the routine meetings, the Maharaja spent his time to liberally soak in the cultural atmosphere of Calcutta. Having heard so much about Gauhar Jaan, the new star of Indian music, he attended one of her *mehfils* and was deeply impressed. He invited her over to his kingdom in the distant Southern province of Mysore. Gauhar's joy knew no bounds. She visited Mysore and left her audience spell bound there as well. She was named as a regular visiting musician during the *Vardhanti* or birthday celebrations of the Maharaja and the famed Dasara festivities of the city. She was accorded special royal honours and rewards at Mysore. Little did Gauhar know then that the city of Mysore that she had fallen in love with was to occupy an important part of her life later on.

While this period in Gauhar's life was a combination of professional success owing to her sharpening her innate skills under numerous practitioners and internalizing their styles to create her own unique musical identity, it was not devoid of the usual distractions. There are some references to her romantic interludes with the rich Zamindar of Behrampore, Nimai Sen. She had met him at a concert at the Hazardwari Palace in Murshidabad and had almost instantly fallen in love with him. Nimai Sen was a great lover of music and invited Gauhar to his hometown. She readily agreed to go and spent some wondrous times at Behrampore. Nimai Sen was excessively lavish in his spending. She was presented expensive gifts of ivory and gold and pampered like the queen of the town. In turn Gauhar gave him her diamond nose-stud as a memento (a possible reference to the *nath uthrai* or a surrender of her virginity.)

Numerous legends abound about their profligate love. One much recounted tale is of a day when Gauhar was down with a bad headache and there was no fuel to boil a kettle of water and prepare tea. When the ardent lover Nimai heard about her predicament, he immediately rushed there and used currency notes to boil the water and prepare her tea!

Nimai Sen also accompanied Gauhar back to Calcutta. Given her great love for handsome stallions, he took her to the Armenian colony where people owned several race horses. Nimai was influential enough to get his lady love try her hand at riding these stallions and thus heady horse-riding marked their courtship! Gauhar is also supposed to have travelled as his wife to another town to listen to the Kirtans of a famous singer Mukund Das.

But the sad turn that her relationship with Chaggan Rai had taken made Gauhar wary and cautious. Moreover she had begun to truly love Nimai Sen and did not want to lose him the way she lost Chaggan. Gauhar therefore insisted that he should marry her and legitimize this relationship. Little did Gauhar realise that women like her were just sophisticated playthings for these rich men, who might shower them with the costliest of gifts in their weak moments, but hesitate to accept them legally. Such a move would lead to a great social backlash from the same society which really would not mind if the illegitimate affairs carried on. In addition, many rich zamindars and princes stood the risk of parental wrath that could result in losing their hereditary claims over the property. An impoverished man would hardly be an attraction at any kotha.

Nimai Sen was no different. Though he loved Gauhar truly he refused to take her as his legal wife. Gauhar was heart-broken but she refused to play into another man's hands like before and began avoiding Nimai Sen. Slowly the relationship broke off and Nimai stopped visiting her.

It is said that many years later on hearing the news of Nimai Sen being on his death-bed, Gauhar rushed to Behrampore to see him. In some corner of her heart she still bore great love and passion for him. But sadly he was dead by the time she reached there. Nimai Sen had carefully preserved Gauhar's nose-stud and had told an attendant to return it to her when she came. Nimai Sen was very sure she would. Gauhar was deeply touched and was drowned in grief and sorrow for many months.

Despite all these personal ups and downs, at the turn of the century, Gauhar was at the threshold of unprecedented glory in the world of music. Indian classical music itself was at a decisive phase of its history, one that would alter the way it was studied, viewed, presented, appreciated and packaged. With the disappearance of old patrons and the appearance of new, democratic ones, the very character of Indian classical music was in for a radical shift. Little did Gauhar know or realise that the other side of the century had the most unimaginable, exciting things in store for her and that her best days were yet to come. Her life and that of many other musicians, both in India and abroad, was to undergo dramatic changes thanks to a certain discovery in America a few decades earlier.

SECTION 2

THE GLORY YEARS

7

'THIS SHOULD TALK'

29 November, 1877; Menlo Park, near New York

It was another day of trial and error for John Kruse, an expert technician who worked with Thomas Alva Edison as his assistant at the latter's 'Invention Factory' in Menlo Park, which was approximately twenty five miles from New York City. In early November 1877, Edison had given Kruse a detailed technical drawing and declared, 'This should talk.' Kruse's job was to assemble the contraption according to the directions of his master. What he was putting together was a device made up of brass and iron cylinders, diamond styluses and several other mechanical arrangements that would facilitate the rotation of these cylinders. Kruse's colleagues watched him at work with great scepticism and were positively amused by a strange horn-shaped metal cone that was fitted with a tiny needle at its end.

Edison entered the laboratory after being told that the work was done. One look at it and he gave a pleased smile to convey his approval to his diligent assistant. He first wrapped a tin-foil tightly around the curved surface of the foot long cylinder. Then he placed the diamond stylus carefully at one end of the foil and began to rotate the cylinder at a gentle and uniform speed, using the handle that was fitted on the right of the turn-table box on which the cylinder was mounted. All the while he ensured that the needle cut a uniform groove in the tin-foil. He then shouted into the horn, reciting the famous nursery rhyme,

'Mary had a little lamb; its fleece was white as snow,

And everywhere that Mary went, the lamb was sure to go.'

The sound of his voice created vibrations in the needle and thereby produced zigzag patterns on the tin-foil. He then brought the horn and needle to its original starting position, changed the stylus, placed the needle in the newly formed grooves and began to rotate the cylinder as before. The people who had crowded around had stopped blinking and breathing and many hearts must have skipped beat. When the entire contraption began to move a terrible noise started emanating from the horn, drawing stifled laughter from the onlookers. Suddenly, as the needle began to pass through the zigzag groove that had been cut by Edison's shouting, the nursery rhyme echoed back distinctly from the device, though feebly. Edison froze with excitement even as the crowd clapped and cheered.

Buoyed by the success of their experiment, the duo worked tirelessly and made changes to the instrument, and came with new and better versions. Finally on 6 December 1877 Edison rushed to the Patents office in New York to file a patent for this new device. On 22 December 1877, Edison proudly displayed his machine in the office of the *Scientific American* which announced the invention of his 'Phonograph' to the rest of the world. Edison was hailed as the 'Wizard of Menlo Park.' Finally on 19 January 1878 Edison received the patent for his invention of the cylinder phonograph.

But Edison realised that though the device was an important break-through in the field of recording and production of sound, it had little value except as a talking toy. So he shelved the project for over ten years during which time he continued to think hard and work harder to find ways to make the device better and more useful. On one occasion he is reported to have got so engrossed in his work that he was at the job tirelessly for 72 hours on end without food and sleep.

By June 1888 Edison was ready with a new model of the phonograph, with a battery operated motor for maintaining uniform speed. However the experimentation and improvements went on till 1911 under the aegis of the Edison Phonograph Company. But frankly, no one, including Edison, realised the commercial potential of this invention and how it could revolutionize the entertainment industry. They had merely thought of it as a scientific experiment that worked at times and failed at others.

Edison had inspired a whole generation of young scientists to experiment in sound recording. It was almost a fad those days to be seen sitting poring over a tin-foil in some shanty laboratory. Everyone wanted to come up with some new discovery like Edison had. Twenty-one year old Emile Berliner of Washington was no different. He was a migrant from Hanover in Germany and earned his living as a draper's clerk. He was obsessed with the solving of electrical problems connected with telephones and phonographs. In the early days of his struggle Berliner was staying in a rented room on the third floor of a dingy house run by a widow and her three children. He frequently tried to simulate long-distance communication, much to the excitement of the children. He would place a soap-box which had been converted into a transmitter circuit on the ground floor where the landlady and the kids would be asked to speak. He would then try and receive these messages in his third floor room which was littered with odd bits of string, wire and batteries.

Around this time, Alexander Graham Bell and Charles Sumner Tainter, the winners of the Volta Prize for the invention of the telephone, came to Washington. With the prize money they had established the Volta Laboratory from which was issued the master-patent for 'cutting a sound line in a solid body.' In this laboratory Bell and Tainter evolved the gramophone.

Meanwhile Berliner's experiments continued. Hearing about the encouragement that the Bell Telephone Company was providing to talented scientists, Berliner decided to submit the idea of his telephone transmitter to the Company. He managed to get it patented and also got a cash prize of $75,000 from the Company. He used this to set up a make-shift laboratory on New York Avenue where he further experimented with the phonographs of Edison.

One fine morning, to this laboratory came a young man of sixteen, Frederick William Gaisberg accompanied by his friend Billy Golden. Gaisberg was a pianist of sorts and made some small money by displaying his musical skills. The most common public entertainment those days was amateur singers accompanied by pianists like him performing by the pavements with Edison's phonograph. For a payment of just five cents the listener would be shown the marvel of human achievement —the machine that could faithfully reproduce the music created by the musicians. Children would clap with delight and believe that one of the musicians had hidden himself inside that cylinder! Apart from such amateur ventures, Gaisberg had also had some formal training in sound production at the Volta Laboratory and the American Graphophone Company at Bridgeport, Connecticut.

The day Gaisberg made his entry into Berliner's laboratory, he had been coaxed by his friend Billy who promised to show him a clown. The outlandish dress sense and queer mannerisms of Berliner had earned him the tag of 'clown' from many people. That day too Berliner was dressed in a monkish frock and was pacing up and down the room. He was buzzing test-messages of 'Hello, Hello' on a diaphragm and repeating the famous English rhyme with his distinct German accent 'Tvinkle Tvinkle little star, how I vonder vot you are.' Concealing his laughter, Gaisberg watched on. After the formal introductions were done, Berliner enquired if the two visitors would participate in his experiment being amateur musicians themselves. Without waiting for any answer, Berliner quickly placed a muzzle over Billy's mouth and connected this up by a rubber hose to a diaphragm. He pushed Gaisberg towards a piano and asked him to play. The piano's sounding-board was also boxed up and connected to the diaphragm by a hose resembling an elephant's trunk. 'Are you ready?' he asked and upon receiving the affirmation he began to crank the recording device as one would a barrel-organ and said 'Go.' Billy was to sing a little song to the accompaniment of Gaisberg's piano. In a few minutes the song finished. Berliner stopped cranking, took a bright zinc disc from the machine and plunged it into an acid bath for a while. Taking it out, he washed the disc and placed it on a reproducing machine which was hand-operated like most coffee-grinders. Much to the astonishment of the visitors, Billy's song and Gaisberg's piano played back from the etched grooves. Berliner went hysterical with excitement. He had made the first 'gramophone record'. He claimed that his technology was far superior to that of Edison's cylinder. This was because when the recording stylus was vibrated laterally on a flat surface it encountered an even resistance, unlike on the cylindrical surface and that accounted for the clarity of tone. Thus was created the first gramophone zinc-disc 'record' in 1891.

Gaisberg's initial amusement turned into awe and respect for the funny man. He begged Berliner to allow him to work with him in his lab. Over the next few months Berliner and Gaisberg conducted several experiments to record a variety of sounds on this new marvel. Till 1897, Berliner used 7-inch zinc discs for the etching process. Ebonite was employed for pressing these zinc records. Ebonite withstood a lot of pressure and would not retain the impression permanently.

Soon a new substance known as 'shellac' began to replace the original zinc as the material for making the discs. Lac was hardened resin secreted by the tiny lac insects which settled on twigs and sucked the plant's sap. These insects were scraped from the twigs, crushed, dried, sieved, winnowed, washed and again dried. The mangled mass was then passed through a hot melting system, filtered and stretched into thin sheets which were known as 'shellac.' This was a non-toxic substance and began to be used as the base material for gramophone records.

Despite all the improvements made to the original model of the gramophone, sales were sluggish. Berliner and Gaisberg realised that unless the gramophone was fitted with a clock-driven motor it would never become a serious commercial proposition and merely remain a toy for the curious. The clock-motor had to perform the task of rotating a turntable at a uniform speed for two minutes continuously against the resistance of a heavy sound-box and thereby produce consistent sound. By chance Gaisberg's eyes caught sight of an advertisement in a newspaper of a sewing machine firm that had made an innovation with the usage of their indigenously developed clockwork motors for their machines. This gave him the answer to the problem they were trying to fix. Gaisberg then utilized the services of a young mechanic in New Jersey, Eldridge R. Johnson, to work on the clockwork gramophone motor which was simple, practical and cheap.

The popularity of the gramophone now began to swell. From popular and comic songs to marches and dialogues, it could play for 1 ½ to 2 minutes anything that the people wished to hear, through its circular records that were 5-inch and 7-inch in diameter. The singers were paid a fee of $3 for each song. Edison's phonograph was steadily losing its popularity despite its superior recording quality, because of the difficulty in duplicating record cylinders. In the case of the gramophones, once an original wax master record was made, multiple copies could be easily stamped. This enabled the gramophone records to overtake the old cylinder.

Buoyed by the success Emile Berliner signed a licensing agreement with Trevor Lloyd Williams, a London-based solicitor on 23 February 1898, in the Hotel Cecil, London. Berliner's agent William Barry Owen worked out the modalities of the deal with Lloyd. Accordingly in April 1898, the Gramophone Company was founded as a syndicate. While the mechanical components of the gramophone were to be made in the United States of America and then assembled in England, the Company decided to take its recordings to wherever its 'recording experts' were located. Berliner's brother Joseph set up the Telephon Fabrik, a factory in Hanover, where the discs reproduced from the master records or matrices were to be manufactured. 31 Maiden Lane, Strand, London became the Head-office of this newly incorporated Company in May that year.

Without wasting much time, the Gramophone Company began its operations in July 1898. Gaisberg became the first recording expert to set off on the maiden recording 'expedition' to London on board the Umbria. The use of the word expedition indicated the excitement that these pioneers felt about the history that they were seeking to create. From 1 November 1898, Gaisberg began numbering the master discs or matrices from #1 progressing with each recording session. Discs were then manufactured from the matrices at Hanover as the first 7-inch, single-sided recorded 'E Berliner's Gramophone discs' with no printed labels on them but merely a tag etched on the centre of the disc. In 1898, the symbol of the 'recording angel' which was to become a famous trademark of the company, was first introduced. Various naming conventions were developed to classify and catalogue the recordings based on chronology, language, geography etc. It was in London that technically the first Indian voices were etched on the shellac discs. There were 47 numbered recordings of Captain Bholanath, Dr Harnaamdas and Ahmed who sang, recited and spoke in several languages. There were 20 records in Persian, 15 in Hindi, 5 in Urdu/Hindustani, 5 in Sikh/Gurumukhi and 2 in Arabic. The musical content was not as important for the company as building up a vast and multi-ethnic, multi-lingual repertoire.

On 15 August 1899, the syndicate was transformed into a limited liability company called the Gramophone Company Limited. Naming procedures were further standardized. The expeditions across the United Kingdom, Russia and Europe were hugely successful and the Company saw brisk business and sales. Exports of gramophones to Africa, China, India and Australia were steadily on the rise and about 500 recordings in European and Oriental languages were catalogued. But despite the success, the new managing director William Barry Owen felt that the gramophone alone was insufficient to run a profitable business and that the Company needed to diversify and bundle its product offerings. The Lambert typewriter was chosen as the odd partner. Thus the unusual marriage of the Lambert Typewriter Company based out of Broadway in New York and the Gramophone Company Ltd, took place on 10 December 1900 resulting in the Gramophone and Typewriter Ltd or GTL. Ironically, years later, it was the typewriter that failed to attract customers. So by 1905 the typewriter portion of the business was sold off to Sidney Herbert of France, though the Company continued to be called GTL till 1907. 'His Master's Voice' or HMV (the label curiously appeared only by 1916) which was the caption that accompanied the Company's trademark popular logo of the dog listening to the record, represented the earliest ventures that aimed at the globalization of a cultural commodity.

The marvellous gramophone had arrived on the world music scene and there was no stopping it.

8

THE GRAMOPHONE COMES TO INDIA

Calcutta, 1900

Even before the Gramophone and Typewriter Ltd. (GTL) stepped into the Indian market, several English and Indian firms were importing blank cylinders, phonographs and records from both America and Europe. The first demonstration of the cylinder phonographs was held around December 1878 at Calcutta. The company, Maharaj Lal & Co, was founded in 1895, and was the oldest dealer for HMV labels in Delhi. Those days the cylindrical records looked like a stack of bangles and hence came to be called 'churis.' Professor H. Bose, a reputed Calcutta businessman, entered this new business under his banner, 'H Bose Records' but in 1908, after a partnership with the Pathe Freres of Paris, became known as 'Pathe-H Bose Records'. His 1906 catalogues list numerous cylinder records including those of the celebrated poet and thinker Rabindranath Tagore. Sadly most of these have been lost along with the working cylinder machines.

Among the English firms in Calcutta, T.E. Bevan & Co of 13 Old Court House Street, Harold & Co, 3, Dalhousie Street, and the Western Trading Co, 17, Chowringhee Lane, were the important ones, while M.L. Shaw, 23/5 Dharamtala Street, and Dwarkin and Son, 267 Boubazar Street, were the Indian ones. They regularly advertised the availability of Edison, Columbia and Pathe brands of phonographs and cylinders in their stores. GTL was aware of the growing demand for recording devices from India. They also wanted to consolidate their business interests in Asia. This meant that they needed to take urgent steps to be a presence in the Indian market before competition took over. As mentioned earlier, they were seldom, if ever, aware of the music of India, its charms. All they were keen on was the business potential that the music of the country had to offer. They hired the Mutoscope and Biograph Co. Ltd to act as their agents in India from early 1900. But the union was short-lived and by 1901, GTL had decided to send their own senior agent to India to assess and evaluate the market and report the business opportunities to the bosses back in England.

John Watson Hawd, GTL's first agent, arrived in Calcutta on 7 July 1901. He toured the country extensively and realised the commercial potential of 'native' music recordings given the all-pervasive nature of music in an average Indian's life. He kept urging his superiors in London not to waste any time and send an expedition to India as soon as possible since several rival companies were already vying for a share in the Indian pie. By 10 October 1901 Hawd had set up his office at 6/1 Chowringhee, and a store was readied at the same venue the following month.

But Hawd's pleas seemed to have fallen on deaf ears in London. By early 1902, Hawd wrote to his bosses in London in sheer desperation:

> 'There will be a big business here when we have goods enough and it is best to own the territory then we know it is well worked...the country is so large that it will take a long time to cover it and as yet we have no dealers to speak of.'

The message was clear—Act fast, or lose out on a potential market. The London Office replied to Hawd:

> 'I am planning to send out Gaisberg to you on the first of February to make records in your vicinity...I am going to have him make haste to go there direct and do work thoroughly and well, and I predict as a result getting a very large business. We will now take up the Indian business on thoroughly business lines and put it on a firm and good foundation.'

But this remained an empty promise. For some reason the London office did not prioritize the Indian expedition. So when by June 1902 Gaisberg had still not arrived, an exasperated Hawd wrote back:

Is he really coming?...of course I don't care, only I had made arrangements with artists which are now cancelled and I am not going to trouble again until he has really landed for by the time he arrives the pooja (religious feast, devotion) will have commenced and nothing can be done till after December.

Finally the Company despatched Gaisberg on the 'Far Eastern Expedition' and the group sailed out of Tilbury Docks on the river Thames, London on Friday, 28 September 1902. 'The Coromandel' that carried the group had the weight driven motors that Gaisberg had specially designed for this long distance voyage tour as part of its cargo. These motors enabled him to dispense with the heavy storage batteries and fragile clock springs that were used to drive the gramophones. Along with this six hundred of the new wax Masters, rather than the previously used zinc discs, were also part of the cargo. They were to be coded according to a special nomenclature prefixed E, with a 1000 numerical sequence for the 7-inch matrices and a 100 numerical sequence for the 10-inch matrices. Gaisberg had a varied set of fellow travellers—from tea planters to railroad and mining engineers, from departmental managers to the inevitable 'Fishing fleet' damsels as well!

The ship slowly sailed along the Hoogly River on Monday, 27 October 1902 and docked at the inland port of Calcutta the next day. Gaisberg was given a hearty and enthusiastic welcome by Hawd and his local colleagues. Speaking about his early days in India, Gaisberg writes:

'It took us three days to unload our thirty heavy cases and pass the customs officers. Our agent, Jack Hawd, had arranged a location and had assembled a collection of artists who watched us curiously as we prepared our studio for recording. It was the first time that the talking machine had come into their lives and they regarded it with awe and wonderment. The rains had passed and India's glorious dry season was ahead of us. We entered a new world of musical and artistic values. One had to erase all memories of European opera-houses and concert-halls: the very foundations of my musical training were undermined. I soon discovered that the Anglo-Indians, whom we contacted and who were acting as our agents and factors, were living on another planet for all the interest they took in

Indian music. They dwelt in an Anglo-Saxon compound of their own creation, isolated from India. They had their own cricket and tennis clubs, tea parties and bridge...the native bazaars never saw them, and even the Eurasians aped them to the extent of tabooing all Indian society.'

However Hawd, who had all along exuded great confidence about the success of the Indian tour, echoed a new scepticism that is revealed in his correspondence to the London office, dated 16 November 1902:

'We are, however, arranging for a room for record making and if it is possible we shall get some native singers, but as this pooja lasts for two months, yet we are not sure we will be able to succeed. We have several wealthy rajas who are interested in the gramophone that have volunteered to help us in every way possible.'

Gone was the assuring tone of his earlier letters and now lame excuses of trying to get native singers 'if possible' and the Durga Puja interrupting the plans were made. Gaisberg and Hawd had fundamental differences on several fronts and the great Indian expedition began amidst these subtle undercurrents of tension between them.

For its first foray into India, GTL needed a local contact point. They found their source in Amarendra Nath Dutt, a gentleman who belonged to a rich zamindar family. Dutt had joined the Indian Dramatic Club in 1893 and got his first break in the play, 'Battle of Plassey' at the Corinthian Theatre a year later. The play was greatly successful as it appealed to the locals' nostalgia for the famous war of the 18th century. It was performed again at the Minerva Theatre.

Modern theatre in Bengal was nourished by several native and folk influences, especially the *jatra*. The jatra was a folk form that had taken on a dramatic presentation and by the late eighteenth century had acquired a theatrical and secular nature. Given its popularity, its influence was bound to be there on the Western style modern Bengali theatre. A string of theatres were opened in Calcutta during the first half of the nineteenth century. The most famous among them was the Chowringhee Theatre (1813-39), which gave its name to Theatre Road (now known as Shakespeare Sarani).

Everything about these theatres was British. They brought in stage actors from London, even their ushers and doormen were British!

By the mid-19th century theatre caught the interest of the neo-literate Bengalis and gradually Indians began gaining an entry into the world of theatre. Private stages were built and some performances attracted 900-strong audiences. The first Bengali production 'Bidyasundar' was staged in 1835 at the private stage of Nabinchandra Basu. The Rajas of Paikpara, the Tagores of Jorasanko and other wealthy patrons encouraged the theatre scene by setting up several private theatres that staged some of the best Bengali classics.

Slowly the demand for bringing theatre out of the private confines of the privileged few began to gain momentum. This led to the rise of several 'amateur' theatres that were set up by the stage-struck middle class. Some enthusiasts even got together and formed a group called the National Theatre. They hired the courtyard of the rich Madhusudan Sanyal's mansion at Jorasanko at Rs 40 a month and had an opening performance in 1872. Numerous luminaries like Ramnarayan Tarkaratna (1822-64), the poet Michael Madhusudan Datta (1824-73), Dinabandhu Mitra (1830-73), Manmohan Basu (1831-1912), Jyotirindranath Thakur (1845-1925), Amritlal Basu (1853-1929), Girishchandra Ghosh (1844-1912) and the Nobel Laureate Rabindranath Tagore (1861-1941) played pioneering roles in ushering in the Theatre revolution in Bengal in the second half of the nineteenth century.

This already well-established theatre scene of the city saw the entry of the Classic Theatre of Amarendra Nath Dutt, in 1897. He leased the Emerald Theatre (earlier known as Star) at Beadon Street to stage its plays. Dutt's fascination for motion pictures led him to become the main patron of Hiralal Sen and his brother Motilal Sen. Motilal had purchased a bioscope cinematographic machine from London and Dutt began learning the art of making motion pictures under him.

John Hawd was quick to notice the vital role played by the Classic Theatre and its artists in the cultural and entertainment scene of the vibrant city. These artists and singers could croon or deliver dialogues that the GTL could record and Hawd had decided to take advantage of this. So when Gaisberg reached Calcutta, Hawd took him to the Superintendent of the Calcutta Police who placed at their disposal an officer acquainted with the city and the language. This officer was to accompany them to various entertainment centres and theatres. Classic Theatre, which was so popular then, was their first destination. 'Romeo and Juliet' was being staged there that evening. It alarmed Gaisberg's colonial European sensibilities to see a 'native' adaptation of an English classic. He thought little of both the acting abilities of the artists and of the singing and dancing of the Nautch girls who had been put into the play arbitrarily. He describes them as being 'heavily bleached with rice powder and dressed in transparent gauze.' To hear them sing 'And her golden hair was hanging down her back,' to the accompaniment of fourteen brass instruments which all played in unison, was nothing short of appalling. Gaisberg was overcome by acute disgust. Writing about his experience of that evening at the Theatre Gaisberg says:

> 'I had yet to learn that the oriental ear was unappreciative of chords and harmonic treatment, and only demanded the rhythmic beat of the accompaniment of the drums. At this point we left.'

It was a classic case of the East being East and the West being West and the twain seldom meeting! Here was a badly arranged, over-enthusiastic Indian band that was attempting to play what they considered 'Western' music to a European audience. They knew that association with the Company would turn their fortunes for the better and hence did not want to let go of the opportunity to impress the Company officials. On his part Gaisberg too was completely clueless about Indian music, even less about what he was looking for. There were cross-cultural misfirings at every level and Gaisberg began to wonder if he made the right decision coming to a musically crass country!

And yet, despite these initial misgivings regarding the repertoire of the Classic Theatre, it was the voices of actors, actresses, dancers and even the house band (which was recorded in various combinations) that amounted to nearly half of the 500 recordings made by Gaisberg on his first expedition to Calcutta during November and December 1902!

But coming back to that first evening at the Classic Theatre performance, Gaisberg and Hawd proceeded to the dinner party hosted by a wealthy babu of the city. They were to be entertained by the 'nautch dance'. (Nautch was the anglicized form of the Hindi/Urdu word '*Nach*' which meant dance.) Gaisberg's account of the evening is interesting and gives valuable insights about these nautch parties that were organized those days. The obvious disdain of the European throbs through every sentence:

'We elbowed our way through an unsavoury alley, jostled by fakirs and unwholesome sacred cows, to a pretentious entrance. The host and his native guests eagerly welcomed the brave band of pukka Anglo-Saxons who bestowed such honour on his house. No native women were present except the Nautch girls who have lost caste. We Europeans ate at a separate table; not even our host sat with us. After a rigidly European dinner we retired to a large salon and were entertained by the Nautch girls. The room presented a most interesting sight. At one end were the native gentlemen in their white gowns; some wore strings of pearls and diamonds and valuable rings. At the other end was our small party of Europeans in evening dress. The Singing Girl advanced slowly around the room singing. Following her closely was her band of five musicians, consisting of two esrag or Hindustani violins, one tumbler player with a right and left tamboora and two mandieras (bells) players. Bringing up the rear were attendants for preparing the betel nut and another holding a silver cuspidor. The singer was heavily laden with gold ornaments and bracelets, anklets and pearl necklaces, and to crown all there was a large diamond set in her nostril. She was a Mohammedan and very popular. She terminated each song with a cleverly executed muscle-dance. I found the performance long and boring and her mouth dyed with red betel nut offended me.'

A little while later a thoroughly frustrated Gaisberg was led to another soiree at the residence of a wealthy Bengali patron. He went in with the same pre-conceived expectation of another offensive evening. This soiree however was a class apart from the previous one, in terms of the arrangements that were made and the audience that had gathered there. It seemed to Gaisberg, to be a concert of a more high profile artist than the ordinary nautch girls he had witnessed earlier that evening. There was a flutter among the crowd as the arrival of the artist was announced. A stately carriage driven by a fine pair of horses stopped at the entrance of the house, and out stepped a young, stunningly pretty, fair, slightly stout figure dressed in a lavish costume. The ornaments she wore too were elegant and not crude and artificial like the ones Gaisberg had seen earlier. She had a regal bearing and a majestic look. As she greeted the host and his friends at the entrance and made her way to the top floor where the soiree was arranged, Gaisberg who was keenly observing her from the balcony felt that perhaps he had finally struck gold. Seeing the Europeans among the audience the lady came close to them and held out her hand with a fluent 'Good evening, gentlemen' stunning Gaisberg and his agents. From close quarters she looked like one of them since she had distinctive Anglo-Indian features and skin colour. She was Gauhar Jaan, the city's most celebrated singer.

In the hall, separate seating arrangements were made, as in the previous venue, for the Englishmen on one side and the ladies of the host's household on the other side. There was a curtain that kept the women from public view. A clearly enchanted Gaisberg watched as Gauhar elegantly took the stage and made preparations to begin her recital. Her accompanists stood around, tuning their instruments and getting ready to start.

As they waited, Gaisberg and the sales manager Addis tried to guess her age. Gaisberg placed her at 22 and Addis felt she couldn't be a summer more than 25. 'But we were wrong,' says Gaisberg 'Though she looked like a young girl, she was forty-five…she was an Armenian Jewess who could sing in 20 languages and dialects.' But Gaisberg was completely off the mark and Gauhar Jaan was all of 29 when he first met her. Gaisberg got her name wrong too and called her 'Goura Jan.'

Gaisberg understood little of what Gauhar Jaan sang but there was something about her voice that enraptured him. He writes: 'She could lay considerable claim to a coloratura voice. She performed with some ease, very difficult vocalizing such as scales and a sort of guttural trill which drew our attention to herself.' The trill was perhaps the famed *taans* of Hindustani music which involve vibration of the voice at varied speeds. As a courtesy to the Europeans among the audience Gauhar sang an English song that evening, 'Silver threads among the gold' which was a great hit and received thunderous applause from the European audience.

During the performance when Gaisberg went to the balcony to catch some fresh air, he was astonished to see all the roads surrounding the building packed with men who were standing wherever they could, some even precariously balanced, so that they could listen to her music. They knew of the concert, but not belonging to the same social class, obviously did not find an entry into the zamindar's soiree, especially one graced by special European guests. So they chose this way to enjoy the music of Gauhar Jaan. This made Gaisberg realise how popular the singer was among the local populace and that recording her would be a commercially fantastic proposition. Thus at the end of 'unsavoury' alleys and frustrating nautch parties and theatre performances, Gaisberg had finally stumbled upon a great find—Gauhar Jaan. She was to be the source of the twentieth century's first commercial recordings of Indian music.

In his search for artists, Gaisberg attended many theatres, parties and fetes along with Hawd. But his disgust for Indian music remained.

'Never again will I be able to summon up an equal enthusiasm for Indian music, for one indispensable accompaniment to most songs was a simple missionary's organ. The keys were played with one hand while the other worked a bellows. I found it produced a dull and uninspiring sound, and I soon came to loathe the instrument. Only one or two male singers were recommended to us and these had high-pitched effeminate voices. There was absolutely no admiration or demand for the manly baritone or bass, and in the Orient vocalists in these categories would starve to death.'

But the lady he met at that famous soiree was a cut above the rest for him. Luckily for Gaisberg, Hawd had already spoken to Gauhar Jaan a couple of months before the arrival of the expedition to India and she had agreed to work with this new Company.

Saturday, 8 November 1902, was a historic day. For on that day, the first 'native' recordings were made. A rudimentary and makeshift recording studio was set up in two large rooms of a hotel in Calcutta. As a trial run, a recording by a local Englishman Walter Stanley Burke, was made. After that, some local artists belonging to Amarendra Nath Dutt's Classic Theatre and Jamshedji Framji Madan's Corinthian Theatre were to be recorded. Two of the recordings were of 'two little nautch girls aged fourteen and sixteen with miserable voices.' They were Miss Soshi Mukhi and Miss Fani Bala, both dancing girls associated with the Classic Theatre. The recordings of theatre artists went on till Monday, 10 November. Gaisberg eagerly waited for the morning of 11 November, when the woman he was besotted with would arrive at the makeshift studio.

Gauhar's entry into the studio on that Tuesday morning in Calcutta was to place her forever in the annals of world musical history. Her imposing persona and her flair in dress and manner had captivated Gaisberg completely. He writes glowing tributes to her in his memoirs:

'When she came to record, her suite of musicians and attendants appeared even more imposing than those who used to accompany Melba and Calve. As the proud heiress of immemorial folk-music traditions she bore herself with becoming dignity. She knew her own market value, as we found to our cost when we negotiated with her.'

She had proved a shrewd businesswoman, as Gaisberg mentions above. She had demanded a handsome Rs 3000 for the recording session and GTL had agreed. While the accompanists tuned their sarangi, tabla and harmonium, a self-assured Gauhar sauntered around the room and investigated the strange device with a huge horn that was fitted on the wall. Amused by the contraption, Gauhar asked the recording expert, 'Am I to sing into this, Mr Gaisberg?' 'Yes madam' was Gaisberg's brief reply. He was busy fixing the recording equipment. At the narrow end of that long horn a diaphragm fitted with a needle was connected to the recording machinery which consisted of a needle placed on a thick wax master on a rotating turntable. Finally, when it was all in place, Gaisberg walked up to Gauhar Jaan and said 'We are done. Are you ready too?' She smiled, nodded and walked up to the horn. Gaisberg cautioned her, 'I hope you remember all that I told you? Sing out into that horn as loud as you can. Don't shake your head or your hands. It will spoil the quality of the recording. Also the timing… I hope you remember? It is not one of your soirees where you can develop your melodies for hours on end. Three minutes is all we have. Aah, a few seconds less than three minutes. Remember the announcement at the end which is for….' Gauhar stopped him politely and asked, 'Shall we start, Mr Gaisberg?' It seemed as if this lady was born to record her voice on these discs, thought Gaisberg. He was amazed at the quiet confidence she demonstrated during a process which had daunted many an accomplished musician before her.

As the first strains of her high pitched, cultured and captivating voice were etched on the grooves of Gaisberg's shellac, Indian classical music took a giant leap forward. From the confines of the courtesans' salons and the rich man's soirees, it was catapulted right into the homes of the common people. In the process it underwent a major transformation in its content, structure and style of presentation.

That same evening Gaisberg also recorded Miss Saila Bai (also catalogued as Miss Sila Bai). But Gaisberg was eager for the next session with Gauhar. She never failed to impress him, both with her talent and her appearance during each of those sessions.

> 'Every time she came to record she amazed us by appearing in a new gown, each one more elaborate than the last. She never wore the same jewels twice. Strikingly effective were her delicate black gauze draperies embroidered with real gold lace, arranged so as to present a tempting view of a bare leg and a naked navel. She was always *bien soignée.*'

Gasiberg was convinced that Gauhar would become the country's first gramophone celebrity and a mainstay for the consolidation of the Company's fortunes in India. He knew that she was hugely talented and tried to get as much variety in her recordings as he could. One day he played the record of 'The Jewel Song' from Faust, sung by Suzanne Adams. Gauhar and her attendants were astonished by the rapidity of those bravura scales and trills. The high pitched song was sung almost in one breath. Gaisberg jokingly asked Gauhar, "Can you sing something like this?" She remained silent and did not answer his question even as she left for the day. When she came in the following morning, she told Gaisberg that she had accepted his challenge and would try something new. She sang a *cheez* or piece in Raga Sur Malhar. Gaisberg was electrified. He simply could not believe what he was hearing. It was a similar 'breathless song' sung in increasing tempo and with single breaths, packing more and more notes with each progression, in a raga that symbolized the monsoons and the accompanying thunder and lightning.

The lyrics, which of course meant nothing to Gaisberg, went:

Ghoor ghoor barasat meharava, bijuriya chamaki anek baar
Gun gaao more piharava, aap jage aur mohi jagaave
Bhar bhar surava, ghoor ghoor barasat meharava.

The rains are pouring down the skies, the lightning flashing across them
many a times
Sing along my beloved one, you keep yourself awake and don't let me
sleep either
Are these torrents of rains or torrents of musical notes that are ushered
in? .

The recording team stood speechless when she finished and then broke into
rapturous applause.

The recording experience, as was mentioned earlier, was a musician's
worst nightmare. The singer had to crane his or her neck into that narrow
horn fixed on the wall and literally scream as loud as possible. The volume
of the voice would ensure that the needle rotated and cut the grooves on
the disc. One wonders how much musical value is lost in this process,
especially the subtle nuances that are so characteristic of Indian classical
music. Since many Indian musicians had the habit of shaking their heads
and gesticulating while singing, a recording agent would literally hold the
head of the singer still, or stretch the poor musician's head further into the
horn and make him / her bellow while two others held his hands! What a
journey the music recording industry has made since those days!

Another interesting feature of most of the recordings of that early era
was the musician screaming her or his name at the end of each recording.
Gauhar had to do it too. This announcement was necessary since the wax
masters were sent to Hanover for pressing the records and the technicians
there would be at a loss to identify the musicians before making the labels.
So they would listen attentively to these 'signature' announcements at the
end of the three minute performance and label the record. Gauhar's thin,
child-like and playful announcement of her name, 'My name is Gauhar
Jaan' in fluent English pierces through all these early recordings. It reflects
the great mirth and enjoyment she possibly experienced during the entire

tiresome process. Some of the records have extended announcements as well. At the end of a melodious Sohini thumri, Gauhar even managed to say that it was a composition by her guru Bhaiya Ganpatrao. Some singers like Malka Jaan Agrewali supposedly narrated their entire address at the end of the rendition! Gauhar makes a three-lined announcement at the end of one of her songs labelled 'Arabic song,' *Aliya habibu aana garibun* in Raga Jogia: 'This is an Arabic song; my name is Gauhar Jaan; you have liked the song'—the statement 'You have liked the song' sounding more like a command rather than as a question!

One of her 1902 recordings is an English song 'My love is a little bird that flies from tree to tree.' It was recorded at a very slow tempo which gave a curiously high-pitched edge to Gauhar's voice. Interestingly the accompanists go on beating at their own pace and rhythm trying to adjust the 8 beat *kaharva taal* or time-cycle to fit this four-square nursery rhyme kind of lyric, but without much success. Midway through, Gauhar seems to have forgotten the lyrics and, makes something up, but that perturbs no one, neither her accompanists nor the recorders! She re-starts from the even beat of the rhythmic cycle and carries on as if nothing had happened.

On 14 November, Gaisberg also recorded Miss Hari Moti and Miss Sushila who were popular performers of the Bengali stage. The Classic Theatre's band was to figure in the session on Sunday, 16 November, while the 18 was reserved for the Corinthian theatre group. Among the two male musicians whom Gaisberg recorded and was not too impressed by, was Lal Chand Boral. Boral, like Gauhar, was a favourite local singer and remained one of the Company's best-selling artists. Interestingly, the majority of the recordings were those of women artists and their names were all prefixed by a curious 'Miss.' Thus Miss Gauhar, Miss Sushila, Miss Binodini, Miss Acheria, Miss Kiron, Miss Rani and others became the first celebrities of the GTL. In fact it was the popularity of the female musicians, the tawaifs in particular, that made many male musicians adopt the high-pitched falsetto voice that Gaisberg spoke about. They probably believed that a shrill, female voice was the only way they could achieve the same kind of popularity as these songstresses, even though they never credited the women singers with any major musical worth.

Several sessions involving the same theatre groups and amateur bands took place in the next few weeks. But Gaisberg was satisfied that he had accomplished what he had come to India for. In Gauhar he had found the Indian voice that would sell across boundaries. He spent the first few days of December 1902 relaxing at the hill-station of Darjeeling and on 10 December 1902, Gaisberg left India for China and Japan aboard the ship 'Chusan' along with Thomas Addis, his wife and George Dillnut.

Gaisberg's six-week Indian sojourn had resulted in some two hundred and sixteen 7-inch matrices and some three hundred and thirty six 10-inch matrices that were shipped to Hanover. Only about half of these were considered suitable enough for commercial sale and the rest were perhaps destroyed as they were considered un-musical or the recording was faulty.

By April 1903, the first stocks of the final commercial pressings were shipped to Calcutta. There were all one-sided records, the 7-inch ones being called 'Gramophone Record' and the 10-inch ones being referred to as 'Gramophone Concert Record'. Hawd was in charge of receiving the consignment and ensuring suitable distribution and marketing. He found to his dismay that many of the records had not been packed properly and had been damaged in transit. He complained bitterly to the London office.

Meanwhile the records registered brisk sales. Especially the records of Gauhar sold like hot cakes across the major cities of the country. Along with the records, the gramophone machines too sold widely. The gramophone became the new status symbol for those middle class Indians who could afford to buy one. This idea was fully exploited by the gramophone manufacturing and distributing companies in its marketing strategies. This is evident from the publicity material and advertisements these companies started putting out regularly in all the leading newspapers of the times. They conveyed multiple socio-cultural messages which are a fascinating depiction of society of those times. One of the advertisements showed the lavishly decorated drawing room of a rich zamindar (inferred from his dress and the style in which the room was furnished, with costly draperies, an expensive clock and carpets). He appears to be proudly displaying the gramophone that sits on a table right in the centre of the room, its gleaming golden horn facing the man. The zamindar's wife stands beside the table looking in wonderment at the device. Curiously, she is not even shown in purdah, especially in the presence of an elderly gentleman who is also present in the picture. His two little children sit on a small stool, leaning forward to have a look. An old man, possibly the rich landlord's father, with his walking stick, also sits on the other side and watches the device with amusement. Interestingly a servant squats on the floor equally lost in the wonder of it. His dark skin is in stark contrast to the other fair-skinned individuals in the picture. And finally, the hero of the piece, the little dog that listens intently, the trademark logo of the Gramophone Company Ltd is also depicted, ready to be regaled. The message the picture conveyed was that the gramophone had something to offer for everyone in the family, young or old, master or slave, man or woman. Using such an image was a master stroke of marketing insight adopted by the Company.

The Company also played on the religious sentiments and the historical nostalgia that Indians revel in. One advertisement shows the Goddess Saraswati, the Hindu symbol of learning, music and the arts, seated by a river-side with her pet swan. All traditional pictures of the Goddess show her playing the ancient and magnificent Indian instrument, the veena. Here too she is shown playing the veena, but the Company's veena is modelled differently. Instead of one of the gourds that constitute the resonator of the veena, out pops a huge gramophone! It was a direct message to the devout that the very embodiment of knowledge and learning had accepted this new medium of reproducing sound and music. To cater specifically to the Bengali audience, the popular local deity Goddess Durga too featured in many ads, sitting blissfully by a river with Her pet tiger even as other animals crowd around her listening to the music in awe.

The other interesting advertisement showed the magnificent durbar of the Mughal Emperor Jahangir (1605-27). He is depicted in all his royal splendour surrounded by his courtiers and attendants. All of them are listening to the gramophone and the caption on top says, 'The Gramophone in the court of Jehangier the magnificent.' Obviously the device was not even invented when the Emperor reigned, but the message was that if it had been around during his time, even he, the Emperor, would have owned it. Thus the publicity blitzkrieg unleashed by the GTL made the gramophone, the records and thereby the artists who sang for them extremely popular.

It was the attempt of selling India back to the Indians at a price of about Rs 250 for a machine.

While the business prospered, relations between Hawd and the company officials began to sour. Differences cropped up between them. Hawd accused Thomas Addis of unwarranted interference in his work. In addition, the London office was quite tardy in its responses. This left Hawd thoroughly disgusted and in sheer frustration he left the services of the Company in mid-July 1903. To make matters worse, he joined a rival company, The Nicole Record Co. Ltd. Addis, who was with Gaisberg on the remainder of the Far Eastern tour, was sent to Calcutta as the replacement for Hawd by August that year. The Company shifted to its sprawling office at 7 Esplanade East that overlooked the Maidan, the large grounds near the Viceregal Lodge.

Hawd meanwhile was so determined to avenge the shabby treatment meted out to him by GTL that he arranged for a recording expedition of the Nicole Record Co. in July 1904 with its recording expert from America, Stephen Carl Porter. Addis immediately wrote to the London superiors about the development and requested for a second Indian expedition to counter the competition. Assessing the market conditions of the time, he writes on 23 December 1903:

'India is a peculiar country in regard to language as if you go 300 miles out of Calcutta you would find a different dialect altogether which would not be understood here and so on through every state and presidency. Each particular district has its own local and popular singers male and female, beside which there are a few amateur singers whose records would sell freely. Now it is this class of work that the better and middle class natives, who have the money enquire for and we are creditably informed the present sales are largely due to the excellent results obtained from the instruments alone, and that it is not the records themselves that are inducing the public to buy instruments.'

Addis was also aware that the expedition so far had covered just the North of India and the South with its own rich and teeming musical heritage had been totally ignored. The London office asked him to prepare a population estimate of the various provinces and regional groups. Like a modern day marketing survey to understand the market they were seeking to conquer, Addis gave a detailed break-up of India and its population as per the 1901 census records. Of the 287,000,000 people who spoke 147 various vernaculars, 60,000,000 spoke Hindi, 44,000,000 spoke Bengali, 47,000,000 Bihari, 20,000,000 Telugu and about 18,000,000 spoke Marathi. This was followed by groups who spoke Rajasthani, Kanarese (Kannada), Gujarati, Oriya, Burmese, Tamil, Malayalam, Pushtu, Urdu etc. This report of Addis was his attempt to impress upon the bosses in London, the diverse amalgam of languages that India was. His purpose was served and the London office instructed him to extend the catalogue, which was to be broken down according to language. Therefore it was to be 300 Bengali, 500 Hindustani, 300 Gujarati, 150 Marathi, 300 Tamil, 250 Telugu, 200 Kannada, 200 Sinhalese, 120 of Bhutian, Nepalese and Tibetan combined, 120 Sanskrit, 120 Persian and 60 Beluchi records.

But like Hawd, Addis too needed to constantly goad his superiors into sending the much awaited second expedition. Time was running out fast. There were a host of issues he had to contend with. Piracy of GTL trademarks by local Indian dealers was a constant threat. The 'International Gramophone Depot' of Dharamtala Street in Calcutta conveniently used the famous trademark 'listening-dog' of the Company in its advertisements by changing its looks to appear a bit rabid! These and many other such illegal activities also entangled the Company in an unending trail of litigations. In his 1903 and 1904 communications Addis outlines other problems that the Company had to contend with:

'We are rather disappointed at the native records coming through so slowly especially when you consider that you have had the original records made here since the beginning of January 1st...we have only a few Bengali records and people are beginning to lose faith saying that they do not believe they are coming at all...it will be quite another year before we shall be in a position to make a big move in the 'Eastern Trade.' (September 1903).

'It frequently happens that we submit the matter for a catalogue to a supposedly reliable man for correct translation, and then, when we submit the same matter to a second party, he discovers great errors.

This is due no doubt to the great difference that exists in methods of writing the various vernaculars.' (7 May 1904)

Competition too was catching up quickly as rival companies sensed the immense potential that the Indian market offered. As mentioned earlier Pathe Freres of Paris had been operating with H Bose to ship cylinder records of many of the same gramophone celebrities of GTL. The Nicole Record Co. Ltd, who began recording in the later months of 1904, were about to introduce their finished discs made of compressed cardboard with a reddish celluloid lacquer coating.

Finally William Sinkler Darby was sent to India assisted by Max Hempe on the second expedition of the GTL from December 1904 to March 1905. Learning from past mistakes and building on their strengths, this expedition was more focused in expanding the repertoire and quality of their records. From recordings in Calcutta, Darby also toured the country, from Allahabad, Lucknow, Delhi, Lahore, Bombay and Madras by train and then by steamer to Colombo and Rangoon. Artists who lived close to one of these centres were brought to the nearest recording location at the expense of the Company and they were also paid a flat fee. Gauhar Jaan, Peara Saheb, Lal Chand Boral, Miss Kali Jaan and others continued to be the mainstays of the Gramophone Company's Indian venture. At the end of the venture some four hundred 7 inch matrices, eight-hundred and twenty 10 inch matrices and sixty-five of the new 12 inch matrices were recorded. A new nomenclature of 'g', 'h', 'i' was assigned to these records of 7, 10, 12 inches, respectively as against Gaisberg's E-series. This expedition was technically more sound, well-planned and better executed and it became a blueprint for the Company's future expeditions.

This time too there were more women than men in the recording catalogue. Down South it was the *devadasis* who were the repositories of music & dance. At a young age they would be 'married' off or dedicated to the deity of a temple to whom they had to render their services through their performances. However they were subjected to sexual exploitation by the clergy. It was Salem Godavari of Madras, a famed devadasi of her times, who was more or less an equivalent of Gauhar Jaan in terms of popularity and number of records she cut. Several compositions of Saint Thyagaraja sung by her are preceded by a brief improvisation or *alapana*. Some Tamil songs and *ragamalika* or mixture of multiple ragas were also sung by her. Bhavani, Ammakannu, Salem Papa and Vadammal were other gramophone celebrities of the South, though it was later Dhanakoti Ammal and Bangalore Nagaratnamma who cut numerous discs and achieved stardom.

Women were more sought after than male artists and they were willing performers for the company. In the 1906-07 tour, about thiry-five women classical singers were recorded by the Gramophone Company, of which about thirty were first-timers. However there was a gradual tapering down of the numbers and eventually in the 1908-10 sessions there were only about eleven new singers.

Several interesting similarities in the attitude of the male musicians of those days come to light, both in the North and the South. They were wary of this new technology and very few of them dared to experiment and adapt to the winds of change. Numerous rumours were spread that recording one's voice through this evil English instrument would result in a loss of voice; that it was against divine sanction, and so on. But it is truly a tribute to the grit, spirit and determination of the early women musicians like Gauhar Jaan and several others, who ignored these warnings, seized the opportunity that came their way, and made the most of it. They stormed into the hitherto largely male bastion of Indian music and conquered the hearts of the listeners through these early recordings. It was only when the commercial success of the women musicians started becoming apparent that the men folk sat up, took notice and meekly followed suit abandoning their superstitions. The records of these women singers started being listened to carefully by many male musicians to understand, evaluate and emulate the content and style. Apart from crooning in a falsetto voice, many male singers even learnt some of the popular renditions of these women musicians and sang them in their soirees or made recordings of the same. For instance, even someone of the stature of Pt. Mallikarjun Mansoor, is supposed to have learnt and recorded for HMV the song 'Bin Badara Bijuri Kahan chamake' that was popualrized by Janki Bai decades earlier. But even as late as the 1919s when the Gramophone Company had almost completed two successful decades in the country, male scepticism lingered on. This is evident in the interesting anecdote recounted by Master Krishnarao of the celebrated vocalist Rahimat Khan Haddu Khan (1860-1922) who was hailed as *Bhoo-Gandharva* or celestial musician on earth.

'Recording session lasted for two days. As it was done acoustically, two large horns were placed before him as microphones. He was very much disturbed by the recording atmosphere and talked too much during the singing. One large HMV emblem frame of dog looking and singing into the horn was placed to catch his attention. However, it irritated him even more and he asked them to remove the doc picture from his sight. When the sample was played back to him, he got angry since someone else like him was singing back through the horn. He got up to leave the hall immediately. With great difficulty, he was persuaded to stay and the recordings were taken.'

Apart from bringing great success and popularity to the women singers, this new technology also did something astounding for the art form. The music of the courtesan's salon was catapulted out of the confines of the kotha and the soirees of the whimsical babus into the mass-market. It was the first step towards democratization of music as music was no longer the preserve of only the rich and privileged. One might not afford to hear a star like Gauhar Jaan in her private, live concerts but could always sit huddled with friends on an evening over tea in 'respectable' surroundings and listen to her magnificent voice over a shared instrument if that was what the connoisseurs could afford. Gaisberg had thus unwittingly pioneered a major revolution in the field of Indian classical music—a fascinating journey from a world of closeted patronage to global mass media.

For the artists the challenge was all the more complex as they were facing a new kind of audience for the first time—one that could not be seen and thereby whose tastes could not be ascertained. Therefore even a singer of Gauhar Jaan's virtuosity and talent, opted to record in as wide a repertoire as possible, cutting across various genres. With the passage of time, as they were able to gather some market intelligence about what was selling and what was not, the recordings could be tailored to the demands of the public, even if only to an extent. Some styles and genres by virtue of being 'uneconomical' obviously got blacklisted on the charts. This led to an informal at first but later, more rigid classification of genres into 'classical', 'light' or 'semi-classical' forms. The same artist could sing a so-called 'pure classical' piece for an hour at a soiree, but sing a 'light' classical item on a record of three minutes duration. Though dismissed as 'light,' these genres had a wider reach, thanks to the records, and achieved commercial success that few 'pure classical' genres could in those times. Thus, the advent of technology led to an intense churning not only in the lives of classical musicians of the time but also in the very content, presentation and classification of classical music as a whole.

Meanwhile, by 1906 GTL had achieved a dominant position in the talking machine and disc record trade in Asia and had some 1500 titles in their Indian repertoire. After Addis, G.E. Gilpin and Percy Rose held his position in India for brief spans before James Muir took over in 1907. Given the immense demand and growing popularity of these records, GTL announced its third recording tour of India between 1906 and 1907 which was to be led by Fred Gaisberg's younger brother, William Conrad Gaisberg (1878-1918). For this expedition only 10 inch and 12 inch matrices were used and the old 7 inch ones were phased out. These were named as the E and F series. Starting May 1906 in Calcutta the tour proceeded to Lucknow, Delhi, Lahore, Hyderabad and Madras, skipping Bombay because of the monsoons. Gauhar Jaan continued to be the hot favourite during this expedition as well. Along with her the other major woman singer whose recordings were taken was her contemporary Janki Bai of Allahabad. About One thousand two hundred recordings in the 10 inch and about hundred and fifty recordings of the 12 inch were added to the already expanding catalogue of GTL. Its almost three thousand Indian titles (700 of the 7 inch, 2200 of the 10 inch and 200 of the 12 inch size) made it by far the largest sound recording company that operated in India.

The next major milestone in the Company's India sojourn was the plan to set up a record pressing factory with cabinet making facilities for the gramophone machines in India by late 1906. Lac was abundantly available in India and accounted for almost 75 per cent of the world's lac production. In later years, gramophone companies placed extensive export orders with India. The ready availability of lac thus became an added incentive. And Calcutta was to serve as the headquarters of not only the India operations of the Company but also service the requirements from all Asia, except Japan. Thus India and in particular Calcutta began to occupy an important place in the global music business. 139 Beliaghatta Road in Sealdah was chosen as the site for the record pressing factory, to be set up in December 1906. By 23 May 1908, the staff and stocks shifted to this new location from the earlier office at Esplanade East. Matrices of original wax masters from all over India, Burma, Ceylon etc began to be shipped to Calcutta.

On 18 December 1908 the new factory was officially inaugurated with an at-home reception. Many senior officials from London, including Fred Gaisberg were guests of honour at this ceremony. Predictably the lady who had become synonymous with the Gramophone Company in India, Gauhar Jaan, was also one of the invited guests. A special concert of Gauhar Jaan was held at this ceremony and songs from that performance were also recorded as a commemorative album. Her famous Kafi composition *'Kaisi yeh dhoom machayi'* which she sang that day was recorded and released commercially later. Her photographs began appearing on the front cover of the records catalogue. Some of them show her posing with the gramophone that sits on a majestic Victorian table and she is seen cradling its sparkling horn. She appears as a fair, stout, pretty woman decked in all her finery —silk and pearls, rings, earrings and necklaces. Her curly hair frames her broad forehead and her arched eyebrows converge at the centre. Closer study even shows a garish varnish on her nails. Gazing away from the camera, she provides almost a three quarter profile with a slightly sulking and wooden expression on her face. Most of the labels of the time proclaim her as the 'First dancing girl of India.'

The location of the pressing factory in India ensured that the artists no longer needed to announce their names at the end of the recording. So even Gauhar Jaan's records post 1908 end without the customary shriek 'My name is Gauhar Jaan!' The 'Made in Calcutta' label was embossed on the records. This was also perhaps in view of the upsurge of nationalism and the increasing demand for the usage of Swadeshi or home-made products that had been spurred by the Partition of Bengal in 1902. The factory began pressing 1000 discs per day and the figure was expected to rise to 5000. The inventories were stocked with over 150,000 discs of varied sizes and in the vernaculars of India. Permanent recording and rehearsal rooms in central Calcutta, along with recording studios at Bombay and Madras were the next major step the company took. Native recording engineers were encouraged and supervised by the Company's European officers who were on deputations for about two years. The distribution and sales network too was totally redesigned. Direct dealing with the retail trade through a large number of dealerships of both Indian and English firms became the chosen vehicle. A branch office came up in Bombay by 1909 to cater to the ever growing demand of records. Thus in just about a decade of its coming to India, the Gramophone Company had monopolized the Indian market.

Calcutta as a seat of entrepreneurial ventures symbolized the enterprising Indian spirit of the times. The Gramophone Company Limited had to contend with many worthy competitors, both local and foreign. Among the numerous rivals the Gramophone company faced in India were Dwarkin & Son, Universal, Nicole (which offered the first double-sided records of Indian repertoire at cheaper rates than the Company's single sided ones), Neophone Disc Phonograph, H Bose who became the first to manufacture records in Calcutta as the 'true Swadeshi' record), the Beka, Royal, Ram-A-phone Disc, James Opera, Singer, Odeon, Pathe, Elephone (catering largely to the South Indian market), Sun Disc and local records like Binapani and Kamala records began flooding the market between 1901-09.

Each one tried to upstage the other to gain a larger slice of the market share by offering some incentive or the other or by convincing some of the greatest names in the world of Indian music to record for them. Some adopted innovative techniques too. The Royal record for example provided the technical knowhow required for recording and carried out the production in Germany. But they used Indian companies and agents to source artists and carry out the sales and distribution. The records too were never issued with the Royal record label but in the names of the local players. A share of royalties among all parties concerned would be worked out. All this eliminated a lot of set-up costs for the company and they also managed to take advantage of the knowledge of the local dealers of the Indian market and its trends.

Interestingly it seems that these companies did not sign any exclusive rights with the artists they recorded. Though Gauhar Jaan was the star celebrity of the Gramophone Company she recorded with many of the competitors as well and some of her records with Nicole, Pathe, Singer, Sun Disc and Royal are extant. In her long and illustrious recording career between 1902 and 1920 she is supposed to have recorded about Six hundred songs in nearly twenty languages that included Hindustani, Bengali, Urdu, Persian, English, Arabic, Pushto, Tamil, Marathi, Peshawari, Gujarati, French etc. Though the thumri was her forte, she did not confine herself to it and she covered the entire range of genres of Hindustani classical music. She sang dhrupad, khayal, dadra, kajri, chaiti, hori, dhamar, tarana, bhajan and even a few Carnatic or South Indian classical songs and English numbers. This just proves Gauhar Jaan's versatility and also her hold on music as a medium. Her phenomenal success was not something either she or her mother, Badi Malka Jaan, would have ever dreamt of. The days of starvation at Azamgarh, the struggle at Banaras and Calcutta and the many years of rigorous training had now consummated into national and international fame, and recognition of a talented diva.

9

INDIAN MUSIC AND THE THUMRI:
A JOURNEY IN TIME

Indian classical music has a hoary and undated past. Being intimately connected with nature and its sounds, Indian music draws its seven basic notes from the sounds of animals and birds. '*Sa*' is associated with the peacock's shrill call, '*Ri*' with the bullock, '*Ga*' with the goat, '*Ma*' with the jackal, '*Pa*' with the cuckoo's cooing, '*Dha*' with the horse and '*Ni*' with the elephant. From the Vedic times this music developed through the rhythmic and melodious chants of the sages.

It is normally believed that until the advent of the Muslim invaders into Northern India in the 12th and 13th centuries, a common system of music prevailed across the country. The music of Northern India was thereafter greatly influenced by Persian and Iranian music, while the South being unaffected by the invasions maintained its own system of music. This led to the bifurcation of Indian classical music into the two prevalent styles of Hindustani or North Indian Classical music and Carnatic or South Indian classical music. But the common foundation, the uniting feature of both these systems of music is the Raga system. Indian music has one of the most advanced and scientific systems of categorisation of the melodic entities known as ragas and an equally sophisticated sense of rhythmic patterns or talas.

One of the oldest forms of Indian classical music is the dhrupad. It was very popular in the North till about the 16th and 17th centuries. A highly stylized, structured and complex genre, dhrupad compositions predominantly eulogized Hindu gods and goddesses. However they were sung without any reservations by Muslim singers as well. Thus the dhrupad became a symbol of the unique Indian ethos of multi-culturalism.

With the consolidation of Muslim rule in North India between the 12th-13th centuries the dhrupad slowly began to lose its importance. Its place was taken by the khayal, a genre not as rigidly bound by technicalities as the dhrupad was. The word khayal comes from Urdu and means 'thought' or 'imagination'. The emphasis was on the imagination of the artist, who was free to expound a raga in a manner he or she wanted, but adhering to the basic rules and norms. Though it is commonly believed that the khayal originated in the 13th century during the time of the celebrated poet Amir Khusrau, many scholars and musicologists like Thakur Jaideva Singh and Kumar Prasad Mukherjee state that it was a later development, as late as the 18th century. Khayal in its present form today owes its existence to the later Mughals and the Nawabs of Oudh. Miyan Tansen in Emperor Akbar's court and his descendants are credited with crystallizing this new genre from the earlier dhrupad and the mystic Quwwali of the Sufi saints of North India.

In this complex galaxy of genres of Indian music, the Thumri presents a bridge between the world of classical and folk traditions. Since Gauhar Jaan mastered the thumri and became almost synonymous with it, a closer look at this genre is warranted.

Though often dismissed as 'light,' the thumri has a hoary past as attested by several scholars. Musicologist Thakur Jaideva Singh traces the earliest form of thumri called '*Chalitham Nrithyasahitam*' to the Harivansh Purana (c.200 A.D.) This was sung along with the dance that Lord Krishna is believed to have learnt in the celestial court of Indra. Similar references have been made by eminent scholar and musician Dr Rita Ganguly where she states that the thumri predates the dhrupad and the khayal, for both of which we have more or less certain dates. Some scholars attribute the creation of this romantic genre to Nawab Wajid Ali Shah. This claim is however exploded with the mention of thumri in the work of Captain Augustus Willard, a bandmaster in the state of Banda in the United Provinces in the early 19th Century. In his work 'Treatise on the music of Hindostan', he mentions that among all the musical forms which he had studied and listened to during his 35 years in India, thumri with its erotic appeal was the one he liked the most. Wajid Ali Shah was then just about 9-10 years old and so could not have created a genre as sophisticated as this at such a young age!

The word thumri is said to be derived from the Hindustani word '*Thumakna*' meaning an attractive gait. So literally it means a song that has an attractive, rather sensuous, gait in both melody and rhythm.

The lyrics of the thumris are largely written in Braj bhasha, a dialect of Hindi spoken in and around Mathura in U.P. This dialect was associated with the Krishna-bhakti movement that raged across the North in medieval times. However Khadi Boli or the spoken Hindi of today and Urdu words also appear in the thumris. Besides, there are entire compositions in dialects of Hindi like Avadhi, Bhojpuri, Mirzapuri, Dingal etc. The language employed is soft and tender and allows the usage of colloquial words to make them sound 'elastic.' For instance, '*Paani*' becomes '*Paniya*' and '*Piya*' becomes '*Piu*' or '*Piyarawa.*' The thumri draws heavily from the popular folk forms like the Hori, Raas and Charachari, as well as the dramas of Oudh and the surrounding areas.

There are two kinds of thumris—the Bandish thumris and the Bol banao thumris. Typically both the kinds have a first part called *sthayi* (sometimes a middle portion or *madhya*) and is followed by single or multiple verses known as *antaras*.

Most Bandish thumris were composed by the Urdu speaking, Lucknow-based poets and musicians and so the favoured language was Khadi Boli mixed with some Urdu. The word 'bandish' means composition and hence in these thumris the lyrics assume a greater importance. The bandish thumris were the popular version of thumri as prevalent in the 19th century and many of these were written by gurus like Bindadin Maharaj. They are light, lively pieces and were generally written as dance accompaniment. Here the focus is seldom on leisurely musical improvisation but on fast taans or melodic trills and intelligent rhythmic manipulation of the lyrics in fast tempo. They have long texts with multiple antaras. Set mostly in medium or fast tempo, they stressed on *bol-baant* or a technique through which the text was aesthetically divided to enable *vistar* (elaboration), *taan* (fast melodic trills) and *layakari* (rhythmic manipulation) and these were largely

Kathak centric compositions. They were set in typical 'light' ragas like Kafi, Piloo, Ghara, Khamaj, Sindhura, Dhani, Manj Khamaj, Des, Tilang, Bihari, Jhinjhoti, Zilla and so on. The talas employed in both varieties of thumri are Deepchandi, Addha, Ikwaai, Sitarkhani and those derived from folk music like Keharawa, Dadra, Khemta, and Charchar and so on.

Bol banao thumris as the very name suggests of 'making or creating a conversation', a musical conversation in this case, dwells on the effective and detailed exposition of the text and the melody through leisurely improvisations. The Avadhi and Bhojpuri dialects occur more in the bol banao thumris that originated from the cities of Banaras and Gaya. Trivial and day-to-day pastimes of Lord Krishna, His flirtations with the gopis of Vrindavan, the festival of Holi, the eternal love of Radha and Krishna—all lend themselves to a textual, dramatic and musical improvisation and form the core of these thumris. The lyrics are not as sophisticated as in the case of the bandish thumris. But it is precisely this rusticity of the lyric, the free rhythmic character and its open-endedness which helps create multiple patterns and gives the singer scope for improvisation. For instance, through this single line verse '*Kaun Gali Gayo Shyam*' (Which road has Krishna taken?) the singer can demonstrate a variety of emotions by shifting the emphasis in the lyrics and varying the rhythmic patterns.

Musicologist Peter Manuel sums this up best in his book *Thumri in Historical and Stylistical Perspectives*:

> 'A good thumri text is 'incomplete'; in that its expression of emotion is sufficiently broad, simple and general so that the singer can interpret it in innumerable ways. At the same time, each line is 'complete' and autonomous in that the emotional thought, however simple, is expressed within that one line, and does not require two or more lines in order to be clear.'

The themes of thumris are predominantly erotic and sensual and could easily be classified as obscene sometimes if seen at a surface level. But there is an inherent spirituality even in eroticism as the propounders of the Madhura Bhakti tradition link it to a form of Krishna worship. They believe that all living souls are deemed feminine and the only masculine super soul is Krishna. It is this pining for union with the man (Krishna in this case) that creates the body-text for these thumri compositions. Thumris are thus written from a woman's perspective. Dr Vidya Rao, eminent thumri singer and scholar, opines that the thumri has echoed the same repressed feminine voice over centuries, though it might have been composed by men.

The *nayikas* or the heroines in the thumri are distinguished by the qualities attributed to them in the classical text of Bharata, the Natyashastra. There is the nayika who is all decked up and ready for union with her lover; then there is one who is suffering deep anguish at being separated from her beloved. One nayika represents a woman who has parted from her lover after a bitter quarrel. Then there is one who is enraged at her beloved's infidelity and his flirtations with other women. Allied to this theme is the plight of the nayika deceived by her lover. Sometimes the memory of a husband who is on a journey or in a foreign or distant land evokes loneliness while in other cases the heroine moves towards her lover's abode, her heart aflutter with excitement and anticipation. In some rare cases the woman is in control and has subjugated her beloved. The pangs of unrequited love, agony of separation, the ecstasy of union and the anger coupled with sorrow at being deceived, form the thematic content of thumris. It is usually Radha and Krishna around whom these themes are woven, but sometimes it is also anonymous men and women who are the heroes and heroines of these stories in verse.

The growth of the thumri is intimately linked with another sister-art, Kathak, the classical dance of North India that originated in the Indo-Gangetic belt. Kathak traced its roots from professional story-tellers called 'kathakas' or 'kathakars' who rendered popular episodes from the Hindu epics. Throughout the medieval and Mughal periods, kathak flourished in the temples and courts, with a strong influence of Vaishnavite themes in its content. By the 18th century it became a popular art form in Lucknow, almost contemporaneous to the popularity of the thumri in the same city. Like the thumri, kathak too drew heavily from folk art forms like the raas and charachari.

Wajid Ali Shah is credited with stylizing the folk raas into a more sophisticated form of dance drama which he called 'rahas.' He is famously known to have donned the role of Krishna himself and danced with his court dancers who were the cowherd girls or gopis. The Mughal and Lucknow courts and later on the Bengali gentry of Calcutta greatly patronized all these allied song and dance forms.

After these art-forms migrated to Calcutta with Matiya Buruj as the epicenter the obvious local influences too crept in. Thumris in Bengali composed by the famous Ramnidhi Gupta became popular as both solo vocal as well as accompaniments for dance performances and were known as *Nidhi-babur tappa.* One school of thought believes that the popular 'nautch' performed by the supposedly debased nautch girls only partially resembled the emergent classical kathak and these girls were freer to improvise. Others strongly hold that it was the nautch that played a major role in preserving the artistic performance practices and that the kathak of today has more resemblances to the nautch than the ancient Brahmin kathakas' style of performance. However there is little documentation of the repertoire and style of nautch, except for the travelogues of Europeans who watched it with sensuous delight, for any clear conclusion on the issue.

It was only by the latter part of the 18th century that the thumri perhaps began to be appreciated as a musical genre in its own right. It was influenced by the emergent genre of khayal and in turn influenced that as well. The more classical 16-beat teental rhythmic cycle replaced the folk meters like kaharava. Khayal recitals were bifurcated into two major sections – a slow, composed one called the Bada khayal or the bigger khayal and a smaller, faster one called Chota khayal. It is commonly believed that the chota khayal was a direct offshoot of thumri, especially the Bandish Thumri. The less-polished and slower expositions of the thumri that derived itself from typical folk themes, ragas and rhythms was the bol banao thumris which, as mentioned before, were most suited for a leisurely and detailed rendition.

It was in the regal courts of Oudh that both the thumri and kathak assumed a crystallized structure. The Lucknow court was more provincial and drew heavily from the local culture, languages and dialects. The Braj folk music thus found great acceptance. There was also an increased amity between the Hindu and Muslim communities in Oudh than in Mughal Delhi and the mutual interactions influenced the art forms too. Since the region they now governed was a strong base of Hindu culture with most of the pilgrimages and mythical heroes of Hinduism coming from here, the Nawabs of Oudh and their musicians and dancers adopted a cosmopolitan ethos. Courtesans began to be celebrated as preeminent exponents of the arts and their genteel sophistication was highly regarded. The situation was quite the same even during the time of Gaisberg's visit to India, as articulated in his own words:

'All the female singers were of course from the caste of the public women, and in those days it was practically impossible to record the voice of a respectable woman. The songs and dances were passed by word of mouth from mother to daughter. They began public appearances at about twelve years of age. The clever brainy ones went on to the top and sometimes travelled all over the country in great demand at the wedding feasts of the wealthy. As they began to make names for themselves many of them insisted that the word 'amateur' should be printed on the record label.'

With the rise of British supremacy came the new concept of the absentee landlord, as postulated in Lord Charles Cornwallis's land code. A new class of landowners of Oudh, known as the *taluqdars,* replaced the zamindars of the time. Taxes to be paid by each estate were now permanently prescribed and both owners and peasants were liable to eviction in case of defaults. These rich taluqdars had little taste for the sophisticated and complex dhrupad, and thumris started gaining immense popularity given their sensuous content.

The dance performance in these private soirees was of two kinds, with and without vocal accompaniment. Thumris, as also *dadras* (faster version of a thumri), Ghazals and Bhajans (devotional songs) formed the vocal accompaniment. The unaccompanied variety of dance had the rendition of the '*Gats*' where swift body movements marked the dance performance. The gats are set to specific rhythmic cycles or talas maintained by a *tabalchi* or a tabla player and a *sarangiya* on the sarangi. The latter plays a repeated melodic verse called *lehra* that lasts for a specific time cycle of the tala. These gats are pre-composed and form a major corpus of the style that developed in Lucknow known as the 'Lucknow Gharana' of Kathak.

In the style of the dance that used vocal accompaniment too, the Lucknow gharana's contribution is immense. The dancer would sing a line of the song; interpret it through her gestures and facial expressions while she was seated on a carpet. After this she would get on her feet to dance.

Most of the tawaifs were trained in both music and dance. However some chose only to sing while others did both. This led to the classification of tawaifs into 'Bai' (the tawaifs who only sang) and 'Jaan' (those who sang and danced.) The seated style of performance was most suited for intimate gatherings in wealthy households. Every subtle nuance, both musical and of body movement, was clearly visible. It also enabled those singers who did not have the physical attributes suited for vigorous dance routines to use their eyes, hands and subtle shoulder and foot movements, while they were seated, to enact the lyrics. Interestingly, even while the dancer sat and performed, her accompanists on the tabla and sarangi always stood up and played their instruments. This indicated their place in the rigidly hierarchical world of the performing arts.

Wajid Ali Shah's reign was the golden period for the growth of both thumri and kathak. He studied dance under Thakur Prasad ji and his brother Durga Prasad ji, who were resident dancers of his court. He produced lavish dance dramas and operas himself and wrote exquisite thumris and dadras under the pen-name of '*Akhtar Piya*.' The most famous of his compositions is of course '*Babul mora naihar chuto hi jaye, chaar kahar mil duliyaan mangao, apna bigana chuto jaye.*' (O! Father! I forsake all my relationships in my maternal home. Four bearers bear my palanquin and take me to my beloved's house) On a literal level, the lyrics speak of a bride leaving her maternal home in a palanquin born by the four bearers, but on a symbolical level, the words can be interpreted to mean a dead body being taken away on a bier by four men, to the funeral. On another, political level, it signified Wajid Ali Shah's exile from Lucknow to Calcutta.

The Nawab patronized many prominent musicians like Sadiq Ali Khan, who has been hailed as the king of thumris, and also about twenty-six sarangiyas and thirteen tabalchis in his court. Performers of folk art forms like *jhoomar* and *tamasha* were also maintained. It is to Sadiq Ali Khan's credit that the refinement of the bandish thumris goes. He is also regarded as the pioneer of the bol banao style. His disciples were great singers and composers of thumri and included the most famous names like Vazir Mirza Bala Qadar (more popularly known by his pen name 'Qadar Piya'), Bindadin Maharaj, Bhaiya Ganpatrao and other stellar musicians like Lucknow vocalist Khurshid Ali Khan, Saheswan gharana vocalist

Inayat Hussain Khan, the khayal singer from Maharashtra Ramakrishna Bua Waze and renowned Lucknow tawaifs like Haider Jaan and Najma. The other prominent male musicians who specialized in the thumri genre and composed too were Lallan Piya whose bandish thumris were extremely popular, Kalle Khan 'Saras Piya' of Mathura (1860-1926), Nazar Ali 'Nazar Piya' of Rampur, 'Sanad Piya' of Bareilly and Rampur, Madho Piya, Chand Piya and others.

The names of many of the courtesans get obliterated in the history of music. Tawaifs generally neither played musical instruments nor did they keep students. The accompaniment was left to male musicians from the Mirasi and Kathaka communities while the Dhadis trained younger tawaifs. Apart from the necessary talent, it was also considered essential for a tawaif to get trained under some *gharanedar* or traditional musician with a long musical heritage and a marked style, to establish herself. If she failed to do this, she remained a mere entertainer and not a professional courtesan. Since the tawaifs seldom taught they had no disciples to perpetuate their names. It was quite a complex equation in itself since many of the male singers got their training in the kothas, as they were born into the families of the accompanists or at times the tawaif herself, but seldom acknowledged the tawaif as their teacher. Yet it was these very gharanedar ustads to whom the tawaif had to turn for her acceptability and recognition! Also, by adopting a high-pitched falsetto voice in the manner of the women singers many male singers including Faiyaz Khan and Anathnath Bose indicated their desire to imitate the erotic and seductive mannerisms of the courtesans. Dr. Amlan Dasgupta sums this up:

> 'Women also learnt in at least two other ways, though they may have used their gharanedar ustads' names for the purpose of publicity…first of all, women artists learnt the great part of their repertoires (of sub-classical forms) from other women singers. These songs seem to exclusively exist in the feminine domain; their striking presence in the repertoires of women artists widely separated in time and place is a subject worth the closest study.'

This explains why Gauhar Jaan too tried receiving *talim* or education under most of the celebrated gharanedar ustads.

After the 1857 War, India saw the emergence of a new middle class consisting largely of educated civil servants, lawyers, teachers, doctors and also merchants and landlords. They had just enough Western education to serve their British masters but more than enough to feel superior to their own people and look down upon all things Indian, especially the performing arts. To them, these activities were seen to be synonymous with a debased and debauched feudal set-up dominated by tawaifs, prostitutes, lecherous nawabs and zamindars. Thumri and kathak were deplored as illicit and decadent entertainment and their accompanists labelled as pimps and social pests. Nautches were believed to be attended only by natives and such less reputable Englishmen who had little or no character to lose. The British administration which had hitherto maintained a stance of neutrality and non-interference, especially towards the cultural traditions of the Indians, changed their stance. Buoyed by the virulent tirades against India and its religions by the Christian missionaries, it was declared that these art forms exhibited unrestrained sexuality and aroused anti-Christian feelings. Puritanical Victorian concepts of 'morality' and 'obscenity' were thrust upon a people who were traditionally known to revel in their knowledge and openness in matters of sex and love. Herein was sown the seeds of the 'Anti-nautch' movement that raged across the country (starting in the 1890s.)

Meanwhile, the early 20th century saw the gradual disappearance of the bandish thumri which had occupied a place of privilege in the courts and salons of oriental Lucknow. This sub-genre got subsumed in the chota khayal format and there was little to differentiate it from the khayal structure. A different fate awaited its cousin, the bol banao thumri. The arrival and consolidation of the recording industry in India sounded the death knell for the bol banao format in the early records. The gramophone discs came with the inherent disadvantage of a limited time-span. In those 2-3 minutes of disc time, the singer had to present fast, lively and crisp tunes that would fit the time slot and also sell well. So even though the thumris were sung and recorded, the leisurely pace of the bol banao was ignored for recording purposes. But singers like Bhaiya Ganpatrao, who honed the bol banao style and used the harmonium to accompany the fast taans in the thumri as against the sarangi, and his students like Mauzuddin and Gauhar Jaan continued to render the bol-banao in their private soirees and concerts.

During the same time, the Banarasi style or *Banaras-ang* of bol banao thumri became popular. It involved singing the thumri in slower tempos and text elaboration. Being strongly influenced by folk forms and rich tradition of seasonal forms like kajri, jhoola, sawan and chaiti, the Banaras style was a beautiful amalgam of these varied sources. It was pioneered by Guru Jagdip Mishra of Banaras, who was Mauzuddin's first teacher. Unlike the Lucknow composers who used 'weighty' and classical ragas like Malhar, Malkauns, Darbari for their bandish thumris, the Banarasi bol banao thumris were generally set to the 'light ragas' and folk talas like kaharava and dadra, as against the classical teental. A rhythmic interlude of *Laggi* in the Banaras style was also a direct folk adaptation. These were sequences of dense and fast tabla patterns built around repeated nuclei of two or four strokes and were set to 8 or 16 beat cycles irrespective of the tala of the preceding thumri.

With the thumri slowly getting away from the kothas of the courtesans to the gramophone records and the public domain, it lost much of its seductive function and transformed into a pure, abstract form. The increasing number of male musicians who took to singing thumri also snatched away the original '*nakhra*' and eroticism associated with the courtesan's rendition of the same thumri. The 1920s and after are considered the prime of the thumri era as the genre was supposedly 'rescued' from the lascivious tawaif by male musicians who appropriated it as yet another component of their classical repertoire. This also ensured a larger social acceptability and respect for the thumri and gave it an unprecedented degree of sophistication and expressiveness like the other classical genres. The bol banao thumri continued to remain the mainstay of all live performances. Thumri and kathak had a formal divorce. The seated abhinaya in kathak to the accompaniment of thumri slowly began to wane. Musicians and dancers began specializing in one of the two arts and seldom combined the two. The deceleration of the thumri's tempo is also noticeable in records as time passed. This was in a way linked to the introduction of new records with increased time-span that were used for recording and much later in 1925 to the birth of Electrical recording that replaced the acoustic/mechanical technique.

The celebrity status that artists of the gramophone era achieved and their travels across the country singing for princes and nobles, was responsible for the bol banao thumri becoming popular all over the country. Banaras continued to remain the citadel of the bol-banao style. Bengal and Calcutta too were important centres from the commercial and popularity point of view. By 1910, along with the Banaras-ang another style that became popular was the *purab-ang* or the eastern style (eastern Uttar Pradesh and Bihar) and the style was imitated and cultivated by many of the leading khayal singers of the times. Apart from Nidhi babu, musicians of Bengal like Girija Shankar Chakraborthy trained an entire generation of Bengali khayal and thumri singers like Sunil Bose and Naina Devi. Zamiruddin Khan, who had even trained under Gauhar Jaan for a while, was another prominent singer of the bol banao thumri.

Thus in this long and interesting journey of the thumri in the world of Indian classical music it is fascinating to note the space it occupies in the scheme of things in Indian music. Much like a woman in a patriarchal society, a thumri is the voice of the female in the world of traditional classical music, largely dominated by men. However it can not be considered as a feminine form merely because it was sung and propagated by courtesans and its theme is essentially from a woman's point of view. But a subtler investigation shows that its interrogative and subversive quality, its wonderful ability to co-exist in harmony with numerous ambiguities, multiple layers of meaning, usage of subtle humour in a way mirrors the myriad roles played by women in our traditional Indian society. Her role is ambiguous, undefined and lends itself to multiple definitions depending on the whim of the male patriarch. The woman creates a space for herself within the limitations that are placed on her by traditional society. Quite analogously thumris too operate within similar limitations of a largely hereditary and orthodox classical idiom, but manage to extend beyond the set pattern. They are set in ragas which themselves do not have fixed structures; they have lyrics which mean multiple things. As Peter Manuel states that in a thumri 'poetry gives up its literary status and becomes a purely musical element.'

The thumri singer negotiates and explores the ambiguities at several levels – the level of the text, the level of the raga and its malleable nature, the tala and the theme. 'A thumri singer would revel in the points of danger and explore just how far and how much otherness can be introduced into the body of the raga. A swar in the raga becomes the door that leads to other ragas; a swar as it is heard in one raga is deliberately punned upon to give it the meaning in another raga. It is not so much that ragas are mixed to create a third new raga with its own identity and personality. Instead the points of weakness, the margins and boundaries, in the raga's structure are used as points at which other ragas are allowed to enter into the body of the main raga.' (Dr Vidya Rao)

As Dr Vidya Rao states in her essay 'Thumri as Feminine Voice':

'Thumri is the small space traditionally given to women in the world of classical/margi music. This is a fine cameo form which uses specific poetic themes, musical embellishments, ragas and talas. It is considered light and attractive but lacking the majesty and range of forms like khayal and dhrupad and is best heard or appreciated in small intimate mehfils...the endeavour of khayal is to guard its thresholds and gates, watch all points of danger, allow for no transgression of the purity of the raga. Thumri on the other hand—like the female body—is entirely open. The style of singing is based on this openness of the form. It is a small form with small scales, small light ragas, small talas. But it leaves itself wide open and vulnerable. As a result it is able, constantly, to expand the space available to it in unique and unexpected ways...as female body, thumri is open, dangerous—yet fecund and regenerative.'

In the midst of this vast and enormous world of Hindustani music, where does Gauhar Jaan and her identity stand? What were the essential features of her music, especially her recordings?

A traditional performance of vocal classical music involves a detailed exposition of the raga through several stages. The khayal presentation falls into the two broad sub-categories of bada khayal or the bigger khayal made up of the slow and composed section and the faster chota khayal. The exposition of a raga through the khayal is not time bound and some singers are known to take hours over it. It begins with the *alaps* or slow and unmetered preludes where characteristic phrases of the raga are sung. The musician then moves towards the lyrics of the composition or *bandish* or *cheez*. The improvisation of these lyrics happens initially in the extremely slow tempo known as the *ati-vilambit laya*. The tempo builds up slowly, picking up speed to become the *vilambit* (slow), *madhya* (medium) and *dhrut* (fast) layas or tempos and the compositions too change. These sections are joined by slow and fast melodic trills and passages called the taans which either use solfa notes (*taan sargam*) or merely in an *akaar* (using the syllable 'a.') Specific usage of improvisatory solfa notes known as *sargam* is also employed in some gharanas and it is said to be an inspiration from Carnatic music.

In this traditional context, it is amazing how Gauhar Jaan pioneered a veritable formula, a kind of prototype that was later copied by all the musicians to present this expansive genre into short bursts of merely three minutes each. Being the first professional Hindustani musician who recorded her music, the onus was on her to create a template to overcome this daunting challenge. She had to ensure that there was no compromise on the traditional aspects of the style and at the same time also present a complete and undiluted picture of the raga, just as she would in a night-long live soiree.

An analysis of any of the khayal recordings of Gauhar Jaan shows a clear sense of shape and balance in the way she structures an expansive form like the khayal into the requisite time span. The alap usually dwelt for a couple of seconds on just one or two notes, usually the tonic 'Sa' only. This was followed by the opening phrase (*mukhada*) of the first line (*sthayi*). The sthayi is important because it sets the rhythmic tone for the rest of the composition. Gauhar would sing this sthayi two or three times in varied ways and quickly switch to the next verse or *antara*, sing it once or twice and then make a rapid return to the sthayi. With clockwork precision she would complete the 'fixed composition' part of the rendition in one to one and a quarter minutes.

The improvisation part of her rendition was primarily through her bravura taans. Blessed with a high-pitched, flexible and highly pliant voice, she could create stunning trills at varied speeds to fit into the time span available before returning to a compressed version of the mukhada at the end of each phrase of taans. The lengths of the taans are in a descending fashion and start with a long, complex phrase and taper down to shorter and further shorter lengths and finally culminate at the mukhada. She concludes with singing the whole sthayi once and then with her customary flamboyance, signs off with, 'My name is Gauhar Jaan'. Thus Gauhar beautifully blended the compositional and the improvisatory aspects of Hindustani music in the shortest time span possible, in the process reaching out to the largest cross-section of aficionados across the country.

Of course for all her precision even Gauhar was sometimes caught unawares and failed to finish on time. Some records trail off in the midst of a packed rendition and lose the time for the customary ending announcement. Since there was no concept of 'retakes' the Company had no option but to work around with these 'incomplete' record masters. This obviously created problems of labelling when the masters were shipped to Hanover for pressing. For the technician there this was just another anonymous voice.

As the bol banao thumris had made way for faster, brighter and lighter versions of the same, the recordings of Gauhar Jaan and Mauzuddin exhibit the fast taans and tempo that is reminiscent of the bandish thumri, coupled with the exposition(*vistaar*) of the bol banao. Gauhar's thumri recording in Raga Bhairavi '*Chhodo Chhodo mori baiyyan*' shows a marked influence of the chota khayal in terms of the tempo and structure. Sung in the classical teental, the lyrics are interspersed with dazzling, virtuoso leaping taans (*sapaat tans*) but the conclusion is at such a frenetic pace that it is difficult to catch the words. Some of Gauhar's taans are of the tappa style employing medium tempo talas like *sitarkhani* and coloured with the frantic, yet ornate trills.

Gauhar recorded in a range of genres—from khayal to dhrupad and from thumri to dadra, bhajan, ghazal, hori, tarana and chaiti. She recorded close to six hundred songs in her illustrious musical career. Of those, the ones still available are her khayals in ragas Jaunpuri, Bhopali, Multani, among others, thumris and horis ranging from Kafi, Bhairavi, Sohini and Pahadi, Piloo, Piloo-Kafi, Pahadi-Jaunpuri, Zila, Ghara and Desh. She has also recorded some tappa-ang horis in Kafi ('*Kaisi yeh dhoom machayi*') and many of her own compositions such as '*Khelat Krishna Kumar, Sab sakhiyan mil gavat nachat aur baajat mridang, Kartaar re, Gauhar Pyaari ki araj yahi hai, Karo Kripa Kartaar.*' (The little Krishna plays joyously, all his companions, the girls get together and make merry by singing, dancing and playing the drums. Oh Creator! It is Gauhar's earnest prayer that you show mercy on her.) Her deep devotion to Krishna is amply displayed in the numerous bhajans she sang in his praise, and in those verses she composed herself. Her renditions of some bhajans like '*Krishna Madho Shyam*' in Malkauns and '*Shyamsundar ki dekhi suratiya, main bhool gayi sudh saari,*' a thumri in raga Khamaj were very popular throughout the country. While most singers pitched their voices at the black 4th (*kaali char*), Gauhar used an amazingly high pitch of the 6th or 7th black note (*kaali* 6 or 7.) Gauhar captivated her listeners with the purity of her notes and the adherence to pitch.

Critics sometimes find Gauhar's renditions repetitive, especially in the improvisatory aspects. But one must acknowledge the challenging task she had of conceptualizing this framework of rendition and executing it with such precision and perfection.

Gauhar also elicited some frowns from the puritans. They felt to record in such a short time was to compromise the integrity of the art-form that they worshipped literally and were reluctant to lend their voices to the machine. But the public approval of these recordings was huge. What, after all, is that art which remains static and does not mould itself in accordance with the popular sentiment? Slowly many of the cynics too fell in line and luckily for them with the advances in technology longer duration records were made possible. This set their fears of having to compromise their art, at rest.

Today the world of Hindustani music has forgotten the pioneer artist of this new technique. But it certainly goes to the credit of Gauhar's grit and her musical ingenuity that despite the criticism and scepticism, she showed her innovative skills and courage to face her peers and evolved a technique suited to the needs of a gramophone recording—a technique which would be adapted thereafter by most artists.

Kataye rishta maut se karta nahin jism naheef
Hai yah sheeraaza kitaab-e-aalam-e eejaad ka.

Death can not separate those who are truly in love!
That has always been the way of the world

—Badi Malka Jaan, Makhzan-e-ulfat-e-Mallika.

10

THE DARLING SONGSTRESS

The success of her gramophone discs, which were among the best-selling records till almost the 1940s, elevated Gauhar Jaan to a celebrity status that even she had not envisaged. Her photograph started appearing on match-boxes which were manufactured in Austria. It shows her as a fair, rose-cheeked young woman dressed in a red velvet gown and adorned with costly jewels. The tag below says 'Made in Austria.' The fact that an Austrian company chose to use her face to sell their products in India underlines the immense fame and popularity, both national and international, that she had earned for herself. She was supposedly the protagonist of many puppet show performances in distant Punjab and Rajasthan. Her photographs began appearing on picture post cards of the times. The coloured ones were priced at 2 annas and the black and white at 1 anna. In some of those pictures, she looks quite imposing in traditional Bengali attire. In another she poses with someone named 'Jaura.' These postcards sold as briskly as her records. Thus at a time when media and publicity were absent and unknown to performing artists, Gauhar Jaan reigned over the world of Indian music like an empress and won the hearts of millions.

The affluent patrons of beauty and the arts showered her with gifts and expensive jewellery. All this adulation and wealth led her to a hedonistic lifestyle. Her mansion at Chitpur, adjacent to the Nakhoda mosque, came to be known as 'Gauhar building.' She owned costly cars, phaetons with exquisite silk-curtains, and imposing victorias (carriages). She often dressed up in all her finery and rode through the streets of Calcutta for the pure pleasure of the drive. Many eye-witnesses have described this stately ride of a beautiful woman who flashed past them in the evenings through the major thoroughfares of Calcutta in a majestic phaeton driven by six white Arabian stallions.

It is said that one evening the Governor's cavalcade passed hers on the main road. Seeing her regal appearance, the Governor thought she belonged to one of the royal families or aristocracies of Bengal. He stopped his cavalcade, doffed his hat, made a quick bow and let her zoom past. When he learnt later that the woman he had encountered on the street and greeted was a mere tawaif, he was furious. He slapped a fine of Rs 1000 on her for flouting the rule which forbade all common citizens from riding in a six-horse carriage. That was the prerogative of only the Viceroy and members of royal families. But Gauhar was not the one to care about such authoritarian dictates. She continued to flout the rule, pay the thousand rupee fine, and yet go on with her evening rides. Such was her spirit!

There are innumerable stories about Gauhar Jaan's extravagant lifestyle and habit of lavish spending on inconsequential things. One of the oft recounted tales is that of the wedding of her pet cat, on which she supposedly spent Rs 1200. And then, when the cat had a litter, she threw a party for the whole city, which cost her Rs 20,000! These are perhaps apocryphal stories which get exaggerated each time they are narrated, but they do reflect the kind of image Gauhar Jaan had created for herself.

With the rising popularity came a flurry of invitations from a host of princely states and wealthy households across the country. They deemed it an honour if Gauhar graced their soirees. She was among the highest paid artists of her time and commanded an extravagant sum of Rs 1000 per concert. An interesting eye-witness account of one such soiree of hers is presented by the eminent musicologist D.P. Mukherjee who had heard her in his youth by sneaking into her house:

> 'In our days there was a singer, Gauhar Jan, and she was unapproachable. Yet, where there is a will, there is a way. I managed to sneak into her house one night in the company of somebody belonging to the underworld of music. She was entertaining a Nabab. She sang Adana, Bahar, Suha and Sughrai, but the Nabab's preference was for thumri, which she sang in one of her sensuous veins with lots of bhava-batana for which she was famous…I vividly remember the occasion when she sang a dhruvapad in Adana, a sadra in the same raga, and yet a third khayal in Adana. Since then, I have found it difficult to concentrate on Adana even when it is sung by the best in the country… Later on, I had more public opportunities of hearing her. It is a pity that today's world does not know what a great khayal singer was lost in the voluptuous folds of thumri. To please her audience, Gauhar Jan would sing Pushtu songs, anything bizarre and clever… She had a magnificent and scintillating personality. There have been many excellent khayal singers among women after her, but I would feign call them masters. They are exceedingly competent, but always fall below the standard that Gauhar Jan occasionally set in khayal.'

On one occasion, Gauhar Jaan was invited to perform at the court of the king of Datia. An incident that occurred during this visit changed Gauhar's perception of herself. Datia, one of the small princely states in Madhya Pradesh, was ruled by the descendants of the renowned Orchha royal family. Maharaja Bhawani Singh Bahadur (1837-1907), was a great patron of the arts and a skilled Pakhawaj player himself. He was the disciple of the illustrious pakhawaj player Pandit Kudau Singh (1815-1910). A story is told about Kudau Singh's prowess on the pakhawaj. Apparently, an elephant in the royal stable was in musth and was creating havoc. Kudau Singh is said to have played his famous 'Gaja Paran' on the pakhawaj and controlled the frenzied creature. Kudau Singh's parans, which involved complex and strong syllables and required considerable strength in playing, were famous. It usually required about 24 tala cycles to complete the rendition of a paran.

Maharaja Bhawani Singh had heard about the prowess of Gauhar Jaan and wanted to invite her to sing at his court. Gauhar, who was at the peak of her musical career then, was selective about the venues she sang at. In her arrogance she turned down the invitation saying it was beneath her dignity to sing for 'small' princely states, having been used to singing in the courts of the likes of Darbhanga, Mysore, Hyderabad, Kashmir etc. The Maharaja was quite stunned by this blunt refusal and he decided that he would not take this insult lightly.

Using his good offices with the British Governor in Bengal, he put intense pressure on Gauhar to perform at the coronation ceremony of the Yuvaraj, the prince of Datia. The immense pressure from the British authorities left Gauhar with little choice but to agree. However she wanted to assert herself and imposed her own conditions to go to Datia. She demanded a special train to be sent exclusively for her! The Maharaja complied with the request and sent a train made up of eleven coaches. Gauhar's entourage consisted of 111 persons. It included ten dhobies, four barbers, twenty *khidmatgars* or orderlies, five *dasis* or maids, five horses and five syces! Her two disciples Doanni and Chuanni (literally, Two-annas and Four-annas!) who usually accompanied her on the tanpura were part of the group. Such was the price that Gauhar had begun to command after her phenomenal rise in the world of Indian music. And people were willing to pay her that to get her to perform at their venues.

Gauhar and her entourage reached Datia. The city was lavishly decorated for the coronation. Gauhar was housed in a luxurious bungalow and was promised Rs 2000 as honorarium for each day she spent in Datia. Some of the best known singers were present and they gave outstanding performances at the coronation ceremony. When Gauhar saw the large number of royals and aristocrats, she realised that Datia was no small kingdom and she had wrongly judged its importance. She had prepared herself for the performance and kept asking the Durbar Bakshi when it would be her turn to take the stage. He simply smiled and said he would let her know soon.

All the performances for the evening were over and the ceremony concluded. Gauhar was perplexed. She had been brought there with all the pomp for the occasion but not given an opportunity to sing. She thought the Maharaja might have planned an exclusive evening only for her concert, so she decided to remain patient. She retired to the bungalow where she was pleasantly surprised to find costly gifts from the Maharaja in her honour. This continued for a day or two. She would get her honorarium every day, and expensive gifts, but no invitation from the Maharaja to sing. Finally a flustered Gauhar sent word to the Maharaja seeking an audience. She was refused permission to meet him. Instead the honorarium was doubled and sent across to her. Gauhar was flummoxed. She did not know what to make of this treatment of her. A couple of weeks passed this way. Gauhar was getting increasingly restless and wanted to do something about it.

Now, it was customary for the Maharaja to go for an early morning ride on his favourite horse. Gauhar knew about this and decided that that would be the right time to confront him. She dressed in male attire, covered her hair with a silk turban and drew a scarf across her face, and waited at the entrance to the fort. When she saw the Maharaja approaching, she accosted him in the manner of a subject seeking justice. Not knowing who this stalker was, the Maharaja stopped and looked at the person questioningly. Gauhar alighted from her horse and made a reverential bow. In the process her turban fell off and out came locks of her thick curly hair. 'Gauhar Jaan! What are you doing here at this hour? Why have you stopped me this way? What is it you desire, a further increase in your honorarium? That can be done too if you so desire!' said the Maharaja. The humbled Gauhar threw herself at his feet and said 'Please forgive me Your Highness! I was too puffed up with pride. I beseech you to pardon me. An artist who is not given an opportunity to showcase his talent feels stifled and I too am feeling terribly suffocated by this idleness. I have come here to sing and to entertain you. I don't need any more gifts or money. All I want is the chance to do what I was called here for.'

The Maharaja knew that he had finally managed to break her arrogance and that she had been humbled into pleading to be heard. He relented and arranged a concert for her that same evening.

After having waited for so long Gauhar came up with one of her best performances that evening and the concert was a huge success. She stayed on in Datia for the next six months and gave numerous performances at the court. She took the opportunity to study music under Ustad Maula Baksh of the Kirana Gharana during her stay here. Finally when she decided to leave, the Maharaja asked her what she desired as a parting gift. Unfortunately, in this instance too Gauhar made a faux pas. She requested the king to present her the same elephant that had been pacified by Kudau Singh through his Gaja Paran. The Maharaja was in a quandary. He had already gifted the elephant to his Guru after it had been tamed. How could he take it back? Seeing his disciple's dilemma, Kudau Singh stepped in and resolved the issue. He declared that Gauhar was like the daughter of Datia and it was customary for all fathers to gift their daughters with costly presents when bidding them farewell. It would be his privilege to present his daughter with the elephant as a parting gift. Tears welled up in Gauhar's eyes. She had never experienced such hospitality before. To be accorded the status of the daughter of the kingdom completely humbled her. She fell at the feet of both the Maharaja and Kudau Singh and said she would come to Datia any time they asked her to.

The Maharaja gave her some parting advice as well: 'Gauhar, success in the field of fine arts is ephemeral. You must realise that today you might be the reigning Empress of music, but you are merely a traveller who will sing till you are destined to and very soon someone else will take your place. The world might forget you and all that you have achieved. But like an unending river, the music will live on irrespective of whether you sing or not. The deeper one delves into the ocean of music, the more one realises how little one knows and how many more lifetimes it would take to explore even a fraction of this vast ocean. Only by subsuming the ego, the 'I', is a true musician born. So never let accomplishments get to your head.'

It was timely advice for Gauhar who had tasted the fruit of unprecedented success. The advice stayed with her and changed her personality to a great extent. She became a more humble and down-to-earth musician.

On her visit to the royal court of Indore, she was given the special honour of singing from a specially prepared dais. At the end of the concert, instead of paying her an honorarium or giving her gifts the Raja of Indore announced that the stage itself would be gifted to her. Gauhar was puzzled. However when the Raja ordered the white sheets and flowers to be removed, she saw that the dais was embedded with silver coins amounting to Rs 1 lakh. And it was all being offered to her. The Raja complimented her saying that she alone was worthy of presiding over that silver stage like Lakshmi, the Goddess of wealth. But Gauhar bowed humbly and told the Raja that being devotees of Saraswati, it was knowledge and music that mattered more to her. She would accept his gift with all humility but distribute it among the poor and needy. This gesture of hers won her great admiration and respect in the Raja's eyes.

In those days, like Calcutta, Bombay too was not just a hub of trade and commerce. It also attracted numerous artists, musicians and theatre personalities who were patronized by the culturally sensitive Maharashtrians. Gauhar too visited Bombay many times and held private soirees there. During one such visit to Bombay around 1904-05, she met Amrit Keshav Nayak, a young and handsome hero of the Gujarati and Hindustani stage. She had met him a couple of times earlier too, in Lucknow where he went to learn Kathak from her guru Bindadin Maharaj. She recalled that he was an assiduous student, keen to master a host of skills —from Kathak to bhava abhinaya or emoting and proficiency in languages like Urdu and Persian. Maharaj ji had always spoken of Amrit in superlatives.

Amrit Keshav Nayak dominated the Hindustani and Gujarati stage in the late 19th and early 20th centuries. He was born in Ahmedabad in 1877 in the Nayak family, renowned for their skills in the Gujarati folk theatre form called *Bhavai*. As a ten year old school dropout, little Amrit migrated to Bombay with his father. Bombay, the city of dreams and opportunities, welcomed Amrit with open arms. He sought employment with Cowasji Palonji Khatao and Sorabjee Ogra. Ogra owned the famous Alfred Natak Mandali and noticing the young man's innate dramatic talents cast him in several plays like '*Gamreni Gori*,' '*Bimare Bulbul*,' and '*Alladin*', where he played the female character Laila.

He soon began to write and direct plays as well. His most significant contribution was the adaptation of several Shakespearean plays into Urdu, a language that he had mastered. His plays '*Khun-e-Nahak*' (Hamlet), '*Bazum-e-Fani*' (Romeo and Juliet), *Muriel-e-Shaque* (A Winter's Tale), and *Shahid-e-Naaz* (Measure for Measure) were huge hits and catapulted him to a top position in Bombay's vibrant theatre world. Since he was himself a skilled actor, he portrayed varied characters with great élan. His *Natak Mandali* toured the North extensively because of the regular invitations from Delhi, Lucknow and Banaras for performances. In addition to being an actor and director, Amrit was also a wonderful writer. He wrote articles for Gujarati weeklies and also attempted a novel '*M.A. Banake kyun meri mitti kharab ki.*' Amrit was married to a young, illiterate girl called Parvati from Kadi in Northern Gujarat at a very young age. She was a complete mismatch for Amrit as she could not provide the kind of intellectual stimulation and companionship that he was seeking. As a result Amrit spent more and more time on his writing, composing verses and theatre activities. But he was desperately looking for someone who could share his passion for the arts.

Amrit and Gauhar met like long lost friends and hit it off almost instantaneously. The shared experiences of Lucknow and of their common guru Bindadin Maharaj bound them in a strange bond of friendship. Gauhar had everything she could ask for, but longed for a true companion. Amrit seemed the right man, though he was younger than her and already married. In spite of that Gauhar decided to stay back in Bombay for a while and moved into one of Amrit's houses in the city.

The heady days of romance were back for Gauhar. In Amrit she found the ultimate soul mate and intellectual companion. Amrit was also a good singer and composed songs and lyrics in his free time. He would pen a verse and they would set it to tune together and Gauhar would render the final version with her characteristic flair. Some of Amrit's most famous hits were *Pardesi Saiyyan neha lagake dukh de gaye, Saar par gagar dhar kar, Dil-e-nadaan ko hum samjhate jayenge* and the evergreen *Aan baan jiya mein laagi.* Of these Gauhar was particularly fond of the last one.

Aan baan jiya mein laagi,
Pyari Chit kyun diya, aan basi kaise phasi
Padan laagi chhab ke paiyyan, Meherban saiyyan
Tum bin mohe kal na pade, tumhare kaaran jaagi
Aan baan jiya mein laagi.

As the arrows of love pierce my heart, I know I have now become a captive
I am reduced to becoming your slave, my beloved one, and falling at your feet beseeching your mercy,
Without you being around, my heart knows no comfort and I have spent so many sleepless nights for your sake.

The lilting music of this dadra greatly fascinated Gauhar. They had set it to Raga Gara in the dadra taal and when Gauhar rendered it in her sweet, melodious tone, Amrit was enchanted. It did not sound like his composition at all, but had acquired a new colour and flavour through Gauhar's voice.

Life had never been so beautiful and perfect for Gauhar. The picturesque Mahalakshmi Race Course of Bombay was and perhaps continues to be, a unique show-piece of the city. With its 2400 metres long racecourse, the turf club was surely a haunt of the daring and adventurous. Given her riotous spirit of self-indulgence, which she shared with Amrit, the Race Course became a weekly haunt for the two. The young man in his English clothes and his pretty companion with Anglo-Indian features and fair skin, dark glasses and binoculars, rooting for their favourite horses, became a regular feature and a cynosure of all eyes at the race course.

An unexpected telegram from Calcutta changed everything for Gauhar. It had a message about Malka Jaan's sudden illness. Gauhar immediately packed her bags, took Amrit's permission and left for home. Malka Jaan had resorted to excessive drinking to beat her loneliness. Her celebrity daughter was now busy travelling across the country and moving in and out of recording studios leaving Malka pretty much to herself. Of course it was the culmination of all her dreams and Malka was supremely happy for her daughter. But Gauhar's increasing absence from home and Calcutta made her infinitely lonely. Also there was growing tension caused by the wayward Bhaglu. Alcohol was her only succour At one mehfil at Motijheel, Malka Jaan had reportedly vomited blood in the midst of the rendition of the famous ghazal 'O! Bewafa Tere liye badnaam ho gaye.' She abruptly concluded the concert complaining of intense stomach pain. The diagnosis was an enlarged liver. When Gauhar saw her mother, she was devastated. She hugged her and cried bitterly at the plight of her constant companion and support throughout her life, the person to whom she owed all her success. Gauhar promised Malka Jaan that she would stay put with her or take her along wherever she went. Her words were like a soothing balm for the aggrieved Malka.

Sadly Malka Jaan's condition never improved. Despite being told not to touch alcohol, Malka could not stay away from it. She secretly gulped pegs every now and then and this spelt doom for her health. Finally, in June

1906, at the age of around 50, Badi Malka Jaan breathed her last. She was buried at the Bagmarie graveyard in Calcutta and the funeral was attended by some of the greatest tawaifs, singers and poets of the city.

Malka Jaan's death was a huge blow to Gauhar. She went into a state of shock and denial and turned into a complete misanthrope. Life without her mother was something she had never imagined. Everything brought back memories of their times together, the highs and the lows, the good times and the bad times, when they had clung to each other for comfort and solace.

Meanwhile Amrit Keshav Nayak was getting increasingly concerned about Gauhar's state of mind. He strongly advised her to consolidate some of her properties back in Calcutta, sell off a few unwanted ones and shift base to Bombay, at least temporarily. Heeding his advice, Gauhar sold two of their properties, one at Beleghata to Prince Qader and another one at the Khirepore slum. She invested some of the money, Rs 15,750, in another house at 22, Bentinck Street, and with the rest of the money and her belongings, she rushed to the open arms of Amrit in Bombay. This change of place and the reassuring company of Amrit was what Gauhar badly needed at that stage. Else she would have lost her sanity. The kind of support she received from Amrit helped her recover and get back to her music and performances.

In early July 1907, Gauhar was invited to perform at a highly prestigious venue in Bombay. The Town Hall, with its tall white Grecian columns was a majestic building. The Durbar Hall inside was equally splendid and imposing. Her concert at this Hall drew one of the city's largest crowds ever. This was a concert meant to help her overcome the personal tragedies she had suffered recently and regain her professional composure. The Gramophone Company was there too, to record the concert. The recording of it was released in 1912. Her beautiful rendition of the khayal in Raga Bhupali, *'Itna joban daman na kariye'* and her melodious *'Chalo Gulzar aalam mein hava-e-fazl-e-rehmani'* were instant hits with the discerning audience. She received a thunderous applause. Amrit Keshav Nayak was present there and gave her a reassuring hug as she hid her face in his arms and sobbed. She thought she had come out of the trauma of her mother's sudden demise. But she was sadly mistaken.

Around that time, Amrit was working tirelessly on his new production 'Zahari Saanp.' Quite determined to make it a runaway hit like the previous plays he had written, acted and directed, Amrit put in long hours on rehearsals and fine-tuning the performances of the cast. In Gauhar's absence he had also taken to alcohol. The morning of 18 July 1907 seemed like any other day. It was back to 'Light' and 'Action' on the stage. Suddenly Amrit complained of severe chest pain and exhaustion and requested for a break in the green room. There he suffered a massive heart attack and died of a cardiac arrest. He was only 30 years old.

When the news was broken to Gauhar, she was hysterical with grief. In less than a year she had lost two of the most important people in her life. She was on the verge of a nervous breakdown. She kept questioning her fate which had struck at her each time she was looking at happiness and success. Meanwhile, some of her well-wishers in Calcutta heard about her condition. They came to Bombay, persuaded her to return home and get a grip on herself and her life. With a heavy heart Gauhar bid farewell to the house of the man who had given her the greatest happiness and the most comforting support at the time when she needed it most.

Life was never a straight path for Gauhar. Disasters and tragedies lurked around every turn and corner. Her flamboyance and self-indulgence may have stemmed from a desire to wash away the memories of these tragedies and live life to the fullest. Gauhar returned to Calcutta, the city that had made her what she was, and decided to pick up the pieces of her tragic life.

Yeh ashk-fishaani nahin hamdam shab-e-gham mein
Aankhon se rawaan hoti hai dariya mere dil ka.

The tears I shed in the dark night of sorrow are not mere droplets of water
The gushing torrents of agony in my heart find an outlet through my eyes.

—Badi Malka Jaan, Makhzan-e-ulfat-e-Mallika.

❦

11

ON PROVING ONE'S PARENTAGE

Calcutta, 1907

Calcutta did not seem the same to an emotionally broken Gauhar. On the one hand she had been through two personal tragedies in quick succession, and on the other, there was the ever increasing pressure of recordings for the Gramophone Company and their rivals. Also she had to travel long distances for her concerts. She hardly had the time to stop, introspect and look back, nor did she have anyone with whom she could share her agonies, insecurities and joys. Her manager Yusuf had proved to be untrustworthy and she decided to dispense with him. A family friend brought to her house a young Pathan boy named Syed Ghulam Abbas Subzwari. Abbas was about ten or twelve years younger than her but was an extremely polite and courteous young man. He was very respectful and was scared to even look Gauhar in the eye while speaking to her. He was in dire need of a job and assured her that he would serve her efficiently as her secretary and manager. Since he appeared trustworthy Gauhar appointed him right away.

When Gauhar got back to Calcutta, she came to know about the increasing trouble that Bhaglu had been creating. After Malka's death he had had a free rein to do as he pleased and had unlawfully occupied a major portion of the building. Gauhar was getting increasingly irritated about his presence. She requested Abbas and his father Ghulam Mehdi Hussain Khan to keep a tab on Bhaglu's activities whenever she was away.

During one of Gauhar's concert tours to Bhopal, Indore and Hyderabad, she received news from Abbas that there had been a major crisis at home. Bhaglu had broken open the locks of the safe and had tried to steal money. As a dutiful manager Abbas had filed a complaint against Bhaglu with the police. Gauhar cut short her visit and returned to Calcutta. Abbas accompanied her to the Chief Presidency Magistrate where she complained about Bhaglu's wayward ways, his drinking problem, forceful appropriation of a portion of her house, siphoning of her money and so on. A notice was accordingly served on Bhaglu.

But Bhaglu was not one to take all this lying down. He decided to strike back. He did not have the courage to directly file a case against Gauhar. So instead, on 4 August 1909, he filed a case against Ghulam Hussain and Hadi, Abbas' father and brother, of harassing him and trying to evict him from his rightful abode. The allegations he made were extremely preposterous. He claimed in his affidavit that he was the only lawful heir and legitimate son of the deceased Malka Jaan and so it was he who had the first right of inheritance over his dead mother's property.

The following was the complaint that Bhaglu lodged in the Court of the Chief Presidency Magistrate of Calcutta against Hingoo alias Ghulam Hussain and Hadi, both residents of Harrison Road, Laskaritola, Calcutta:

"The complainant is the adopted son of one Malka Jan and the complainant has been living in the aforesaid 49, Lower Chitpore Road for upwards of 42 years as the adopted son and heir of the said Malka Jan. One Gaharjan is the daughter of the said Malka Jan. For sometime past, one Abbas has been on friendly terms with the said Gaharjan. The said Abbas and his father have been instigating the said Gaharjan to expel the complainant from the house. The accused no 2 is the brother of the said Abbas and the accused no 1 belongs to the party of the said Abbas. On the 30th July '09 the accused

no 1 showed a knife to your petitioner and threatened to stab; on the 31st July '09 both the accused abused your petitioner and the members of his family; on the 1 st August '09 Golam Mehendi- the father of the said Abbas abused and threatened your petitioner. On the 3rd August '09 the accused persons accompanied by Peshwaris threatened the son of your petitioner named Farhan. The accused persons have been systematically molesting the complainant and others of his family. The complainant prays that Your Honour will be pleased to direct the H Town to warn the accused persons not to molest the complainant.

Gauhar was shocked to see the allegations that were being made by an ungrateful man on whom her mother had showered utmost affection all her life. She decided to take legal help to evict Bhaglu from the premises and accordingly employed the solicitors F.R. Surita & Co to send a letter to this effect to Bhaglu.

Finally on 10 January 1910, Bhaglu's Attorney G.N Dutta & Co sent a legal notice to Gauhar's attorney F.R. Surita:

'To F.R. Surita Esqr.

Dear Sir,

Re: Premises No 49 Lower Chitpore Road

Your letter of the 21st ultimo to the address of our client Shaik Bhagloo has been handed to us today with instructions to state in reply that your client is fully aware that our client is occupying a portion of the above premises as a co-owner with your client and she has therefore no right to ask him to quit the same. If inspite of this knowledge of hers, she chooses to take any steps against our client she can do so at her own risk and our client will be fully prepared to defend the same.

Yours faithfully,
G.N.Dutta & Co.
2, Hastings Street, Calcutta.'

The High Court too issued a summons to Gauhar. It read that Sheikh Bhaglu had filed a court case on 29 January 1910 to claim his legal inheritances from Gauhar, who he alleged was his mother's illegitimate daughter. It was claimed that in 1868, in Azamgarh, his father Sheikh Wazir had married Malka Jaan and a year later he was born. The father had apparently died when Bhaglu was merely two years old and that was when Malka shifted to Banaras and Calcutta and became a courtesan. She also ended up as the mistress of an Armenian gentleman and the result of that illegal union was his step-sister Gauhar, the famous tawaif of Calcutta, born in 1873. Though Malka died a sudden death in 1906 and hence left no will behind, it was the 'legitimate son' who could claim all her property—the estates at 49, Chitpur Road and 22, Bentinck Street. He also claimed there was a net amount of Rs 2, 38,955 in dues that were recoverable from Gauhar. *(The original version of the affidavit filed by Bhaglu can be found in the Appendix.)* It was the most outrageous claim ever made. Gauhar had always suspected Bhaglu's intentions and would chide Malka for pampering him so much. But even she never expected that he would stoop so low.

She discussed the entire matter with Abbas who suggested that she employ one of the city's best attorneys, Ganesh Chandra Chandra of G.C. Chunder & Co. to fight her case. Gauhar cut down on many of her professional commitments, recordings and concerts and decided to give this case her full attention; else she could be left on the streets. The Attorney was a pleasant natured gentleman who welcomed Gauhar in his huge study. The case papers were laid on his table and he perused them carefully. 'Miss Gauhar, it is a complicated case. I am afraid you will now have to prove in the Court that you are indeed the only legitimate daughter and legal heir of late Madam Malka Jaan. She being a courtesan makes things all the more difficult, but then we will have to strive for direct evidence if we are to win this case.' Gauhar did not know what to say. Was her very identity now in question? The issue of her parentage had troubled her many years back and it seemed to have returned now to haunt her.

In the counter-affidavit filed by Gauhar on 19 March 1910, she gave all the details of her lineage, of the marriage of her parents Robert William Yeoward and Adeline Victoria Hemmings in 1872, her birth on 26 June 1873, the divorce of the parents and the move to Banaras and Calcutta by the mother and daughter who had now taken on a new religion and new names. She reiterated that she had never heard of Sheikh Wazir who was

Nautch girls in a performance in Delhi, circa 1830.

Nautch performance in the 1900s.

Nautch performance.

Durga Puja in Kolkata.

Nawab Wajid Ali Shah of Oudh.

Badi Malka Jaan

The ghats on the shore of the Ganga, Varanasi.

The cover page of Makhzan-e-ulfat-e-Mallika of Badi Malka Jaan.

Old Calcutta: bazaar

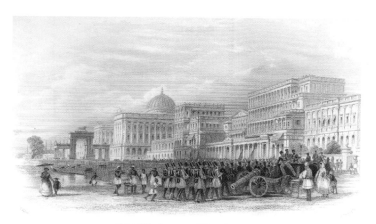

Old Calcutta: Esplanade

Old Calcutta: the Howrah

Darbhanga Maharaja Lakshmeshwar Singh, 1888

Maharaja of Mysore Chamaraja Wodeyar X

Young Gauhar

Gauhar Jaan, 1896

A painting of Gauhar Jaan.

Emile Berliner, the inventor of the gramophone.
(Photo courtesy: The Music goes round by F W Gaisberg)

Frederick William Gaisberg, the first recording expert to India.
(Photo courtesy : The Music goes round by F W Gaisberg)

Advertisements of the gramophone company.

The gramophone Saraswati- an advertisement.

Janki Bai of Allahabad in a recording session
(Photo courtesy: Music goes round by F W Gaisberg)

Gauhar Jaan in a recording studio.
(Photo courtesy: Vikrant Ajgaonkar)

Gauhar Jaan's Picture on the post cards of the times.

*Gauhar's picture on match boxes
made in Austria, 1905.*

*Gauhar and Jaura:
picture post-card of the times.*

Gauhar Jaan and her favourite pastime of horse-riding.

The talented Amrit
Keshav Nayak

Amrit Keshav
Nayak

Ustad Faiyyaz Khan of
Agra gharana

Zohra Bai

Bal Gandharva, the doyen of
Marathi natyasangeet, circa 1915.

'Singer' record of Gauhar Jaan.

Gramophone concert record of
Gauhar Jaan.

Nicole record of Gauhar Jaan.

Sun Disc record of Gauhar Jaan.

Ustad Abdul Karim Khan,
the doyen of the Kirana Gharana.

Hand-sketch of an ageing
Gauhar by Debaprasad Garg,
Raja of Mahishadal.
Carries her signature as well,
dated 3 April 1928.

The sprawling Mysore palace

Maharaja Nalwadi Krishnaraja
Wodeyar of Mysore.

City Magistrate of Mysore
Mr M. Chennaraj Urs who dismissed
the property claims cases.

Obituary Column in the 'Statesman'
dated 28 January 1930.

Chitpur Road, Kolkata

Gauhar building adjacent
Nakhoda mosque

Gauhar building, Kolkata

Gauhar building, now Salim Manzil

Nakhoda Mosque, Kolkata.

being named as her dead mother's husband. Bhaglu was the son of their maid Ashia at Azamgarh, whom Malka had adopted and both Ashia and Bhaglu accompanied them to every city they lived in. Bhaglu's father was a groomer of horses in Robert's household at Azamgarh and had eloped with another woman leaving Ashia and Bhaglu helpless. That was when they sought her deceased mother who had taken pity and sheltered the two. They had belonged to the '*chamar*' or cobbler caste and had converted to Islam when they came to Calcutta. This too had been facilitated by Malka. (*The original of the counter-affidavit filed by Gauhar can be found in the Appendix.*)

The Court hearing finally began. Bhaglu had lined up a series of witnesses, all of whom he had bought. His father-in-law Noor Ali was the first to testify. He claimed that he had never heard of anyone called Ashia and that Malka was the mother of his son-in-law and had come to him personally to plead for his daughter's hand for her son. Maulvi Mohammad Wazid who solemnized Bhaglu and Rehana's *nikah* also testified that he had received a request from Bibi Malka Jaan that he should do the honours for her son's wedding. Hence Bhaglu was indeed her son and he had read the same in the wedding vows as well. The case proceeded this way for a few months.

By April 1911, Bhaglu filed a petition seeking permission for presenting more witness to bolster his case. The witnesses were located outside Calcutta and were too old to travel and hence requested a joint commission of attorneys from both sides to travel and hear the witnesses. Accordingly a Commission headed by District Judge, Justice Baijnath Mishra was constituted to interrogate the witnesses. It consisted of lawyers from both sides, Rajendranath Sen representing Bhaglu and S.A. Haidar representing Gauhar. The Court issued the following directive on 1 May 1911:

'High Court, O.O.C. Jn   Suit No 92 of 1910
Harrington J.

Shaik Bhugloo
-Vs.-
Gauhar Jan

Upon reading on the part of the plaintiff a Master's summons bearing date the 22nd day of April last and an affidavit of Nibaran

Chunder Mukerjee of the due service thereof affirmed on the 24th day of April last and an affidavit of the plaintiff affirmed on the 22nd day of April last all filed on the 25th day of April last and an affidavit of the plaintiff affirmed on the 29th day of April last and an exhibit thereto and marked 'A' and an affidavit of Yakub Khan affirmed on the 26th day of April last, all filed this day and upon reading on the part of the defendant an affidavit of Syed Gholam Abbas affirmed and filed on the 25th day of April last and upon hearing Mr A.N. Chowdry, advocate for the plaintiff and Mr Gregory, advocate for the defendant—it is ordered that a commission do issue out of and under the seal of this Court directed to the District Judge of Azamgarh in the United Provinces of Agra and Oudh authorizing him to swear or affirm and examine viva voce Oli Mahomed Chowdry and Golam Khan, both of village Gomra in the District of Azamgarh as witnesses on behalf of the plaintiff with liberty to the defendant after service of this order forthwith to join in the said commission for the purpose of cross-examining the said witnesses. And it is further ordered that the District Judge be at liberty if he is unable to act under the said commission to appoint some pleader of his Court to act as Commissioner under the said Commission so to be issued to him as aforesaid. And it is further ordered that the said commission be made returnable on or before the 15th day of May instant and that the evidence to be taken thereunder be read and used at the hearing of the suit saving all just exceptions as to the admissibility therefore. And it is further ordered that the hearing of this suit be stayed for a fortnight from the date hereof and that this suit be placed at the bottom of the peremptory list of causes after the expiration of fortnight from the date hereof. And let the consideration of the question of costs of and incidental to this application be reserved until the final determination of this suit or unit the further order of this Court.

Dated this 1st day of May 1911

G.N.Dutt & Co—Attorneys
G.C.Chunder & Co.—Attorneys   Registrar'

Accordingly the Commission made its journey to Gomra and the testimony was recorded on 11 May 1911. The first witness was a sly, eighty-five year old man called Wali Muhammad Chaudhry. He was the *chowkidar* of the tawaif community in Azamgarh and Banaras and settled petty disputes among them. He confidently told the Commission that he had known Malka for a long time. She was the daughter of an Englishman Hardy and his Indian mistress Rukmani, a tawaif herself. Their union resulted in two daughters Biki and Bela and all of them were converted to Christianity by Hardy. After Hardy's death, the two sisters took to the trade of tawaifs as they were very poor. Sheikh Wazir was a *khansama* or cook who was in the service of Hardy. He was Biki's secret lover. After Hardy's death he married her and converted her to Islam renaming her as Malka Jaan. Bhaglu, he claimed, was the son of Biki and Wazir. When the son was barely six months old, Wazir died of cholera. Malka then met Khurshid who had come there from Lucknow and the two eloped with the boy to Banaras. Wali also claimed that about ten years later when he visited Calcutta he was told that a very famous courtesan from Banaras had now made that city her home. Out of curiosity he went to visit her and was surprised to see that it was the same Malka Jaan that he had known. He had also seen Bhaglu then, whom Malka introduced to him as her son. She was extremely kind and hospitable and served him eatables and drinks. While they were talking, Wali saw a beautiful young fair-skinned girl playing in the house and enquired from Malka as to who that was. Malka had smilingly replied that she was the 'gift' from a white-sahib whose keep she had been. With this long and fanciful story Wali concluded his testimony.

It was the turn of Mr Haidar to grill Wali. Haidar's repeated questioning brought forth contradictory answers. Wali also claimed he had attended the conversion ceremony of Malka Jaan which was solemnized by the Qazi Miya Nanku. Each time he was cornered he would blame his old age and failing memory and ask that he should be spared the torture.

The next witness was a man in his 60s, Ghulam Khan. He recounted the same story almost verbatim. Ghulam was in an inebriated state and just repeated all that he had been told to say, like a parrot. Mr Haidar cross-questioned him. When asked why he had been spotted in Calcutta recently and at whose behest he had travelled there, Ghulam was baffled. He mumbled that it was to meet Wali's son Ali Hussain who had assured him of a job. The enraged lawyer persisted and asked him to speak the truth. Why would he want to go hunting for a job at that age? After persistent questioning, Ghulam capitulated and broke into tears. He said he was just told by Wali and his son to memorize a few facts and blurt them out in front of the Commission. Given the dubious nature of both these 'witnesses,' Justice Mishra dismissed the two and chided Bhaglu's attorney for wasting the Court's precious time and money on this wild goose chase.

The case shifted back to Calcutta for further hearing. Once again, Bhaglu lined up a series of witnesses, Sheikh Jangi, Wazir Hussain and Hussain Asghar, who all toed the familiar script. The court then summoned Gauhar to depose. There was a huge crowd that morning at the court. Lots of people had thronged to catch a glimpse of the celebrity who was being dragged to court. Oozing supreme confidence, Gauhar gave her entire testimony right from the role played by her biological father Robert William Yeoward until the time when conditions forced them to migrate to Banaras and later Calcutta. She also mentioned to the Court that Bhaglu and Ashia had been given shelter out of kindness by her deceased mother and far from being grateful, the wretch was trying to appropriate her property. She also declared that she had Maluvi Ekramuddin Sahab of the Dharamtala Mosque where Bhaglu and Ashia had converted to Islam as a witness. Where was the need to convert if he was already the son of a Muslim man, Sheikh Wazir, she questioned. The counter-questioning from Bhaglu's lawyer was highly offensive and virulent. He asked several personal questions and tried to malign the reputation of both Gauhar and the late Malka. Seeing her mother's life becoming a subject of ridicule in an open court, Gauhar was suddenly seized by an impulse. She declared that she would somehow trace her biological father and produce him in Court to depose in her favour. She sought time from the Court to enable her to do this. The Court was adjourned for a few weeks.

Gauhar had no clue how she would manage to locate Robert. It had been her desire from the day the truth of her parentage was made known to her to confront Robert. But Malka had left no clues about her ex-husband. Even as her attorneys chided her for displaying such brazenness in court, Gauhar had made up her mind. She would go looking for Robert Yeoward.

She took a train to Azamgarh in disguise, lest the revelation of her identity make for juicy gossip given her celebrity status. To her dismay there was no one in Azamgarh who had any idea about Robert. Finally an old man in the dry-ice factory where her grandmother Rukmani had worked told her that he vaguely recalled Robert shifting to Allahabad after his break-up with his wife. Gauhar took the next train to Allahabad. It was a journey into the past and was fraught with intense anticipation and sorrow. Rediscovering her roots, her parentage was something she desperately needed to do, not only to win that case, but also to redeem her spirit.

A few people in Allahabad had heard about the Armenian gentleman from Azamgarh who had settled there a few decades ago and directed the young *burqa* clad woman to a mansion adjacent to the sugar mill. Gauhar's heart was pounding fast as her steps hastened towards her father's mansion. With great trepidation she knocked the door and it was answered by a charming and elegant gentleman aged about 55 with a cigar in his mouth and a questioning look on his face. Gauhar froze. The resemblance she bore to this man almost proved that he was indeed her father Robert William Yeoward. She was overcome with emotion. On the one hand she wanted to fling herself in his arms and cry out aloud. On the other she wanted to chide him for needlessly ruining the lives of her poor mother and herself. The man kept looking at her questioningly and asking her whom she desired to meet. Gauhar composed herself and told him that she was his daughter, from his ex-wife from Azamgarh. The man's face turned pale. He denied having any knowledge about such a liaison. He was a respected gentleman of the city and lived there for long with his own family and that he should not be blackmailed into such a thing, he told her. Gauhar then showed him the wedding ring that he and Malka had exchanged. Robert was flustered. He summoned her inside and asked her where she had been all these years. Gauhar broke down and narrated the whole story to him. She said she was no longer his little Angelina, but Gauhar Jaan, the famous tawaif of Calcutta and a gramophone celebrity. Robert was astonished. He had seen her name in the newspapers and also her picture on the match-boxes. It had never occurred to him then that this was his daughter. Gauhar requested him to depose before the court in the hearing of the case that could decide her fate, her future and give her legitimacy in the eyes of society. Robert was not amused. He coldly replied that he wouldn't mind doing that but she would have to pay him Rs 9,000 for this favour. Gauhar was stunned. With tears rolling down her cheeks, she looked at him with utter contempt. Was this the price that a father demands to declare to the world that this was his offspring, she seemed to ask. In a fit of rage she stormed out of the house and hurried back to Calcutta.

The events of the previous day lingered in her mind. She was extremely disturbed and hurt by Robert's attitude. There was not a word of kindness or comfort, but cold calculative money-talk. She reached home and finding Abbas there flung herself in his arms and sobbed like a child. Abbas was greatly shocked. He had remained faithful and dependable all this while and had looked upon her with great respect. Her physical intimacy startled him. He shrugged away and asked why she was so distressed. After hearing the entire incident relating to Robert Yeoward, Abbas took her to Mr Ganesh Chandra Chandra. The latter advised her that now that she had located Mr Robert, she could rest assured that the Court would ensure that he deposed in the case.

The Court accordingly summoned Robert William Yeoward to present himself or else face heavy penalties. With no option left, the man finally reached Calcutta. He corroborated all the details that Gauhar had mentioned in court earlier. He also produced the marriage certificate and ring along with Gauhar's baptism papers and birth certificate. He testified in the presence of everyone that Gauhar was indeed his daughter and that no one could call her a child born out of wedlock. He also spoke of one Hemraj who groomed horses in their house at Azamgarh. His wife Ashia was their maid but had become a close confidante of the lady of the house, Victoria. Hemraj had run away with some woman after having abandoned Ashia and her little son, whom Robert had also seen. They had eventually been taken in by Robert's wife. However after he divorced his wife, whom he suspected of infidelity, he dismissed the maid and her son as he was planning to shift base to Allahabad. He knew that they would seek shelter with his ex-wife given their close friendship.

Robert stuck to his story despite the intense hammering that he received from Bhaglu's lawyers. From where she was sitting in the audience, Gauhar gave Robert a smile of gratitude. Robert had finally fulfilled his duties towards his daughter and his testimony almost clinched the case in Gauhar's favour.

To bolster her case further, Gauhar also managed to locate Nathu Bai, the mid-wife in Azamgarh, who had delivered her. She too reiterated the statements made by Robert.

Finally after long months of hearings and adjournments, the case was headed to its logical conclusion. On 2 August 1911, Justice Harry Lashington Stephen began to deliver his verdict. He said that there were three issues that the court had to consider before delivering a judgement: Was the plaintiff Bhaglu the legitimate or adopted son of deceased Bibi Malka Jaan; was the defendant Gauhar Jaan the legal or illegitimate daughter of the same deceased and did Bhaglu retain any legal claims to the dead lady's properties. That Bhaglu was a part of Malka's household was proven beyond doubt. There had been numerous witnesses who had testified that Malka had taken great pains to ensure that his education, employment, marriage and business went on smoothly. That all the people in her household referred to him as '*Miyaan*' proves that he was not a servant but an important member of the family. His status too was more that of a son rather than a slave. The accounts ledgers with payments to different servants did not carry his name, again proving this point. Also the fact that he carried out the last rites of Malka indicated that he was more than a son to her.

But the court noted that numerous cases were pending against him by his creditors. These had been lodged with the Land Acquisition Collection office, the Alipore Court and the Calcutta Police. Here Bhaglu clearly mentions his parents' names as Sheikh Wazir Jan and Ashia. Either he had lied in his testimony there or was deliberately misleading the court now. Also given the unreliable nature of his witnesses, it was appropriate for the court to conclude that it was Gauhar Jaan and she alone who was the legal heir and legitimate child of the deceased Bibi Malka Jaan and the adopted son Bhaglu, driven by greed, had tried to misappropriate the property.

Accordingly, on 10 August 1911, Justice Harry Lashington Stephen decided the case in Gauhar's favour with costs against Bhaglu. (*The original version of the judgement delivered by Justice Harry Lashington can be found in the Appendix.*)

Celebrations broke out in Gauhar's camp. She profusely thanked her witnesses and gave a warm smile and hug to Robert William Yoeward, who wished her well and left for Allahabad. There was a massive display of fireworks and sweets were liberally distributed to everyone that evening at 49, Chitpur Road. Gauhar had proved a point to herself and the world.

Within a month, on 4 September 1911, Gauhar filed a counter case (Suit No 946 of 1911) against Bhaglu and requested the court to evict him from her residence. The defendant (Bhaglu) was ordered to be removed from 49 Lower Chitpore Road and that he be restrained by injunction to enter the said house. A writ of summons was served on 17 September 1911, by affixation, upon the refusal of the defendant to accept the order. A warrant of the attorney was filed on 5 December 1911.

Bhaglu meanwhile filed an appeal petition against the earlier verdict through his lawyer A.N.Chaudhury. That came up for hearing at the Division Bench of the High Court. The Chief Justice Sir Lawrence Hugh Jenkins and Justice John George Woodroff dismissed this appeal on 27 February 1912. Finally on 16 June 1913, Justice Ashutosh Chaudhury passed the final decree in this case and Bhaglu was asked to file no more petitions and leave the residence of Miss Gauhar Jaan with immediate effect.

Thus after a long legal battle Gauhar finally exorcised the ghost of Sheikh Bhaglu and hoped to live in peace thereafter. She thought she had found a dependable and trustworthy manager in Abbas. But Gauhar was never destined to lead a predictable and uneventful life.

Jo saaz se nikli hai woh dhun sab ne suni hai
Jo taar pe guzari hai woh kisko pata hai?

The beautiful music from the instrument catches everyone's attention
But who has thought of the plight of the string which is played on?

—Saahir Ludhiyanavi

꧁ ꧂

12

THE GLORY YEARS

Delhi, 1911

The 19th century was called the British century as it saw the emergence and consolidation of a vast and powerful British Empire across the various colonies of the world. In 1876, Queen Victoria had been proclaimed as the Empress of India or *Kaiser-i-Hind*. The Viceroy, Lord Lytton had decided to commemorate this event with a grand imperial durbar. The durbar, an age-old Indian tradition of holding magnificent coronation ceremonies, was adopted by the British from the late 18th century to display their imperial might and power to both the native rulers and the people. They realised that the exercise of power and authority should be associated with these outwardly symbols of magnificence and splendour. Emulating the Mughal style, the durbars evoked a lot of nostalgia among the people who had been accustomed to such displays.

With the exile of the last Mughal Emperor Bahadur Shah Zafar to Rangoon, after the 1857 War, Delhi became an important seat of power, though it was Calcutta that was the capital of British India. Each time the British felt the need to flaunt their might, Delhi was chosen as the venue to host a durbar. Queen Victoria's 1876 Durbar was held in Delhi and history seemed to repeat itself by the end of 1911. Emperor George V was coming to India by the end of that year and hectic preparations were on for a grand Imperial durbar for him.

The visit had symbolic importance too. The nationalist movement in India was gathering momentum. The Partition of Bengal in 1905 into East and West Bengal, largely on communal lines, had been unwittingly initiated by the Viceroy Lord Curzon. This had triggered off a series of protests not only in Bengal but in the whole country. The spirit of swadeshi had been aroused in the minds of the Indians. Various groups within the Congress Party were galvanizing this emotion into a strong movement. The Durbar was aimed to assuage the aggrieved feelings of the people of Bengal and counter the nationalist sentiment by annulling the Partition plan. The preparations for the royal visit went on for months.

George V was crowned Emperor at Westminster Abbey in London on 22 June 1911. The Emperor then set out on a tour of all his colonies along with his wife Queen Mary. The royal couple were to visit India by the end of that year and the grand durbar was planned for 12 December 1911. Queen Mary wore 4149 cut diamonds, 2000 rose diamonds, 22 emeralds, 4 rubies and 4 sapphires for the occasion!

Emperor George was not new to India. He had visited the country as the Prince of Wales in 1905-06 and had attempted to blunt the swadeshi movement by openly advocating the impropriety of the Partition. During the 1911 Delhi Durbar, the Emperor doled out sops to various interest groups. In the presence of about 80,000 specially chosen guests, that included Rajas and Nawabs of various princely states, King George announced a plethora of concessions. The Bengal Partition was annulled and a Governor-in-Council for united Bengal was created. Bihar, Orissa and Chhotanagpur were separated from Bengal's jurisdiction and integrated into a new Lieutenant Governor's province. Assam was reduced to a Chief-Commissionership.

Along with these administrative and political announcements, the Emperor generously gave away titles to the assembled subservient princely states and their rulers. The most important announcement he made towards the end of his speech was that regarding the transfer of the capital to Delhi. 'We are pleased to announce the transfer of the seat of the Government of India from Calcutta to the ancient capital of India...' (Delhi). There was first of all a stunned silence in the audience followed thereafter by wild and incredulous cheering all around.

The *Leader* newspaper of Allahabad of 14 December 1911 reported the grand event in an article titled 'History-making at Delhi'. The editor observed that 'once again history has been made on the site of Delhi, in which the central figure is and will always be the great Monarch who announced his coronation to his faithful princes and dutiful subjects. The gracious words of the Emperor delivered by his own tongue will be treasured up by the present generation of Indians...perhaps the most important and certainly the most far reaching in its consequences was that which His Majesty was pleased to make himself at the conclusion of the durbar. The transfer of the Government of India from Calcutta to Delhi means the recovery to Delhi itself of a lost heritage, the revival of its faded glory and the opening of a new chapter of progress and prosperity...transfer of capital from Calcutta to Delhi will not be popular with Calcutta, which will contemplate the loss of its prestige as the first city of India with uneasiness.'

The editor was right. A pall of gloom descended on Calcutta after the announcement was made. Newspapers were flooded with letters from the citizens of the city criticizing the move. Many entrepreneurs and businessmen who had invested money in the city felt cheated. There was nothing left to lure new businesses to Calcutta any more. One letter bemoans: 'We have spent a very great deal of money in recent years in order to cope with the business which the influx of the Government officials and cold-weather visitors has brought us. Now it seems to me that there will be no cold-weather season in Calcutta and we need not have extended at all...we are the people who will suffer...'

While the Durbar spelt doom for Calcutta and its residents, it brought glory to one Calcuttan. That was Gauhar Jaan. A few months prior to the Durbar she had received a letter from the Governor's office informing her of a rare privilege that was to be bestowed upon her. In view of her celebrity status and her glorious accomplishments, she had been selected to perform in the presence of Emperor George V at the Delhi Durbar. Buoyed by her recent victory in the infamous court case, Gauhar's joy knew no bounds. She immediately sent her acceptance.

On that memorable day in Delhi, she was to sing along with her contemporary Janki Bai, the well known singer from Allahabad. At that glittering ceremony in the presence of the King Emperor of England and his Queen and all the royal families of India, Gauhar Jaan and Janki Bai presented their melodious duet. Among other items was a piece they had specially composed for the occasion titled 'Yeh Jalsa Taajposhi ka, Mubarak ho, Mubarak ho!' or 'Congratulations to His Majesty on this grand coronation ceremony.' The two were then escorted to the Emperor, who praised them profusely for their talent and presented a hundred guineas to each of them as a token of his appreciation. It was truly the pinnacle of professional success that any musician of those days could have aspired for and Gauhar was especially blessed by the fortune of such recognition and fame.

Although the British Government had decided to invite her to the durbar since she was one of the leading singers, the moral police of the country did not grant her that recognition and credibility. The Government of the United Provinces had planned a unique exhibition, the first of its kind, at Allahabad in 1910-11. Several leading citizens of the city were also involved in its preparation. The three month long exhibition, which would showcase arts and crafts, agricultural produce, industrial equipment, entertainment shows and amusement parks, was intended to create a veritable paradise on earth and a show of the century. An obvious choice for the entertainment section of the event was Gauhar Jaan of Calcutta. She was to be felicitated with a gold medal at this concert.

As news of her inclusion trickled out, widespread protests in the form of letters to the editors of various newspapers were made for weeks on end. The objection was against the government's decision to invite a tawaif to perform at a public function; thereby in a way legitimizing their status in society. It was argued that the inclusion of a tawaif would be a bad influence on society and would corrupt the youth. The conservative section of the city that included both Hindus and Muslims wrote bitter letters condemning this decision.

A look at some of the newspapers of the times shows the intensity of this disapproval. The *Saddharma Pracharak* of 28 December 1910 from Bijnor remarked that the sanctity of the exhibition would be defiled by the intemperate use of wine within its walls and the music and dance of the nautch girl of Calcutta. The editor deplored the fact that the convenors of the Exhibition had included the performance of the 'dancing girl' Gauhar Jaan merely as a crowd-pulling stunt and to make up for the loss they had incurred due to their mismanagement. He expressed surprise that while the students of the Muir Central college and Hindu Boarding House were encouraged to witness her performance at a reduced fee, they had to apply to the principal of the college for permission to attend Arya Samaj meetings. The editor thundered that this only reflected the skewed priorities of the Government and urged people like Pt Madan Mohan Malviya to help save the situation.

The *Fitna* of Gorakhpur dated 8 January 1911 protested the inclusion of a tawaif's performance in a public event of this magnitude and remarked that if entertainment and money-making was the only aim of the Exhibition, the Committee should have allowed twenty prostitutes instead of one to perform at the venue.

The renowned newspaper of Allahabad, the *Leader* dated 21 January 1911 contains a lengthy letter from Mr Satish Chandra Banerji in which he expresses his disapproval of the Exhibition Committee's decision to present Gauhar Jaan with a gold medal. Barely a week later on 27 January 1911, the *Musafir* of Agra took exception to Gauhar Jaan's presenting a concert and receiving a gold medal, as also the inclusion of Acchanbai of Rampur who also sang at the same venue. It asked the people of Allahabad not to take this lightly and protest against such 'immoral' acts.

The *Abhyudaya* of Allahabad of 9 February 1911 published a translation of articles in the *Prabasi* (Calcutta) regarding the inclusion of Indian and European music in the United Provinces Exhibition and remarked that although political dependence was inevitable in the prevalent circumstances of the country, still people should try and cultivate independence in the arts. In the *Hindustani* of Lucknow dated 20 February 1911 a writer protested against Gauhar Jaan's singing and dancing at the event and remarked that its 'effects on the social and moral progress of the people of the Provinces will be very injurious.' Continuing the tirade the writer remarked that European officers should discourage nautch parties which are given in their honour and they should try and assist the people in introducing social reforms.

However despite this orchestrated campaign, the concert of Gauhar Jaan was held as scheduled. The protests could do nothing to undermine her popularity. Her concert was a huge success. It drew one of the largest crowds and proved to be the most profitable investment of the whole exhibition. The already highly priced tickets were sold for three or four times the original price and were sold out in no time leaving thousands disappointed. On the day of the concert there was a stampede at the venue and the police had to be called in to control the crowds. Gauhar's popularity had not diminished despite the tirades against her in the newspapers across the state.

Of course the exhibition was a matter of discussion till almost the end of 1911 with some disparaging comments or the other about its organization appearing in the newspapers of the times. The focus slowly shifted away from Gauhar's inclusion to the colossal waste of money at the exhibition by the Government.

Even as the protests raged in the North, her popularity did not diminish. On the contrary it had spread to the South as well. She was invited to Madras by C. Gopala Chetty, a wealthy businessman of the city. Madras was emerging as an important centre for artists of the Carnatic or South Indian classical style. While in Madras, Gauhar stayed with her friend Salem Godavari, a devadasi, in Thambu Chetty Street, in George Town. Like Gauhar, Godavari too had attained great fame through her gramophone records. Gauhar's concert at Victoria Public Hall in Madras in 1910 was a huge success and was attended by many of the musical luminaries of the city including the grand old dame of Carnatic music, the eminent Vainika Veena Dhanammal. Dhanammal was an artist par excellence and very parsimonious when it came to praise. Her daughters and granddaughters who learnt under her trembled to sing in her presence and longed to get a glimpse of an appreciation from the lady. The fastidious Dhanmmal was supposedly enthralled by Gauhar's performance and decided to host a dinner in her honour. A lavish party, costing about Rs 1000 and catered by the reputed caterers of Madras, Harrison's of Broadway was held.

Dhanammal received Gauhar with great affection and during her stay in Madras taught her a Carnatic *kriti* or composition in Raga Surutti, '*Bhajana Parula*' composed by the saint Thyagaraja. Gauhar released a record of it later on. During her stay in Madras, many artists visited her. Among them was the famed Ariyakudi Ramanuja Iyengar who is considered the pioneer of the modern concert format of Carnatic music. Iyengar expressed a desire to learn some of her songs, especially the Krishna bhajans like *Radhe Krishna Bol Mukhase* and *Krishna Murari Binat Karat* that she had popularized across the country. Gauhar readily agreed to teach him and Ramanuja Iyengar picked up some gems from her repertoire. Later, many of her Hindustani and Urdu compositions were published in a Tamil book titled '*Gandharva Kalpavalli*' by P.S. Ramulu Chetty in 1912. (*Nigahen phirake dil bar se laahe, Aarey saiyyan padoon main tore paiyyan; Haq nahin rahi mere dard-e-jee; Dina ratiyaan chhedo saiyyan chhodo baiyyan dhadake satiyaan; Maza dete hain tere baal ghunghroowale* are her compositions that have been published in this book.) The lyrics of those songs were all in Tamil and published with notation for people to learn and follow. Many old timers in Madras, including the veteran scholar, musician and musicologist Shri S. Rajam, recall both hearing and learning Gauhar Jaan's songs with great interest.

While her concerts were widely reviewed, not all music critics were impressed. Her concert in Bangalore in 1912 was reviewed by H.P. Krishna Rao, the South Indian editor of the *Indian Music Journal*:

'Miss Gauhar entertained the public of Bangalore with her dance and music on the 20 April. The Bowring Institute was packed to the full and the entertainment lasted over two hours. The programme consisted of a variety of pieces- Hindustani, Karnatic and English, some of which were sung with style, expression and beauty. Miss Gauhar possesses a sweet voice which when prolonged seems uniformly grand, more so, as it is produced without any physical strain. The notes are faultless and simple. The gradual transition from one note to another and the wave-like ascent and descent (the *andolitam)* which produces in the mind of the hearer that kind of agreeable illusion which one experiences when rocked in a cradle are special points of beauty in her singing. Everything is precise and accurate. North Indian dance is a simpler process not involving the more scientific, elaborate and wonderful display of command over the body and the limbs as required in the South Indian system. It consists of a few simple rhythmic movements of the feet and the hands, but Miss Gauhar's gesticulation in which facial expression plays an important part is far above the standard we have observed in Northern Indian dance.

But we failed to notice in her rendering any of those intelligent flourishes of Hindustani music that we are accustomed to find in first-rate Gavois. The pieces she sang, though suited to the middle class of hearers, were not adorned with any skilful improvisations which an expert can not possibly avoid even in ordinary singing…Miss Gauhar is known through the Gramophone records even to the villager. Her records are enjoyable but there is a disparity between the copy and the original leading to disappointment. She has made a name and fortune far above the reach of even masters of the art, of whom there are plenty in India and if the key to such success is to be sought for, it will be found to lie in the invisible and self-advertisement through the Gramophone: MY NAME IS Gauhar Jan.'

The same negative opinion seems to be shared by Pt D.C. Vedi who heard her in Amritsar, Patiala and Bombay in the early part of the century. He recalls her being accompanied on the sarangi by the famous Ustad Mamman Khan at the performance in the court of the Maharaja of Patiala, Bhupinder Singh that he had witnessed. Not disagreeing about the marvellous voice she possessed, Pt. Vedi claimed that as a khayal singer she was only average and did not follow any established style.

Thus opinions about her singing were sharply divided. The Maharaja of Kashmir Hari Singh ji who was a great patron of the arts had heard her on a number of occasions and was deeply impressed by her virtuosity. He thought she was the greatest classical singer of her times.

But perhaps the greatest tribute was paid to her by none other than Pandit Vishnu Narayan Bhatkhande (1860-1936). Bhatkhande is an iconic figure of modern Hindustani classical music. It was thanks to his tireless efforts that the hitherto unstructured corpus of Hindustani music, which was in the hands of illiterate ustads, sycophantic court musicians and sensuous tawaifs, got a scientific structure and format. His seminal work on standardizing and notating Hindustani music as also his tireless efforts at rationalizing the teaching and learning of the art gave a new life to this ancient art form. He created a notion of '*Thaats*' whereby he classified the various existing ragas into groups. He had toured the country extensively and met up with musicians of different genres including the renowned Carnatic musician Subbarama Dixit who had authored the famous '*Sangeeta Sampradaya Pradarshini*.' Pandit Bhatkhande attempted to create one unified system of music for India that drew from all the musical styles of the country, but this was too ambitious a project to accomplish. It is said that on his visit to Calcutta somebody suggested that he listen to the famous Gauhar Jaan in a concert. He had snapped back 'Do I now have to descend to the level of learning about music from a mere singing and dancing girl?' Later though, he did get an opportunity to listen to her and was apparently bowled over by her brilliance. After that he is said to have remarked that Gauhar was the greatest singer of khayal and thumri among women in India those days. (His views have been shared by Prof D.P. Mukherjee as well.)

By the time she went back to Calcutta from Madras, Gauhar had recovered from all the personal travails that she had been through and got back into her professional life with complete enthusiasm.

One day when she was shopping with some friends in a famous perfume shop of Calcutta, in walked an extremely handsome and dignified youngman. He took one look at the beautiful Gauhar and couldn't take his eyes off her. She noticed him too but pretended to ignore him. Her friends caught sight of this charming gentleman and whispered to her, 'Wonder who he is; must be the prince of some kingdom.' In a tone of indifferent arrogance Gauhar loudly replied, 'What do I care who it is? My music reaches everyone eventually.' The man managed to overhear the conversation, gave a long look to her and hurriedly walked away in embarrassment.

That evening Gauhar received a letter saying that the Nawab of Rampur was in Calcutta and desired to meet her over dinner. Gauhar went fully decked up for the royal dinner. She was stunned to see that the man whom she had met and spoken disparagingly of at the perfume shop was none other than Nawab Hamid Ali Khan, the celebrated Nawab of Rampur. He told her in a soft voice, 'Madam, yes indeed I too have been affected and attracted by your music. I would request you to visit Rampur and stay there and entertain us for a while.' Gauhar was overjoyed and readily agreed to visit Rampur.

Rampur State was established in 1774 by Nawab Faizullah Khan. From the time of the fifth Nawab, Yusuf Ali Khan (1816-65), Rampur started emerging as a major center of Hindustani music. Post the Sepoy Mutiny and the fall of Delhi and Oudh many musicians started migrating to Rampur. This led to a mixing of styles and helped in creating a new gharana known as the 'Rampur Sahaswan' gharana. It was famous for its renowned Beenkars who played the '*been*' (a stringed instrument like the veena) in the dhrupad style.

Nawab Hamid Ali Khan's reign (1875-1930), which is known as the golden period of Rampur, saw the crystallization of the musical traditions of the State. He was often referred to as the 'Shahjahan of Rampur' for his eclectic tastes in music, architecture and literature. It was not surprising then that Pandit Bhatkhande had been invited to Rampur for discussions on the theory of music, when the Nawab heard of the former's project to document and standardize classical Hindustani music. He commanded his ustads, who were reluctant to attempt notating classical music, to provide all support to Pandit Bhatkhande. Thus a large portion of the compositions in Panditji's *Kramik Pustak Malika* and the *Hindustani Sangeet Paddhati* are from the Rampur tradition. As per musicologist Pt. S.N. Ratanjhankar, the princely state represented 'one of the purest strongholds of conservative and uninterrupted classical tradition.' Some of the greatest names of Hindustani music like Bhaiya Ganpatrao, Ustad Inayat Hussain Khan, Wazir Khan, and others received the liberal patronage of the musically conscious Nawabs, particularly Nawab Hamid Ali.

Gauhar Jaan was always accorded a most grand welcome each time she visited Rampur. Her concerts were arranged regularly and she lived along with the women of the royal family in the zenana each time she visited the city. The Begum Sahiba's memoirs of the times mention a grand mehfil she had arranged in 1912. It was an exclusive all-women's concert for the zenana to which singers like Gauhar Jaan, Rajeshwari Bai of Banaras and Zohra Bai of Agra were invited. They regaled the audience. While in Rampur, Gauhar Jaan took some lessons from Ustad Nazir Khan and by incorporating some elements of the Rampur Gharana into her already versatile musical style; she made her music more diverse and colourful.

After spending some happy months in Rampur, Gauhar decided to return to Calcutta. Nawab Hamid Ali had great affection and regard for her and told her that she could come to Rampur any time she desired, that she should treat it as her second home and the state would welcome her with open arms.

Back in Calcutta, Gauhar's busy professional life carried on. Soirees at the houses of the rich and famous aristocrats of the city were common. Many eye-witness accounts of the time speak highly of her stage presence and talent. The music historian Dilip Mukhopadhyay speaks at length about her concert at the Mullick Bhawan in Jorasanko on a summer evening of 1913. The venue was historical in itself as it had seen numerous plays and musicals including the first performance of the National Theatre. The house was owned by Banamali Mullick and Motilal Mullick. Their elder brother Govindlal Mullick too was a great patron and was in fact the father-in-law of the legendary singer L C Boral. Gauhar's concert had been arranged on the occasion of the marriage of Motilal's son Murari Mohan Mullick. Mukhopadhyay mentions that while people thought Gauhar was middle-aged, she looked very youthful and pretty. As she ascended the stage the lights were all turned on and she looked more dazzling under the spotlights.

Gauhar had the ability to make an accurate assessment of the audience before she began her concert. That evening too she saw several familiar faces in the crowd that was made up of Englishmen, Bengalis, Marwaris, Rajasthanis, Punjabis and others. Before beginning, she requested the organizers to seat the audience according to their linguistic backgrounds. The organizers and audience were puzzled by this request, but decided to follow the diva's orders. She then alighted from stage even as her accompanists played on. She went to each and every group present in that small and intimate gathering and sang in their language. The Englishmen and the memsahibs were delighted to hear an English song rendered in chaste English. After the song a short expressive piece, the '*bhaav batana*' and dance would follow. Similarly, songs were sung exclusively for the Punjabis, who were treated to some Punjabi tappas, while the Rajasthanis and the Marwaris were entertained with thumris and dadras in Hindi and Urdu. Since the Bengalis were in the majority she shifted her attention towards them at the end. Mukhopadhyay mentions the two Bengali songs she sang that evening:

'Phanki diye praner pakhi, ude galo, aar elo na aar, elo na aar
Bujhiba premer dore, bendeche keo pran moina
Bolo Sakhi kothai jabo, kothai gele pakhi pabo
Emon Dhani ke shohore amar pakhi rakhlo dhore
Dekhaley tare kede nebo aar debo na.'

'The bird of life has been tied down by the strings of love, yet the
bird has deceived and flown away, never to come back again.
Where do I go my friend and search for this bird?
Who is the rich man in the city who has captured my bird in his
golden cage?
The minute I meet him, I shall take back my little bird and never
let her go again.'

This song in Raga Zilla set to dadra tala has been commercially recorded
as well.

The other song she sang that evening at the Mallicks was another soulful
tune, a composition of Tagore:

'Keno Choker jale bheijiye dilem na
Pother shukno dhulijatho
Ke janitho ashbe tumi go
Emon anahuter moto'.

'Why didn't I wash away all the dirt on the way with my tears?
Who knew that you would make an unprecedented entry in this
fashion?'

That evening every single member of the audience felt she had sung exclusively
for him or her and it was this personal rapport that she built up during her
live performances that set her apart from most other singers.

A similar anecdote is reported from Bombay. On one occasion she was to
perform immediately after Zohra Bai of Agra. Zohra Bai was an unparalleled
exponent of khayal gayaki and could expose the raga for hours with great
finesse. That evening at the concert Zohra Bai was again in her element and
went about exploring every nuance of the raga. But sadly the audience was
unable to follow her exposition since they were not expecting such a detailed
presentation and quickly lost interest. Gauhar Jaan, who was observing the

reactions of the indifferent audience from backstage felt great sympathy for poor Zohra whose exquisite music was literally falling on deaf ears. She had planned to render weighty khayal renditions herself given that she was performing after an artist of the eminence of Zohra Bai. She had discussed the plans with the accompanists too. But having seen the reaction of the audience, Gauhar told her accompanists that she had changed her mind and would sing something different that evening. Gauhar was aware that *natya sangeet*, the songs from popular Marathi plays, would go down well with the audience. So she started with one of those and expectedly the audience was immediately hooked and gave her a loud applause. Having won their attention, she proceeded to present a chota khayal directly, skipping the ati vilambit and vilambit layas and also the expansive tankaris. Her rendering of the khayal obviously did not match the standards set by Zohra Bai that evening but Gauhar had consciously chosen a style which appealed to the audience far more than her predecessor's weighty presentation. At the same time she did not reduce the concert to a mere collage of small songs, which would have insulted the taste of the audience.

Dilip Mukhopadhyay refers to several other instances of Gauhar's concerts and the techniques she adopted to woo her audience. She performed quite a lot for Star Theatre. Those days the dramas would be preceded by a music performance. If it was a high profile baiji like Gauhar performing, then the large crowds that came to hear her would stay on for the play as well. At one such performance at the Star Theatre that Mukhopadhyay attended, the audience was made up primarily of Bengalis with some Hindi speakers too. Therefore Gauhar decided to sing several Bengali songs including Nidhu babu's famous tappa '*Jatona jotone mone mone monei jaane*' (My heart still remembers that pain), the popular Bengali kirtan '*Jamuno ei ki tumi shei jamuna prabahini*' (O! Yamuna, are you the same eternal river that flowed then during the times of Krishna?) and her signature song '*Radhe Krishna bolo mukha se*' among others.

Shrewd as she was Gauhar knew she could gain the goodwill of the Bengali Babus by singing as many Bengali songs as she could in her soirees. Although she spoke Bengali with an accent, when she sang, no one could tell that she was not a Bengali. She was so innovative that she had begun to include the songs composed by Rabindranath Tagore in her repertoire even before the word 'Rabindra Sangeet' was coined. Gauhar was not afraid to defy the norms and in fact she seldom used the tunes that Tagore had set his songs to. She rendered them in her own style, giving them a classical lilt. Several Bengali songs find a place of pride in her long and versatile discography.

Between 1900 and the 1920s there were two famous singers heading the tawaif community in the United Provinces known as the Chaudhary sisters Badi and Chhoti, better known as Nanuan and Bachchuan. Nanuan learnt dance from Nanda Devi, a leading dancer of the Lucknow Gharana, while the younger learnt *shayari* or poetry from Manju Saheb, an ustad in Urdu poetry. They were considered as stalwarts in both literary and performing arts, and their daughters, Rashke Munir and Badre Munir, were skilful musicians. Badre Munir was a close friend of Gauhar Jaan. Nanuan and Bachchuan hosted several prominent soirees at their kotha in Lucknow. On one such occasion the two famed divas, Gauhar and Zohra Bai again performed back to back at the kotha. Gauhar was overcome by the same diffidence when she heard about Zohra Bai preceding her. Each time she was to sing after or before her, she would ensure that her rendition was markedly different from Zohra's. That evening began with Nanuan and Bachuan's concert. Then Zohra Bai gave yet another sterling khayal rendition. Gauhar was hard put to wipe away the impact that the khayal had made. So instead of presenting another khayal and appearing as a weak mimic, she switched to her forte, the thumri. With 'Pani bhare ri kaun albelo ki naar' and her captivating composition 'Ras ke bhare tore naina' accompanied with wondrous animation and bhav batana, Gauhar captured the imagination of the audience. Bashir Khan, a direct disciple of Bhaiya Ganpat Rao and a frequent accompanist for Mauzuddin as well, accompanied her on the harmonium and ably reproduced the subtle nuances of these emotionally surcharged thumris. At the end of the evening, the people had totally forgotten what had preceded Gauhar's performance.

The renowned musicologist Thakur Jaidev Singh speaks highly of Gauhar Jaan as being without 'peer in her thumri singing and in her rendering of other light classical types.' He even recalled attending unforgettable night-long sessions starting at 8 p.m. between Gauhar Jaan and Agrewali Malka Jaan. In these fascinating sessions of *Sawal-Jawab* or musical repartees between two veteran singers, the audience would find it difficult to decide who the better of the two was.

Gauhar was also famous for her immaculate dress sense. She was extremely consciously of herself, her mannerisms and appearance as she was of her audience. She would dress in the richest of garments, seldom repeated her dresses and jewellery and matched the colours of her dress to the mood of the genre or rendition that she had planned to sing. A grave and sombre person in personal interactions, she would effortlessly don the role of an enchanting seductress on the stage. She took great care of all her guests and visitors.

Gauhar's hedonistic lifestyle too became a matter of legend. She spent most of what she earned on her pleasure and fetishes. It was said that she wore an invaluable diamond brooch on her left shoulder, to guard which she sometimes had two rifle-wielding soldiers on either side of her while she performed. Such flamboyance and ostentation was perhaps unheard and unseen in the world of Indian music. But that was Gauhar; she loved being her true self and couldn't care less for the jibes of her detractors.

This is illustrated in an anecdote where she offended the famous maestro of the Agra Gharana, Ustad Faiyaz Khan. This interesting incident has been recounted by an eye-witness, Amiyanath Sanyal. Sanyal was a doctor of medicine but more than that, a true "Rasika", an aficionado of North Indian classical music and a respected musicologist though not a performing musician. In his youth, he trained under Shyamlal Khatri and later from the legendary sarangi maestro Ustad Badal Khan. He first met Gauhar as a student of Medical College, when he was in his early twenties around the time of the World War I. A translation of his long, yet picturesque account gives an insight into the subtle politics of the times and also into Gauhar's indomitable spirit.

As mentioned earlier, the homes of patrons like Shyamlal Khatri and Seth Dhulichand were regular venues for musical activity. On one such occasion at Shyamlal Khatri's house, many musicians including Amiyanath Sanyal had assembled for an evening of discussions on music. Sanyal recounts the arrival of Agrewali Malka Jaan with an anonymous, but dignified looking gentleman who wore a long lightweight green coat and a red velvet cap with a zari border that tilted carefully to the right. After some humorous repartees, they eventually got the gentleman to join in a ghazal they had started singing and they were stunned into silence when he began singing in a rich and trained voice and with a professional competence that was quite unexpected. After he finished, Khatriji who was standing by the side, introduced the gentleman as Ustad Faiyaz Khan the doyen of the Agra gharana. The Ustad had been a rage all over the country and was in the service of the Gaekwad of Baroda for a long time. The Maharaja of Mysore had honoured him with the title of 'Aftab-e-Mousiqui' which became synonymous with his name. Despite his reputation and the recognition he was accorded elsewhere, the Ustad had never performed in Calcutta. The reason, it later emerged, was that he hated Gauhar Jaan and many of her kind and was of the view that as long as the tawaifs had a captive market in Calcutta, there was no room for male singers from heavy-weight gharanas like his. But there was one tawaif whom he did not hate and that was Agrewali Malka Jaan. Although she was much older than him, he had had a torrid affair with her over several years. In fact this became the reason for the downfall of the other legendary musician Mauzuddin. Mauzuddin was madly in love with Agrewali Malka but the latter kept rebuffing him, given her involvement with Faiyaz Khan. With his love going unrequited Mauzuddin took to drinking heavily and that spelt doom for his voice and career.

Now, coming back to that evening at Khatri ji's house, just as the mood of the mehfil was getting more lively, in walked Gauhar Jaan. Her entry brought a frown to Faiyaz Khan's face and a curl to his lip. Gauhar's mere presence made the young sarangi players like Sanyal and others move away quickly from the Ustad, both out of respect for her and anxiety about what would transpire. With Gauhar one never knew what to expect.

Speaking about her appearance Sanyal says that it was impossible to ascertain her age by looking at her. If anyone had questions about whether she was young or old, thin or fat, these became inconsequential because her words and actions were encased in the beautiful fluster of a young girl and this would distract anyone's thoughts. Her normal dress was one that would befit a sixteen year old. Her gait had the imperiousness of a king elephant. Her facial expressions and gestures sometimes highly animated and at other times highly suggestive, would make all tawaifs blush. In the mehfils she attended she would show the maximum respect towards her guru Bhaiya Ganpatrao, Ustad Badal Khan, Shyamlalji and Seth Dhulichand. Anyone else in the group would be considered by her as a contemporary and friend who was either tamed or tameable.

At mehfils, touching the shoulder of a gentleman or a lady of her acquaintance, just for friendship's sake, while taking her seat on the floor never seemed strange or ill-mannered when it was Gauhar who did it. She used her eyes most effectively to convey a range of emotions. These killer looks varied depended on whether she intended to humiliate the other person or flirt innocently. Sanyal too had been a victim of these 'looks' and at their first meeting he had thought it was a deliberate coquettish act. But by the time of the second meeting he was convinced that irrespective of whether her behaviour was justified or odd, it arose from the depths of her character and was spontaneous and absolutely natural. Some people would be offended by her occasional outbursts which reeked of a lack of decorum. But Shyamlal Khatri and others were used to her and forgave these minor lapses of a great musician. Her unusual talents and her uncontrollable and spontaneous playfulness would win them all over. When Ustads and aficionados like Badal Khan, Shyamlal ji, Vishwanath Rao, Lakshmi Prasad Mishra, Tannulal ji and others witnessed any musical soiree of exception they would be forced to comment, almost involuntarily, that it was nothing but a shadow of Gauhar's performance. Such was her reputation in the field of performance at least.

That evening, on entering the room, she paid her respects to Khatri ji and to all others in the room and took her seat on the other side of where Malka and Faiyaz Khan were seated. She had seen everyone in the room in a flash. It was usually her eyes that reflected her thoughts and emotions before they became words. From across the room, she exchanged quick pleasantries with Malka, who was a friend despite the competition and rivalry between them. Faiyaz Khan sat stiffly and did not even bother glancing towards her

Then, with a respectful look in her eyes Gauhar turned towards Khatri ji and innocently questioned him 'Babuji, will you go to Shelley's (a baiji) mehfil? The carriage is ready.' Khatri ji said 'No,' they had an important guest that evening and asked her if she could recognize who it was. Gauhar fixed her eyes on Khan Sahab, her face flushed with concentration. Her left index finger, accompanied by a beautiful dancer-like movement of the slightly bent neck had hardly moved to her chin when the astonished look in her eyes disappeared, relieving the bowlike brows of their tension. Her face glowed with delight and the enlarged pupils of her eyes seemed to speak of some long forgotten memory. Babuji had asked her to get her thoughts together and concentrate and she had done so successfully.

With a luminescent smile and in a sweet voice she said 'Babuji! How could he ever leave my memory! This would be impossible! The blow he dealt is something I shall never forget!' She was referring to a musical contest between them many years ago in Delhi. Gauhar and Agrewali Malka Jaan, though extremely good friends, were also great professional rivals. In this particular back-to-back musical soiree in Delhi, Gauhar's recital had followed Malka's and she had surpassed Malka in all aspects. Malka was red-faced about her reputation having taken such a beating. It was then that her new-found lover, the young and good-looking Faiyaz Khan had taken it upon himself to redeem his lady-love's prestige as also of Agra and their gharana. He had rendered such an outstanding performance that the effect of Gauhar's rendition was totally lost on the audience. This act of his had endeared him further to Malka and paved the way for their affair.

Recalling that evening in Delhi, Gauhar became a little thoughtful, lowered her head and played with the lace border of her pink georgette sari. She then declared 'Babuji, he is the one and only Ustad Faiyaz Khan Sahab of that Delhi mehfil fame.' And with an air of great familiarity, she directly addressed Faiyaz Khan as though he were a dear friend of many years: 'So Khan Sahab? I was not even informed that you had come to Calcutta! Malka why didn't you tell me? Anyway, what has happened has happened; now tell me Khan Sahab, when will you sing for us?' It was customary for Gauhar to invite any reputed Ustad who came to the city to her house for a soiree and she would honour them after the concert with costly gifts. Gauhar's eyes lit up the way those of a child are when it sees a tangerine in the hands of another. The last sentence was uttered in a pleading tone and was full of genuine emotion.

Even as Gauhar enthusiastically waited for a reply, Faiyaz Khan adopted a very reserved and snobbish tone and chose Khatri ji as an intermediary rather than address Gauhar directly. 'Babuji! We are from the west (meaning

Uttar Pradesh) and are not accustomed to the ways of the east. So it will be impolite for me to reply to her directly; please forgive me. Please be kind enough to explain to her that it is against the principles of our Gharana to wander about with a tanpura under our arms and sing. If she is so eager to hear us, she will have to take the trouble of going to Agra and soak in the flavour of the music of our Gharana. I, moreover, have not come here to sing.' The unexpected reply startled everyone present. An uncomfortable silence descended on the gathering and no one knew what to say. Most people would have felt deeply humiliated by such a reply and would have perhaps walked away from the room. But Gauhar was cast in a different mould altogether.

She turned her face with a strange kind of indifference and a distinct look in each of her eyes. In an innocent voice, as though nothing had happened, she addressed Purushottam Das, a businessman who sat beside her: 'Purushottam bhai! Would you be kind enough to tell me how far Agra is from Calcutta?' Purushottam was a veteran witness to many such ego-battles. With a big smile on his face he said 'Gauhar! You really amaze me! You don't know how far Agra is from Calcutta? Well, let me tell you: Agra is as far from Calcutta as Calcutta is from Agra. If you don't believe me measure and see, you understand?'

Gauhar feigned such amazement as if she had just fallen from the sky. 'Ya Allah! Is that so? Well maybe it is and you are right.' Then, with one palm on a cheek, she gave a cunning knit-brow look at Khan Sahab and Malka and said, 'I don't really know the distance, but it seems Agra and Calcutta are no longer far apart, it seems they have come quite close! Puroshottam bhai, what do you have to say? Did my tired eyes see anything wrong and my vile tongue blabber any blasphemy?' All the while poor Malka who was caught in this embarrassing cross-fire between her lover and her friend kept looking helplessly at Khatri ji pleading with him to control Gauhar. But Khatri ji too seemed to be enjoying this battle of wits and avoided her gaze. Faiyaz Khan was terribly vexed by the innuendo. He got up abruptly, took Babuji's permission and stomped out of the hall in anger. Malka quickly excused herself and followed him.

All the while Gauhar kept looking around with complete indifference. After Faiyaz Khan and Malka left, Shyamlal took Gauhar to task and reprimanded her for her uncouth behaviour. But Gauhar just bowed her head and listened to all he said as though it were a blessing from an elderly well-wisher.

Gauhar's outspokenness was legendary in the concert circles. There would be exciting competitive performances among singers in many soirees. It was perhaps the secret desire of every tawaif to equal Gauhar's professional success, affluence and popularity. Benazir Bai who had received generous patronage from the Darbhanga Raj was one such tawaif who had got the opportunity of performing in the same soiree as Gauhar. Benazir had stunning good looks and in an attempt to enhance them and thereby make herself more attractive to her audience, she had come loaded with the most exquisite jewelry from head to toe. But her performance was just about average and totally at variance with her gorgeous attire and looks. When she reached Gauhar to take her blessings at the end of her recital, Gauhar gave her some pertinent advice laced with her characteristic sharpness. 'Benazir, your *zewar* (ornaments) may shine in bed, but in a concert it is only the musician's *hunar* (art) that matters and impresses.' Benazir went pale. She hadn't expected an acidic comment like this. She waited quietly for Gauhar to perform. But Gauhar gave a scintillating performance that evening. Benazir, who was hoping to get back at Gauhar, was shamed into silence. She apparently took off all her ornaments and rushed to Bombay to the residence of Ustad Kale Khan, father of the doyen of the Kirana Gharana Ustad Abdul Karim Khan. She placed the ornaments at his feet and asked him to make her a worthy musician. The elderly Ustad rejected those ornaments and said the spirit and dedication with which she had come would suffice and she would mature into a talented artist. After about ten years of rigorous training, she emerged as a fine singer. Many years later, she had the opportunity of encountering Gauhar again in the durbar at Darbhanga. After listening to Benazir even Gauhar was stunned. She had truly metamorphosed into an accomplished singer. Gauhar hugged her and expressed her deepest appreciation saying, 'Benazir! God bless you! Now your diamonds are really flashing!'

Yet another famed ustad who visited Calcutta was Ustad Kale Khan, of the Patiala Gharana, the uncle and teacher of the legendary Ustad Bade Ghulam Ali Khan. Known to be an eccentric man, Kale Khan was usually lost in his own thoughts of music. Eye-witnesses like Sanyal who had heard him sing, say that his voice was like a sarangi, without the sharp edges. Though it reminded people of Ustad Abdul Karim Khan's singing, his voice did not resort to falsetto in the upper octaves and retained its original well-rounded character. Despite being gluttonous in his eating habits, he would commence a concert immediately after a heavy meal of oily *puris* and *rabri*, a sweet dish, and yet maintain the virtuosity of his presentation. He was famous for his fanatic *riyaz* or practice sessions during which he would sing just the scale(s) of a raga for hours on end. His expertise at various kinds of taans, like the heavy *halaq* taans and the lighter *sapaat* ones were legendary, as also his skill at *badhat vistaar*, or step-by-step exposition of a raga. Gauhar was fortunate to hear him at one soiree in Calcutta. After the concert she reverentially requested him to accept her as his disciple, stay at her palatial 'Gauhar Building' on Chitpur Road and train her in these specific techniques. This was typical of Gauhar. Despite her accomplishments as a celebrated musician, she was humble enough to want to learn new things and absorb new ideas.

Kale Khan agreed to take her on as his pupil and since he had few options for residence in Calcutta, readily consented to stay in a portion of her house. The teaching sessions began in right earnest. Gauhar was a meticulous student and very quickly assimilated all that he taught her. But sadly the teaching sessions and the proximity to Gauhar bred evil ideas in Kale Khan's mind. According to Dilip Mukhopadhyay, one day he held her close and told her, '*Tum mera dil bhar do aur main tumhe dil bhar ke gana sikhaoonga.*' (Satisfy me and I shall happily teach you all the music that I know.') Gauhar was both enraged and outraged. This indecent proposal from the man she respected as her guru was an affront. She asked him to leave her house immediately and not show his face to her again. A chastised Kale Khan tried to make up but Gauhar was firm. She shut her doors on him forever. Kale Khan then took refuge in Biden Street. Given his maverick nature, he had some misunderstandings there too with Imdad Khan, the ace sarangi player who was also Gauhar's regular accompanist. Kale Khan kept hopping from one place to the other and finally left Calcutta for Patiala in utter despair. But by then gossip about Gauhar and Kale Khan's alleged affair became the talk of the town. Kale Khan too never let any opportunity pass to malign her and call her names—a witch and an '*ajagarni*' (a serpent) in public. Gauhar however maintained a studied silence and never answered questions regarding this incident. It was Bijoy Lal Mukhopadhyay, another student of Kale Khan who was present at 'Gauhar Building' when the incident took place, who revealed the truth to the world.

The Kale Khan episode underscored a common and generally accepted phenomenon in the teaching and learning of Hindustani music those days. Many eminent women singers, including the legendary Begum Akhtar have spoken about the casual and repeated misdemeanours of the male ustads with their female disciples. Expecting sexual favours from them or molesting them in return for knowledge rarely evoked anger, outrage or surprise. It was yet another indication of a debased system where music was equated with a variety of vices.

Closely allied with this was the tendency of the ustads to be half-hearted in teaching their tawaif students. This point is borne out in Muhammad Ali Ruswa's celebrated novel 'Umrao Jaan.' The famous tawaif of Lucknow, Khanum Jaan despite being so knowledgeable in music herself, had employed an ustad to train her girls because tawaifs could gain musical legitimacy only through association with gharanedar musicians. However, the resident ustad hardly made any attempt to correct the mistakes of his female students when they sang scales of ragas wrongly. It was Khanum's intervention that forced the ustad to mumble the actual notation of the raga, but again in a half-hearted fashion.

Scholars like Kumar Mukherjee have elucidated three kinds of musical training that these hereditary male musicians imparted: that given to their own male relatives, that given to the tawaifs and that given to the non-kin male students. Obviously their own kin were top on their priority list in terms of the quality and dedication put into their training. They were taught the choicest compositions and special features that distinguished their particular gharana. After all it was 'family property,' and the next of kin had the first right over it as the future torch-bearers. While the ustads might have maintained strict discipline and expected the same rigour from their tawaif students, they purposely kept their training incomplete. They were taught just as much was necessary to become skilled entertainers and there were no esoteric underpinnings, just cold pragmatism. Mukherjee speaks of a famous incident in this regard. Munnibai, a tawaif, was a famous student of Ustad

Abdul Karim Khan and was a highly talented artist. Her rendition of Ragas like Bilaskhani Todi would go on for a minimum of one to one and a half hours, with no repetitive sounding phrases and passages. Ustad Alladiya Khan heard one such concert of hers and was stunned. He immediately chided the guru saying, 'What are you doing? Just teach her as much as is required. If she starts singing for one and a half hours, who will listen to us?'

Sometimes the ustads tried to be such perfectionists with their female disciples with regard to vocal perfection and pitch fidelity that the strenuous practices they were required to put in led many women musicians to lose their voices or develop serious problems with them. It was this complex world of teaching music that people like Bhatkhande tried hard to change.

However, gradually the mindsets of the ustads of these gharanas changed. Doyens like Ustad Alladiya Khan and Ustad Abdul Karim Khan began to induct women from both 'respected' backgrounds and from the tawaif lineage as well, into their hallowed fold and groom them into consummate artists. In fact, when one analyzes the list of women artists who ruled the roost in the last three quarters of the last century as gharanedar musicians, most of them came from the Jaipur and Kirana gharanas.

Besides these Ustads, a tawaif had members of her own community to train her and this was basically the major training she received. The other important source of learning for her was her sarangi player. These players were from the lowest rung of the socio-musical pyramid in terms of both prestige and pedigree. They were often looked down upon as pimps. They lived off the tawaifs, many a times in their salons, and were considered as hangers-on. But at the same time they could impart quite a bit of musical knowledge to the baijis. Sometimes they even corrected them while they were performing or prompted them when they forgot the lyrics once in a while. The status of the tabalchi was no better and he was considered yet another parasite at the kotha, though he had a major role to play in the success of any soiree.

Gauhar Jaan too had several such hangers-on. Pandit Gowri Shankar Mishra, the second son of her guru from Banaras, Pandit Bechoo Mishra, was her long-time sarangiya. Pandit Bechoo would often visit Calcutta to train Gauhar. In his absence his son would also do the same even as he accompanied her in her performances. Most baijis usually had two sarangiyas on either side of them. The one on the right would be the more senior and respected one while the other was a junior sarangiya. In the early days Ustad Imdad Khan of Patna donned the role of the second sarangiya for Gauhar. The tabalchi, Laddan Khan, who normally accompanied Gauhar, was relegated to the back, thus underlining his status in the social hierarchy of the musical world.

In the performance and transmission of Hindustani classical music, where gender and social identity played such a complex role, it is remarkable that Gauhar Jaan and women like her achieved such phenomenal success despite all odds.

But Gauhar was quite unlike the male ustads in that she was ever ready to share her knowledge with those who came seeking it. As a result, almost an entire generation of upcoming women musicians, especially those specializing in genres like thumri and ghazal revered Gauhar Jaan and looked up to her as a role-model.

Five year old Bibbi was one of them. On the morning of 5 December 1919 the lady inspector of schools, Miss Lin entered Bibbi's classroom of the Mission School in Faizabad with her friend, the celebrated 'Madame Gauhar Jaan.' Bibbi was enchanted by Gauhar's elegant dress, a white *garara* complemented by a Dhaka *Jamadani dupatta* with gold pom-poms hanging at the edges and her flashing diamonds. So imposing was her appearance that the little children stared spellbound. Little Bibbi who was sitting in the front row was tempted to pull the pom-poms and draw the attention of the woman. Seeing the pretty child with her pink cheeks tugging at her garment, Gauhar picked up the child and asked her if she knew how to sing. Bibbi had heard her mother Mushtari's musical rendering of the *marsiya,* and she very confidently agreed to sing for the celebrity guest. She sang a well-known composition, '*Amma mori bhaiya ko bhejo ri ke saawan aaya, beta tera bhaiya to baala ri*' (Dear mother, send my brother as the monsoons have arrived, and the mother replies – dear daughter your brother is still young.) Her neat and clear rendition greatly impressed Gauhar. She asked her whose daughter she was. When told that she belonged to a respected Muslim household, Gauhar lamented that she would not be allowed to sing in that case. She then made her famous prediction about the girl that if given the right training she had all the makings of a '*Mallika-e-ghazal*' or the Queen of Ghazals. That Gauhar's prediction turned into a benediction for young Bibbi who went on to become the sub-continent's most popular ghazal singer, Begum Akhtar, is something that Begum Sahiba often quoted with great pride throughout her life.

Another story goes that Begum Akhtar, who at one time seriously contemplated a career in theatre and films, changed her mind after she heard the live concerts of Gauhar and was greatly influenced by her rendering and her style. Incidentally, it was Gauhar's sarangi player Ustad Imdad Khan, who became Begum Akhtar's guru. Gauhar was the trend-setter of the 'fashion statement' that went along with being a woman singer of those times.

Another contemporary of Begum Akhtar who was also a star of her times was Siddheshwari Devi of Banaras. As a child she had listened to Gauhar's records and nursed a great ambition to sing like her. Many years later, in the 1930s when she sang in Calcutta at a famous conference, Siddheswari Devi was overcome with emotion. She was after all, singing at the same venues where the likes of Gauhar Jaan, Agrewali Malka Jaan, Mauzuddin and others had sung. When she started singing the thumri *'Piya pardes mora man hara,'* the audience was reminded of the eminent singers of the yester years and applauded her. She concluded the recital with a fantastic rendering of a thumri in Bhairavi *'Kahe ko dare gulal.'* Incidentally Ustad Faiyaz Khan, Gauhar's bête-noire was also present there and appreciating the young singer, had commented: *'Baad Gauhar Jaan aur Malka Jaan ke yeh sehra tere hi sir hai—tu thumri ki rani hai.'* (After Gauhar Jaan and Malka Jaan, the crown of thumri queen rests on your head!).

In an interview to a Calcutta-based music critic, Siddheshwari Devi said:

'Gauhar Jaan and Malka Jaan were like the stars of the sky for me. I had heard their records on the gramophones of my neighbours as a very young child. They had been sources of deep early inspiration for me when even to dream of being a singer seemed such impossibility. The fact that my name was even mentioned along with theirs brought a kind of fulfillment that defies all description. That too from a distinguished artist like Faiyaz Khan whom I held in great esteem and awe. I get a special feeling whenever I remember that occasion...'

There was another little girl from Amritsar who had migrated to Calcutta with her mother. The story of her early life was quite similar to that of Gauhar's. Her mother, Rajbala was a trapeze artist in The Great Bengal Circus of Motilal Bose. She became Bose's mistress and in 1899 gave birth to a daughter in Amritsar. She was named Indubala. Soon Bose's interest in Rajbala dwindled and the mother and daughter shifted to Calcutta in search of a livelihood. A wealthy man, Jiban Krishna Ghosh, sheltered them and Rajbala remained loyal to him till the end. Once in Calcutta, Rajbala trained herself as a singer and this was where Indu's musical training began. She was initially supposed to become a nurse and was admitted as a trainee in the Pataldanga hospital in Calcutta. But Indu had absolutely no interest in the profession and she ran away from there. Motilal Bose however was very fond of his daughter and kept in touch with her though he had renounced the mother. At one of her mother's soirees, the twelve year old Indu also performed and won appreciation from the audience. She was then enrolled as a student of Pandit Gowri Shankar Mishra and his brother Kali Prasad Mishra.

It was customary for Pandit Mishra to organize all-night concerts at his rented house in Jorasanko for the Janmashtami festival that marked the birth of Lord Krishna. On one such occasion, Gauhar Jaan was also invited as the chief guest and all of Gowri Shankar's students were to perform. Indu was terribly nervous to see Gauhar sitting right there in the first row and began to sing with great trepidation. She sang a thumri and got up to leave. But Gauhar asked her to sit down and sing another song and then yet another. Gauhar embraced her warmly at the end of her performance and complimented her rich voice quality. She told Pandit Mishra to bring the girl to see her the following day. All night, little Indu could hardly sleep because of the excitement. Being complimented by the prima donna of Indian music was a great achievement for the little girl. That evening was to change the course of Indu's life.

Gowri Shankar was Gauhar's main sarangiya. He knew that Gauhar intended to take Indu under her wing as a student and was alright with it. His brother Kali Prasad greatly resented the idea, but gave in to his elder brother's wishes eventually. The next morning when they reached Gauhar's house all the arrangements had been made for a formal gandabandhan ceremony and about a hundred *laddoos* were ready for distribution. Indu's first recollection of Gauhar was that of a completely down-to-earth and humble musician who did not have the airs of one who was a nationwide celebrity. She embraced the girl and tied the *ganda* or thread formalizing her acceptance of Indu as a student. She asked her to sing something and the little girl sang a Bengali tappa, '*Shuno rajkumari hathe dhori, prane diyo na aar betha*' (O! Princess! I am pleading with you; do not pain my heart any more.) Gauhar showed her appreciation and encouragement, even though she corrected her mistakes. She commenced her teaching with a tappa in Raga Bhupali '*Aa mila mehera miyan.*' However, because of her hectic tour schedule and personal problems, Gauhar was not very regular with the classes. But whenever she was in Calcutta, she would call Indu Bala home and teach her. Other than music, Indu learnt valuable lessons in etiquette, performance dos and don'ts, stage manners and so on that stayed with her all her life. It was the most valuable and first-hand experience that a performing artist of the stature of Gauhar Jaan was sharing with her.

Indu Bala's diary jottings provide many valuable insights about Gauhar Jaan, the woman she admired, loved and respected. She talks of Gauhar's fluency in many languages and her ability to compose verses. She laments that sadly the lady never got her due for all this. She particularly recalls an exquisite khayal composed by Gauhar herself in a rare Raga Lakshmi Todi that was set to jhap taal.

'*Tum hazarat khwaja, sab rajan ki raja; Hoon aayi hoon tero darwaja*
Gauhar pyari ki araz yahi hai, jag mein raakho meri laaja.'

(Oh Khwaja! The king of the world, I have come to your doorstep beseeching your mercy, the only request of Gauhar is that you shower your grace on her.)

Indu remembers seeing Gauhar driving along in her horse-carriage at a great speed across the wide roads of Calcutta near Eden Gardens. What stuck her was the huge, round sun glasses Gauhar wore during her jaunts. A girl called Loila Jaan always accompanied her and people said she was her daughter as she resembled Gauhar in colour and features. Indu mentions that her father was once standing at the bandstand near Eden Gardens, when Gauhar saw him. She greeted him with a loud shriek of *'Adab Arz Hai Maharaj'* and he had replied, very politely *'Tasleem, Bai!'* When not in her horse carriage Gauhar took evening walks in the Eden Gardens, stopping for tea at a restaurant on the Promenade, at Outram Ghat, then took another stroll once the lights at Eden were on and then move on to either Shyamlal Khatriji's house at Harrison Road or Surbahar player Harendranath Sheel's house for a brief chat session. Another friend she often visited was Narendranath Chatterji. She liked to have a paan and exchange the news of the day with him before returning home. The letters that Gauhar sometimes wrote to Indu's father were also steeped in courtesy and politeness, in which she comes across as utterly self-effacing

Along with Indu there was another student Gauhar had, named Anathnath Bose. She taught these two just for the love of teaching and expected no fees from them. Bose was a young boy born in Jossore, in Bangladesh of today, and driven by his love for music came to Calcutta when he was fifteen or so. Gauhar had heard him at Seth Dhulichand's house and when requested, agreed to take him as a student. Speaking of their lessons Indu recounts that while practicing if the student lost a beat or a note Gauhar merely raised one eyebrow and that was enough to tell the students that they had erred. Her extremely eloquent eyebrows could convey all emotions, pleasure, satisfaction, contempt, displeasure and anger. If the student was unable to correct the mistake, she would sing herself and demonstrate the right way.

Indu acknowledges with gratitude the debt she owed to Gauhar. In the few years of their association Gauhar influenced her deeply. She expressed deep admiration for her teacher and friend, saying that Gauhar was a genius but few knew her real worth. And yet she was simple, humble, devoid of jealousy and pride and was generous with her praise, be the singer a junior or senior artist. One thing Indu observed with some amusement was that Gauhar, like a true woman, never revealed her age. 'I am as old as people perceive me to be,' she would retort if Indu jokingly asked her her age!

Unfortunately for Indu, her former teachers, especially Kali Prasad Mishra, began resenting her association with Gauhar. Indu continued her regular lessons with them as Gauhar was often out of town for long stretches of time. After a while, they told Indu that they would not teach her if she continued to go to Gauhar. Rajbala had to plead with the Mishra brothers and finally they arrived at a compromise. On a predetermined day, a *yagna* or sacrificial fire was performed at the Mishra household. Indu was summoned to this ritual and was forced to cut off the thread or ganda that bound her to Gauhar as her pupil, and offer it to the sacrificial fire. It was an extremely distressing ritual for Indu. And she was heartbroken. It meant that she was breaking that unique bond with a woman whom she genuinely loved and respected and from whom she had learnt so much. Indu Bala went on to become one of the greatest singers and actresses of her times, and she always referred to Gauhar Jaan as her favourite guru, one who had the major share in shaping her talents.

From Indu Bala's diaries the impressions one has formed of Gauhar so far get concretized. Gauhar was a woman who evoked strong reactions from people. Those who liked her, loved her, those who didn't, well, they hated her and everything about her! What is remarkable is the equanimity with which she handled both. She lived life on her own terms and to the full. But fate had its own plans for her. She went from one personal disaster to another and by the time she was about forty she seemed to be heading towards what was going to prove the biggest blunder of her life.

SECTION 3

THE FALL FROM GRACE

Rehmat nahin kuch cheez par ae waaiz naakas
Jo had se guzar jaaye woh banda nahin hota.

Of what use is the advise of the preacher
To a slave who has crossed all limits and has made up his mind to defy
his master?

—Badi Malka Jaan, Makhzan-e-ulfat-e-Mallika.

॰॰॰

13

THE BECKONING OF DOOM

The famous poet Akbar Allahabadi was a great fan of Gauhar's, and he had made that famous comment about concerts being lifeless if she wasn't part of them. The same Allahabadi, however, had a very sarcastic verse about her personal life:

'Aaj Akbar kaun hai duniya mein Gauhar ke siwa
Sab khuda ne de rakha hai use, ek shauhar ke siwa.'
(Who in the world today is as great as Gauhar?
God had showered every gift on her except that of a husband!)

In another verse he addresses her directly saying:

'Ada hai, husn hai sin hai, sabhi jauhar hai e Gauhar
Magar yeh ek kami hai ki tu rakhti nahin shauhar'

(Grace you have and beauty, O Gauhar, youth is yours and every ornament,
The one thing you don't have and that is a husband.)

All Gauhar's romantic liaisons had turned out to be temporary escapades which did not withstand the passing of time. The irony was that she spurned many rich men and talented Ustads who pined for her love, but chose to fall for the most unlikely suitor.

When Gauhar was facing the messy court case that Bhaglu had slapped on her, Abbas, her Peshawari manager, had stood firmly by her side. She was impressed by the support he had provided during that time, and she began to repose more and more faith in him. Her gratitude and appreciation soon turned to affection, and before long, she started looking to him as a panacea for her loneliness. Abbas was initially flustered by her overtures since he looked upon her as an employer, one he deeply respected. But then Abbas was human too and after a while, succumbed to her charms. It was hardly surprising, considering that Gauhar was being wooed by the whole world!

As early as 1913, Gauhar entered into a 'muta marriage' with Abbas. Muta is a practice in Islam which allows two people to enter into a short-term contractual relationship that lasts for few hours, days or months. The man is supposed to give some item of value to the woman and they 'marry' and have the legal sanction to engage in sex. With the expiry of the contract period, they part ways. A nikah, on the other hand, was a permanent and religiously solemnized wedding. One is not sure what 'valuable' item Abbas gave Gauhar or the duration of the contract. But they began to spend an increasing amount of time as man and wife. According to Indu Bala, one of Gauhar's students, Abbas would be present at most of the concerts as an irritating fixture. At the end of a performance, he would try to hobnob with the wealthy people in the audience and ask them annoying questions like 'Don't you think she was amazing? Don't you think she deserves more?' He probably believed that that was what the ideal manager-secretary should do.

Gauhar had noticed that Abbas was an amateur tabalchi of sorts. When he was about eight or ten years old, and lived in Lucknow he had a distinguished neighbour, Pandit Ram Ram Mishra, who was a skilled tabla player. Constant association with Mishra generated some interest in Abbas as well and he too learnt to play the tabla, but never pursued it seriously. However, for Gauhar that was another point in his favour.

When Gauhar gave her affection, she gave unstintingly. Abbas was at the receiving end of not just her love, but also her implicit trust in him.

But in all fairness to Abbas, he had earned that trust through his steadfast support and loyalty. Such was her feeling for Abbas that within a week of the court quashing the cases filed by Bhaglu and ordering his eviction from the Chitpur Road residence, Gauhar signed a deed (on 20 June 1913) by which she gifted the palatial 49, Chitpur Road residence to Abbas. The deal stipulated that the rent from the three holdings of the house were to go to Gauhar. Since her attorney Ganesh Chandra Chandra was ill, Mr B.K. Basu of No 2, Old Port Office Street prepared the deal and had it signed by the attorney. He also read it out to Gauhar and she agreed to the terms. Basu added this to his files saying 'Read over and explained by me and consented by her.' Herein began Gauhar's litany of woes.

Abbas's father who had hitherto remained in the background, but had stood by his son and his employer during those trying days of the court case, moved into the house claiming rights over his son's residence. He brought with him a whole set of cacophonous relatives who marred the tranquil atmosphere of the house. Their presence greatly interfered with Gauhar's riyaz/practice sessions and soirees that she used to hold. But rather than offend her 'father-in-law' Gauhar decided to move out of that house herself. She sold her house on Bentinck Street and bought one on Free School Street. She moved into this new residence in early 1914.

The romance between Gauhar and Abbas lasted for a while. Gauhar felt reassured by the presence of a man in her life, who was willing to take charge of her legal tangles, her concert and recording schedules and also her financial accounts and property matters. It gave her the freedom to engage entirely and completely with music. Abbas handled his responsibilities sincerely, meticulously coordinating Gauhar's busy schedules.

But soon he came under the influence of his wily father, Ghulam Mehdi Hussain Khan's machinations. Mehdi Khan wanted to extract the maximum out of his son's association with the richest and most popular tawaif of Calcutta, rather, India. Gauhar suddenly started noticing changes in Abbas' behaviour. He started staying away from the Free School Street house, and spending more time with his relatives at Chitpur Road.

Having seen so many ups and downs in life and having faced the treacheries and betrayals of her loved ones, Gauhar became increasingly suspicious and possessive of Abbas. Her insecurities led her to do and say many irrational things. She would repent later and beg for forgiveness, but the very next day she would get incensed by some act of his that she perceived as disloyal and indifferent and the scene would repeat itself.

Abbas in the meantime had begun to widen his network and was becoming quite popular among the tawaifs of Calcutta, especially as he was known to be the blue-eyed boy of the city's most famous musician. His friendships turned into liaisons before long and Gauhar began to hear many stories about his escapades with some of the younger tawaifs of the city. When she confronted him, he would feign innocence and plead for mercy. But there was something about Abbas that made Gauhar melt. All her anger and agitation would dissipate once she saw him and heard his protestations of innocence. Either she was blindly and madly in love with him or desperately craved the support of a man who could protect her and guide her life in the right way. That made her reluctant to give Abbas up.

The Gauhar of this period as seen from some of her letters to Abbas comes across as a woman battling her insecurities and swinging violently from one extreme mood to another. Every time she went out of Calcutta for a performance, Abbas would be constantly in her thoughts. From each venue she wrote letters that contradicted each other.

In 1915 Gauhar Jaan set off on an extensive concert tour that saw her criss-cross the length and breadth of the country. She began with Bombay, a visit that brought back the old memories of Amrit Keshav Nayak and the heady days they had spent together. He was one person whose memory she always cherished. While at Bombay, she stayed with her friend, the noted vocalist Anjanibai Malpekar.

But even during this tour she was waging an intense personal battle. On 7 May 1915, she wrote a letter to Abbas from Bombay, in a tone that sounded like she was serving an ultimatum. She specifically asked him to leave her alone. 'Please do not try to keep any contact or relationship with me henceforth. You have shown me the utmost kindness and loyalty. God has made you the recipient of my property. I pray that you stay there in happiness and peace by the grace of God and if God wills, you will be able to live there in comfort.'

In complete contrast to this harsh letter was the missive she sent him on 10 May, also from Bombay. Expressing deep regret for her harshness she beseeched him to show mercy. 'Abbas, I beg your forgiveness with folded hands. You have not done anything bad to me neither have you acted with dishonesty. Deep down in my heart I know that you mean good and have my welfare in your thoughts always. For the sake of Immam Hossain, excuse me and I will never forget your obligation for the rest of my life. I know that you have been and will remain loyal to me and will neither allow nor cause harm to befall me. I am also confident that you will never indulge in any misconduct vis-à-vis me. I deeply love you Abbas and I know it is the same from your end.' Just a few days later another letter reached Abbas on similar lines as the earlier one. 'Abbas till now I have respected your loyalty towards me. I shall never forget the dutifulness and obedience with which you have behaved with me so far. This letter is intended to formally communicate this deep and sincere sentiment of mine to you.'

These letters reveal the terrible mental conflicts that Gauhar was battling. Being impulsive and insecure and to an extent naive too, she kept raving and ranting at Abbas as and when she was seized by a particular emotion. In a vein of supreme detachment and matronly concern for the man who was actually much younger than her, she writes another letter to him from Bombay. 'Do not have any doubts in your mind. You fix up your marriage with any one you want. It will be my responsibility to make arrangements for the wedding and also fund it. Whatever your heart desires ask me and I shall buy that for you.'

Gauhar also visited Pune and paid her respects to the doyen of the Kirana Gharana Ustad Abdul Karim Khan. Khan Sahab had set up his music school in that city and Gauhar decided to visit and perform there. Though she had an eclectic mix of various gharanas, she considered her singing to be closest to the Kirana style and hence offered her respects to the man who is believed to have pioneered the style. She became very fond of Khan Sahab's eleven year old daughter Champakali, who later came to be known as Hirabai Barodekar, one of the most famous vocalists of the 20th century. She was the daughter of Abdul Karim Khan and his Hindu wife Tarabai Mane. Tarabai was in some way related to the Baroda royal family, in whose court Abdul Karim was the court musician. Their affair and marriage led to their banishment from the State. They, with their five children, Hirabai, Saraswati Rane (Sakina or Choutai), Kamalabai (Gulab), Suresh Babu Mane

(Abdul Rehman) and Papa (Krishna Rao Mane), took refuge in Bombay. Hirabai's sweet and melodious voice caught Gauhar's attention too. She taught her and also Sunderabai, the other famous female vocalist of her times, a number of bhajans and thumris. They in turn recorded these on gramophone discs thereby popularizing many of Gauhar's trademark bhajans like *Radhe Krishna Bol Mukhase* and *Krishna Murari Binat Karat*. In fact when Abdul Karim Khan separated from his wife and Tarabai moved to Pune with her five children, Gauhar had even offered to adopt Hirabai, so fond was she of the little girl.

The period between 1910 and 1940 was the golden age of the Marathi theatre—the age of the musical plays which were known more for their songs or *natya sangeet* than themes. The play titled '*Maanapamaan*', written by Kakasaheb Khadilkar, first staged on 12 March 1911, ushered in a whole new era in Marathi natya sangeet. The reigning deity of this era was *Nat-Samrat* Bal Gandharva. In an article entitled 'Titans of the Golden Age of the Marathi Stage' in *The Hindu*, Sri R.M. Kumtakar says: 'Few indeed symbolized in person that glorious era more than Bal Gandharva, the legendary singer-actor, the brightest and the most enduring among the idols of the Marathi musical drama which brought unprecedented and also unequalled popularity, prosperity and prestige to the Marathi stage during the first three decades of this century...' With his divine voice and histrionic talents, he was a household name across Maharashtra.

Born in 1888 as Narayan Shripad Rajhans, he was christened as 'Gandharva' when he was only ten years old, by none other than Lokmanya Tilak who listened with amazement to the child's musical prowess. Bal Gandharva took to theatre early and joined Annasaheb Kirloskar's 'Kirloskar Natak Mandali.' He received excellent musical training from the maestro Pandit Bhaskarbuwa Bakhle. The young, petite and extremely handsome man became a hit essaying female roles on stage. From a debut as Shakuntala, he is said to have played more than 36 roles in about 27 musical plays. By 1913, he started his own company, '*Gandharva Natak Mandali*' and along with veterans like Govindarao Tembe, Master Krishnarao, Ganpatrao Bodas, transformed the Mandali into a near cult with a huge fan following. It also created a rich corpus of songs of Marathi natya sangeet. Most of the reputed musicians of the time, Pt Bakhle, Sawai Gandharva, Buwa Waze, Shankar

Rao Sarnaik, Dinanath Mangeshkar, Pandhakarbuwa, and even maestros like Ustad Alladiya Khan, Ustad Bande Ali Khan and Agrewali Malka Jaan, gladly associated themselves with the Mandali.

Despite presenting pure classical *ragdari* or raga based music, the natya sangeet caught the imagination and attention of even those in the audience who had no fondness for nor knowledge of traditional Hindustani music. Bal Gandharva was ably supported by Govindarao Tembe, a harmonium player. Govindrao evolved a very distinctive style of harmonium playing which he could adapt very beautifully to the different genres, including natya sangeet. Tembe was a prolific writer, a playwright, an interesting speaker and a music director with a grand vision.

It was quite obvious that an outstanding class of artists and musicians like these would have heard and appreciated Gauhar's records too. Her three-minute presentation formula impressed and inspired them. So much so that they would imitate some of her immensely popular songs, and set Marathi lyrics to the same tunes but with minor modifications. Inspired by Gauhar's music Tembe introduced the Purab-ang thumri and dadra kind of songs into Natya Sangeet and that became an instant hit among audiences across Maharashtra.

During the visit to Maharashtra Gauhar was determined to see one of the Mandali's plays herself and decide whether her tunes were being plagiarised. She was shocked to see how her famous songs and tunes (for instance, among other songs her *'Garajat aaye'* in Raag Sur Malhar was sung by Bal Gandharva in the play *'Swayamvar'* as *'Anrutachi Gopala,'* her popular dadra in Pahadi *'Pardesi saiyyan'* as *'Dhanarashi jaatha'* in *'Maanapmaan'* by Bal Gandharva and later Krishnarao Gore, the evergreen Malkauns piece *'Krishna Madho Shyam'* was sung in *'Swayamvar'* by Bal Gandharva as *'Vairi maara yaala'*) had been adapted with great élan. It is said that she picked up a quarrel with Bal Gandharva on this, though not much is known of whether the misunderstandings were resolved and they maintained cordial relations thereafter. But it underscores the wide influence that Gauhar's music had on various genres and forms across the country.

Once Gauhar was back in Bombay, her attention turned to Abbas again. In her typically spiteful, impulsive manner she wrote to him saying 'Abbas! Let me go! Give me my freedom. If you leave me, you will also be free and no one would mock you. You can always say and continue to remain the owner of property worth lakhs. You may enjoy this property for the rest of your life with pride, twirling your moustache!' It was tragic that an artist of her stature should let herself descend to such irrational behaviour

On the invitation of the Nizam, Gauhar visited Hyderabad where she was given a royal reception at the resplendent Chow Mahalla Palace and stayed at the Begum Mahal in style. But her mind was still occupied by thoughts of Abbas. Despite the scores of letters she wrote to him, in varying states of mind, Abbas remained silent and chose not to reply a single one of them. His protracted silence riled her further and she wrote to him again from Hyderabad on 4 August 1915: 'I write to you with great regret that if any other person had inherited my property at Lower Chitpur Road, they would have remained grateful to me for the rest of their lives. They would have acknowledged the fact that they have become wealthy because of my grace. But you?'

Before getting back to Calcutta, Gauhar had a couple of concerts at Lucknow and Rampur. She decided to spend some time at Rampur, the home of her beloved Nawab Hamid Ali. On 21 October 1915, she wrote to him from Rampur. 'I had acknowledged you as my muta husband. If I had not given this property to you, then the question would have arisen as to who would inherit it. Till now I have not shared any of my assets or properties with any one other than you. But I am sorry to say that you have greatly disappointed me and I have had to listen to a lot of unsavoury comments from society because of this. I now realise how big a mistake I have made by taking you as my muta husband. If I had kept the Chitpur Road house and stayed in the Free School Street house, then with the rental from the former itself I would have lived like a queen. Do you admit this?'

Finally, on 6 January 1916, she fired the last salvo at him from Lucknow: 'Please accept my advice to you. Whatever you have received in life so far, far exceeds what you deserve or are worthy of. So enjoy whatever you have got in life, through dubious means and otherwise, in peace and happiness. Set me free.'

The news from Calcutta about Abbas's continued affairs and reports of his operating her bank accounts without informing her, infuriated her. He had also stopped crediting the rent from the Chitpur Road holdings to her account as per the gift-deed. She decided to cut short the tour and get back to Calcutta in June 1916.

By then Gauhar had made up her mind to terminate this farcical relationship. She was exhausted and the relationship had taken its toll on her. She approached one of the most popular solicitors of the city, Mr Arddhendra Kumar Ganguly, popularly known as O.C. Ganguly. He had earlier prepared the legal documents for the many houses that Gauhar had bought and sold. In his memoirs, Ganguly recounts this case which turned out to be one of the most sensational ones of his career. Ganguly appointed Barrister Sir B.C. Mitra and advocate Charu Chandra Ghosh to fight the case. Given the reputation of Mr Ganguly's firm and the eminence of the lawyers, Gauhar had to pay a huge fee of Rs 510 for each session. Sir Mitra would joke and take a jibe at Ghosh that while his fees was a mere Rs 510, his client earned as much as Rs 1000 for a single night's performance.

The main thrust of the prosecution was that Abbas had exerted 'undue influence' on the plaintiff Gauhar and trapped her emotionally, thereby appropriating all her property and wealth. Now that she wanted to terminate the relationship, she wished to get back all that she had gifted to him. The suit (Case No 678 of 1916) was filed on 19 June 1916 by Badre Munir Chowdharayan alias Nanhua Jaan of 250, Bowbazar on behalf of Gauhar. Badre Munir had been given the power of attorney to file the case, dated 7 March 1916, as Gauhar had to go to Rawalpindi for an important concert.

The argument of the case went as follows:

'Gauhar Jan of 46, Free School Street, at present residing at Rowalpindi in Punjab; by O.C. Ganguly Vs. Syed Gholam Abbas Sabzwari, lately residing at 46, Free School Street, but at present at 49, Lower Chitpore Road by C.C. Bosu.

- The defendant had been in the employ of the plaintiff for last eight or nine years, looking for her business and other affairs and had been treated by the plaintiff with implicit trust and confidence and remained in sole charge of all the properties movables and immovables, used to collect rents. In course of such service, the defendant acquired considerable influence on the plaintiff.

- That in or about the month of June 1913, the defendant taking advantage of his position and influence induced the plaintiff to execute in his favour a Deed proposing the transfer of 49, 49/1, and 49/2 Lower Chitpore Road and enjoy the rents by the plaintiff in her lifetime.
- The plaintiff further states that the defendant was in love with the plaintiff and had great intimacy with her.
- That since the execution of the Deed, the plaintiff was in possession of the profits and the defendant was paid the rents until about a year when she left Calcutta on business.
- The plaintiff called upon the defendant for cancellation of the Deed whereupon the defendant refused.
- Declaration that the plaintiff is the absolute owner of the property notwithstanding execution of the Deed dated 20th June 1913. Deed be declared null and void.'

Accordingly a warrant was filed on 7 July 1916 by Abbas's lawyer C C Bosu. Summons was served on Gauhar by affixation on 30 June 1916.

Gauhar's legal team began investigating the case and examined the entire set of letters that Gauhar had written to Abbas over the last couple of years. They were all written in chaste Urdu and were highly poetical in nature. An Urdu specialist was hired to get these letters translated into English. The fun-loving Sir Mitra would enjoy a hearty laughter reading those lengthy declarations of love that Gauhar had showered on Abbas in her letters.

A case of fraud was made against Abbas and much later a criminal case too was filed against him to intimidate him further. Ganguly mentions in his memoirs that Abbas's father made many a visit to his office and pleaded with him to request his client to withdraw the criminal case against his son and also not strip them of all their property.

A written statement was thereafter filed in the High Court on 7 August 1916:

'From 1907 to 1911, the defendant generally managed the affairs of the plaintiff. In 1910 and 1911, the defendant was directed by the plaintiff to look after the suit filed by Bhagloo. After disposal of the suit the defendant had no concern in management but his father used to manage and sometime in 1914 he was appointed for the sale of 22, Bentinck Street house. The plaintiff in all important matters used to consult and was guided by Mr G.C. Chunder, an attorney.

The defendant states that he was married in Muta form to the plaintiff but he denies that the plaintiff was in the habit of carrying out his wishes and suggestions and denies that in execution of the deed the plaintiff was not acting out of her free will.

The plaintiff is a shrewd and intelligent woman. The plaintiff is desirous to make the defendant agree to nullify the Muta marriage and having failed, filed this suit.'

All the correspondences between Gauhar and Abbas were annexed along with this written affidavit.

This infamous case was headed for an interesting denouement. It had attracted enough headlines in the media and was the talk of the city. A lot of dirty linen was washed in the court with fiery accusations and counter-accusations by both sides. People thronged to watch the proceedings and entertain themselves. With luminaries of the legal world like Ganguly, Mitra and Ghosh on her side, it was difficult for Gauhar to not win the case. On 21 November 1918, the judge, Justice George Clause Rankin dismissed the case in favour of Gauhar. Abbas was slapped with a fine of Rs 3000 which was payable to Gauhar and their muta marriage was also nullified.

Justice Rankin decreed the following in his ruling of 21 November 1918.

- That the plaintiff will withdraw this suit unconditionally and without any right to institute a fresh suit.
- That the defendant will pay to the plaintiff Rs 3000 for costs. Defendant shall not be entitled to costs incurred in appointment of interlocutors.
- That the plaintiff if so required by the defendant will execute in his favour a proper release in respect of the premises of No 49, Lower Chitpore Road.
- That the plaintiff will withdraw the police proceedings instituted against the defendant.

Taking pity on Abbas and as a recompense for all the good things he had done for her, Gauhar decided to part with him with a conciliatory gesture. She gifted him a house and asked him to live there happily and never again cross her path. Thus ended the 'marital' life of Miss Gauhar Jaan.

Gauhar was glad that she had finally managed to exorcise the ghost of Abbas. She thanked Mr Ganguly profusely for his efforts and even promised to sing at his son's wedding.

But it was a pyrrhic victory for Gauhar. All along, she had left the management of her finances entirely to Abbas and so didn't even know exactly how much she was worth. When the case started she found she was dreadfully short of funds. She had to sell property and jewellery to pay the fees of those high profile lawyers of the city. Her extravagant lifestyle had finally caught up with her.

Emotionally drained and financially impoverished, Gauhar withdrew into a shell. Her finances were dwindling rapidly and concert offers were not forthcoming. People seemed to have got disenchanted with her, especially after the entire court fiasco.

Once again Gauhar stood at the crossroads of her professional life not knowing where to go. But she was not alone. There were thousands of women like her were also affected by the waves of a movement that were sweeping across the nation for sometime now.

Ibteda aawaargi ki josh-e-vahshat ka sabab;
Hum tho samjhe hain magar naaseh ko samjhayenge kya?

I know fully well about the wild times when I started going astray,
But Oh! Advisor! How do I make you give up finding faults and understand
my plight?

✤

14

THE ANTI-NAUTCH CAMPAIGN

Miss Tennant was a British Anglicist, who, like the Christian missionaries, deemed it a divinely ordained responsibility to check the moral decadence of Indians. She had come all the way from England to India with a specific purpose in mind. In a circular dated 19 June 1893 that appeared on behalf of the 'Punjab Purity Association' in all newspapers, she made a passionate appeal to the educated elite of the Punjab seeking their opinions on a matter of great importance according to her. The letter read as follows:

> 'The custom of celebrating festive occasions by nautches prevails in our country. The nautch girls are as a rule, public prostitutes. To encourage them in any way is considered immoral by some people. They hold that the nautches only give opportunities to the fallen women to beguile and tempt young men. There are some, again, who consider dancing girls to be the depositaries of our music and see nothing objectionable in attending nautches. This is a question of vital importance for the moral welfare of young men.

May I, therefore, respectfully solicit your valuable opinion on the subject? If you are of the opinion that nautches are really dangerous to the moral well-being of our youth, I would also invite your suggestions as to how nautches may be done away with, or young men may be restrained, from attending them. All opinions collected will be published.'

The 'Anti-nautch' movement that was unleashed in the country starting the 1890s had its roots in several important social developments in England. The 19th century was one of rising Christian evangelism in Great Britain and decades later this was to have an influence on the cultural life of Indians. The seeds of the anti-nautch movement in India were in a way sown through two important events in the socio-religious life of Britain—the 'Second Great Awakening' (1790-1840s) and the 'Third Great Awakening' (1880-1900). These were evangelical movements that were largely aimed at maintaining the 'moral fabric' of society through religious means. The pressure of the Church forced the British Parliament to create a 'Missionary clause' in the 1813 renewal of the East India Company charter, thereby opening India to missionary activities.

By the middle of the 19th century, the 'Social purity movement' started gaining ground in Britain, influenced by the Max Nordau's concept of 'degeneration' and the Lamarckian theory of evolution. These theories maintained that a preoccupation with gambling, alcohol, sex and other vices would spiral into further indulgence and thereby degeneration. The effect of this physical and moral decadence would be passed on to future generations as well. Of all the vices sexual indulgence was most harmful to the 'health' of society and the State needed to come down on licentious behaviour with a heavy hand, they declared. The spread of sexually transmitted diseases like syphilis both in England and India in the 1850s, seemed to vindicate their claims and made the authorities sit up and take notice.

Several 'Social purity organizations' sprang up in Britain like the National Vigilance Association, the White Cross Army, The Salvation Army and The Church of England Purity Society of the White Cross League (CEPS). Members of these groups harassed people on the streets if they felt they were behaving in an immoral and indecent fashion. Prostitutes and their patrons were their primary targets.

After India was placed directly under the British Crown, post the 1857 War, the British had a greater political clout over the country. This coupled with technological advancements as well as the activities of the missionaries who had entrenched themselves in the country by then, gave the British a free rein to interfere in the lives of Indians.

Since the beginning of the nineteenth century, British opinion had been divided on how India should be handled. The 'Orientalists' believed that local traditions, languages, customs and political structures should be exploited for the effective control of the sub-continent. The 'Anglicists' on the other hand argued that the country should be moulded to reflect British standards, beliefs and mores. The only way to do this was to Christianize the country.

The 1857 War bolstered the ambitions of the Anglicists. The 'Mutiny' was termed as a total failure of the accommodative Orientalist philosophy. The Anglicists set out on the most ambitious social engineering projects in India. One of the first things they advocated was a restriction or ban on free social interaction between the British and the Indians. British residents in India were no longer permitted to have bibis or mistresses. Those who dared to associate with Indian women, especially the tawaifs, were severely reprimanded.

This resentment towards the tawaif had its roots in the proximity of the aristocracy and the feudal lords of the time to the tawaifs. These women were no strangers to court intrigue and many a kotha served as centres of sedition during the 1857 'Mutiny.' After the suppression of the revolt, the British were quick to bring in laws against the tawaifs, especially in the Oudh region which had seen a large uprising. Properties of the tawaifs were seized and zoning laws were enacted that adversely affected them.

The class of neo-literate Indians, armed with modern, English education in schools set up by Christian missionaries, freely embraced Western ideals. They began to look down upon various aspects of their own culture and traditions, especially the performing arts which were now seen to be synonymous with a debased and debauched feudal set-up dominated by tawaifs, prostitutes, nawabs and zamindars. Coincidentally, from this very same class of neo-literate Indians emerged the various social reform movements and the freedom movement. They too held the tawaif in utter contempt.

As the eminent reformer Keshab Chandra Sen postulated: 'Hell is in her eyes. In her breast is a vast ocean of poison. Round her comely waist dwells the furies of hell. Her hands are brandishing unseen daggers ever ready to strike unwary or wilful victims that fall in her way. Her blandishments are India's ruin. Alas! Her smile is India's death.'

The growing disdain for Indian art forms is illustrated by the incident that occurred during Prince Albert Victor's visit to India in 1890. A performance of traditional Indian nautch was organized in his honour. Widespread protests broke out across the country, largely spearheaded by a Christian missionary Reverend J. Murdoch. He chastised the British Government for going back on its 'divinely ordained duty' of cleansing Indian society of the evils of the tawaifs. He issued a number of pamphlets strongly condemning these nautch parties and called upon all British officials to refrain from attending them and thereby legitimizing the nautch. Publishing houses printing mostly religious literature like the Bible started bringing out a huge quantity of anti-nautch literature in the form of books, pamphlets and journals. One of the early agitators against Indian music and dance was the 'Madras Christian Literature Society'.

The clarion call for an abolishment of the nautch was first given in Madras around 1892-93. In 1893 a formal appeal was made to the Governor of Madras and the Viceroy asking them to refrain from attending any 'pernicious entertainment.' The protests and submissions continued unabated for several years. On its part, the Government came up with an official declaration whereby all 'nautch girls' were branded as mere prostitutes. This led to a further hardening of the negative sentiment and in a way painted all the tawaifs, baijis and devadasis with the same brush as those indulging in the flesh trade. The complex and subtle hierarchy that existed within the tawaif and devadasi communities was something that the 'reformers' could not understand. This group of Christian puritans and the elite natives succeeded in preventing a nautch performance in honour of the Prince of Wales in Madras in 1905.

The first formal and legal step to abolish the devadasi system was taken by the Government of the Maharaja of Mysore as early as 1909. Temples in the state were forbidden from utilising the services of devadasis after that. Dance performances in public places, known as '*taffe*' was banned across the

State. The news was received with great jubilation across the country and gave a further boost to the reformers'zeal. Mysore was hailed as a pioneer of social reform.

The anti-nautch movement launched against the devadasis of the South quickly spread to the North, where the tawaifs became the targets. 'Social purity' organisations like the ones seen in Britain in the mid-eighteenth century were established in Northern India to rid society of the pernicious influence of the tawaif. The 'Punjab Purity Association' (Lahore), the 'Social Service League' (Bombay), and a host of others took it upon themselves to work for this hallowed goal.

All these moves sounded a death-knell for the entire class of performing women. Many of them died in penury. A popular proverb of the times describes their plight most aptly: 'The dancing girl was formerly fed with good food in the temple; now she turns somersaults for a beggar's rice.' With no plans for the rehabilitation of these 'fallen' women, the social purists left these condemned practitioners of an ancient art to fend for themselves or reinvent their art and adapt it to the modern situation. Having no options for an alternate profession, most of them resorted to prostitution. Many tawaifs in the North slowly gave up the dance element in their performances and concentrated on music only since it was perceived as a more 'pure' art. Even there, the 'intelligentsia' censored what they considered as erotic or obscene lyrics and genres. All these changes had their impact on the musical instruments as well. The sarangi became synonymous with the decadent tawaif tradition. The harmonium gained respectability as a worthy accompaniment and replaced the sarangi. The word 'Bai' acquired derogatory connotations in the North, and many tawaifs gave up the title in favour of 'Devi' or 'Begum' which signified their 'respectable' background.

Gauhar Jaan, the ever resourceful one, was quick to reinvent herself and adapt to the changing political and socio-cultural scenario. The anti-nautch movement made little difference to the lives of the high-class baijis like Gauhar. The fact that Gauhar took the music out of the kothas and into the more largely accessible format of the gramophone discs, which could be heard and appreciated by a large cross-section of society, was in itself the first major step towards liberating the arts. Performance standards and protocols as also the life-styles of performing musicians, especially women, changed dramatically with this recording revolution.

But even as the reformers amputated an important arm of the performing arts, there was an upsurge in art-revivalism and oriental discourse. It was agreed that a suitable alternative to nautch culture that complied with the scrutiny of the reformers needed to be found. As one respondent to Miss Tenant's circular, Lala Harkrishan Lall, Bar-at-Law, stated:

> 'According to our ancient beliefs and ideas, music and dancing are heavenly, while prostitution is hellish. With you the question ought to be how to divorce blessing from curse and separate one from the other, in this way you may increase purity of life in India and lessen the chances that the devil has to ensnare the youths of the country.'

Intertwined closely with the concepts of cultural nationalism, swadeshi and the freedom struggle, was the discourse on the glory of the performing arts in terms of their antiquity and history, their degeneration at the hands of women who exploited them for their own debased ends and how the arts should be liberated from such misuse. India's ancient civilsation, heritage and culture were utilized to pave the way for a present in which tradition and modernity co-existed. The intention was to create an awareness of the shared culture and history of the entire country, give a sense of national identity and a sense of self-esteem to a people who had seldom thought as one united whole but rather as disparate elements. The arts were easily the most important component in defining this national identity and they had to be sanitized.

As the nautch forms of the north and its variants in the south like the *sadir* dance of Tanjore, started getting increasingly marginalized, a new impetus was given, especially to the revival of the classical dance forms. Between 1920 and 1940 many dancers like the legendary ballerina Anna Pavlova from Russia and Ruth St Dennis and Ted Shawn from the United States contributed to this new awakening by sanitizing the themes of dance and giving it a more structured and modern base. The Indian pioneers included Rabindranath Tagore, Uday Shankar, Madame Menaka, E.Krishna Iyer, Rukmini Devi Arundale, Ragini Devi and others who strove to free dance and music from the social stigma that was attached to them. Kathak and Bharatnatyam rose from the ashes of the nautch and sadir, retained elements of the ancient traditions and adapted them to create a new modern idiom suited to the present times and prevalent socio-political conditions. Ironically, the art of the tawaif was rescued and reinvented, but the tawaif herself was destroyed.

Music saw a similar revival. Organizations like the Gayan Samaj and later the Madras Music Academy played important roles in defining what constituted classical, how it needed to be performed and perpetuated and created a common system of appreciation and valuation in the context of the South Indian classical idiom.

The North too was witnessing major upheavals in this field of modernization of music. Pandit Vishnu Narayan Bhatkhande (1860-1936) and Pandit Vishnu Digambar Paluskar (1872-1931) began a movement to make Hindustani classical music a nationalistic project. Bhatkhande writes in an article titled 'A short historical survey of the music of Upper India (1916): 'The advent of Muslims led to the decline of Hindu arts. They preferred Muslim musicians who distorted the language and purity of Sanskrit verses. The only music heard now is that of tawaifs and their sarangis. The old arts need to be restored.' The duo created a corpus of knowledge in Hindustani classical music. They attempted to standardize its notation so that learning and teaching became simpler. Also, they set up well-accepted models for the performance and transmission of Hindustani classical music. Bhatkhande travelled extensively across the country to study the classical texts on music and interview contemporary ustads and pundits, and wrote a four volume magnum-opus *'Hindustani Sangeet Paddhati'* that clearly defined concepts of ragas and the ideas of notation. Bhatkhande also spent his time in rewriting several bandishes or compositions, expunging them of their original erotic content.

Paluskar had established the first modern music school of North Indian music known as the *Gandharva Mahavidyalaya* in Lahore as early as 1901. This school was open to all, and was structured along the lines of the numerous missionary-run English schools which had been set up in India in the later half of the 19th century. Bhatkhande's 'Tawaif School' was an attempt to bring the tawaifs into the mainstream. It was ironic that the custodians and practitioners of the art form for generations needed a modern school of this kind to hone their skills! And surprisingly, tawaifs like Nanuan and Bachchuan wrote letters to Bhatkhande requesting him to appoint them as teachers in this new school, so that they could earn an honest living. Their appeals fell on Bhatkhande's deaf ears.

An interesting observation made by H.C. Mukerji in response to the Punjab circular makes the purpose of this arts-revival project amply clear. He says:

> 'Let us teach our wives and daughters to practice music at home, so that they may entertain their husbands and brothers. Musical clubs should be organized at all important places, not simply for the private entertainment of the members among themselves but for giving performances on festive occasions.'

In 1921 when the tawaif community organized a meeting and offered to be a part of Mahatma Gandhi's non-cooperation movement, Gandhiji is reported to have unequivocally rejected this 'obscene' proposal. The discrimination continued even after Independence. The Home Ministry under the new Home Minister Sardar Patel issued stringent orders to All India Radio not to permit 'those women whose public lives were a public scandal' to enter their studios!

Thus what the early decades of the 20th century witnessed was not mere changes in the repertoire or style but a major recontextualization in the way the arts were perceived, performed and propagated. With this new approach, the nautch girls, the tawaifs and the devadasis became a thing of the past.

As author Pran Nevile puts it in his *Nautch girls of India*:

> 'Honoured by royal lovers, rewarded by nawabs and nobles, patronized by the European elite, immortalized by poets and chroniclers, pursued by love-sick gallants, the Indian nautch girl, a symbol of glamour, grace and glory and a queen of performing arts, passed into the pages of history.'

Sun chuke haal tabahi ka meri, aur suno
Ab tumhe kuch meri taqreer maza deti hai.

You have heard the tale of my destruction,
There is more to it, so listen on! By now, being accustomed to the sad
tale, you might enjoy it!

❧

15

LIFE AFTER ABBAS

The separation from Abbas left Gauhar bitter and heartbroken. She turned into a misanthrope and seldom appeared in public. But she could not give up her concerts altogether as she needed the money even more now to sustain herself. Most of her wealth had either been swindled away or spent on the case. Despite this dire need for money, she had lost interest in public performances and started being selective in choosing her concerts. One venue where she chose to perform in the 1920s was the home of Bhupendra Kumar Ghosh of Pathuriaghata, a wealthy patron of music and dance. He was the organizer of the famous Music conference known as the '*Banga Sangeet Sammelan*'. The occasion was the wedding of Ghosh's nephew Siddheshwar. Gauhar and Agrewali Malka sang and danced at the wedding all through the night. But Gauhar's soul was not in the performance. Though it wasn't apparent to her audience, she knew that something was missing, and that her involvement in her music was not total, as before. This caused her some anxiety.

In 1920 Gauhar had her first interaction with Mahatma Gandhi. Gandhiji was rasing funds for the Congress Party in Calcutta, in the name of the 'Swaraj Fund,' he requested Gauhar to help his cause. He had heard about her popularity across the country and felt that she could contribute significantly. Gauhar readily agreed and wrote back to Gandhiji saying that she would be very glad to assist the Congress in its struggle for freedom and would perform at a fund-raising concert, but on one condition. She would do this only if Gandhiji attended her concert too and met her in person. Bapu was amused by the lady who laid down pre-conditions for her help and readily agreed to grace the event. On the day of the concert, Gauhar scanned the audience many a times, looking for Gandhiji among the crowd. Unfortunately, some political developments had taken place, so Gandhiji had to stay away. However, he sent Maulana Shaukat Ali as his representative. All the tickets for the concert were sold out and the organizers had collected Rs 24,000 from that one show.

When Shaukat Ali met Gauhar after the concert to collect the donation amount, he was shocked to find her giving him only Rs 12,000. Smiling at him, she said: 'Malauna Sahab, please go and tell your Mahatma that while he speaks of honesty and sincerity, he doesn't seem to keep his word given to a mere tawaif. Since he chose to absent himself from my concert, despite promising to be present, he has kept up only half of his promise. Therefore, I too will give him only half the amount that I originally intended to donate.' The Maulana couldn't say anything. He smiled sheepishly, took the money and left. Gauhar had not quite lost her spirit, and was ready to take on even a person like Mahatma Gandhi!

While Gauhar still did not venture out much, one place she never refused to visit was the zamindari of Mahishadal in East Midnapore district of Bengal. The zamindars there were known as the Rajas of Mahishadal. The family, especially its young heir Maharajkumar Dev Prasad Garg, was an artist, painter and patron of music. He was a student of Muzaffar Khan of the Sikandara gharana. The Mahishadal family were the official hosts and patrons of Ustad Faiyaz Khan in Calcutta. Gauhar had been performing here for a very long time. In fact the first time she had gone there was for the *annaprasan* or rice-eating ceremony of baby Dev Prasad Garg. The relationship had since grown into one of mutual admiration and respect. Whenever their carriages crossed near Eden Gardens, Gauhar would stop and make a polite bow to the Maharajkumar and her greeting was suitably reciprocated.

But for these occasional outings, Gauhar confined herself to her Free School Street House and seldom met visitors and guests there. One hot afternoon, a couple of young students knocked at her door. Gauhar was taking a nap and hearing the maid arguing with someone at the door, she came over to find out who they were. She was surprised to see two youngsters in their late teens standing there and staring at her in complete awe. The frown of annoyance at being disturbed left them completely tongue-tied. One of them finally mustered up enough courage and told her that they had heard so much about her, they wanted to hear her live. In the same breath they also confessed that they were students still and could not afford her fees for a private soiree. The maid was preparing to throw these penniless intruders out, but Gauhar stopped her and asked them to come inside. Concealing a smile, she spoke to them in English, to their amazement. 'So you two young men have come here to listen to me sing? I will gladly do it, but before that I need to note down the names and addresses of your guardians in the city.' The boys were flustered. They got worried that Gauhar would complain to their guardians and they would be punished for visiting the home of a tawaif. 'Hurry up, boys! I don't have all the time in the world to wait for you. If you cannot do even this, I don't see why I should be obliging you.' The youngsters finally gave her the names and addresses and she sang for them with as much sincerity and involvement as she would have in any major soiree. After the concert they thanked her profusely and were about to leave, when she gave them some parting advice. 'Look here, boys, I would never again want to hear that you have gone to the house of a baiji. In case such information comes to my ears or you land up here again, rest assured that I will immediately inform your guardians about your improper behaviour.'

The men hurried away with her music still ringing in their ears. They were overwhelmed at having heard the most famous singer of India in a live, intimate concert, and also pleased at the maternal advice she had given them.

Around 1921-22 a young journalist, Goswami Sudhadhar Dev Sharma, wished to interview her on some topics related to music. Gauhar agreed to meet him after repeated requests from him. Goswami recounts the experience of that interview with her in an interview that he gave to Dr. Trilokinath Brajwal for the *Dharmayug* dated 12 June 1988. On the pre-determined day, Goswami arrived at her place with an assistant who was to take notes during the interview. The interview was to be conducted over two sessions, on two mornings. Goswami states that the very first time he saw her in person he was captivated by her magnetic personality. Although she was almost fifty years old, he says, she had a rare youthful charm that was enhanced by her genteel disposition, her sweet voice and warm hospitality. After some pleasantries when the discussion turned to matters of music, Gauhar immediately guessed that the 30-odd year old Goswami was still trying to 'understand' what music was. She smartly confused him with numerous remarks in Braj bhasha, over which she seemed to have a terrific command, as she did of other languages. He recounts that in her wise presence, his arrogance in his own 'learning' evaporated in a few minutes; so profound was her knowledge.

After a general discussion about the various genres of Hindustani music, Goswami asked her about her favourite form, the thumri. She smiled at him and asked him a counter question. 'Goswami ji, I would request you to kindly let me know what in your opinion is the thumri? What is its scope? Where does it belong?'

Facing three questions simultaneously had Goswami stumped. He started fumbling for words. Seeing his discomfiture she smiled, and expressed sympathy, said, 'Please do not misunderstand me. It is not my intention to make you appear foolish. I am just reminded of one of Kabir's couplets: '*Main kehi samjhaoon, sab jag andha, ek-dui hoi unhe samjhao, sabahi bhulana pet ke dhandha.*' (It is not my business to educate the world, one or two I could still explain but if the whole world is blind (ignorant) then who all do I go around enlightening?) Not wishing to pull his leg any more, she changed the subject and narrated an anecdote of a different kind.

'Just a few days back, Gandhiji had sent his representative Ali Bhai to meet me. He said that Gandhiji wanted me to convey the message of the country's freedom movement through my voice. I was taken aback by this request. He wanted a *hajjam* (barber) to do the work of a *hakim* (doctor)! Moreover, what did I have to do with the freedom struggle? They wanted a donation which I gladly gave. The matter ended there.' By narrating this

incident she was trying to deflect attention from the embarrassing position she had put Goswami in.

As the interview moved to other topics Goswami was stunned to find how well-read Gauhar was, and by her ability to spontaneously quote Sanskrit *shlokas* related to music, Captain Villard's '*Music of Hindustan*' and Hakim Muhammad Karan's book in Urdu called '*Ma-adnul Mausiqui*' written during the time of Nawab Wajid Ali Shah.

Coming back to the subject of the thumri, Gauhar said:

'Much has changed over the centuries, Goswamiji. Dhruvapad is called Dhrupad; Mumbai has become Bombay; Varanasi has become Benares and numerous such alterations of names by people with little knowledge. So it is not for me to conjecture where the word 'thumri' originated from. That is left to intellectuals like you! But I have read of its presence in the musical world for about 300 years and more. Legend has it that in paradise there was a teacher of dance known as Tumburu who was also considered a singer of the Kouthum branch of the Sam Veda. His special singing renditions, replete with dance-like movements and facial expressions, were called '*Kauthumari Pada.*' In fact mention of this *gandharva* or celestial musician has been made by Acharya Sarangdev in his '*Sangeeta Ratnakara*' too. It is likely that the word 'thumri' is a corrupted version of 'Kauthumari Pada' of Tumburu.

Some also claim that the thumri has its origins in Gwalior where the Raja Man Singh Tomar had composed songs and created ragas for his beloved Gurjari wife. Four Gurjari ragas that are still in vogue can be traced back to this time. One raga was called '*Tanwari*' named after the Raja himself. His original treatise on music '*Maan Kutuhal*' is nowhere to be found but the Persian translation of the book by Fakirullah is titled '*Raagdarpan*' and is available. Though it does not mention all that I just spoke about, it says that all music had three dimensions to it—*Gayan*, *Vadan* and *Nritya* i.e. Singing, Playing an instrument and dancing. ('*Geetham Vaadyam Nrityam trayam sangeetamuchyate.*')

The other theory is the one that traces it to the holy land of Vrindavan where Lord Krishna played his famous raas with Radha and the other gopis. To commemorate this celestial dance the priests there sing stories of the leelas or dalliance of Krishna and Radha ('*thumak thumak ke*' as they say in Hindi). Perhaps these songs of the raas leela were set to the lilting rhythm ('thumak') and became known as thumris. Not even one thumri of antiquity exists in any language other than Braj Bhasha. So thumri neither belongs to Lucknow nor to Banaras. It is the sweet butter and jaggery from the place of the Lord's divine playfulness Braj. Wonder how the people of Banaras and Lucknow appropriated the form to themselves.'

Even as Goswami sat speechless at the eloquence of Gauhar Jaan, she broke into a song, a thumri of Kumbhandas

> 'Sakhi ri! Boond achanak laagi
> Sovat huti madanmad maati ghan garjyo tab jaagi
> Dadar mor papeeha bolai, komal shabd suhagi
> 'Kumbhandas' Lal Giridhar so, jaai mili badbhagi'

(O! friend! The rain drops suddenly touched the parched earth that was in deep slumber and the thunder claps awakened it; the frogs croaked, the cuckoos and peacocks cried,
Their sweet and auspicious voices seemed like a celebration of my union with Lord Krishna!)

And then another one:

> 'Udi Jaa panchi, khabar la pee ki
> Jaai Bides milo peetam se
> Kaho bitha birahin ke jee ki
> Sone ki chonch madhaao main panchi
> Jo tum baat karo mere hi ki
> "Madhavi" lao piya kau sandesava
> Jaani bujhao biyoginati ki.'

(Oh bird, fly and carry my message to my beloved who has gone far away. Tell him about the turmoil in my heart. If you promise to keep talking only about me to my beloved, I will gild your beak with gold. Your message will bring succour to my troubled heart.)

Goswami was overwhelmed by this impromptu performance, which, despite the absence of accompaniments, was beautifully rendered, with melody and emotion. Gauhar too realised that she had got carried away a little, and quickly pulled herself back to narrating the history of the thumri.

'The English Captain Villard must have heard such soulful thumris and has written extensively in his book '*Music of Hindustan*' published in 1838 in praise of this form. Similar analyses had been undertaken by Hakim Muhammad Karan in his Urdu compilation, '*Ma-adnul Mausiqui*' written during the time of Nawab Wajid Ali Shah. An elderly gentleman once gifted me a hand-written copy of this lovely book, I had read the whole book with great interest, especially the section on thumri.'

Speaking of the ground that the thumri had traversed Gauhar continued, 'My mother Malka Jaan used to say that when she was young, it was considered absolutely necessary for thumri singers to be trained not only in raag, taal, lyrics and other aspects of vocal rendition, but also abhinaya. Since most women singers were illiterate, they would be at it for years. Occasionally, the sarangiya and tabalchi prompted them and sometimes explained the song. But even their understanding was limited. If a singer decides to sing a thumri, she must know the meanings of the songs, the importance of each word, its context and the 'cultural setting' of the song as a whole. My Ammi was aware of the hazards of thumri singing so she gave it a totally new treatment. She would spend a lot of time understanding the lyrics and their meanings, give it her own interpretation and set it to an appropriate tune. She integrated her dance movements beautifully into the singing as well. Ammi was always sensitive to the audience and the general atmosphere that prevailed in the soiree. She adapted her repertoire to the audience's mood and that helped her to establish an instant rapport with them. This ability of hers was admired by the most eminent khayaliyas and dhrupadiyas of the time. Whatever little I have achieved in my life is only because of the strong foundation that my Ammi laid for my training and understanding of music.

'Unfortunately Nawab Wajid Ali Shah's innovations which were an indecently choreographed version of the raas and called Rahaas corrupted this beautiful lyrical form. But he has been sufficiently punished for this. Even to this day, he stands as a statue in Vrindavan. Don't you know this?'

When Goswami pleaded total ignorance she laughed and said, 'Indeed, a temple in Vrindavan houses his statue. What greater punishment for a Muslim than to be idolized?'

At the end of this two-day interview Goswami came out an enlightened man. The fact that Gauhar had spent so much time and effort on educating this young man shows that the ageing diva was a thinking musician, one who understood the historical and social contexts of her art and had read widely about it.

The threat of oblivion is one of the greatest fears all performing artists have to deal with. Therefore the desire to remain constantly in public gaze and memory becomes an overriding preoccupation for a musician. Gauhar's self-imposed sabbatical, when she consciously withdrew for a while from public concerts and soirees to reconstruct her life, turned out to be disastrous for her. When she finally decided to make a comeback, she was already a spent force in the minds of the public. Some new singer had caught their attention and listening to an ageing diva who had just made a public spectacle of her personal life was not an attractive proposition. As a result, no offers came her way. Gauhar's finances were dwindling, and she was a worried woman.

In her glory years Gauhar could have at least fifteen mujras every month and about seven or eight performances elsewhere, apart from recording sessions. But now things had changed. The Chitpur Road house had been sold to finance the legal battle against Abbas. Other properties she owned too were sold off randomly. She had taken up a small two room house on the fifth floor of a building near the city's Maulana Azad College on Wellesley Street. She began giving music lessons to earn money. But Gauhar once again resorted to her habit of profligate spending. She had some money in the bank which she withdrew and on the advice of some friend decided to invest it in the share market. But as luck would have it, the markets crashed and she lost all her money there as well. Brokers to whom she owed money started harassing her. They filed cases of fraud against her and battling them from one court to the other left Gauhar thoroughly exhausted, physically, emotionally and financially. She sold her houses on Free School Street and also the Gauhar Building to take care of immediate payments to various creditors. Never known for her financial acumen, she had mismanaged her resources to such an extent that she was on the verge of bankruptcy. She began charging her students one rupee as a fee, something she had never done before. It is said that she started selling her compositions for a rupee each to musicians and recording companies. Gauhar Jaan, once the empress of the music world, feted and fawned on by those who mattered in Calcutta society, was reduced to just another ageing, impoverished tawaif.

Her plight became a self-perpetuating loop of misery. Because of her straitened circumstances, she became more reclusive. This reclusiveness meant fewer and fewer invitations to perform, which in turn meant less and less income. On the rare occasions of a public performance, she would request the organizers to send her a vehicle and get in and out of it as unobtrusively as possible. She had started looking and feeling very old. Her eyes became weak and she had to wear spectacles. A sketch of her, done by Maharaja Kumar Debaprasad Garg of Mahishadal, shows an old woman with unkempt hair, wearing huge round glasses, looking downwards with a frown on her face. The sketch carries her signature in Urdu and her name written below in English, possibly by Garg—the date, 3 April 1928.

One of the things Gauhar Jaan could not handle was loneliness. Being alone in her house soon got to her, so she started staying with Agrewali Malka Jaan, a professional rival, no doubt, but someone with whom she shared a warm friendship. When reports of her impoverished condition spread, many people came forward to help her. The Gramophone Company gave her a small honorarium. After all it was her records that had laid the foundation for the Company in India. Bhupendra Krishna Ghosh of Pathuriaghata was another patron who regularly helped old and needy musicians with almost missionary zeal. But his philanthropy was low-profile and unpublicized. It was only after his death, when his private cupboard was opened, did his family discover bills and receipts for the medical treatment of many artists whom he had supported.

Gauhar had been a regular visitor at Bhupendra Krishan Ghosh's home, '*Bagan Bari.*' The concept of the garden house was peculiar to the zamindars of Bengal. Most aristocratic families built palatial houses in the midst of the few acres of farm land they owned, usually outside the city. Women who were 'maintained' by the zamindar were housed in these 'baris' and the place was used for musical mehfils and parties. The produce of the garden, fruits, flowers, would be despatched regularly to the main residence of the owner. The women of the household seldom visited the garden house and generally chose to stay away.

Though Gauhar had performed regularly at the Pathuriaghata house and knew Ghosh to be a very affluent and generous patron, her self-respect prevented her from approaching him directly. She found in Gyan Dutta a well-wisher who would eventually act on her behalf.

Dutta was a cloth merchant and had been a great fan of Gauhar's. He had never missed a single one of her soirees. Despite being totally at variance with both melody and rhythm, Dutta was very keen on learning music. One day he mustered enough courage to approach Gauhar and request her to teach him. She agreed, and taught him a few songs, most of which he made a mess of when singing before an audience. However his spirit and his enthusiasm did not diminish and Gauhar indulged him. She introduced him as 'my friend' and that pleased Dutta no end. He would boast among his circle of friends that Calcutta's most famous baiji called him her friend. He would often land up at Ghosh babu's house as he knew the latter well, and insist on singing the new songs he had learnt from Gauhar. Ghosh would endure the man's singing and then ask with feigned bewilderment, 'Does Gauhar also sing like this?' Gyan Dutta was too naive to catch the sarcasm and would consider it a blasphemy to be compared with her. Embarrassed, he would remark, 'Oh no! She is many times better than this. I am nothing, just trying to learn...' and grin sheepishly.

Gauhar too had never taken him seriously and looked upon him to provide comic relief in her stressful life. She had lost touch with Dutta and for a long time had no contact with him. One day, however, Gyan Dutta happened to see her at Malka's house. She was sitting alone by the window, a pall of gloom on her face. She seemed the very personification of despair and desolation. She wore thick glasses, ordinary clothes and looked preoccupied. When Dutta approached she was terribly embarrassed and tried to quickly rush inside. But he managed to speak to her. He was shocked to see the apparition that Gauhar Jaan had become. Determined to help the lady who had been a kind teacher to him, Dutta decided to speak to Ghosh babu about her condition. Ghosh babu immediately agreed to help her, but all his help would be in kind.

But Gauhar had too much pride to accept anyone's charity. If they paid for her art, it was fine, but living off their largesse was something she couldn't stomach. That thought gradually killed her spirit. She decided to leave Calcutta and find peace elsewhere. A rich patron offered to resettle her in Darjeeling and so she moved there from Calcutta in 1924. In the idyllic and serene mountains of Darjeeling she hoped to find some peace. She was given a big bungalow to live in, practice and teach music. Things were going just fine. Her neighbours were enthralled by her long riyaz sessions and the classes that she held for students from the neighbourhood. But when some people noticed the presence of a young man called Bal Mukunda who frequented her place at all hours, they became suspicious. The same neighbours, who had admired her and marvelled at her musical skill, began questioning her respectability. So they started making loud protests against the presence of a 'prostitute' which was causing the moral degradation of their neighbourhood. It did not take long for a respected tawaif to be viewed as a characterless prostitute! Gauhar Jaan's patron was not very happy with these developments and so he gently asked her to move out and find alternative accommodation.

The entire Darjeeling episode rattled Gauhar. She was growing increasingly restless and constantly looking for some place where she would find peace. But to a tortured mind, peace would not come from the outside. She would have to battle her demons wherever she went. She stayed for a while at Darbhanga but she couldn't really settle down, and she decided to move to Rampur, the place where she had once found great happiness.

But things had changed. Nawab Hamid Ali was no longer the young and romantic prince who had met her in that perfume shop at Calcutta, nor was she the pretty damsel who caught the attention of every passer-by. But the Nawab kept his promise—that the doors of Rampur would always remain open for her, and she was graciously welcomed to the palace. Gauhar was invited to stay in the zenana with the royal women. She blended so well with them that the seven year old daughter of the Nawab, Nawabzadi Nanni Begum Sahiba became very attached to her, and affectionately addressed her as Gauhar Amma. The Nawab Sahab was a linguist, fluent in English, German, French, Persian, Urdu and Hindustani. He was also a lover and practitioner of music. So he recognised Gauhar's intelligence and scholarship, and his respect for her remained as before.

In 1926, Lord Irwin took over as the Viceroy of India. His was an eventful Viceregal tenure when lots of important politically turbulent events took place. In 1927, Lord Irwin planned to make a state visit to Rampur. He was accorded a warm welcome by the Nawab and his officials. Irwin had heard a lot about the famous 'singing and dancing girl from Calcutta' and wished to hear Gauhar Jaan in concert while there. The Nawab readily agreed. An ageing Gauhar seated herself on the stage with two students behind her for vocal support and to play the tanpura. She had dressed in the same flamboyant style that she used to in the good old days. But in addition she had pinned on to her dress, all the medals that she had received in appreciation from various British Government bodies and native Maharajas and Nawabs. It was an impressive array indeed.

Gauhar Jaan's concert that evening did not reflect either her age or her mental state. She was outstanding and her performance enthralled Lord Irwin. He went up to her and congratulated her on her brilliant music. He also expressed a wish to see the array of medals she wore. Breaking protocol, and in an act of questionable decorum, especially in a Muslim Nawab's court, he reached out for the medals. Gauhar was terribly embarrassed to see a white man place his hands close to her chest in an open durbar. Nawab Hamid Ali was livid. But he could do little as he was subservient to the British. After Lord Irwin left, he marched up to Gauhar and with a look of utter contempt, said, 'So you did manage to get a white man to touch your breast, didn't you?' and stormed out. Tears welled up in Gauhar's eyes. She was being accused of indecent behaviour when it was not her fault at all.

After that incident the Nawab's attitude towards her changed. He started avoiding her, seldom gave her opportunities to sing in the court and refused to grant her an audience when she requested it. Gauhar was humiliated and heartbroken at being punished without reason. This coldly hostile atmosphere prevailed for a few months. But when Gauhar discovered one day that the diamonds gifted to her had been replaced by cheap and worthless imitation stones, it was the ultimate blow to her self esteem. This was possibly done by someone in the court who was jealous of her closeness with the Nawab and given their estranged relationship after the Irwin incident, wanted to make the final strike to ensure she was ousted from the Palace. And then continue saying "Gauhar decided to leave Rampur for good. It was early 1928.

She decided to move to Bombay where she had found happiness early in her life. Bombay had a distinctive musical culture and the necessary commercial prosperity to support it, so it attracted hordes of Hindustani classical musicians. In May 1928, she was invited as a guest to Gamdevi in

Bombay, by Seth Madho Das Gokul Das Pasta. He rented a house for her, and made all arrangements for a comfortable stay there. He called Gauhar his sister and showed immense regard and respect for her. To ensure that she stayed there for a while at least, he made her sign an agreement that she would stay for six months in that house and sing at private soirees organized by him.

During one of her concerts in Bombay, the Yuvaraja of Mysore Kanthirava Narasimharaja Wodeyar happened to hear her. He was a colourful personality, deeply interested in the arts and music, especially Hindustani and Western music. He frequently visited Bombay. Gauhar's stellar performance totally captivated the Yuvaraja. He went back to Mysore and recommended to his elder brother, the Maharaja of Mysore, Nalwadi Krishnaraja Wodeyar that the talented Miss Gauhar Jaan deserved to adorn the court of Mysore and not languish as a guest of some Seth in distant Bombay.

Accordingly Gauhar received a telegram from the Dewan of Mysore, Sir Mirza Ismail, stating that the Maharaja wished to appoint her as his court musician. Gauhar was overjoyed. Mysore had always been a pleasant memory for her as she had frequently visited the place right from the days of Chamaraja Wodeyar, the father of the present Maharaja. She requested Gokul Das to let her proceed to Mysore, and offered to pay the rent for the months she had stayed in his house. The Seth graciously waived the rent, saying that as a good brother it was his duty to bid farewell to his sister and wish her well on her new journey. A delighted Gauhar packed her bags and made the final shift of her life, to the kingdom of Mysore.

Sab khadi hain dasta-basta naavke kaatil ke paas;
Ab umeedon ki nishaan kya khaak honge dil ke paas?

Can there be any glimmer of hope for me when everyone I know stands
obediently by the side of my assassin?

—BADI MALKA JAAN, MAKHZAN-E-ULFAT-E-MALLIKA.

❦

16

BLACK HOLE: THE DEATH OF A STAR

Mysore, August 1928

The State of Mysore was one of the largest princely states of India
at the turn of the century. All princely states were under the direct
supervision of the British Resident who was a representative of the
Viceroy. The British had introduced a system of bestowing honours upon
the native princes. One of them was the gun-salute. The greater the number
of gun-salutes, the higher the prestige of the state. Princes and Nawabs
vied with each other for the largest number of gun-salutes. The Nizam of
Hyderabad, the Maharaja of Mysore, the Maharaja of Jammu and Kashmir
State, the Maharaja of Baroda and the Maharaja of Gwalior were the only
five princes to be accorded the 21 gun-salute. Of course the King Emperor
and overlord of all these native princes, the British monarch, was given a
101-gun salute at the 1911 Delhi Durbar.

The lifestyle of some of these princes is what perhaps made Rudyard
Kipling comment that 'Providence created the Maharaja to provide mankind
a spectacle.' They were indeed a spectacle and many of them led debauched

lives far-removed from the aspirations of the common people. There are legendary stories of the marriages of dogs and cats between princely state and the huge expenditure that it entailed on the State exchequer. All this when their people battled intense famines, droughts, poverty and disease. Many of these princely states were thus islands of splendour in an ocean of misery.

But Mysore was an exception. Barring a brief fifty year interregnum under the Muslim usurpers Haidar Ali Khan and his chivalrous son, Tipu Sultan, Mysore was under the reign of the Hindu rulers known as the Wodeyars. They had ruled the state from 1399 and were among India's longest reigning royal families.

From the end of the 19th century, under the enlightened rule of the later Wodeyars, Mysore State pioneered several measures in the fields of political democracy, economic revitalization, social emancipation, infrastructure development, irrigation and power, the spread of education and healthcare. In fact the reign of the Maharaja of Mysore, Nalwadi Krishnaraja Wodeyar (1894-1940) was called the 'Golden era' as it ushered in unprecedented prosperity and growth. Gandhiji in fact likened the kingdom to *'Rama Rajya'* or the ideal government and hailed the Maharaja as a *'Rajarishi'* or a saint among kings. He had in fact wondered if a province that was as progressive, enlightened and prosperous as Mysore even needed freedom.

While Mysore State achieved an all-round growth in social and economic indices, it also emerged as a cultural crucible in the South. With the decline of the Tanjore Court which had been the nucleus of cultural activities until the middle of the 19th century, there was a mass exodus of scholars, musicians, dancers and painters to Mysore. They received generous patronage and encouragement from the culturally sensitive Maharajas. Mysore evolved its own style of playing the veena, the *'Mysore bani'* or *'shaili.'* Several luminaries in the field of South Indian classical music, like Veena Sheshanna, Veena Shamanna, Veena Subbanna, Mysore Vausdevacharya, Bidaram Krishnappa, Mysore Sadashiva Rao, Dr Mutthaiah Bhagavathar, Veena Venkatagiriappa, Mysore Chowdaiah and others adorned the royal court. Under the benign rule of Nalwadi, Mysore also adopted a very modernizing role in the propagation and promotion of music. Scientific theoritization and systematization of musical concepts was greatly encouraged by the musically sensitive Maharaja. For the first time in India, public address systems or microphones were stationed in the palace grounds to enable the public to enjoy the private durbar concerts. Collaborations between Western classical, Hindustani and Carnatic musicians, grand instrumental ensembles and orchestras, musical discourses and debates, healthy competitions among musicians on matters of music, creation of a vast corpus of new compositions and ragas and evolution of a distinctive Mysore style of music were all part of this grand musical revolution.

The most important aspect of the musical environment in Mysore was the element of synthesis, harmony and integration. Eminent Hindustani singers like Ustad Faiyaz Khan, Ustad Abdul Karim Khan, the Calcutta sitarist Aftab Barkatullah Khan and others were invited and honoured in Mysore. Their stay in Mysore over a long period enabled great cultural synthesis and symbiosis. The Carnatic musicians of the court adopted many Hindustani ragas into their repertoire. Abdul Karim Khan got an opportunity to learn under the master, Vasudevacharya, and he incorporated the Carnatic style of *kalpana-swarams* or extempore renditions of solfa notes in the midst of composed music, into the Hindustani tradition as *sargams*. During a short stay of about two years, Sarala Debi Choudhrani, Rabindranath Tagore's niece was exposed to Carnatic music and the Veena of Mysore. On her return to Calcutta she sang these to her uncle Gurudev, who was so impressed by the Carnatic tunes that he composed songs based on them. This entire corpus of songs based on Carnatic tunes created a new genre of Rabindra Sangeet, called '*Bhanga Gaan*.'

It was into this musically steeped atmosphere of Mysore that Gauhar arrived, in the August of 1928. The *Avasarada Hobli* was the department in charge of maintaining the records and emoluments paid to various artists who were in the service of the court. In a memo dated 20 August 1928, Gauhar was formally appointed as the court musician of the Mysore durbar.

'Miss Gohar Jan is appointed a Palace Musician on a pay of Rs 500/- (Rupees Five hundred) per mensem (inclusive of salaries of her musicians and accompaniments) with effect from the 1st August 1928.

Dil Kush Cottage will be given free for residence.

Miss Gohar Jan will be at Mysore during the Birthday and Dasara seasons and on other important occasions when her presence may be required. At other times, she may leave Mysore with permission. She will work under the orders of the Durbar Bakshi.

(For Huzur Secretary)
1. The Durbar Bakshi, Palace, Mysore.
2. Miss Gohar Jan, Palace Musician, Dil Kush, Mysore.'

Dil Kush Cottage was a nice little bungalow nestling amidst the hills, on the way to the Lalitha Mahal Palace of the Maharaja. She had with her a maid servant Sheriffen Patan and a steward Abdul Rahiman, his wife and three children. Patan was a native of Kanpur and was paid Rs 10 per month with food; while Rahiman was from Calcutta and was paid Rs 16 per month with food for the entire family. It was a new chapter in Gauhar's troubled life and she hoped it would usher in good times.

When she received her first month pay, she was a little puzzled to see a deduction which she could not comprehend. She sought the help of Ustad Barkatullah Khan, the sitar maestro from Calcutta who knew her well. He informed her that this was the normal government procedure in Mysore and the deduction was towards income-tax. The issue of the honorarium had already left her a little sore. From the days of spending Rs 20,000 on a kitten's birth to living on Rs 500 per month, which was inclusive of the payments made to all her accompanists was a gigantic come down. This additional deduction upset her even more. While she was grateful for being given a shelter at a time when she was getting increasingly marginalized, she was certainly not the kind to accept things quietly.

In a signed letter dated 24 September 1928, Gauhar Jaan wrote to the Durbar Bakshi requesting him to exempt her from the income-tax deduction:

'Sir,

Aftab-e-Sitar Barkatullakhan, who is my ustad, showed me your letter and also Huzur Secretary Saheb's memo.
You were not pleased to tell me about this deduction towards income-tax when I was entertained. As regards the amount that goes to my musicians, I regret my inability to say about it since it

varies very much. I shall be grateful if you could exempt me from this payment; otherwise the deduction may be made out of my pay as per the rules and I have not the slightest objection.

With respects
I am,
Yours faithfully,
Gohar Jan.'

Along with this letter was enclosed one from Ustad Barkatullah Khan, who was residing at the Barkhat Manzil in Mysore's Nazarbad area. He writes to the Bakshi:

'Dear Sir

As desired by you, I explained to Miss Gohar Jan about the deduction towards income tax and I beg to enclose her letter addressed to you.
The Huzur Secretary's memo is also herewith returned.

I am,
With best regards
Yours faithfully,
Barkatullah Khan.'

These letters were then forwarded to the Finance department, the Huzur Secretary on 27 September 1928 with specific queries about what portion of her salary was taxable and also if the rental value of the free quarters would come under the purview of tax.

The Huzur Secretary perused the documents for a fortnight and sent back a reply to the Durbar Bakshi on 18 October 1928, refusing to grant her any such special status or exemptions.

'Income tax may be deducted as per rules on the whole pay of Miss Gohar Jan, i.e. Rs 500/- as also on Rs 45/- being the rental value of the free quarters Dilkush allowed to her.'

Despite her protests, Gauhar had no option but to comply with these rules. As if this was not enough, another misfortune awaited the already battered Gauhar.

The month of October ushered in the grand festival of Dasara. Mysore was known all over the country for the pomp and splendour with which the Dasara festival was celebrated, keeping up the traditions of the erstwhile Vijayanagara Empire. For ten days there would be lots of religious activity in the Palace and in temples across the State. Along with the puja rituals, each day would witness wrestling bouts, competitions, music and dance performances to regale the royals and the subjects. The royal armoury, weaponry, infantry, cavalry, musical instruments and books in the library would be duly worshipped by the Maharaja. The ten-day celebrations would conclude with an extravagant *Jumboo-savari*, a procession with the Maharaja, the Yuvaraja and his son Jayachamaraja Wodeyar, seated in richly bedecked howdah, carried by an elephant. Preceding them would be colourful displays of folk dancers and performers, musicians, military bands, marches of soldiers and orchestras even as an excited public gathered on the streets to witness this spectacle.

While the whole of Mysore was engrossed in the mirth and merriment of the Dasara festival and Gauhar was attempting to be a part of it, she received the most unexpected blow. She was shocked to receive a legal summons from Bombay. It was to do with a case of defaulting on payments filed against her by Seth Madho Das. He had accused her of not paying the rent that was due to him when she had occupied the house in Bombay; that she had broken the agreement to stay there for six months and suddenly shifted to Mysore. Gauhar could not believe that a man who addressed her as his sister could do this to her. She replied to the Court stating her inability to go to Bombay as her presence was required at the ongoing Dasara celebrations in Mysore, as per the rules of her appointment. After this she wrote several letters to the Seth to sort out the matter but he remained silent.

By then the condition of her eyes was deteriorating and she was advised to go in for eye-surgery in Bangalore. While in Bangalore, she received an exparte decree from Bombay to the 1st Munsiff's Court in Mysore to attach her monthly salary of Rs 500 in lieu of her non-payment and fraud cases filed by the Seth. Her salary was accordingly deducted and she considered the matter settled.

She wished to return to Calcutta for a brief while in February-March 1929 and left with the Durbar Bakshi's permission. Back in Calcutta, the

ghost of Bombay continued to haunt her. Another decree for Rs 500 came
to the Munsiff Court and her salary was again attached.

In great exasperation she wrote a lengthy letter directly to the Dewan
of Mysore, Sir Mirza Ismail from Calcutta, on 6 March 1929, giving him
a detailed description of the sequence of events:

34, Marsden Street, Calcutta

Respected Sir,

I beg first of all to state that there is no other benefactor of mine
in this world after God the Almighty and the Holy Prophet, save
and except the Maharaja Bahadur of Mysore and your goodselves,
his Vazier.

A new calamity has befallen me to add to my several misfortunes
and I may be permitted to give you a detailed information of all
that has put me to further trouble inspite of the fact that I have
taken refuge at your threshold. Considering the fact that your honour
has saved me already from total destruction, I may again place the
holy personality of the same Prince Ali Asghar, the beloved child
of Imam Hosain between myself and your honour, requesting you
to be kind enough to help me at this juncture.

Last year in the month of May '28, I was a guest at Gamdevi,
Bombay, of Seth Madho Das Gokul Das Pasta. The rent of the
house I lived in was paid in the first month by the same Seth and
he had also made arrangements on his own account for my boarding
etc. Mr Seth called me his 'sister' and had shown great regards for
me. He told me to sign an agreement for the house for six months'
residence but for the rent he assured me that he would pay it of
himself regularly. Meanwhile I went over to Mysore as I received
your telegram. At the time of my departure, I enquired from the
Seth if I was to pay the rent but he again assured me that he would
clear it himself.

After a few months of my stay in Mysore, in October last, I received
a Court Summons from Bombay to which I replied that on account
of Dasahara I was unable to attend the court personally. And just after

this I wrote several letters to settle the matter, but he kept silence. One day, Barkatullah Khan Sahab, Aftabi Sitar, came to me and I informed him all about my case. He introduced me to Mr Narasimhayya, the Advocate and I gave him too necessary information. Mr Narasimhayya wrote a note to the Pleader of the Complainant and meanwhile relieved me from my anxieties, saying that the State of Mysore never allowed the enforcement of any foreign decree.

But while I was having my eye operation at Bangalore an exparte decree had come from Bombay to the Mysore 1st Munsiff's Court from where the attachment of my monthly salary was ordered. The decree was for Rs 500/- and half of it was paid from my salary while the other half I paid further from my own pocket.

But again at Calcutta, I was taken with surprise to learn that another decree of Rs 500 had come for a second time to the 1st Munsiff's Court of Mysore and again the attachment of my salary was enforced; as I got from the Durbar Bakshi my monthly allowance only in half. Both the decrees now amounted to Rs 1000/-. I am never sorry for the money in this connection but I am astonished to find this enforcement of second decree without any notice or court summons sent to me at any time before this. This was also exparte decree. I am at such a distance from Mysore that I can do nothing myself. My doctor has advised me to take complete rest for a month more.

May I respectfully solicit your favour to be kind enough as to render a helping hand towards my case and save me from all this. There is none to help us after God and the Five Holy Souls, except the Maharaja Bahaddur and yourself. If you will help me, as you have already obliged me, I am sure I shall be relieved from all my troubles. The Pasta Seth of Bombay being a millionaire himself has broken his pledge with me, though I was his guest, for a few hundred rupees. Had he told me to pay off the rent I would have gladly settled everything before my coming to Mysore. I had left the key of the house with him. Your Honour fully knows that I have got no other means of support except the State monthly allowance. I do hope that Your Honour will not forget me.

With respectful regards to Bari Begum Sahiba and Chhoti Begum Sahiba, and love to Sahibzadi Sahiba.

Yours obediently,
Gowhar Jan.'

The letter was reviewed by the Dewan's secretary and a terse official noting in pencil on the top of the letter sealed Gauhar's fate. It read: 'Please tell her that this is not a matter in which I can interfere. I am sorry and I am unable to meet her. She must consult her legal adviser and act according to their counsel.'

Elaborating on the entire course of action the Palace office filed a status report, dated 13 March 1929.

'Miss Goharjan was appointed as a musician on Rs 500 per month with free quarters with effect from 1ˢᵗ August 1928. A warrant to attach Rs 510/- from her salary was received by the Durbar Bakshi from the First Munsiff Court, Mysore in connection with a civil suit against her in the Bombay Court and in pursuance thereof a portion of her pay was attached and remitted to the Court in January 1929. Before the balance could be remitted information was received from the court that the attachment warrant was withdrawn as she had paid the money out of courts.

Subsequently in connection with another civil suit in Bombay by the same party, another attachment warrant for Rs 511/2 was received by the Durbar Bakshi and in accordance therewith portion of her pay viz. 245-12-0 has been attached from her salary and remitted to the first Munsiff court. She has been asked by the Durbar Bakshi to state if she has settled the claim out of court as she had done in the previous case or else the balance due by her viz. Rs 265-6-0 will be recovered from her salary of February and remitted to the Court. She has wired to him in reply to remit her half other salary.

In her letter to the Dewan Saheb, Miss Goharjan submits that she was duped by one Seth Madhodas Gokuldas Pasta in regard to the rent of the house he rented for her for six months at Gamdevi, Bombay, while she was his guest, that the supreme courts can not execute civil warrants of British courts and she may be kindly helped to extricate herself out of this difficulty. She seems to have been informed in reply by the Private Secretary to the Dewan Saheb that in a matter like this, he could not interfere and that she might act as per advice by her legal advisors. It is seen from her letter that through Prof. Barakatullakhan she has engaged Advocate Narasimhayya who has told her that the State of Mysore never allowed the enforcement of any foreign decree. Apparently she misunderstood the advice of her Advocate and living as at present at Calcutta she can not consult him again presumably till she returns to Mysore.'

Gauhar returned to Mysore and the case was somehow settled with the help of her Advocate. But the loss of money, the deception of the Seth and the precious little help she got from the Mysore State left her further disenchanted. She grew increasingly irritable and restless and the maid and the steward became the favourite targets of her ire.

On their part, the Mysore State authorities seemed to be getting increasingly restive about this new guest from distant Calcutta who brought with her a series of problems which they were now being asked to tackle. Gauhar withdrew further into her shell and in her short stay in Mysore her performances were very infrequent. The Palace records maintain information regarding just 3 performances for which she was paid a handsome Rs 3000 and presented khillats or gifts worth Rs 300.

The ones she did perform in were marked with great ceremony. As old time Mysorean and eminent journalist Mr H. Y. Narayandutt, son of renowned music composer and court musician Shri Yoganarasimham recalls, Gauhar would have a host of orderlies follow her at every soiree. They would attend to her every need, help her on to the stage, and take off her velvet slippers which they would slip into the pockets of their long coats. At the end of the soiree, they would rush back to put the slippers on and assist her to alight from the stage.

The January of 1930 was exceptionally cold and as Mysore froze, Gauhar fell sick. More than a physical illness it was extreme mental fatigue and the chronic depression she suffered from that had taken its toll. Her will to live, to sing, to dance had long died. Her body was getting increasingly affected by the vagaries of her mind. She was admitted to the Krishnarajendra Hospital in the city with high fever. Sheriffen sat by her side for many nights trying to give her a cold pack to reduce the fever, but the fever would not come down. The Durbar Bakshi ensured that she got the best of treatment to help her recover from her illness. But Gauhar had given up the fight. Finally on 17 January 1930, Miss Gauhar Jaan of Calcutta, the Empress of Indian music, the Cuckoo of Calcutta and the first Indian voice to be recorded on the gramophone, was silenced forever. She passed away in a desolate corner of the Krishnarajendra Hospital, lonely and forlorn, with none by her bedside to shed tears for her.

Kasam janaaze pe aane ki meri khaate hain Ghalib
Hamesha khaate the jo meri jaan ki kasam aage.

The ones leading my funeral procession are those who earlier swore by my life!

—Mirza Ghalib

Mera kabhi zabaani poocha na haal dam bhar;
Likhte hain dushmanon ko woh laakh baar kagaz.

They did not bother to even ask me about my welfare,
Now they write reams to my enemies!

—Badi Malka Jaan, Makhzan-e-ulfat-e-Mallika.

※

17

AFTER THE END

Mysore, 1930

The death of the famous singer-dancer of Calcutta and the gramophone celebrity was widely publicized across the country in several newspapers. *The Statesman* of Calcutta reported her demise on Tuesday, 28 January 1930 in its 'Stage and Screen' section:

'A loss has been sustained by the death in Mysore of Madame Gauhar Jan, where she was court singer and danseuse to H.H the Maharaja of Mysore. Born in 1873, of European parentage—her father being Mr Robert William Yeoward, planter and engineer, and her mother, Adeline Victoria Hemmings, Gauhar Jan was christened Eileen Angelina Yeoward. At the age of 6, Miss Eileen embraced Islam at Benares, with her mother. The mother adopted the name of Malka Jan, and the daughter that of Gauhar Jan. It was in 1883 that Gauhar Jan first came to Calcutta under the patronage of H.H. the late Nizam of Hyderabad, and she had lived practically all her life here, with the exception of two years in Bombay and occasionally tours of the country, and the last two years in Mysore.

Her fame as a songstress earned her the title of 'Indian nightingale' and when gramophone records were first made of Indian songs, she was the first to be approached. When Maud Allan, Madame Anna Pavlova and Madame Calve of Paris visited India, they were entertained by Gauhar Jan. Pavlova's praise for Indian saris brought her from Gauhar a most expensive sari and a choli (jacket) which she still treasures. Sir Harry Lauden was also introduced to Gauhar Jan and was delighted by her singing. She leaves a number of pupils in India to perpetuate her art.'

Meanwhile, back in Mysore, the Durbar Bakshi's office submitted a letter to the Huzur Secretary informing him about the death of Miss Gauhar Jaan. It was settlement time and the various arrears that were due to the Mysore Government by the deceased had to be settled. In the letter dated 22 January 1930, the Bakshi's office states:

'Miss Goharjan was an inpatient in the Krishnarajendra Hospital and died there on Friday, the 17th instant. She was in receipt of a pay of Rs 500/- per month in the Sangeetha firka of this Elakha and after deducting a sum of Rs 8-8-0 towards the payment of income tax, the net amount payable to her for the month of December 1929 was Rs 491-8-0. Under orders of the Assistant Secretary, out of the above amount of Rs 491-8-0, a sum of Rs 250/- was paid to Miss Goharjan on the 15th instant to meet certain of her expenses at the Hospital. Now a sum of Rs 241-8-0 is to her credit in the pay bill and she is entitled to her pay till the 17th instant of this month.

It is ascertained that she maintained one maid-servant by name Sheriffen Patan and one Steward by name Abdul Rahiman with his wife and 3 children. The former viz., maid servant, it is ascertained, was paid Rs 10/- with food and the latter Steward with his family Rs 16/- with food per month and that the maid-servant is a native of Cawnpore and Steward is a native of Calcutta. They complain that they have nothing to eat and that they want to go back to their native places.

As may be observed from the Huzur Secretary's No 4845 dated the 21st January 1930, a sum of Rs 18-12-0 is due by Miss Goharjan to the City Municipal Council, being the water charges for the Palace building occupied by her.

Finally, I am submitting herewith the D.O. letter dated 22nd instant, received from the officer in charge of Krishnarajendra Hospital regarding the dues to the said hospital from late Miss Goharjan.

The matter is submitted for kind orders

Achappa (SD/-)
(For Durbar Bakshi)'

The Huzur Secretary's office perused all the accounts in detail provided by the Bakshi's office and decided to settle the matter. Gauhar owed the hospital 4 Rupees and 8 annas and the city municipality water charges of 18 Rupees and 12 annas. These were paid off from the balance due to her. The Maharaja's government also decided to bear the railway fare for Sheriffen and Abdul to enable them to return to their native places. In addition they were to be given a bonus of Rs.50 and Rs.100 respectively as they had lost their jobs. Whatever amount remained was to be given to any legal heir who was entitled to it.

However there were many more people to whom Gauhar owed money and they demanded a settlement of their dues. Dr A.J. Ram & Sons, the 'Chemists, druggists and scientific opticians' who had their shop at Sayaji Rao Road in Mysore wrote to the Huzur Secretary on 20 February 1930 informing him that the deceased had to pay them about 17 Rupees and 11 annas for medicines and appliances supplied to her. They enclosed a detailed bill for the medicines she had purchased from August 1929 that had remained unpaid. These payments too were duly made by the Palace. The palace electrician sent in his claims on 13 March 1930 of 7 Rupees anc. 5 annas. Similar claims were made by Mohammad Jabber of Ghulam Humza & Sons, Bakers and Confectioners, for the sum of 3 Rupees and 14 annas for thirty-one loaves of bread supplied to Dil Kush cottage; Adishesha Rao, the tailor, for making shirts, jackets and other garments for 18 Rupees and 6 annas; Linga the milkman, for 6 Rupees and 14 annas; Krishnaiya the washerman, Rs 4; and Siddha the scavenger, Rs 4. The Huzur secretary's office settled all these claims which totalled 354 Rupees and 2 annas. A balance of 156 Rupees and 13 annas still remained in the credit account of the deceased.

Sheriffen and Abdul bid their farewell to Dil Kush Cottage and Mysore. Some people believe that Gauhar's body was taken to Calcutta and buried there, as no references to the site of her grave in Mysore have been found. However this theory doesn't seem plausible, given the distance between Mysore and Calcutta and the absence of a direct train or any other mode of transport between them. So it is quite likely that Gauhar was buried in Mysore itself, but since she did not have any family as such, no one bothered to mark her grave with a tombstone or monument.

It took 2-3 months for the Durbar Bakshi's office to settle all the financial matters of Gauhar and they were about to close the case when several 'family members' flooded the Palace offices with letters claiming close relationship with the late singer and demanded their share of her 'estate.' Gauhar, who, when alive didn't really have the comforting shoulder of a loving relative or friend to cry on, suddenly had innumerable 'relatives' mourning her loss!

Gauhar Jaan's obituary in the Statesman was noticed by one man who deemed it fit to write directly to His Highness, the Maharaja of Mysore on 3 February 1930 enquiring about the deceased:

42, Grand Square, Dinapore Cantonment.

To His Highness the Maharajah of Mysore

Your Highness,

I beg that you will pardon me my presumption in writing to inquire about my daughter, Madam Gauhar Jan, who was a singer at your Highness' court. I beg to state that I, Robert William Yeoward, am living and that I am Madam Gauhar Jan's father. On reading the account of my daughter's death in the 'Statesman' of the 29-1-30, I, being her sole living parent, would be very grateful if your Highness will condescend to order that full particulars be sent to me of her death and also information regards her property and who has taken possession of the same.

Thanking your Highness in anticipation,

I beg to remain
Your Highness' Obedient servant ·
R.W. Yeoward.

A man who had asked for Rs 9, 000 to acknowledge his daughter in the court and had never bothered to keep in touch with her thereafter suddenly seemed to have been overcome by paternal love!

Mr Rama Rao of the Huzur Secretary's office wrote back to Yeoward on 11 February 1930 stating that the property of the late Miss Gauhar Jan was before the City Magistrate in Mysore and that he should apply to them directly for any more information regarding the same. The letter skips any details about the cause of death. In fact none of the records, including the hospital discharge summary, make any reference to the cause of Gauhar's death. The Mysore records have every detail of how much she owed whom, but nowhere is the cause of death or the place of internment mentioned. Not even in her death certificate (No 1559/159) registered by the Mysore City Corporation's Registrar of Births and Deaths on 18 January 1930!

On 1 February 1930 the Dewan's office received another letter, this time from the office of a leading solicitor of Calcutta. N.C. Bose & Co:

10, Hastings Street, Calcutta

To
The Dewan,
Mysore Government

Dear Sir,

Estate Gouhar Jan-decd.

We are instructed by our client Mr S.G. Abbas Sabzwari, the husband of the deceased above named to apply to the High Court

Calcutta for letters of Administration to the estate of the above named. Our client is informed that the jewelleries, ornaments and other belongings of the said deceased are in the custody of your Government for protection. As our client will have to set out in his affidavit of assets the particulars thereof, we have to request you to be good enough to furnish us at your earliest convenience with a complete list of the jewelleries and other belongings of the said deceased in the custody of your Government.

An early reply is solicited,

SD/-

They too received an identical copy of the reply sent to Yeoward.

After having ended his marriage with Gauhar following a public spat, Abbas suddenly resurfaced to proclaim his love for his deceased wife! Abbas' requests to the City Magistrate seeking details of her property in Mysore elicited another sharp reply that advised him to come to Mysore and inspect the property and prove the legitimacy of his relationship before making his claim. The tenacious Abbas had the audacity to write to the Government of Mysore requesting State accommodation, as though he was coming to Mysore as a royal guest! Interestingly another letter to this effect, dated 8 March 1930, reached Mysore from 34, Marsden Street, Calcutta —the same address that Gauhar had used when she had written to the Dewan of Mysore, seeking his help.

'His Highness
The Maharaja of Mysore,
The Palace, Mysore.

Respected Sir,

I have received a letter from Your Highness' Private Secretary, along with one from the City Magistrate of Mysore, to the effect that I should reach Mysore personally to lay my claims in Court for the possession of the property left by my wife, the late Madam Gohar Jan during this past month. I intend to start for Mysore now, but as I shall be quite a stranger there, I do hope your Highness will be kind enough as to allow me some place of accommodation in any of the State houses, for my short stay there. Formerly, I used to put up at 'Dilkusha' which had been so kindly given to my wife for residence; but now alas! She is no more!

Praying for an early and favourable response,
I remain,
Your Highness' obedient servant
S.G.Abbas Subzwary.'

The demands made by Abbas in the letter were preposterous. In a terse reply dated 19 March 1930, the Huzur Secretary wrote back that 'his request for accommodation during his stay here can not be granted.'

At about the same time, a letter arrived from a Mysore-based solicitor Advocate Mohammad Waleeullah. He had enclosed the power of attorney to handle the case given to him by his client, one Mir Kumbharhal Ali. Kumbharhal Ali was a Mysorean and claimed that he had wed Gauhar Jaan when she was in Mysore! Through his advocate he wrote to the Huzur Secretary on 8 February 1930.

'Most Respected Sir,

Please allow me to bring a few lines for your kind consideration and perusal.

The Petitioner's legally wedded wife Goharjan was an employee in the Mysore palace for the purpose of singing on a monthly pay of Rs 500/. She died on or about the 17th January 1930 in Mysore, leaving this petitioner, to all her properties, as her sole heir and also as a sole legatee under a will. To the best of information and knowledge of the petitioner, Goharjan has no other heir at law.

For the purpose of treatment when my wife Goharjan fell ill last, for burial expenses, for performing her 3rd and 10th day religious ceremonies, this petitioner as becoming her husband and heir has so far spent more than 300 rupees from his own pocket. Now the 20th day and 40th day ceremonies are yet to be performed. All this means an additional expense of Rs 500/ and more.

This humble petitioner prays that you may be pleased to pay him Goharjan's arrears of pay, if any, money usually granted to the relatives of employees who are deceased towards funeral rites, and money which Goharjan would have been given as her marriage present had she been alive.

I need hardly say that the sums thus to be bestowed upon me will go towards the performance of remaining rites with view to give peace and rest to the departed soul of my wife Goharjan.

For this act of your kindness I shall ever remain grateful to you.

Begging to be excused for this trouble and heartily thanking you in anticipation.

I beg to remain,
Most respected Sir,
Your most obedient servant
Mir Kumbharhal Ali.

Interestingly, the husband who did not even know the exact date of the wife's demise, as mentioned in the letter above as 'on or about 17 January,' seemed so keen to perform the funeral rites according to religious customs!

To complicate matters further, Abdul Rahiman, the Steward, returned to Calcutta and sent in his prayer for monetary assistance.

'One Sheikh Abdur Rahaman, son of late Shaikh Doma of Sirajuddowla's bazaar, Murshidabad, now residing at 23/1, Canal East Road, Seth Bagan, P.O.Sham Bazar, Calcutta represents that the memoralist was serving under late Miss Goharjan, that since her death he has been struggling hard for the maintenance of the family, that he has to make provision for the following according to the wishes of late Miss Goharjan from her estates and properties:

1) The grave of Miss Goharjan should be made pucca and Mullah should be appointed for recital of the Holy Koran at the place.

2) A sum of Rs 5000/ should go to the Mohamaden orphanage at Calcutta.

3) A sum of Rs 2000/ should go to the Shiah Fund at Mysore, and prays that in order to fulfil the wishes of late Miss Ghorajan and to maintain his family orders may be passed and some pecuniary help granted.'

The Mysore Government was thus bombarded with letters from a host of claimants. Given Gauhar Jaan's popularity, success, lifestyle and tastes, all these people believed that she would have amassed a huge fortune while in Mysore and they spared no efforts to try and lay their claims to it. The Government on its part left it to the discretion of the City Magistrate Mr M. Chennaraj Urs (B.A., L.L.B.) to settle the matter in the favour of anyone whom he deemed as the rightful legal heir.

Mr Urs directed both the major claimants, Abbas and Mir Kumbharhal, to present themselves in his Court, place their arguments and claims which would help him in settling the matter. Not one to give up to an anonymous Mysorean, Abbas used all his contacts and managed to enlist the support of Mr J.C. Mukherjee, the Chief Executive Officer of the Calcutta Municipal Corporation. Mr Mukherjee was persuaded to travel to Mysore and testify before the Magistrate that Gauhar was indeed Abbas' wife and that he was the sole heir of her immense wealth. Mr Urs gave a patient hearing to the arguments of both sides but Mr Mukerjee failed to impress or convince him. He finally dismissed the claims of both the parties and decreed that if there was any other claimant he should approach his Court within the next six months with all relevant proof to the assets, failing which the said property of the deceased would be taken over by the Government of Mysore.

This farce that was going on in Mysore captured the imagination of the press in Calcutta too. The famous Bengali journal *Kheyali,* published a detailed article on the entire drama on 17 January 1931. It started with a verse addressed to the late Gauhar Jaan, in an obvious reference to Abbas:

'Kutile kutil prane chinali nako, shyam je ki rothon'

Hidden as it was in darkness, you did not realise how crooked it was, what you considered as a jewel.

The report then goes on to say that 'the finest singer-dancer Gauhar Jaan has died. After her death, in distant Mysore, the battle has begun between

Shunda and *Upashunda*, the mythological demons who fought with the Goddess Chamundi. The City magistrate Mr Urs is seized of the matter. Abbas Subzwari of Calcutta has claimed to be her husband and legal heir, while in Mysore Mir Kumbharhal declares he is her spouse. To prove Abbas's legal claims on her estate, Mr J.C.Mukherjee, the Chief Executive Officer of Calcutta Corporation, has travelled all the way to Mysore to depose before the Court.' Taking a dig at Abbas's efforts, the article says, 'Obviously his witness is of great value. Abbas Subzwari is no mean *jauhari* (jeweller) himself and knows the value of good witnesses. No wonder he has taken the best jewel of Calcutta, Mr Mukherjee, as witness to Mysore! But alas! Mukherjee's evidence has been dismissed by the Magistrate Mr Urs, as also that of Mir Kumbharhal. The Magistrate has passed an order stating that besides these two claimants if there is any one else who professes to be her legal heir, he/she should depose before the court with proper evidence within the next six months.' The article comments on how all of Abbas Miya's efforts went in vain, leaving him sad and frustrated. It also states: 'What happened in Mysore? Even the evidence of the venerable Chief Executive Officer has not been admitted. This is an insult and affront to the people of Calcutta. Why don't we organize mammoth protest meetings in the Town Hall of the City to condemn this insult to our first citizen?'

A poem was also published in the same journal, along with this article, highlighting the absurdity of the whole matter. It was titled '*Chief-Gahar Jaan samvad*' or a dialogue between the Chief of the Calcutta Corporation and the late Gauhar Jaan, a free translation of which is given below:

> Everyone knew that Gauhar Jaan was a great singer and dancer.
> But did people know what else she did besides this?
> What kind of rice she ate, what time she retired to bed, whether she slept at all,
> None of this has come out in any newspaper – monthly, daily or fortnightly
> Which reporter of any reputed newspaper has ever bothered to gather these details?
> Just because you are the Chief of a city's corporation are you privy to every personal detail of the citizens?

If you are the cook in a large feast, do you taste all the dishes being cooked?

Gauhar has left for her heavenly abode, abandoning all the insignificant possessions of this world,

But seeing the extent of her assets, people's hopes of their own glorious future have brightened,

Whether her property got her happiness one does not know, but it certainly got her two husbands, Mysore's Mir Kumbharhal and Abbas of Calcutta

Watching this drama from her heavenly abode, Gauhar seems to be having the last laugh!

To prove you are someone's husband you need evidence, my dear friends,

Both husbands are now worried about where to cook up this evidence from

After a lot of search and consideration, Abbas Ali got the Corporation Chief's witness,

The bees are stealing the honey from the city of gardens (Mysore)

Abbas is convinced that the evidence of the honourable Chief should seal the case in his favour and the claims of his marital status would carry more weight,

The Chief condescended, packed his briefcase and left for Mysore's court.

After all he is the Corporation Chief and must have all the news,

What is happening in the city? Who is whose wife or husband? Is it a legal or unlawful relationship?

Whose calf has drunk milk from whose cow's udder?

Whose cot has a mattress that is smaller than the length of the cot?

Yes, indeed, the Chief is a knowledgeable man and knows all of this!

Both husbands have submitted their evidence, and much drama ensues

But the case is dismissed, both the *miyas* are deprived

The judge passed an order, any relative if alive, present yourself in the court.'

It was tragic that Gauhar's life had become a subject of ridicule in local newspapers and journals.

The persistent Abbas kept making repeated claims even after the dismissal of the case. Eight years after the death of Gauhar, he still kept filing petitions with the Government of Mysore. In a report dated 2 November 1938, the Palace office notes that S.G. Abbas Subzwari had written to the Private Secretary to the Maharaja of Mysore:

'The Petitioner prays that the properties belonging to the late Madam Gauhar Jan be handed over to him. Similar application received in May 1938 has been forwarded to the Chief Secretary to the Government, Bangalore for disposal. Submitted for kind orders, whether this too may be sent to the Government.' In the official noting it is stated that 'the property was confiscated to the Government as it was held that there were no legal heirs. This petition too may be sent to Government.'

The Mysore records speak no more of Abbas after November 1938.

Two years later on 24 July 1940, Abdul Rahiman made his final attempt at soliciting help from the Mysore Government.

'To His Excellency the Maharaja of Mysore,
Re: Late Gouharjan's properties
Most respectfully sheweth,

'That your memorialist was in personal attendance to the said Miss Gouharjan till her death at the Rani hospital in Myseor. That your memorialist submitted a petition to Your Excellency, requesting to grant a provision out of the properties of late Gouherjan on which your memorialist has been informed 'that the Mysero Govt. can not do anything in the matter.

'That the said Miss Gouherjan used to maintain your memorialist with his whole family consisting of 4 members, besides paying your memorialist a monthly allowance of Rs 18/ p.m.

'That several persons of her heirs have got their shares out of the properties of late Gouherjan, but instead of my so long honest and faithful services, I have been deprived of the provision.

'That your memorialist is in a great deal of difficulty and starving with his family in these hard days.

'In the circumstances your memoralist most humbly prays that Your Excellency may be graciously pleased to appoint me to the post of Durwan in any of Your Excellency's Calcutta properties or grant me some pecuniary help, and thus save your memoralist and his family, from dying in starvation.

'And your humble memoralist, as in duty bound, shall ever pray.

Abdul Rahman
1, Damzen 2nd Lane,
Room No 5, Tiretta Bazar, Calcutta.'

Apart from an official noting of 16 August 1940 with the terse 'May be filed' it is not known whether he received help or not. Nor is there any information on what became of both Abbas and Abdul.

This is also the last reference to Gauhar Jaan or any of her acquaintances in the Mysore Palace records. She was slowly pushed into the recesses of memory of not only Mysoreans, but of Hindustani musicians, music lovers and connoisseurs across the country.

Na pooch naamaye aamaal ki dil aawezi
Tamaam umr ka kissa likha hua paaya.

Do not ask me how fascinating the record of my deeds is,
I found the entire story of my life narrated there!

Hum tho markar bhi kitabon mein rahenge zinda;
Gham unhi ka hai jo mar jaayein tho guzar jaate hain.

Even in death I will remain immortal in the books that are written about me,
Pity those who don't just die, but 'pass away' into oblivion!

❧ ❦ ❧

EPILOGUE

The recording and entertainment industry in India continued to make great strides. Electrical recording replaced acoustic/mechanical recording in 1925. The Radio emerged as a popular medium and after an era of silent films, sound started entering Indian movies. The Gramophone Company Ltd. and the Columbia Graphophone Company Ltd. merged and registered a holding company known as the Electrical and Musical Instruments (EMI) in 1931. Stereo recording and reproduction was patented. By 1952, EMI started launching its first Long Playing (LP) and Extended Play (EP) vinyl records. With Independence, the Governments and music associations donned the role of the new patrons for the art. By 1960 the last 78 rpm records were issued and finally stopped completely in the 1970-80. By then the advent of television changed the way Indian households looked at entertainment.

Starting with the first ever CD factory in England, launched by EMI in 1986, the 1990s ushered in a new era of hi-fi equipments, audio/video cassettes, recorders and players. Gramophone records were now antique pieces that were in the private and closely held possession of jealous collectors, each wanting to vie with the other in terms of quantity of their possession. They were and continue to be sold at princely sums in the *chor-bazars* of many cities like Delhi, Mumbai, Kolkata and Bangalore. With the dawn of the new millennium and the advent of the CDs, DVDs, the MP3 players, the iPods, the iPhones, state of the art modern recording studios, digital mixing and remastering and a host of technologies, the old, three minute clips sung in great speed and in a high pitch by someone like Gauhar Jaan might appear shrill and unsophisticated. Who would care to remember the doyen of the Indian recording industry in the wake of such momentous and mind-boggling changes? She was thus slowly reduced to becoming a barely discernible figure who did not warrant even a casual mention in the annals of Indian musical history. Hindustani music had found new icons and idols and the cuckoo from Calcutta was nowhere in their gallery of fame.

However there were some genuine connoisseurs who occasionally congregated and celebrated her life and its achievements. In April 1968, a photograph of Gauhar Jaan presented by one Mahmudbhai was unveiled at the Deodhar School of Indian music (Trinity Club, Bombay) by its President Seth Khataubhai Vallabhadas. In his address he told the gathering: 'Gauhar Jan conquered the hearts of *rasikas* (aficionados) through her emotion-filled, lyrical, and melodious thumris in which she was declared the queen.' The function was attended by the who's who in the then world of Hindustani music in Bombay. 'Gayan Tapaswini' Moghubai Kurdikar, Dhondutai Kulkarni, Ustad Azmat Hussain, Ustad Latafat Hussain, Masit Khan, Mohammad Ahmad Khan, Gulu Seth Dasdanwala, Vamanrao Deshpande and others. Shri Deshpande recalled how her style had influenced Govindrao Tembe to introduce the Purabi-ang in Marathi Natya Sangeet. Mahamudbhai who had studied under Gauhar Jaan for a short period of time demonstrated the salient features of her music through some of her famous khayals and thumris like '*Aan baan jiya mein lagi,*' '*Hamse na bolo raja,*' '*Tan man din ja sanwariya,*' '*Maika piya bina kacchu na suhave,*' '*Raske bhare tore naina,*' her own thumri composition which was a favourite among singers like Begum Akhtar and Siddheshwari Devi and '*Piya chal hat tori banawati bat na mane ri.*'

For researchers seeking to know more about Gauhar Jaan there are just too many road-blocks. The fact that there were many women with the same name with slight variations in spellings complicates matters. Gauhar Jaan of Patiala, Gauhar Jaan Jaipurwali, Miss Gohar (associated with the Parsi Theatrical Company in Bombay), Gohar Mamajiwala (singer and actress who was also the mistress of film producer Chandulal Shah of Ranjit Studios in Bombay) and Miss Gohar Bai Karnataki of Bijapur (who was associated with Bal Gandharva and was his mistress for long) among others, were celebrities who bore the same name. Some scholars tend to mistake one for the other in their research and often come up with contradictory facts about her life.

For instance, it has been mentioned that Gauhar acted in films and plays in 1924-27 while in Calcutta and Bombay. Given her physical and mental state, this seems highly unlikely and could be a case of mistaken identity. At best, Gauhar might have lent her voice for some musical productions in Calcutta. But acting in them and that too at the fag end of her life, when she was an emotionally broken woman seems highly unlikely.

Another controversy that revolves around Gauhar's ethnic origins is the oft repeated assertion that Gauhar was an Armenian Jewess. This also seems misplaced. Though she was of Armenian Christian descent thanks to her father and of Anglo-Indian origins due to her mother's mixed parentage, there is nothing to suggest her Jewish origins. It must be recalled that Jews seldom or never convert to Islam and hence the fact that Gauhar and her mother did convert debunks the claims of her Jewish descent.

Meanwhile, the Gramophone Company in its new Indian avatar of HMV/Saregama reissued 18 songs of Gauhar Jaan in 1994 on audio tape and CD under the banner of 'Chairman's Choice,' which sadly went unnoticed. Meanwhile committed enthusiasts of organizations like the Society of Indian Records Collectors and its zealous and devoted honorary Secretary, Shri Suresh Chandvankar and others have been conducting lecture-demonstrations, presentations and listening sessions of Gauhar's music, thereby trying to keep Gauhar's memory alive to an extent. But in this age of information explosion and media invasion, the lives of gramophone celebrities of India hardly hold public attention.

◆

I took a long look at the garish, pink building that is now named 'Salim Manzil.' My car had difficulty navigating the road that once was Chitpur Road, but is now known as Rabindra Sarani. Bursting at its seams with numerous hawkers, shopkeepers, road-side eating joints, vehicles and cattle, all jostling for space in its narrow confines, the road would be any motorist's worst nightmare.

Pandey ji, my hitherto affable driver, refused to get into those narrow lanes and stopped the car far away from the entrance to the Nakhoda Mosque. Calcutta was smouldering in the heat of May at 45 degrees. Putting on my cap and goggles, I decided to leg it out. Being unsure of the exact location of the mansion called 'Gauhar Building', I made a couple of enquiries. One of the shopkeepers selling chappals by the roadside was an old man with a goatee and skull-cap and a face crowded with wrinkles. When he heard my query his face lit up, and with a broad smile, said, 'Gauhar Bai? You are looking for her house? Whatever for? Are you a journalist?' I replied in the affirmative and told him I was just filing a short story about her. '*Haan*, Sahab, she is now just a story for you journalists. But in her heyday, she ruled this street, this city, and in fact the whole of Hindustan. I am about 90 years old now and have fond memories of Gauhar Bai's enchanting music. My parents too would somehow manage to listen to her at some of the community gramophone playing centres. *Wah sahab! Kya zamana tha*, what an era it was!' He closed his eyes recalling those days. I woke him from his reverie and asked him where I could locate 'Gauhar Building.' He pointed to a massive structure right next to the large and imposing Nakhoda mosque.

As I neared the building, I was overcome with numerous unknown emotions. Having set out on a journey with no end or road-map in sight, I was now standing right in front of ground-zero—the place where the 'Cuckoo of Calcutta' spent a large part of her life. Images of her famed horse-drawn carriage trotting across these very lanes, the sounds of the melodious music that must have emanated from behind those walls during the numerous mehfils that this venue had witnessed and the buzz of guests clamouring to get inside, played in my mind's eyes. When I asked why the building was now called 'Salim Manzil' and not 'Gauhar Building,' another old Muslim gentleman who was selling fruit juice from his portable vending machine told me that after the court cases with Abbas, Gauhar was forced to sell the house. Since then it had changed many hands and was now named this way. The three-storeyed building had clothes drying from the parapet grills on the upper floors while the fleet of shops on the ground floor sold a variety of goods from hardware to foreign currency! I wondered if any of them knew the historical significance of the building they occupied.

Calcutta has come a long way since the time Gauhar left it for Mysore. Its name has changed, generations have passed and new musical interests, icons and patrons have taken over. But while Gauhar's memory is completely lost in most of the other parts of the city she called her home, she still lives on in this narrow lane. People here have neither forgotten her life nor her exquisite music. She might still be the topic of discussion in many a tea-time *adda*.

Pandey ji decided to become his usual affable self again. Even as I stood there lost in thought, he navigated the car through the narrow, crowded lanes and halted it near the place where I stood. His honking interrupted my chain of thoughts. 'Babu, do you plan to stand here and stare at that ugly-looking building? What do you find so attractive about it that you have come all the way looking for it? We must leave now; the traffic will get worse in the evening.' I smiled, didn't answer any of his questions, took one more deep, long look at that pink building and got into the car.

The opening verses of Badi Malka Jaan's *Makhzan-e-Ulfat-e-Mallika* passed through my mind. They seemed so appropriate not only for herself, but also for her beloved daughter, Gauhar.

'In the loneliness of my grave, I opened my eyes and looked around
The mourners had come, cried, given me my ceremonial burial and left.
It was when I was left all by myself, far removed from the colours of life
That the real thrust of my miserable existence hit me hard,
I mourned my life, while my near and dear ones mourned my death.
In the loneliness of my grave, my mourning continued
But wasn't it too late?'

APPENDICES

꧁

APPENDIX I

THE COMPLETE DISCOGRAPHY OF GAUHAR JAAN

(*Courtesy: 'The Record News,' the Journal of the Society of Indian Records Collectors, Volume 9, January 1993*)

Company name: The Gramophone and Typewriter Ltd and sister companies.
Location: Calcutta
Date of recording: November 1902
Recorded by: Frederick William Gaisberg
Type of record: 7-inch – originally single-side recorded disc.

SI No	Matrix	Catalog	Title	Pressing & Issue date
1	E1022	13037	Miss Gauhar Jan (1st Dancing Girl) – Calcutta Dagar Na Jaani Jaabe Kaise-Tune Dadrah [Mahomedan Song] s/s s/s c/w 2-12303 c/w 2-12303 Re: HMV E 9	Hanover 1903 Calcutta 1908 Jun 1913 Jun 1916

2	E1023	13038	Gauhar Jan Tune (From Indravoli) – Toran s/s s/s	(Mohamedan Song) Hanover 1903 Calcutta 1908
3	E1024	13039	Gauhar Jan (Song) – Dadrah (Dadra) s/s	(Madrasi) Hanover 1903
4	E1025	13143	Gauhar Jan Fee Mashi Nao s/s	(Burmees) Hanover 1903
5	E1026	13144	Gauhar Jan Jna Bali Champali s/s	(Gajarai) Hanover 1903
6	E1027	13145	Gauhar Jan Sobkoina Taria Jhali – Tarda Jhala s/s	(Tailungi) Hanover 1903
7	E1028	13146	Gauhar Jan Bhalo Basibe Baley Bhalo Basiney s/s	(Bengali) Hanover 1903
8	E1029	13147	Gauhar Jan (Song) – Pahail (Pahari) s/s	(Peshwari) Hanover 1903
9	E1030	13148	Gauhar Jan My Love is Like a Little Bird (English Script) s/s	(English) Hanover 1903

Company name: The Gramophone and Typewriter Ltd and sister companies.

Location: Calcutta

Date of recording: November 1902

Recorded by: Frederick William Gaisberg

Type of record: 10-inch – originally single-side recorded disc.

10	E118	13050	Miss. Gauhar Jan – (1ST Dancing Girl) Calcutta (not issued) (not on register)	

11	E119	13051	Miss Gauhar Jan – Calcutta Mainwari Bichuya Baje – Kaal (Jaunpurl) s/s c/w 13052	(Mahomedan Song) Hanover 1903 Calcutta 1908
12	E120	13052	Gauhar Jan Sawariya Ne Man Har Lino – Thungri (Tumri) s/s c/w 13051	(Mahomedan Song) Hanover 1903 Calcutta 1908
13	E121	13053	Gauhar Jan Ghor Ghar Barsat Mehrva Surkhi Malhar (Thumri Malhar) s/s c/w 13054	(Mahomedan Song) Calcutta 1908
14	E122	13054	Gauhar Jan Tohe Bachan De Mai Hari Balma – Dadra s/s c/w 13053	(Mahomedan Song) Hanover 1903 Calcutta 1908
15	E123	13055	Gauhar Jan Jabse Hai Tujhse Ankh Sitamgar Lagi Hai Maritaki Gajal (Gazal) s/s c/w 13056 c/w 13056 Re. HMV P 13	(Mahomedan Song) Hanover 1903 Calcutta 1908 Jan 1916
16	E 124	13056	Gauhar Jan Dil Jani Meri Meri Tune Kadar Nahin Jane – Dadra Manah (Dadra) s/s c/w 13055 c/w 13055 Re. HMV P 13	(Mahomedan Song) Hanover 1903 Calcutta 1908 Jan 1916
17	E 125	13057	Gauhar Jan Mere Subah Tere Kurbaan (English Tune) s/s c/w 13058	(Mahomedan Song) Hanover 1903 Calcutta 1908
18	E 126	13058	Gauhar Jan Aainta Habibi Ana Garibun – Tune Jogla s/s c/w 13057	(Arabic) Hanover 1903 Calcutta 1908

19	E 127	13059	Gauhar Jan Aayu Na Maal Hain Jo — TARJ s/s	(Kutchi) Hanover 1903
20	E 128	13060	Gauhar Jan Paad Shahem Majook Yesha s/s	(Turkish) Hanover 1903
21	E 129	13061	Gauhar Jan Nazar Teri Ho Gai Jigar Ki Paar — Gara (Gara — Dadra) s/s c/w 13063	(Hindustani) Hanover 1903 Calcutta 1908
22	E 130	13062	Gauhar Jan Nam Main Mohi Saasur Murdani — Gara s/s	(Sanskrit) Hanover 1903
23	E 131	13063	Gauhar Jan Chhabi Dikhila Ja Banke Sawariya — Pilu s/s c/w 13061	(Hindustani) Hanover 1903 Calcutta 1908
24	E 132	13064	Gauhar Jan Fanki Diye Pran s/s s/s c/w 13860 c/w 13860 Re. HMV P 14	(Bengali) Hanover 1903 Calcutta 1908 Calcutta 1908 Jan 1916
25	E 133	13065	Gauhar Jan Dil Kise se Lagana Bura Hai Khamach (Khambaj) s/s c/w 13066	(Hindustani) Hanover 1903 Calcutta 1908
26	E 134	13066	Gauhar Jan Tan Man Tope Karu Vaar — Kafu (Kafi) s/s c/w 13065	(Hindustani) Hanover 1903 Calcutta 1908
27	E 135	13067	Gauhar Jan Aaye Ghar Mat Badarwa Mollar Khial (Malhar Kheyal) s/s c/w 13068	(Hindustani) Hanover 1903 Calcutta 1908

28	E 136	13068	Gauhar Jan Sunori Nadiya Tora – Gandhar (Gandhari) s/s c/w 13067	(Hindustani) Hanover 1903 Calcutta 1908
29	E 137	13069	Gauhar Jan Shyam Rang Mein Bigodi Chunriya – Khmach (Holi – Kahmbaj) s/s c/w 13070 c/w 13079 Re. HMV P. 15	(Hindustani) Hanover 1903 Calcutta 1908 Jan 1916
30	E 138	13070	Gauhar Jan Jagai To Hari Dhola Jage Na – MAND s/s c/w 13069 c/w 13069	(Hindustani) Hanover 1903 Calcutta 1908 Jan 1916

Company name: The Gramophone and Typewriter Ltd and sister companies.

Location: Calcutta

Date of recording: December 1904

Recorded by: William Sinkler Darby

Type of record: 10-inch – originally single-side recorded disc.

31	2584h	13854	MISS. Gauhar Jan – Calcutta Choro Choro Mori Bahiya Piya – Bhairabi Tumri s/s c/w 13858 c/w 13858 Re. HMV P 21	(Hindustani) Hanover 1905 Calcutta 1908 Jan 1916
32	2585h	13842	Gauhar Jan Nahak Laye Gawanwa Mora – Bhairabi Tumri s/s c/w 13856 c/w 13856 Re. HMV P 17 c/w 13856 Re. HMV P 17 (285h-T1)	(Hindustani) Hanover 1905 Calcutta 1908 Jan 1916 c.1927

33	2586h	13855	Gauhar Jan Mere Darde Jigar Ki Khabar Nahin − Jangoti Tumri (Jhinjhoti Thumri) s/s c/w 13867 Blace c/w 13867 Violet c/w 13867 Re. HMV P 22	(Hindustani) Hanover 1905 Calcutta 1908 Nov 1915 Jan 1916
34	2587h	13843	Gauhar Jan Paniya Jo Baran Gayi Bhich Dagar Ghero − Desh Tumri s/s c/w 13857 c/w 13857 Re. HMV P 18	(Hindustani) Hanover 1905 Calcutta 1908 Jan 1916
35	2588h	13856	Gauhar Jan Aan Baan Jiya Mein Lago − Gara Tumri s/s c/w 13842 c/w 13842 Re. HMV P 17 C/W 13842 Re. HMV P 17 (2588h − T1)	(Hindustani) Hanover 1905 Calcutta 1908 Jan 1916 c. 1927
36	2589h	13857	Gauhar Jan Krishna Madho Ram Narayan − kheyal s/s c/w 13843 c/w 13843 Re. HMV P 18	(Hindustani) Hanover 1905 Calcutta 1908 Jan 1916
37	2590h	13858	Gauhar Jan Hai Gokul Ghar Ke Chora − Khyal Multani s/s c/w 13854 c/w 13854 Re. HMV P 21	(Hindustani) Hanover 1905 Calcutta 1908 Jan 1916
38	2591h	13859	Gauhar Jan Eshahey Pran Hrideye − Zila (Zila Gat) s/s s/s	(Bengali) Hanover 1905 Calcutta 1908
39	2592h	13860	Gauhar Jan Aaj Keno Bandhu − Zila (Zila − Dadra) s/s s/s c/w 13864 c/w 13864	(Bengali) Hanover 1905 Calcutta 1908 Calcutta 1908 Jan 1916

40	2593h	13861	Gauhar Jan Jangala Kakhano Posh Meneng Jhijit Medley (Jhinjhit Misra – Jalad Ektala) s/s	(Bengali) Hanover 1905
41	2594h	13862	Gauhar Jan Na Janena Jane Pran – Medley (Misra Ragni – Dhimey Tetala) s/s	(Bengali) Hanover 1905
42	2595h	13863	Gauhar Jan Nimesher Dekha Jadi – Khambag (Khambaj – Gat) s/s s/s c/w 13865 c/w 13865 Re. HMV P 23	(Bengali) Hanover 1905 Calcutta 1908 Calcutta 1908 Jan 1916
43	2596h	13864	Gauhar Jan Ke Tumi Nideye – Desh (Desh Kawali) s/s	(Bengali) Hanover 1905
44	2597h	13865	Gauhar Jan Hari Baley Dako Rasana – Gowri (Gouri Ektala) s/s s/s c/w 13863 c/w 13863 Re. HMV P 23	(Bengali) Hanover 1905 Calcutta 1908 Calcutta 1908 Jan 1916
45	2598h	13866	Gauhar Jan Tomari Birahe Sahey – Bhairobi (Bhairavi – Gat) s/s	(Bengali) Hanover 1905
46	2599h	13867	Gauhar Jan Piya Bin Nahin Awat Chain – Soruth (Surat) s/s c/w 13855 Black c/w 13855 Violet c/w 13855 Re. HMV P 22	(Hindustani) Hanover 1905 Calcutta 1908 Nov 1915 Jan 1916

47	2600h	13868	Gauhar Jan Jayo Ji Jayo Na Nakhre Dikhawa – Gara s/s c/w 13875 c/w 13875 Re. HMV P 24	(Hindustani) Hanover 1905 Calcutta 1908 Jan 1916
48	2601h	13869	Gauhar Jan Hai Saiyon Paron Mein Tori Paiyan – Zila s/s c/w 13874 Black c/w 13874 Violet c/w 13874 Re. HMV P 25	(Hindustani) Hanover 1905 Calcutta 1908 Nov 1915 Jan 1916
49	2602h	13870	Gauhar Jan Dildar Dildar Tan Man Dhan Khurbaan Karoon – Pahaki (Pahari Jhijhit) s/s c/w 13872 Black c/w 13872 Violet c/w 13872 Re. HMV P 26 c/w 13872 Re. HMV N 6323 (2602h T1)	(Hindustani) Hanover 1905 Calcutta 1908 Nov 1915 Jan 1916 C. 1935
50	2603h	13871	Gauhar Jan Chal Gayo Gum Ka Yah Warke – Pahari Jhijit s/s c/w 13873 c/w 13873 Re. HMV P 27	(Hindustani) Hanover 1905 Calcutta 1908 Jan 1916
51	2604h	13872	Gauhar Jan Bari Jaun Re Sawariya Toope Wariyan – Soruth s/s c/w 13870 Black c/w 13870 Violet c/w 13870 Re. HMV P 26 c/w 13870 Re. HMV N 6323 (2604h T1)	(Hindustani) Hanover 1905 Calcutta 1908 Nov 1915 Jan 1916 C. 1935
52	2605h	13873	Gauhar Jan Shyam Re Mori Bhaiyan Gahona – Soruth s/s c/w 13871 c/w 13871 Re. HMV P 27	(Hindustani) Hanover 1905 Calcutta 1908 Jan 1916

53	2606h	13874	Gauhar Jan Savariya Ne Mara Nazar Bharke – Jangoti Pahadi (Pahari Jhijit) s/s c/w 13869 Black c/w 13869 Violet c/w 13869 Re. HMV P 25	(Hindustani) Hanover 1905 Calcutta 1908 Nov 1915 Jan 1916
54	2607h	13875	Gauhar Jan Chinat Tahi Badal Gaye Naina—Piloo s/s c/w 13868 c/w 13868 Re. HMV P 24	(Hindustani) Hanover 1905 Calcutta 1908 Jan 1916
55	2608h	13876	Gauhar Jan Savariya Man Bayo Re Bhako Yaar -PILOO s/s c/w 3-13013 c/w 3-13013 Re. HMV P 28	(Hindustani) Hanover 1905 Calcutta 1908 Jan 1916

Company name: Nicole Freres, Ltd., 21 Ely Place, London
Indian Branch Office located at 3/4 Council House Street, Calcutta.
Location: Calcutta
Date of recording: December 1904
Recorded by: Stephen Carl Porter and John Watson Hawd
Type of record: 10-inch – Brown Celluloid Coated Cardboard Disc – single and double side recorded disc.

56	1283. C-1	1283	Miss. Gauhar Jan – Calcutta Sham Ki Base Surat Mein – Hindustani s/s c/w C-188 Nicole Record 1283 c/w C-188	(Hindustani) London 1905 Stockport 1906

Company name: The Gramophone and Typewriter Ltd.
Location: Calcutta
Date of recording: April 1906

Recorded by: William Conrad Gaisberg

Type of record: 10-inch – originally single-side recorded disc.

57	3764e	3-13013	Miss Gauhar Jan – Calcutta Aitne Jowan Daman Na Kariye – Khyal Bhoopali s/s c/w 13876 c/w 13876 Re. HMV P 28	(Hindustani) Hanover 1906 Calcutta 1908 Jan 1916
58	3765e	3-13014	Gauhar Jan Tan Man Ki Sudh Bisar Gayi Kaisi Bajai Thoomri – Pahari Junjowti s/s c/w 3-13015 c/w 3-13015 Re. HMV P 174	(Hindustani) Hanover 1906 Calcutta 1908 Jan 1916
59	3766e	3-13015	Gauhar Jan Jao Jao Mose Na Bolo Savten Ke Sang Raho – Dadra – Pahari Junjhouti s/s c/w 3-13014 c/w 3-13014 Re. HMV P 174	(Hindustani) Hanover 1906 Calcutta 1908 Jan 1916
60	3767e	3-13016	Gauhar Jan Sawar Bhanke Jobanwa Chupaye Jaat – Holi Jut s/s c/w 3-13018 c/w 3-13018 Re. HMV P 175	(Hindustani) Hanover 1906 Calcutta 1908 Jan 1916
61	3768e	3-13017	Gauhar Jan (Song) – 'Gazal Pushto' s/s	d.3/10/06.C (Pushtoo) Hanover 1906
62	3769e	3-13018	Gauhar Jan Jo Piya Aaye Mose Dukh Soha Jaye Na – Khambag Jogia s/s c/w 3-13016 c/w 3-13016 Re. HMV P 175	(Hindustani) Hanover 1906 Calcutta 1908 Jan 1916

63	3770e	3-13039	Gauhar Jan Chaila Hatja Tumahar Jai Hai Desh Dadra s/s c/w 3-13021 c/w 3-13021 Re. HMV P 176	(Pushtoo) Hanover 1906 Calcutta 1908 Jan 1916
64	3771e	3-13023	Gauhar Jan Masta Diwana – Theatre Tune—gazal s/s c/w 3-13024 c/w 3-13024 Re. HMV P 177	(Pushtoo) Hanover 1906 Calcutta 1908 Jan 1916
65	3772e	3-13024	Gauhar Jan Malapaani Mishyaraani – DHANI – Gazal (Includes Talking) s/s c/w 3-13023 c/w 3-13023 Re. HMV P 177	(Pushtoo) Hanover 1906 Calcutta 1908 Jan 1916
66	3773e	3-13020	Gauhar Jan Aaj Pajaai Man Chaak Gerba – Gazal Pharsee (with Spoken introduction) s/s s/s c/w 3-12198* (Recording by Keeti Jan) c/w 3-12198* Re. HMV P 158	(Persian) Hanover 1906 Calcutta 1908 Dec 1912 Jan 1916
67	3774e	3-13021	Gauhar Jan Aise Sawan Ke Mahinna Mein Godale Godna – Kajiri Haliya s/s c/w 3-13019 c/w 3-13019 Re. HMV P 176	(Hindustani) Hanover 1906 Calcutta 1908 Jan 1916
68	3775e	3-13022	Gauhar Jan Chalu Nahinwa Madmati Gugriya Rama— KAJIRI s/s s/s	(Hindustani) Hanover 1906 Calcutta 1908

Company name: Gramophone Monarch Record.
Location: Calcutta
Date of recording: April 1906
Recorded by: William Conrad Gaisberg
Type of record: 12-inch – originally single-side recorded disc.

69	614f	013041	Miss Gauhar Jan – Calcutta (Matrix defective) (Song) – Gazal Dhani	d.14/8/06.c (Hindustani)
70	615f	031042	Gauhar Jan Chuo Des Dharve Bhare – Savan (Sawan) s/s c/w 13045 c/w 13045 Re. HMV K 12	(Hindustani) Hanover 1906 Calcutta 1908 Jan 1916
71	616f	013043	Gauhar Jan (Song) – Thoomri Kawali (Matrix defective)	(Hindustani) d.13/7/06/c
72	617f	013044	Gauhar Jan Yah Chal Tori Namanu – Thoomri Kawali s/s c/w 13048 c/w 13048 Re. HMV K 13	(Hindustani) Hanover 1906 Calcutta 1908 Jan 1916
73	618f	013045	Gauhar Jan Dhar laage Oonchi Aatriya – – Mallar (Malhar) s/s c/w 13042 c/w 13042 Re. HMV K 12	(Hindustani) Hanover 1906 Calcutta 1908 Jan 1916
74	619f	013046	Gauhar Jan (Song) – Tarana – Bhimpalassi Matrix Defective	(Hindustani) d.10/7/06.c
75	620f	013052	Gauhar Jan Gairat Aaz Chashm Barm Royete – Gazal Mand s/s c/w 13053 c/w 13053 Re. HMV K 16	(Persian) Hanover 1906 Calcutta 1908 Jan 1916

76	621f	013047	Gauhar Jan (defective) (Song) – Chait s/s (one pressing only)	..../08.c (Hindustani) Hanover 1906
77	622f	013048	Gauhar Jan Maza Dete Hain Kya Yaar Tere Bal – Dadra s/s c/w 13044 c/w 13044 Re. HMV K 13	(Hindustani) Hanover 1906 Calcutta 1908 Jan 1916
78	623f	013049	Gauhar Jan Chalo Gooviya Aaj Khele Holi – Holi Jut s/s c/w 13050 c/w 13050 Re. HMV P 14	(Hindustani) Hanover 1906 Calcutta 1908 Jan 1916
79	624f	013050	Gauhar Jan Ya Baraj Mein Kaisi Phag Machire – Holi Jut s/s c/w 13049 c/w 13049 Re. HMV P 14	(Hindustani) Hanover 1906 Calcutta 1908 Jan 1916
80	625f	013051	Gauhar Jan Yeh Nathi Hamari Kismet Ke Visaa – Gazal Desh Pahari s/s s/s c/w 13058 c/w 13058 Re. HMV K 15	(Hindustani) Hanover 1906 Calcutta 1908 Dec 1912 Jan 1916
81	626f	013053	Gauhar Jan Hui Zalf Sanr Kushd Hama Cheen Cheen – Gazal – Jhunjowtti— pahadi s/s c/w 13052 c/w 13052 Re. HMV K 16	(Persian) Hanover 1906 Calcutta 1908 Jan 1916

Company name: Gramophone Company Ltd,
Location: Calcutta
Date of recording: April 1908
Recorded by: Frederucj William Gaisberg.
Using George Walter Dillnutt's recording book and numerical series.
Type of record: 10-inch – double sided discs, Hanover Calcutta.

82	8892o	4-13248	Miss Gauhar Jan Jabna Khuli Bhin The Aarje Muddakelie – Bhairavi Gazal Dadra c/w 4-13249 c/w 4-13249 c/w 4-13249 Re. HMV P 356 c/w 4-13249 Re. TWIN FT 406	(Hindustani) Hanover 1908 Sep 1909 Jan 1916 1931
83	8893o	4-13249	Gauhar Jan Raskebhare Tere Nayan – Bharivavi Dadra c/w 4-13248 c/w 4-13248 c/w 4-13248 Re. HMV P 356 c/w 4-13248 Re. TWIN FT 406	(Hindustani) Hanover 1908 Sep 1909 Jan 1916 1931
84	8894o	4-13250	Gauhar Jan Rasili Matwaliyon Ne Jadu Dala – Bhairvi Titala c/w 4-13257 c/w 4-13257 c/w 4-13257 Re. HMV P 357 c/w 4-13257 Re. TWIN FT 407	(Hindustani) Hanover 1908 Jul 1909 Jan 1916 1931
85	8895o	4-13251	Gauhar Jan Aayee Kari Badariya (Kyan Gauharki Rachit (Composed by Gauhar Jan) – Kajri Tilak Kamod c/w 4-13253 c/w 4-13253 c/w 4-13253 Re. HMV P 358	(Hindustani) Hanover 1908 Sep 1909 Jan 1916
86	8896o	4-13252	Gauhar Jan Piya Kar Ghar Dekho Dharkat Hai Mori Chatiya – Des Ektala c/w 4-13256 c/w 4-13256 c/w 4-13256 Re. HMV P 356	(Hindustani) Hanover 1908 Feb 1910 Jan 1916

87	8897o	4-13253	Gauhar Jan Najariya Lage Mayka Pyari – Khamach Dadra c/w 4-13251 c/w 4-13251 c/w 4-13251 Re. HMV P 358	(Hindustani) Hanover 1908 May 1909 Jan 1916
88	8898o	4-13254	Gauhar Jan Shama Ferake Dil Main Jalakar Chale Gaye – Gazal Khammach Dadra c/w 4-13274 c/w 4-13274 c/w 4-13274 Re. HMV P 360	(Hindustani) Hanover 1908 Aug 1910 Jan 1916
89	8899o	4-13255	Gauhar Jan Shyam Sundar Ki Dekh Suratiya Bhulgaee Sudhsari Re – Toomri Khamach Titala c/w 8-13166 c/w 8-13166 Re. HMV P 361	(Hindustani) Dec 1909 Jan 1916
90	8900o	4-13256	Gauhar Jan Aau Gale Lage Jau Mai Vari Saiyana – Des Jhinjhoti Titala c/w 4-13252 c/w 4-13252 c/w 4-13252 Re. HMV P 359	(Hindustani) Hanover 1908 Feb 1910 Jan 1916
91	8901o	4-13257	Gauhar Jan Mayka Piya Bin Kachu Na Sohayee (Bhai Ganpatro Randhya Ka Rachit) – Sohni Titala c/w 4-13250 c/w 4-13250 c/w 4-13250 Re. HMV P 357 c/w 4-13250 Re. TWIN FT 407	(Hindustani) Hanover 1908 Jul 1909 Jan 1916 1931
92	8962o	4-13225	Gauhar Jan Mere Barachhi Nighon Ki Tirchhi Jigar Par Mari – Dadra Zila c/w 4-13273 c/w 4-13273 c/w 4-13273 Re. HMV P 352	(Hindustani) Hanover 1908 Aug 1910 Jan 1916
93	8963o	4-13262	Gauhar Jan Woh Sitamgar Aata Najarhi Nahi – Dadra Kafi c/w 4-13263	(Hindustani) Feb 1910

94	8964o	4-13263	Gauhar Jan Ao Piya Chal Hath Tori Banvat Ki Baat Nahi Bhave – Dadra Des c/w 4-13262	(Hindustani) Feb 1910
95	8965o	4-13264	Gauhar Jan Khelan Ko Hari Radhe Sang Vah Krishna Bihari Aavat Hai – Holi Desh Chachar c/w 4-13267 c/w 4-13267 c/w 4-13267 Re. HMV P 362	(Hindustani) Hanover 1908 Feb 1912 Jan 1916
96	8966o	4-13265	Gauhar Jan Ambawaki Dali Tale Jhulna Dolave – Sarang Dadra c/w 4-13270 c/w 4-13270 c/w 4-13270 Re. HMV P 363	(Hindustani) Hanover 1908 Sep 1909 Jan 1916
97	8967o	4-13266	Gauhar Jan Aailo Kali Ghata Chhatahi Matwali Ghata Pyari Pyari – Pahari Jhinjhoti c/w 4-13269 c/w 4-13269 c/w 4-13269 Re. HMV P 364	(Hindustani) Hanover 1908 Feb 1910 Jan 1916
98	8968o	4-13267	Gauhar Jan Kaisi Yah Dhummachai Kandaiyare – Holi Kafi Jat c/w 4-13264 c/w 4-13264 c/w 4-13264 Re. HMV P 362	(Hindustani) Hanover 1908 Feb 1912 Jan 1916
99	8969o	4-13268	Gauhar Jan (Sung by Gauhar Jan at the Town Hall, Bombay, July, 1907) Chalo Guljar Aalam Main Havaye Fazle Rehmani – Dhun Kalyan c/w 9-13000 (Zohra Bai) c/w 9-13000 Re. HMV P 365	(Hindustani) Aug 1912 Jan 1916

Note: The label of this disc suggests that it was recorded at the Town Hall, Bombay, During July 1907. Although the 'sound' of this disc has a certain 'live' ambience, the company did not have a recording expert operating in India at the time. Thus it may be presumed that this recording was taken at a later date.

100	8970o	4-13269	Gauhar Jan Khelat Krishna Kumar Re – Kafi Jat c/w 4-13266 c/w 4-13266 c/w 4-13266 Re. HMV P 364	(Hindustani) Hanover 1908 Feb 1910 Jan 1916
101	8971o	4-13270	Gauhar Jan Mere Dilko Churake Kidharko Chale – Dadra Bhairvi c/w 4-13265 c/w 4-13265 c/w 4-13265 Re. HMV P 363	(Hindustani) Hanover 1908 Sep 1909 Jan 1916
102	8972o	4-13271	Gauhar Jan Rasiya Kidhar Ganvai Balam Harjai – Dadra Bhairvi c/w 4-13272	(Hindustani) May 1909
103	8973o	4-13272	Gauhar Jan Bhor Bhi Tum Ghar Ayee Ho Mere – Desh Dadra c/w 4-13271	(Hindustani) May 1909
104	8974o	4-13273	Gauhar Jan Yeh Kya Kaha Ke Merin Balabhi Na Aayegi – Pahari Jhinjhoti c/w 4-13225 c/w 4-13225 c/w 4-13225 Re. HMV P 352	(Hindustani) Hanover 1908 Aug 1910 Jan 1916
105	8975o	4-13274	Gauhar Jan Bevafa Tum Ho Kabhi Ahle Vafa Ho Jaana – Behag-ki-dhun Dadra c/w 4-13254 c/w 4-13254 c/w 4-13254 Re. HMV P 360	(Hindustani) Hanover 1908 Aug 1910 Jan 1916
106	8976o	4-13275	Gauhar Jan Basohe Deya Meliya Mai Nahi Rahna – Pahadi Dadra Single Sided	(Punjabi) May 1909

Company name: Gramophone Company Ltd,
Location: Calcutta
Date of recording: December 1908
Recorded by: George Walter Dillnutt
Type of record: 10-inch – double sided disc.

107	10173o	8-13166	MISS Gauhar Jan – CALCUTTA Jao Sakhi Piyako Le Aao – SINDHU KAFI c/w 4-13255 c/w 4-13255 Re. HMV P 361	

Note: This Single recording is most likely- retrospectively – numbered from an earlier recording session in April 1908.

SUN DISC RECORD

Company name: F.B. Thanewale & Co., (The Sun Record Co., Bombay) 143 Kalbadevi Road, Bombay and 13 Esplanade, Calcutta.
Location: Calcutta
Date of recording: 1909
Recorded by: Polyphon Musikwerke, A.G., Wahren-Leipzig, Germany.
Type of record: 10-inch Sun Disc Record.

108	21.	21	Gauhar Jan Pardesi Suniya Neha Lugay Dulan Ek Gayo – PAHARI (Dadra) c/w 22 (Made in England)	Hindustani
109	22.	22	Gauhar Jan Piya Ke Milan Ko Muyen Kuyese – Bhairvi Thumri c/w 21 (Made in England)	Hindustani
110	c/w	23	Gauhar Jan Not verified	
111	c/w	24	Gauhar Jan Not Verified	

112	- 25	25	Gauhar Jan Piya Bin Nahin Avat Chen – Piloo c/w 26 (Made in England)	Hindustani
113	- 26	26	Gauhar Jan Chinata Nahin Budul Guyo – Sohni c/w 25 (Made in England)	Hindustani
114		105	Gauhar Jan (Not verified)	Hindustani
115	115.	115	Gauhar Jan – Gazal Desh – c/w 116	Hindustani
116	116.	116	Gauhar Jan Hamare Piya Mere Pran Ke Jalamewar – Pilu c/w 115	Hindustani

Company name: Pathephone & Cinema, Co., Ltd., 7 Lindsay Street, Calcutta.

Location: Calcutta

Date of recording: December 1910

Recorded by: T.J. Theobald Noble

Type of record: 11-inch – Vertical Cut – Centre Start. (Pathephone)

117		46047 c/w	Gauhar Jan Mopa Baro Jori Kar – Sone Holi	(Hindustani)
118		46048	Gauhar Jan Borwa Badrowa Ra – Janga – Thumri	(Hindustani)
119		46054 c/w	Gauhar Jan Choro Choro Mori Baiya – Bhairavi Thumri	(Hindustani)
120		46067	Gauhar Jan Bo Tera Somajaya Ra – Bhairavi – Dadra	Hindustani
121		46068 c/w	Gauhar Jan Sada Pran Chay Jare	(Bengali)
122		46069	Gauhar Jan Je Jatona Jatone	(Bengali)

123		46070 c/w	Gauhar Jan Nimeseri Dekha Jodi	(Bengali)
124		46071	Gauhar Jan Ke Tumi Niday Loye	(Bengali)
125		46072 c/w	Gauhar Jan Borsa Negara Wachra – Posthu	(Hindustani)
126		46073	Gauhar Jan Chapamon Pajra – Posthu	(Hindustani)
127		46044 c/w	Gauhar Jan Nazara Marda – DES – TAPPA Punjabi	(Punjabi)
128		46082	Gauhar Jan Teri Moy Chekar Rohalda – Tappa – Jhijhouti	(Punjabi)
129		46083 c/w	Gauhar Jan Hari Saiya Poroma Tora Paieya – Zila	(Hindustani)
130		46084 c/w	Gauhar Jan Moja Da Taha Kaya Year – Dadra	(Hindustani)
131		46085 c/w	Gauhar Jan Sono Nanadia Tora Boyer – Gandhar – Khemta	(Hindustani)
132		46086	Gauhar Jan Tarana – Gujri Tori	(Hindustani)

Note: Apart from the above listing, no actual copies of these Vertical cut, center-start 11 inch disc records have been found to verify the catalog and matrix numbers.

SINGER RECORD

Company name: Singer Phono and General Agency, 10-12 Kalbadevi Road, Bombay.

Location: Bombay

Date of recording: 1910

Recorded by: Expert of Schallplatten Fabrik-Favorite, G.M.b.H.,

Type of record: 10-inch – double sided disc, Hanover 1910

133	7780.	7780	Gauhar Jan Har Chhou Saichi Chal Sang Mere – PAHARI c/w 7781	(Hindustani)
134	7781	7781	Gauhar Jan Oh Piya Chal Hui Tori Banavao ki Bar – DESH c/w 7780	(Hindustani)
135	7785.	7785	Gauhar Jan Aaja Savaria Tose Gnva Lagalu BHAIRVI Dadra c/w 7788	(Hindustani)
136	7786.	7786	Gauhar Jan Nahi Parai Muika Chain – BHAIRVI THUMRI c/w 7787	(Hindustani)
137	7787.	7787	Gauhar Jan Tori Bholi Bholi Suraiye Pe Jadu Balihari ASHA JOGIA c/w 7786	(Hindustani)
138	7788.	7788	Gauhar Jan Maika Piya Bin Kachhuna Suhay – SOHINI c/w 7785	(Hindustani)

These SINGER RECORD discs are later recordings than those made for the JAMES OPERA RECORD; but as stated above, there may also be reissues of the 'James' discs, coupled with European recordings on SINGER RECORD.

Company name: Gramophone Company Ltd,
Location: Calcutta
Date of recording: December 1913
Recorded by: Arthur Spottiswoode Clarke
Type of record: 10-inch – double sided disc.

139	2982y	12-13012	MISS Gauhar Jan Ham Jam Muhabbat Jan – Sindh Kafi c/w 12-13026 Re. HMV P 3551	(Hindustani) May 1917
140	2983y	12-13013	Gauhar Jan Peari Peari Mori Jia Men – Kedara c/w 12-13016 as. HMV P 2267	(Hindustani) Feb 1916
141	2984y	12-13014	Gauhar Jan Meri Agan Lagi Manva – Dadra c/w 12-13025 Violet c/w 12-13025 Re. HMV P 2099 c/w 12-13025 Re. TWIN FT 554	(Hindustani) Oct 1914 Jan 1916 1931
142	2985y	12-13015	Gauhar Jan Nainon Say Naina Mila – Singh Kafi c/w 12-13022 .HMV P 4015	(Hindustani) Jul 1919
143	2986y	12-13016	Gauhar Jan Gari Dungi Saiyan – Dhani c/w 12-13013 as. HMV P 2267	(Hindustani) Feb 1916
144	2987y	12-13017	Gauhar Jan Aashakn Hun Me Laknaye Risalat Mav ka – Pahari Jhinjoti c/w 12-13018 .HMV P 4143	(Hindustani) Feb 1920
145	2988y	12-13018	Gauhar Jan Shafaiya Rojen Mahashar Rojen Jajan Tum Hai – Mand c/w 12-13017 .HMV P 4143	(Hindustani) Feb 1920
146	2989y		Gauhar Jan (Not issued) (No details known)	
147	3001y	12-13021	Gauhar Jan Mere Hazrat Ne Madine Men Manahi Holi – Gazal Holi c/w 12-13038 c/w 12-13038 Re. HMV P 2101	(Hindustani) Aug 1915 Jan 1916

148	3002y	12-13022	Gauhar Jan Manwa Lubhao Chhail Saiyan – Pahari Jhinjuti c/w 12-13015 .HMV P 4015	(Hindustani) Jul 1919
149	3003y	12-13023	Gauhar Jan Palchhan Tarpey More Jia – Pilu Kafi c/w 12-13030 c/w 12-13030 Re. HMV P 2102	(Hindustani) Oct 1915 Jan 1916
150	3004y	12-13024	Gauhar Jan Daray Khwaja Yato – Pahari c/w 12-13044 .HMV P 5001	(Hindustani) Oct 1919
151	3005y		Gauhar Jan (Not issued) (No details known)	(Hindustani)
152	3006y	12-13025	Gauhar Jan Hato Hato Saiyyan Balhar Tore Jaiyyan – Bhupali c/w 12-13014 Violet c/w 12-13014 Re. HMV P 2099 c/w 12-13014 Re. TWIN FT 554	(Hindustani) Oct 1914 Jan 1916 1931
153	3007y	12-13026	Gauhar Jan Furqat Men Abto Ho Gaye – Pahari Jhinjuti c/w 12-13012 .HMV P 3551	(Hindustani) May 1917
154	3008y	12-13027	Gauhar Jan Kisko Ham Yad Kia Karte Hain – Asawari c/w 12-13043 c/w 12-13043 Re. HMV P 2103	(Hindustani) Jan 1915 Jan 1916
155	3009y	12-13028	Gauhar Jan Maftun Zulf Chehraye Jananan Ban Gaya – Sindh Khamach c/w 12-13029 .HMV P 3351	(Hindustani) Dec 1916

156	3010y	12-13029	Gauhar Jan Gamse Hai Sina Figar – Pahari Jhinjuti c/w 12-13028 .HMV P 3351	(Hindustani) Dec 1916
157	3011y	12-13030	Gauhar Jan Hat Chhor Sakhi Chal Sang Meray – Punjabi Pahari c/w 12-13023 c/w 12-13023	(Hindustani) Oct 1915 Jan 1916
158	3022y	12-13038	Gauhar Jan Holi Khelat Khwaja Mionuddin – HOLI c/w 12-13021	(Hindustani) Aug 1915
159	3023y	12-13038	Gauhar Jan Holi Khelat Khwaja Mionuddin – HOLI c/w 12-13021	(Hindustani) Aug 1915

Note: Replacement recording used between first and second issue c/w 12-13021 Re. HMV P 2101 Jan 1916

160	3024y	12-13039	Gauhar Jan Esrab Ka Banka Sanwaria – Mand c/w 12-13040 Violet c/w 12-13040 Re. HMV P 2108	(Hindustani) Oct 1914 Jan 1916
161	3025y	12-13040	Gauhar Jan Kea Hamse Pia Taqsir Huyee – Mand c/w 12-13040 Violet c/w 12-13040 Re. HMV P 2108	(Hindustani) Oct 1914 Jan 1916
162	3026y	12-13041	Gauhar Jan Alwar Ke Kandhaiya Hori Khele – Sindh Kafi (Holi) c/w 12-13042 c/w 12-13042 Re. HMV P 2109	(Hindustani) Feb 1915 Jan 1916

163	3027y	12-13042	Gauhar Jan Na Maro Pichkari Chhaila – Paraj Holi c/w 12-13041 c/w 12-13041 Re. HMV P 2109	(Hindustani) Feb 1915 Jan 1916
164	3028y	12-13043	Gauhar Jan Phans Gaya Dil Betareh Ya Rab Karun Tadbir Kea – Ghazal Sohni c/w 12-13027 c/w 12-13027 Re. HMV P 2103	(Hindustani) Jun 1915 Jan 1916
165	3029y		Gauhar Jan (Not issued) (No details known)	
166	3030y	12-13044	Gauhar Jan Rasul Khuda Bansiwala Hai – Bhairavi c/w 12-13024 .HMV P 5001	(Hindustani) Oct 1919

Note: Matrix numbers 3031 y, 3032 y have not been traced.

APPENDIX 2

MISCELLANEOUS ORIGINAL DOCUMENTS

2.1. Affidavit of Bhaglu in the Court:

Suit No. 92 of 1910

Shaik Bhagloo of 49, Lower Chitpore Road, Calcutta by G.N. Dutta & Co.
- VS-
Gauhar Jan of 49, Lower Chitpore Road, Calcutta by G.C.Chunder & Co.

Plaint filed on 29/01/1910 states:

1. One Malka Jan, a Mahomedan female governed by Sunni school of law was married in 1868 at Azimgarh in United Provinces and Oudh to one Shaik Wazir.

2. Plaintiff is the son of this said marriage born in or about 1869. Plaintiff till death of Malka Jan lived with her and acknowledged as her son.

3. In or about 1870, Shaik Wazir died and Malka Jan came to Calcutta, took profession of a dancing girl and earned considerable fortune both movables and immovables.

4. While Malka Jan was a dancing girl, she was in the keeping of an Armenian gentleman and the defendant Gauhar Jan was born of such illicit union in or about 1873.

5. Malka Jan died in 1906 leaving her surviving said son, the plaintiff and illegitimate daughter Gauhar Jan, the defendant and as such the plaintiff is entitled to the whole estate of Malka Jan and the defendant has no right title and interest.

6. Since the death of Malka Jan, the plaintiff is in possession of a portion of 49, Lower Chitpore Road and the other half is by the defendant. Plaintiff came to know that the defendant had her name registered with Land Registration Office her name as the sole owner.

7. The defendant is in wrongful possession and wrongfully collecting rents. On 17/1/1910 the defendant wrongfully filed a suit in S.C. Court to evict the plaintiff.

8. Plaintiff prays
   a. What estate Malka Jan seized and possessed at the time of death.
   b. Declaration that the plaintiff is entitled to the whole estate and the defendant has no right title.
   c. Defendant be ordered to deliver possession.
   d. Accounts.
   e. Receivables
   f. Injunctions.
   g. Costs
   h. In the alternative declaration that the plaintiff is owner of 2/3rd and defendant of 1/3rd.
   i. Properties 49, Lower Chitpore Road; 22, Bentinck Street; 7, Beliaghata Road; 11/1 Koilasarak, Kidderpore.

Plaintiff signed in Urdu, explained by Golam Zahoor, interpretor.

2.2. Counter-affidavit of Gauhar in the Court

Written statement of Gauhar Jan filed on 19/03/1910:
1. Story told by the plaintiff is false and to blackmail the defendant.
2. Defendant is the legitimate daughter and the only child of Malka Jan. Defendant learnt that her mother in her early life professed Christian religion as she was born of Christian parents, with maiden name Victoria Hemmings.
3. On 10/09/1872 she, a spinster of 15 years, married to Robert William

Yeoward in Holy Trinity Church of Allahabad according to Christian rites by Rev. Mr J. Stevenson, officiating Civil Chaplain. Defendant born on 26/06/1873 and baptized at the Methodist Episcopal Church at Allahabad on 03/06/1875 by the name Allen Angelina.

4. Defendant learnt, some time after her birth her father filed a divorce suit against her mother, had a decree and her custody was given to the mother. After that her mother came to Benares, became a Mohamedan and took the name as Malka Jan. She made the defendant a follower to that religion. Malka Jan adopted the calling of a dancing girl and began to train the defendant.

5. That in 1883, when the defendant was 10 years of age and attained considerable skill as a singer and dancer, her mother came to Calcutta with her and put up at Coolootola Street.

6. In Calcutta, her mother gained great skill and reputation and the defendant also and both of them earned large sums as pay and presentation.

7. In 1887 defendant's mother purchased 49, 49/1, 49/2 Lower Chitpore Road from one Haji Mohammad Karim Siraji and removed there with her daughter.

8. From 1887 upto the death of her mother both of them continued as dancers and in 1903 Malka Jan bought a garden home in Beliaghata and also a land at 11/1 Koila Sarak Road, Kidderpre and during that period purchased precious stones and jewels.

9. After the death of her mother, defendant got her name registered as sole heir and legal representative in the Land Registry records.

10. In August 1906, the defendant purchased with her own earnings the house being 22, Bentinck Street at Rs 15, 750/-. On 22/09/1909 the defendant sold the Kidderpore property to one Prince Kamar Kader of Circular G.R. Road for difficulty in realizing rents.

11. The defendant does not know who Shaik Wazir was, as mentioned in the plaint.

12. The defendant has learnt from her mother that the plaintiff is the son of a chamar woman, named Assia, who was in service in a Christian family in Azimgarh, a relation of the defendant's mother. The father of the plaintiff also working in the same family as a Syce. In Benares, the plaintiff and his mother was appointed by Malka Jan as servant and maid-servant.

13. Again when Malka Jan came down to Calcutta, the plaintiff and his mother were employed in the same capacity. Thereafter the plaintiff and his mother, originally chamars, made conversions to Mahomedanism. After the death of the plaintiff's mother, the defendant's mother kept him in service and got him married and allowed to stay in her house with wife. After the defendant's mother's death, the defendant also allowed his service at Rs 10/- per month.

14. In 1907, the defendant went to Bombay for performance and after return came to know that the plaintiff was in concert with Syed Wazir Hasan, her manager and Dil Narayan Sing, her Durwan to rob her money and blackmail her. His conduct showed that he intended to hasten the death of the defendant. The defendant dismissed Wazid Hassan on recommendation of her Doctor, Late Dr. Masoom and engaged one Golam Abbas, an educated Mahomedan young man to take charge of her financial business. Upon such arrangement the plaintiff was angry. The defendant started proceedings against him in Police Court and Small Causes court for evicting him.

Plaintiff A/D: Nothing to be noted.
Defendant A/D: Original conveyance of 29/07/03 between Satya Sanker Ghose, Ram Golapurni Debi, Satya Bhushan Ghosal, Tara Sundari Debi and Malka Jan and Gauhar Jan.

2.3 List of Exhibits and Depositions:

Witnesses of the plaintiff:
1. Wali Mohammad
2. Mirja Noor Ali
3. Nati Dai (Midwife)
4. Shaikh Jangi (Broker of houses)
5. Syed Wajid Hasan
6. K. Ahmed
7. Shaik Nabban
8. Asghar Khan
9. Mohammed Wajid
10. Dhirendra N. Banerjee.

Witnesses of the defendant

1. Gauhar Jan
2. R.W. Yeoward
3. Ekramuddin
4. Esther Mordecai
5. Syed Fida Hossain
6. Golam Mahiuddin
7. Fayaj Hasan.

2.4. Judgement delivered by Lushington in the Bhaglu case.

Judgment Copy

Suit No. 92 of 1910
In the High Court of Judicature at Fort William in Bengal
Ordinary original Civil Jurisdiction

Present:

The Hon'ble Mr Justice
Stephen.
The 2nd Day of August 1911.

Shaik Bhagloo
–VS–
Gauhar Jan

The Court: The plaintiff in this case pleads that he was born in 1869, the son of Malka Jan and Sheikh Wazir both Mohammedans, who were married at Azimghar in the United Provinces in 1868. His father died in 1879 and afterwards his mother had an illegitimate daughter Gauhar Jan the defendant. The plaintiff lived with his mother and Gauhar Jan, till the death of the former in 1906 after she had amassed a considerable fortune as a dancing girl. Since her death the plaintiff has been in possession of part of her property, but the defendant is wrongfully in possession of another part to which the plaintiff is entitled. He denies the legitimacy of the defendant, but if she is legitimate he claims to be entitled to two thirds of the estate. He therefore sues for a declaration in his favour and for other reliefs. The defendant on the other hand denies the plaintiff's allegations and pleads that she is the legitimate daughter and only child of a woman who was originally a Christian called Victoria Hemmings, who was married to Robert William Yeoward on the 10th September, 1872 at Allahabad. The defendant was born of that marriage on the 26th June 1873, which her parents were living together, and was baptized at a Methodist Episcopal Church on the 2nd June 1875 in the name of Allen Angelina. Subsequently what the defendant calls divorce proceedings were instituted between her parents, and they separated. The mother and daughter went to Benaras, where the mother was converted to Mohammedanism and took the name of Malka Jan. The defendant's case is that she was converted at the same time and took the name of Gauhar Jan, though this is not pleaded. She further pleads that about 1883 her mother who had become a dancing girl brought her to Calcutta, where the plaintiff took to the same pursuit. Malka Jan lived in Calcutta till her death in 1906, when the defendant succeeded to all her property which was of considerable value. As to the plaintiff, she says that he is the son of one Assia who was a maidservant in Azimghar, and came to Benaras as maid to Malka Jan bringing her son with her. She followed Malka Jan to Calcutta and she and the plaintiff were afterwards converted to Mohammedanism. Assia died in Malka Jans' service, and the plaintiff, who had been dismissed from that service and afterwards taken back, was allowed to continue in service and never lived in Malka Jan's house in any other capacity than that of a servant. Issues have been settled as follows:

1. In the plaintiff the son of Malka Jan, legitimate or otherwise?
2. Is the defendant the legitimate daughter of Malka Jan?
3. Could the plaintiff acquire legal rights, by his acknowledgement by Malka Jan? Was there such acknowledgement?

Questions relating to the interest of the parties in any property were reserved.

The first and the main question in the case is whether the plaintiff is the son of Malka Jan, as if he is not, his case fails.

The case he makes for himself on this point is follows:-

The first relations that he remembers are his grandmother Rukminia and his mother Malka Jan, and his information about his family before the time when he can remember for himself comes from them, and Wali Mohamed a witness who was examined on commission. Its effect is that his grandmother was an Indian and his mother a Eurasian, her father being a man called Hardy. He himself was born at Azimghar forty or forty five years ago. He does not remember his father but remembers living at Azimghar. From there he went to Allahabad, Azimghar again, Benaras for four or five years, and eventually to Calcutta, always with his mother. In Calcutta they lived in two houses in Colootollah and afterwards in Chitpore Road during which time the party consisted as it as appears of his mother, his grandmother, his aunt, the defendant and himself. After Malka Jan came to Calcutta the circumstances of the family improved and he was always provided with good clothes and later with money. He had his meals with the rest of the family, and the servants whom he names, served him as they did the others. His marriage was arranged 20 or 21 years ago. It was negotiated through the family cook, who was also a professional match maker, and celebrated with considerable display at the expense of Malka Jan. His wife received jewelry from Malka Jan and the defendant, and she and her children were always treated by them as near relations would be. He is the father of children, and all expenses connected with the eldest, including his education were met by Malka Jan on a scale suitable to the case of a grandchild. The general expenses relating to the other children were met by Malka Jan, though we have not heard of their education. On Malka Jan's death the plaintiff first raised her body to have it carried out to burial, he with the defendant arranged the ceremony of Phylpan and he instructed a Mouler to recite certain prayers. He was addressed in the family by the appellation of *Mia*, a word that would never be applied to a servant and Malka Jan and the defendant always addressed him and his family in terms denoting relationship. Such is the story put forward by the plaintiff on his own behalf. Before considering how far it is affected his cross-examination or by the defendant's evidence, I will consider how far it is supported by his other witnesses. The first of these is Wali Mohamed whose evidence was taken on commission. He is 80 years old and the chowkidar of prostitutes in Azimghar. He corroborates the plaintiff as to Malka's parentage, and says that after Hardy's death Malka, who was then called Bika, became a prostitute at Azimghar. In time she became intimate with one Wazir, a Khansama, and on trouble arising between Wazir and his people because she was a Christian, was converted to Mohammedanism, married Wazir and took the name of Malka while they were married Bhagloo was born, and Wazir died six months later. Malka then made the acquaintance of one Khurshed who left Azimghar with her, her mother and son. Afterwards the witness saw Malka at Calcutta where he asked after Bhagloo who was shown to him, and he also saw the defendant, who Malka said, was the daughter of a Sahib. He saw Malka and Bhagloo about a year later. This story is without dates; but does not seem to have been shaken in cross-examination.

The next witness of importance is Mirza Nur Ali whose daughter (she was really an adopted niece) the plaintiff married. He relates how the marriage was suggested to him by Naziba the match maker who said that Bhagloo was Malka's son by Wazir Jan, and how at first he refused the match because "the bridge-groom's mother was a dancing girl". He was persuaded to consent however by Malka, who referred to Bhagloo as her son, said he was born in wedlock, offered to pay Rs.500/- to defray the wedding expenses, and told him that the defendant would be his daughter's sister-in-law, and would be companion of hers and treat her well. Afterwards as ceremonial visit was paid to his house by Malka and Gauhar, and they came again on the day of the marriage. With Bhagloo and Mirza Nur Ali, Nabha may conveniently be considered, as he completes the family witnesses. He does not in fact add much in the way of oral evidence to what has gone before, but he speaks to having been educated and provided with Medical attendance as though he were a member of the family.

Other witnesses who support the plaintiff's story are Nathu Bai the midwife, Shaik Jungi who knew Malka Jan in Benaras and afterwards, Wazid Hussain for a considerable time a trusted friend or servant of Malka Jan and the defendant. Hussain Ahmed Ashgar Khan a man who at one time kept Malka Jan, and Mohammed Wazid who performed the plaintiff's marriage ceremony. These persons between them with various means of knowledge speak to the plaintiff living in Malka Jan's house as a son might live, and being addressed by her and the defendant as a relation. There is a certain quantity of documentary evidence to the same effect. These are partly letters, see exhibits E.F.G. and partly account books, see Exhibits H, L, N and O, among which we find entries where the plaintiff is referred to as a member of the family as could be, a list of jewellery which seems to be a list of what was given to Bhagloo's wife, and a list of servants in which his name is not found. Some of these entries have been satisfactorily traced to Malka Jan or the defendant, particularly the N. Series, the O Series, and I incline to believe the L series, other have not. But in my opinion there is enough to corroborate the evidence that has been offered as to the way in which the plaintiff was treated and addressed in Malka Jan's house. This is how the plaintiff's case appears at its best, and it is at once apparent that there is a weak point at each end of the story. In the first place Wali Mohammed's evidence is all the evidence that there is, that the plaintiff's father ever existed. It is of course quite likely that it would be impossible to get evidence relating to such a man 45 years after his death and I do not say that the absence of such evidence is suspicious, but it does weaken the plaintiff's case. In the second place, if the plaintiff was Malka's son why is he not in possession of her property? His answer is that the defendant persuaded him to give up all the keys to boxes and so forth to her, so that is his property was attached, and he had certain litigation in progress, he might be able to defeat his creditors. This I do not believe. There is no evidence that he ever had any control over the property in Malka's lifetime, and I see no reason to suppose that he ever grave anything to Gauhar.

Besides these inherent defects in the plaintiff's case, there must further be considered admissions which he has been forced to make in cross examination. The most important of these refer to statements he made in Land Acquisition proceedings in Alipore in 1905, in the Police Court in Alipore in 1907, and in the Presidence Magistrate's Court in 1909. On the first occasion he deposed that he was the son of Shaikh Wazir Jan and that he lived in the house of Malka Jan, who he described as a dancing girl adding "I do not serve her...I have been in her house three years".

On the second the father's name given may be the same as Shaikh Wazir, but he deposes "I reside at the house of Malka Jan (Bijie) as a tenant – she is the mother of Gauhar Jan". On the third he described himself as "the adopted son of one Malka Jan" and as "an adopted son and heir" of Malka Jan. Taking the plaintiff's case as it thus stands I think it may be fairly summarized by saying that it rests almost entirely on the fact that he lived in Malka Jan's house on terms of familiarity that suggest a relationship to her, and that she did on several occasions represent him as her son. I cannot attach much weight to Wali Mohammed's evidence but I cannot overlook the testimony of Nur Ali and others who speak to the way in which the plaintiff was treated. Whether the plaintiff has made out a case on which I could give him a decree I need not decide as I must discuss the defendant's evidence, and will therefore consider whether it has met the case made by plaintiff, that is in fact within it accounts for the fact as I hold it to be, that the plaintiff lived practically all his life in Malka's house, at her expense, on terms of familiarity that suggest relationship.

Before proceeding further however I will once for all state my general opinion on the character of the witnesses in the case as persons entitled to credit. The defendant has been a prostitute from her youth, as apparently her mother was before her. It may therefore be presumed that as a witness she is usual, and I see no reason to think otherwise of her as far as this case is concerned. The same may probably be said of Malka Jan. The plaintiff has been brought up and supported by a prostitute mother and sister; he brings this suit to acquire the proceeds of their prostitution. I gather from part of Gauhar's cross-examination that he considers that Gauhar failed in her duty in not helping his daughter to become a prostitute. I am therefore probably justified in attributing to him the venality of a prostitute combined with other moral defects which I had rather not considered too closely. Also I suppose that the arrangements of Malka's household were not governed by the conventions that obtain elsewhere, or at least not without serious aberrations from what is usual in their application. I think I may safely say that all the other witnesses are tainted with the moral defects I have attributed to the parties to a greater or less degree, and consequently in this case I think it is particularly necessary to pay attention to such facts as I consider certain and important rather than to those that are more uncertain and comparatively trifling. Having said so much in connection with this aspect of the case I need not refer to it again.

The story put forward by the defendant in which she seeks to prove that the plaintiff is not the son of Malka Jan, and incidentally that she is her legitimate daughter, is derived from the witness Yeoward, about whom I will say more hereafter. On the 10 October 1872 at Allahabad, Yeoward, a Eurasian aged 20 married a Christian Eurasian girl then aged 15 called

Adeline Victoria Hemmings. She had not been married before and was daughter of Mr Hemmings, who Mr Hemmings was Yeoward does not seem to know, but she was a Eurasian and an English name which was not Hardy, was mentioned to him in connection with her parentage. A girl was born of the marriage on the 26 June 1873 and subsequently Christened in a Methodist Episcopal Church. Yeoward's wife, it may be well to say at once according to the defendant, afterwards became Malka Jan, and his daughter is the defendant.

Yeoward was engaged in various places in the manufacture of artificial ice, and did not live much with his family; but in 1876 he received an offer from one Safuzzil Hossain to set him up in an indigo plantation at a place four miles from Azimghar, and he accordingly moved there, while his wife and daughter lived in Azimghar itself. Here he heard something about his wife which caused him to leave that place and take work elsewhere. In 1879 however he returned and brought a charge of adultery against one Jageswar Bharthi. The charge was struck off, as we find from a copy of Register. Yeoward says it was compromised, and this is the occasion of what is called in the written statement of decree of divorce. Documentary evidence was offered to show what actually happened, but the whole proceeding was so irregular that it was impossible to admit it. The husband and wife however both appear to have acted in the belief that they were divorced and as supposing, this story to have any truth in it, I see no reason to suppose that the belief was not genuine. Yeoward thenceforth had no correspondence with his wife, and heard nothing more of his daughter till January 1910 when he received communications from Gauhar Jan in connection with this case.

Gauhar Jan's own evidence carries on the story after a gap as to which there is evidence that I will consider later. What she first remember is being at Benaras when six or seven years old. She lived with her mother and grandmother and certain servants who she names, as particularly Assia, a maid, and the plaintiff her son who was a boy doing menial service in the house. Assia eventually died in her mother's service, but the evidence relating to her is important and will be better considered by itself. The first definite event that Gauhar seem to remember is the conversion of mother, herself, and her grandmother, to Mohammedanism, by one Khurshed, at a time when she and her mother were receiving dancing lessons. After a time the party including the plaintiff came to Calcutta, but Assia came later, after paying a visit to her husband at Azimghar. They lived there at various houses, the identity of which is not of importance, and eventually as settled at 49, Lower Chitpore Road, the conveyance to Malka Jan of which is dated 20th December 1887. This may be considered as the family house, and is part of the property which is now in dispute. Before they moved there however two events occurred names the grandmother's death, which is not of much importance, and the plaintiff's conversion to Mohammedanism by one Ekramuddin, which is very important indeed, as it is destructive of the plaintiff's case if it actually occurred. At some date, which it seems impossible to fix with any approach to certainty, Gauhar Jan became the mistress of first one man and then another at Benaras, but says she still constantly come to Calcutta. In 1889 she and her mother went to Benaras to defend two suits brought there for the price of clothes, a very important matter because Malka Jan pleaded the infancy of her daughter, and if her evidence is to be believed, said that Yeoward was her father, and produced a marriage certificate. After these suits no incident of much important occurred, till Malka Jan's death in 1906 but during this time Gauhar Jan seems to have been living chiefly at her mother's house, earning a good deal of money, which she says she paid to her mother. On her mother's death she took possession of her property, with no objection from the plaintiff and on consulting her mother's attorney, who is now acting for her, procured a mutation of names in the Alipore Registry. Malka Jan's funeral was carried out under her instructions and the plaintiff took no part in any of the ceremonies on the business connected with it. Gauhar Jan denies generally that Bhagloo was even treated as a member of the family, though he was treated with indulgence. She denies that he was ever called Mia but says he was addressed in a way consistent with his being a servant. She denies her presence at the negotiations for Bhagloo's marriage, or that he or his wife ever received presents of the value he alleges. He received regular pay, and was at one time dismissed and obtained service in an establishment quite unconnected with Malka Jan's.

Of the other witnesses who support the story told by Yeoward and Gauhar Jan the two most important are Ghulam Khan and Keder Hossain. The former was examined on a Commission taken out by the plaintiff who did not tender his deposition. I have however treated it as evidence in the case in accordance with the decision in Khan Ram Mahto-Vs- Murli Mahto 36 Cal, 466, and contrary to the rule laid down in Kusum Kumari Roy – VS – Satta Ranjan Dass 30, Cal, 999 and followed in Hemanta Kumari – VS – Banku Behari Sikdar, 9b, W.N. 794. Also in case this should be incorrect I have tendered it myself, and further I wish to add that I consider it was open to the defendant to tender it as false in some particulars and true in others. He says that Malka alias Beki was the daughter of Rukmania who had lived with a Sahib called Hardy by whom she was converted to Christianity. After Hardy's death, Beki lived with her sister Bela in Benaras as a prostitute. Later Beki, Bela and their mother went to Allahabad where Beki married "Robert Sahib". Beki and Robert Sahib were employed by Havajah Hossain to work in an ice factory. Keder Hossain is, or is described as a Mouhre. He has Mohurrir to the Government pleader in Benaras, in 1879 or 1880 when he says that Malka Jan, her mother Victoria Hemmings, and Gauhar Jan came there. He became muta husband to Victoria Hemmings' mother for a term of eight years, about a year after the party came to Benaras, in order to do which he had her converted to Mohammedanism. He taught Persian to Malka and Gauhar Jan; but did not teach it to Bhagloo, because he was only a boy who filled chillums, and the son of chamar woman, namely Assia. The party including his muta wife apparently, all came to Calcutta in 1883, where he sometimes visited them. Before the term of his marriage with Victoria Hemmings' mother, who changed her name on conversion, expired, she died at Benaras. He saw the family in Calcutta after they had moved there, and always found Bhagloo in the position of a servant.

Ekramuddin speaks to the ceremony of Bhagloo's circumcision, and says that he was then 14 or 15 years old. Esthen Mordecai identifies Bhagloo as the man who as a boy served in her house about twenty-two years ago; and in this she is corroborated by Golam Mohiuddin Tayak Hossain also speaks to his being in the service of his sister Abbassi Jan in 1890 or 1891.

Before considering how far this evidence has been broken down on cross-examination I will consider the documentary evidence produced by the defendant still leaving the evidence as to Assia to be separately considered. The earliest document on the record is a copy of the marriage certificate of

Robert William Yeoward and Victoria Hemmings, showing that persons of these named were married at Allahabad on the 11th September 1872. One copy of this was made out on the 21st July 1889; it is said for use of Malka Jan's case in Benaras. The other was made out on the 3rd December 1910 for use in this suit. We have next two depositions taken in Malka Jan's suits in Benaras. They both contain as statements of the marriage in Allahabad, and one mentions Robert Yeoward as the deponent's husband, and a statement that her marriage with him was dissolved. There are several objections to these documents. They both purport to have been made in the same suit as far as the number is concerned, but the name of the Munsiff is different in the two suits. There are other minor mistakes, and it appears that under the Rules obtaining in the United Provinces the depositions ought to have been destroyed before the copies were made. The copies appear however to have been made quite regularly and there is no evidence that they were made otherwise. I have already referred to the depositions made by the defendant on three occasions.

The effect of the cross-examination of the defendant and her witnesses leads me to the conclusion which I have already stated, that the plaintiff was treated much more like a member of the family then the defendant has admitted, and I believe the documents in the L. series to be Gauhar's. Also I do not consider it to be proved that he paid any rent for the part of the house that he occupied. On the other hand he seems, from his own account, to have received money from the man who kept Gauhar, or at least from one of them. I cannot however attach great importance to these matters taken by themselves when the very irregular constitution of Malka's household is considered and I came to consider the evidence relating to Assia I think an obvious explanation of the familiarity with which the plaintiff was treated will be apparent.

As to the substantive case put forward by the defendant, it is not necessary, as perhaps it is not possible, to go further back in the family histories of the parties concerned than Malka Jan. She was, it is admitted partly of European descent, of which there is no trace visible to me in the appearance of the plaintiff. If she was married to Yeoward as he states she was, it is perhaps physically possible that she may previously have given birth to the plaintiff, supposing Yeoward to have been grossly deceived in certain matters. But Yeoward's story is inconsistent with Wali Mohomed's, and if Yeoward is to be believed the plaintiff's account of his parentage is very much discredited, if not actually disproved. On the whole I find it impossible to treat Yeoward's story as a fabrication. As told by him it does not in its main features seem to me very improbable, it is supported by the marriage certificate, which I see no reason for doubting, and it was put forward by Malka Jan in 1890, when she had not chance of calling Yeoward to corroborate it and made no attempt to have him personated. It was not suggested that the witness before me was not Robert Yeoward, and he challenged cross-examination on the point. The only flaws in the marriage certificate that can be suggested are that the names of Yeoward's grandfather, is, as he says, put for that his father, and Eliza Hemmings is entered in the place for the name of Malka Jan's father, which seems consistent enough with Yeoward's story. I find it impossible therefore not to believe Yeoward in the crucial point of his marriage with Victory Hemmings.

If this is so, there is no difficulty in accepting his story of Gauhar's birth and his separation from his wife, thought here there are some dark places. I accept this part of his evidence the more readily because he has attempted to corroborate his evidence by the production of a copy of what would have been a public document had it been as regular in substance as it was in form. Taking his evidence as it stands therefore I accept it in its main points, and consider that as I have said, it is practically inconsistent with the story put forward by the plaintiff. There is however one point about Yeoward's credit that must be specially noticed. Shortly before the case came on for hearing is an application was made to me on behalf of Gauhar Jan, asking for the arrest of Yeoward on the ground that he was demanding to be paid Rs 9000/- before he gave his evidence, and that he threatened that if he were not paid he would withdraw to beyond 200 miles from Calcutta, in which case his evidence would be procurable only on Commission. I procured him to appear before me and he gave me an undertaking that he would appear when required. It now appears that the Rs 9000/- was to be the price of a house at Dinapore but there could be no doubt that he was attempting to exact payment for this evidence. Fortunately Gauhar Jan was well advised in the matter, and, though on further consideration, I am inclined to fear that there is no statutory enactment enabling the court to deal effectually with such a case, I have no doubt that he gave his evidence without having been paid for it, thought he is of course a deeply interested witness. The circumstance of course must be borne in mind in weighing his evidence, and I may add that he seemed to accept the very curious position in which he represents himself to be without any truce of some of the feeling that it might be expected to evoke. I feel however that in considering his position I am as far removed from any state of affairs within my experience, personal or judicial as I am in reference to any other witness of importance in this case. All that I can say about him with any confidence is that I believe the most important parts of his evidence.

Under these circumstances I consider that such case as the plaintiff has made out has been discredited to such an extent that he must fail. There remains however the case made out by the defendant relating to the woman Assia, who is said to be the mother of the plaintiff. The story is briefly as follows:-

When Yeoward was living on an indigo plantation near Azimghar with his wife and child living in the town, he had a Syce named Hemraj, married to a woman called Bodissia who had a son by him who is Bhagloo. When Malka Jan or Victoria Hemmings left her husband, Bodissia, who is the same Assia, left her husband, and thereafter attached herself to Malka Jan as a maid till her death in August 1888 in Malka Jan's house. If this story is true it accounts for the favour shown to the plaintiff and for the terms of familiarity on which Bhagloo was treated by Malka and Gauhar Jan. The presence of the father, the woman and the child at Azimghar is spoken to by Yeoward. I find it difficult to believe that he really remembers all he describes, though the fact that he gives the name of the woman not as Assia, but as something like it, is in his favour. Later Assia's presence in Benaras and her subsequent arrival in Calcutta after that of Malka Jan, is spoken to by Gauhar who describes her as a servant then and afterwards. In this she is supported by Teder Hossain, and a photograph is produced in which as woman alleged to be Assia is represented sitting among the other servants. The most important piece of evidence as to Assia is however, an extract from the corporation register of deaths, where we find the death of Assia recorded. The date is 8th August 1888, but as this is not mentioned by any of the witnesses it is not of much importance, though it seems to suit the rest of the defendant's story. Her age is stated as 70, per medical attendant is Rakhal Babu who has been mentioned as a doctor who attended Bhagloo, her residence is stated to be 39, Lower Chitpore Road, which may easily be a mistake for 49, and the signature, description and residence of the informant is "Bhagloo, Son No. 39". This part of the case is met by a general denial of Assia's existence by the plaintiff, and some of his witnesses, and the woman in the photograph is said to be maid of another name. Were it not for the death certificate I should regard the evidence of the plaintiff and his witnesses as equivalent to that brought forward by the defendant, but as the case stands the corroboration to the defendant's story afforded by the certificate seems to me very strong indeed. Consequently I am of the opinion that the evidence as to Assia goes to overthrow the story told by the plaintiff.

I hold accordingly that the plaintiff is not the son of Malka Jan and decide the first issue against him. Accepting Yeoward's story as I do, I hold that the defendant is the legitimate daughter of Malka Jan and decide the second issue in her favour.

The suit is therefore dismissed with costs.

H.L. Stephen
10-08-1911

Mysore,

24th September 1938.

The Darbar Bakshi,
The Palace,
MYSORE.

Sir,

who is my Ustad

Aftabe-sitar Mr. Barakatullakhan showed me
your letter and also Huzur Secretary Saheb's memo.

You were not pleased to tell me about this de-
dution towards incometax when I was entertained. As
regards the amount that goes to my musicians I regret my
inability to say about it since it varies very much. I
shall be greatful if you could exempt me from this payment; otherwise the deductiona may be made out of my pay
as per rules and I have not the slightest objection.

With respects,
I am,

Yours faithfully,

34, Marsden Street,
Calcutta,
March 6th - 1929

Respected Sir,

I beg first of all to state that there is no other benefactor of mine in this world after God the Almighty and the Holy Prophet, save and except the Maharaja Bahadur of Mysore and your goodself his Vazier.

A new calamity has befallen me, to add to my several misfortunes, and I may be permitted to give you a detailed information of all that has put me to for the trouble inspite of the fact that I have taken refuge at your threshold. Considering the fact that your honour has saved me already from total destruction, I may again place the holy personality of the same Prince Ali Asghar, the beloved child of Imam Hoosain between myself and your honour, requesting you the kind enough as to help me at this juncture.

Last year in the month of May /'28, I was a guest at Gamdevi, Bombay, of Seth Madho Das Gokul Das Pasta. The rent of the house I lived in was paid in the first month by the same Seth and he had also made arrangements on his own account for my boarding etc. The Seth called me his "Sister" and had shown great regards for me. He told me to sign an agreement for the house for six months' residence but for the rent he assured me that he would pay it off himself regularly. Meanwhile I went over to Mysore as I received your telegram. At the time of my departure I inquired from the Seth if I was to pay the rent but he again assured me that he would clear it himself.

After a few months of my stay in Mysore, in October last, I received a court summons from Bombay to which I replied that on account of Dasahra I was unable to attend the court personally. And just after this I wrote several letters to Pasta Seth to settle the matter; but he kept silence.

One day Barkatullah Khan Sahib Aftab; Silair came to me and informed him all about my ——. He introduced me to Mr. Narsimayya, the advocate, and I gave him too necessary information. Mr. Narsimayya wrote a note to the Pleader of the complainant and meanwhile relieved me from my anxieties, saying that the State of Mysore never allowed the enforcement of any foreign decree.

But while I was having my eye-operation at Bangalore an exparte decree had come from Bombay to the Mysore 15th Munsiff's Court from where the attachment of my monthly salary was ordered. The decree was for ₨ 300/- and the half of it was paid from my salary while the other half I paid further from my own pocket.

But again at Calcutta, I was taken with surprise to learn

to learn that another decree for Rs 500/- had come for a second time to the 1st Munsiff's court of Mysore and again the attachment of my salary was enforced; as I got from the Durbar Bakhshi my monthly allowance only in half. Both the decrees now amounted to Rs 1000/-   I am never sorry for the money in this connection but I am astonished to find this enforcement of second decree without any notice or court summons sent to me at any time before this. This was also exparte decree. I am at such a distance from Mysore that I can do nothing myself. The doctor has advised me to take complete rest for a month more.

May I respectfully solicit your favour to be kind enough as to render a helping hand towards my cause and save from all this. There is none to help me after God and the Five holy souls, except the Meharaja Bahadur and your self. If you will help me as you have already helped me, I am sure I shall be relieved from all my troubles.   The Parsi Seth of Bombay being a millionire himself has broken his pledge with me, though I was his guest, for a few hundred rupees Had he told me to pay off the rent I would gladly have settled everything before my coming to Mysore. I had left the key of the house with him.   Your honour fully knows that I have got no other means of support except the State monthly allowance I do hope that your honour will not forget me.

With respectful regards to Bari Begum and your other Begum Sahiba, and love to Sahibzadi Sahiba.

yours obed in P.S.,

Gowhar Jan

To

His Highness The Maharajah of Mysore

Your Highness,

        I beg that you will pardon my presumption in writing to inquire about my Daughter, Madam Gauhar Jan, who was a Singer at Your Highness' Court.

        I beg to State that I, Robert William Yeoward, am living and that I am Madam Gauhar Jan's Father

        On reading the account of my daughter's death in the "Statesman" of the 29.1.30. I, being her Sole living parent, would be very grateful if Your Highness will condescend to order that full particulars be sent to me of her death and also information regards her property and who has taken possession of the Same.

        Thanking Your Highness in Anticipation I beg to Remain Your Highness' Obedient Servant

        W. Yeoward

Mr R. W. Yeoward
H 8 Grand Square
      Dinapore
          Cantt.
31/2/30 —

ಸಂ.
No.

ನಮೂನೆ- 6
Form - 6

ಕರ್ನಾಟಕ ಸರ್ಕಾರ

GOVERNMENT OF KARNATAKA

ಜನನ ಮತ್ತು ಮರಣಗಳ ಮುಖ್ಯ ರಿಜಿಸ್ಟ್ರಾರರು

Chief Registrar of Births and Deaths

ಮರಣ ಪ್ರಮಾಣ ಪತ್ರ

(ಜ.ಮ.ನೋ. ಅಧಿನಿಯಮ,1969ರ 12/17 ನೆಯ ಪ್ರಕರಣ ಹಾಗೂ ಕ.ಜ.ಮ.ನೋ ನಿಯಮಗಳು, 1999ರ ನಿಯಮ 8/13 ರ ಮೇರೆಗೆ ಕೊಡಲಾದ)

DEATH CERTIFICATE

(Issued under Section 12/17 of the RBD Act, 1969 and Rule 8/13 of the KRBD Rules, 1999)

ಈ ಕೆಳಕಂಡ ವಿವರಣೆಯನ್ನು ಕರ್ನಾಟಕ ರಾಜ್ಯದ ____________ಜಿಲ್ಲೆಯ ____________ ತಾಲ್ಲೂಕಿನ ____________(ಗ್ರಾಮ/ಪಟ್ಟಣ)ದ ರಿಜಿಸ್ಟರಿನಲ್ಲಿರುವ ಮರಣ ಸಂಬಂಧವಾದ ಮೂಲ ದಾಖಲೆಯಿಂದ ತೆಗೆದುಕೊಳ್ಳಲಾಗಿದೆಯೆಂದು ಪ್ರಮಾಣೀಕರಿಸಲಾಗಿದೆ.

This is to certify that the following information has been taken from the original record of death which is the register for ......V.W. 20...... (village/town) of ......M.C.C......taluk of ......Mysore......district of Karnataka State.

(1) ಹೆಸರು
Name ...G.ahar Jan

(2) ಲಿಂಗ
Sex ......Female

(3) ಮರಣದ ದಿನಾಂಕ
Date of Death ...17.1.30

(4) ಮರಣದ ಸ್ಥಳ
Place of Death ...K.R. Hospital

(5) ತಾಯಿಯ ಹೆಸರು
Name of Mother ......—......

(6) ತಂದೆಯ/ಗಂಡನ ಹೆಸರು
Name of the Father/Husband......—

(7) ಮರಣದ ಸಮಯದಲ್ಲಿ ಮೃತರ ವಿಳಾಸ
Address of the deceased at the time of death:
.............................—
....
....

(8) ಮೃತರ ಖಾಯಂ ವಿಳಾಸ
Permanent address of the deceased
....
.............................—
....

(9) ನೋಂದಣಿ ಸಂಖ್ಯೆ
Registration No 1559/159

(10) ನೋಂದಣಿ ದಿನಾಂಕ:
Date of Registration 18.1.30

(11) ಷರಾ (ಯಾವುದಾದರೂ ಇದ್ದಲ್ಲಿ)
Remarks(if any) ......—......

(12) ಪ್ರಮಾಣಪತ್ರ ನೀಡಿದ ದಿನಾಂಕ:
Date of issue 21.8.09

(13) ಪ್ರಮಾಣ ಪತ್ರ ಕೊಡುವ ಪ್ರಾಧಿಕಾರಿಯ ಸಹಿ
Signature of the issuing Authority

Registrar of Births & Deaths
Mysore City Corporation
MYSORE

(14) ಪ್ರಮಾಣ ಪತ್ರ ಕೊಡುವ ಪ್ರಾಧಿಕಾರಿಯ ವಿಳಾಸ
Address of the issuing Authority

....

ಮೊಹರು/ Seal

"ಪ್ರತಿಯೊಂದು ಜನನ ಮತ್ತು ಮರಣದ ನೋಂದಣಿಯನ್ನು ಖಚಿತಪಡಿಸಿಕೊಳ್ಳಿ"

"Ensure registration of every birth and death"

ವಹಿಯಲ್ಲಿ ನಮೂದಾದ ರೀತಿಯಲ್ಲಿ ಮರಣದ ಕಾರಣಗಳ ಬಗ್ಗೆ ಬಹಿರಂಗಗೊಳಿಸುವಂತಿಲ್ಲ. ಪ್ರಕರಣ 17/(1)ರ ಪರಂತುಕ ನೋಡಿ.

No disclosure shall be made of particulars regarding the cause of death as entered in the Register. See proviso to Section 17(1).

W. D. No. 2361–7,50,000 ಹಾಳೆಗಳು–ದಿನಾಂಕ 22-11-07–ಸರ್ಕಾರಿ ಹೊರವಲಯ ಮುದ್ರಣಾಲಯ, ಬೆಂಗಳೂರು-59

APPENDIX 3

GAUHAR JAAN'S FAMOUS COMPOSITION
'RAS KE BHARE TORE NAINA':

Arey pathik giridhari sun itni kahiyo ter
Dig jhar layi raadhika ab brij bhoolat pher
Aa ja sanvariya tohe garava laga loo
Ras ke bhare tore nain, saanvariya
Ras ke bhare tore nain
Jehi chitavat tehi bas kari raakhat
Naahi pade maika chain sanvariya
Ras ke bhare tore nain

O traveller, just tell Girdhari (Krishna) when you see him that Radha has run out of tears, When would he come back to Braj?
Come to me Saanvariya (One with dark skin, Krishna), let me embrace you. Your eyes full of elixir.
O Krishna, your image is in my heart and I can find no peace.

APPENDIX 4

SELECTED VERSES FROM
'MAKHZAN-E-ULFAT-E-MALLIKA':
THE TREASURE OF MALKA JAAN'S LOVE

Badi Malka Jaan published her collection of verses on 22 October 1886. The Dewan or collection of her poetry is exquisite and covers a wide range of topics. From spirituality and philosophy to sensuality, unrequited love, pessimism, betrayal and romance, they cover a wide gamut. It reflects the sensitivity of the poetess and the way the experiences of her life had moulded her into a consummate artist and composer of verse. References to Allah and the Holy Prophet, repentance of the sins committed and a sincere plea for pardon throb through the collection.

Besides the ghazals in Urdu, numbering close to 600, the collection also has some of her thumris. Listed below are a couple of them:

1. *Mero Man liyo cheen, akhiyaan raseeli waaki*
   Mori aali woh baanki chitavan, batiyaan karat pyaari pyaari
   Moorakh nipat anaari baat chalat bholi bholi boli tholi ki mag mag thak thak mohe muskaa de
   Dagar chalat nit garava lagaave baari basi, vaako Krishna bhes hum unhi par tan man Malka taj dein.

   His eyes, full of elixir, have captured my mind. Being naïve and immature, I have been swayed away by his sweet talk and make some innocent conversation with him. As we walk the path, he tries to embrace me. But even if this attractive captor is not the original Krishna and an imposter, Malka would still submit her body and mind to him.

2. *Baasuri baaj rahi dhun madhur,*
   Kanhaiyya khelath jaavat hori antar jan
   Jaao sakhi sang Malka woh tho nith
   Khath thak thak ang bori na chori gori.

The sweet sound of the flute is enchanting; the mischievous Krishna enjoys playing Holi. Come along with me my friend, to join this eternal game with the Lord.

3. *Ghar aaye bhor tum mor peer vaapeet tihari nyaari*
   Malka piya to rahe sautan ghar tarap tarap hum rain gujaari.

You have come in the morning, Oh! Krishna! Wearing the elegant crown adorned with a peacock feather. You stayed all night at my step-wife's house, even as Malka suffered the pangs of separation all night.

The Dewan has a series of laudatory messages by people from varied walks of life. They complement the literary beauty of the collection and Malka's expertise at versification. In Urdu poetry, the common practice for people writing laudatory messages is to try and determine the date of the composition through intelligent arrangement of words in a verse, by counting the place value of the alphabets of which, the date is deduced—in this case, the date being Hijri 1303 or AD 1886.

Right from Muhammad Karim Shah, descendant of the Tiger of Mysore Tipu Sultan to rulers of states, contemporary poets, the son of the Deputy Magistrate of Dhaka Maluvi Muhammad 'Shams' of Calcutta to tawaifs of the time like Umrao Jaan, Bibi Naseeran Jaan, Chatta Jaan, Bibi Manjoo Sahiba Yahoodan, Khurshid Jaan, Gunaa Jaan of Darbhanga, Shireen Jaan of Lucknow, Bibi Ajooba Jaan, several eminent persons from across the country have written in praise of the work. Presented below are some of these, starting with the verses written by Gauhar Jaan in praise of her mother's poetry. This also demonstrates Gauhar's command over the Urdu language:

1. *Likhake Malka ne jo chapvaya yeh dilchasp kalaam; Lab-e-haasid pe bhi hai soz-e- tarannum larayeb.*

   The collection of poems that Malka Jaan has published is so interesting and splendid that even on the lips of those who are jealous of her there is undoubtedly praise for the pain in the melody.

2. *Fikr taareekh ki jab hone lagegi Gauhar, Rang laayegi bahut mauj-e-tabassum laarayeb.*

   When one is consumed with worries about the exact date of the composition of these verses, there is undoubtedly a colourful smile on one's lips.

3. *Na milega kahin taareekh ka koson jo patha; Honge us raah mein sab hosh-va-khirad gum laarayeb.*

   But there is no indication of the date even if one traverses long distances. But without doubt, if one traverses the path taken by Malka, they would forget their agonies.

4. *Nuktaacheen banke phiregi jo tamannayein dili; Maahir-e-ilm-o-hunar samjhenge har dam laarayeb.*

   When our heart's desires themselves become critics, this would be considered right by the experts of the art.

5. *Band ho jaayenge haatif ki nidaa ke lab bhi; Hain zabaan daani mein woh sheereen-e-takallum laarayeb.*

   The pleading tones of Haatif (arch angel Gabriel, who is also considered a source of creativity) too are silenced by this exquisite collection of Malka Jaan. Undoubtedly her verses are filled with such sweetness.

Maharaja Padmanada Singh Sahab Bahaddur, ruler of the state of Baneli, Kharagpur in the district of Bhagalpur writes:

Mukarrir hai yeh deewan-e-murassa
Gul-e-ummeed baag-e-fikr-e-naadir
Makaula sach hai yeh haatif ka 'afsar'
Tarakki kar rahe akhlaak-e-shaayar.

This splendid collection of poems is studded with such exquisite gems. It is a rare garden where the flowers of hope are in full bloom. I commend the composer of such rare talents and I wish that the literary skills and virtues of the poetess increase with every passing day.

Sahib-e-Diwan Maharaj Yuvaraj Birbar Thakur Harkishan Singh Bahaddur, the ruler of the Kishankot State in Punjab writes a lengthy praise in chaste Persian!

Mir 'Asghar' Ali Lucknowi, pupil of Nawab Gulshanuddaulah Bahaddur writes:

Gul-e-majmoon tarah tarah ke hain;
Yeh chaman doston ke khaatir hai,
Hai yeh misra-e-saal, Aei 'Asghar'
Fikr-e-Malka ki khoob nadir hai.

The Dewan of Malka Jaan has such exquisite flowers of varied hues. This garden of poems has been created by her for her friends. If anyone needs to know the date of the composition, Asghar recommends the following verse- *Fikr Malka ki khoob nadir* (the verse means she has presented rare poems and the place value of the alphabets adds to hijri 1303.)

Among the others who have written similar verses of praise are eminent poets like Hazrath Shams Lucknowi, Munshi Yaqoob Sahab 'Asar' of Oudh, Hafiz Ali 'Najaf' (a disciple of Dagh Dehlvi), Raghunath Sahai 'Ibrat' of Azimabad in Patna, Munshi Abdussamad 'Qasir' Banarasi (disciple of the Mughal Sahibe Aalam bahaddur), Ghulam Haidar Khan 'Muztar' and others.

Writing about the verses, the publisher Mahomed Wazeer of Ripon Press, Calcutta, states:

Bandish mein khoobiyaan hain maani mein shookhiyaan hain;
Kyun na ho is sukhun ke ahl-e-kamaal taalib?
Magloob banke haatif bola 'Wazeer' mujhse
Hai rang-e-shaayari mein Malka ka rang ghaalib.

This composition is full of such splendid literary values; its meanings are attractive and full of depth. Why will it not attract admirers from among the masters of the art?

Captured by the meaning of the Dewan of Malka, Hatif himself ordered Wazeer to bring this collection out in print. After all the colours of the poetry of Malka are akin to those of the renowned Ghalib. (Or Malka's poetry has an upperhand among the contemporary literary works.)

Given below is a collection of some selected Urdu poems of Badi Malka Jaan covering a wide range of themes:

1. *Banaya Haamilaane arsh ne maidan nabuwwat ka;*
    Bichaya aks zaat-e-haq ne usmein farsh kudrat ka.

    When the Leader of the Skies, the Almighty, decided to send His Last Prophet to this world, He decided to send someone who was a reflection of His own image. Thus in His own holy persona, He dispatched the Holy Prophet Muhammad to this world.

2. *Hue juzwe badan sab paak seele ashq-e-furqat se;*
    Ke aalam abr-e- rahmat ka hua chashmaane ummath ka.

    Every particle of this Prophet's body was washed in the holy stream of the Almighty's grace. The Prophet was then sent as a symbol of His grace and mercy to the world, so that His followers could get a new vision.

3. *Ajab hikmath se khaake laamakaan bunyaad mein daali;*
    Banaya jab khuda ke qasd ne aiwaan risaalath ka.

    When the Almighty made up His mind to dispatch His Prophet to the world, He used the choicest ingredients to create such a Messenger. The Prophet was made unbounded by time and space and was created for the whole world as a symbol of His Mercy.

4. *Nigaah-e-lutf se Malka ki jaanib aap agar dekhein;*
    Rahe nazzaara phir mohtaaj kyun chashm-e-inaayat ka.

    If such an epitome of mercy and forgiveness casts a glance on Malka, all her sins would be washed away and she would be blessed. She would no longer depend on any one else's grace thereafter.

5. *Woh tho gardan par churi phera kiye;*
    Main shahadat ke maze chakha kiye.

    Even as my assassin moves his knife menacingly on my throat
    I enjoy suffering martyrdom at the hands of my beloved.

6. *Lakho lahadein aa gayi thokar ke mukaabil;*
    Is par bhi maseehayi ka daawa nahin hota.

    There have been several dispirited and dejected souls whom I have
    revived through the balm of love. I have brought back hopes in the
    lives of many.
    But never did I ever claim to be a messiah who brings the dead back
    to life.

7. *Dekhakar tegh-e-sitam yeh badduwa deta hoon main;*
    Noor mit jaaye ilaahi deedaye saiyyaad ka.

    (Speaking on behalf of the captured bird that looks on at her captor
    from the cage.) Seeing the sword of atrocities that my captor is using
    to torment me,
    All I can do is curse that the evil captor loses the light of his eyes.

8. *Duzdeeda nigahon se na agyaar ko dekho;*
    Khulta hai dhaka rehne do parda mere dil ka.

    Don't look at strangers with such piteous eyes
    The long concealed secrets of the heart would be revealed by this.

9. *Sar khole hue saath tamanna ki hain foujein;*
    Kis dhoom se uthata hai janaaza mere dil ka.

    The armies of my desires would attack me with such ferocity
    That there is little doubt that my coffin would be taken out in great style.

10. *Meri tarah bechain karega tujhe zaalim;*
    Gar zikr teri bazm mein aaya mere dil ka.

    In a gathering when you happen to hear the sad plight of my heart
    I am certain that you would become as restless as I have been in your
    absence

11. *Ummeed roti hi thi aarzoo bhi rooth gayi;*
    Jo hamne dil pe kabhi jabr ikhtiyaar kiya.

    No wish of mine gets fulfilled; there is no hope to look forward to
    As a result my mind has become barren and hopeless ever since I
    forcibly suppressed it and made it accept the inevitable.

12. *Shobadaabaaz abhi dast-e-dua ban jaaye;*
    Gar nikale nikalti asar ki soorat.

    A prayer that has emanated from the depths of the heart with all
    sincerity gets answered
    How could a trickster's pretensions of worship be ever rewarded?

13. *Dil nikal aayega pehloo se mere teer na kheench;*
    Rooh-e-berabth tu marg-e-guloogeer na kheench.

    Do not remove the arrows that you have fired on my arms. The pain
    that you have been inflicting on me is something that I have got
    accustomed to. I now wish to end my life in the same agony and if I
    am denied even the pain that I have got so used to now, what would
    happen to me?

14. *Mujhe shaam-e-wislath ki ummeed hogi;*
    Dikhaye jo muh Subh-e-roushan kisi ka.

    Seeing his bright face early in the morning
    Lights up hopes in my heart of our union by night.

15. *Tera naas ho jaaye aei subhe peeri;*
    Dhala jaata hai haai joban kisi ka.

    Addressing the 'morning' that has been occurring for ages with the rise
    of the sun each day, the poetess says: Oh! You old and infirm morning!
    I curse you to destruction since you have not shown me my beloved's
    face. I wait for him for so long even as my youth fades away.

16. *Do vaar mein Malka nazar aaya naya aalam;*
    Dam bhar bhi na khanjar se sitamgar ke ladi chot.

Portraying a weak and submissive nature, largely due to the sufferings she faced, the poetess says: Two blows were sufficient to kill Malka. The wound could not put up a fight, even for a moment, against the atrocities of the enemy. The victim had no fear of her death as the agony of the living world had made her indifferent to both life and death.

17. *Naamaabar se poochte hain leke khat bashauk woh;*
    Kya shab-e-taareeq furqat ka afsaana mizaaj.

    My beloved receives the letter I sent through the messenger with great anxiety and asks him: What was her condition in the dark and miserable night of separation?

18. *Gair thokar se sataate hain nishaan-e-turbat;*
    Jo na hota tha sitam mujh pe hua mere baad.

    Wasn't it sufficient for my enemies who troubled me all my life with their atrocities? The tortures they failed to inflict on me while I was alive, they try to fulfill upon my death. I am not given peace even in my tomb where my enemies come and kick my tombstone.

19. *Gar fase dafn rahenge yu hi aahon ke hujoom;*
    Sham-a-baalee ne lahad hogi khafa mere baad.

    I fear whether my moans would continue in my tomb, long after I am buried. If that happens the lamp lit beside my final resting place would be in a precarious condition. Each lament is like a blow of wind that would threaten the lamp's existence. Let the crowds assembling on my tomb also not grieve and moan for me.

20. *Malka sitam maut ka dekh ke ghabrayi;*
    Jeene pe sahib kare khaak na insaan ghamand kare.

    The most resplendent of lives meet their end in the silence of the grave. Malka is rattled by the spectacle of death. But she rationalizes it as the ultimate and unescapable truth. Every well meaning human being must realise this eventuality and not be puffed up with pride over earthly accomplishments and possessions.

21. *Soz-e-jigar ka aapne likha tha haal usmein;*
    Aei naamaabar na hota kyun sholaabaar kaagaz.

Oh! Messenger! Don't be startled by the sight of my letter which has volcanoes of fire emitting from it. My letter is just a frank representation of my condition and my agonies make my letter appear so fiery. Either this could burn the letter that carries this piteous message or break the heart of the one who reads it.

22. *Unko yakeen jazbe muhabbat pe kuch na tha;*
    Kaayal hue hain aah ki taaseer dekh kar.

He did not have faith in the sentiments of love that I had towards him. But my laments and moans seem to have convinced him about the depth of my emotion.

23. *Yusuf azeeze misr zulekha kaneez ho;*
    Hairaan hoon main husn ki tauqeer dekh kar.

The beautiful Queen of Egypt Zuleikha had willfully become the slave of the handsome Yousuf, with whom she was madly in love. In a tongue-in-cheek remark based on this historical episode, Malka says she is surprised to see the disrespect of beauty in this case!

24. *Paasbaan hain deedaye laila ilaahi khair ho;*
    Kais ka saaya khada hai pardaye mehmil ke paas.

Love is a two-sided relationship. Quoting from the story of the legendary lovers Laila and Majnu, Malka says that while Majnu risked his life and tried to get as close to Laila who was in her howdah surrounded by his enemies, her sight too kept a protective cover of him all the time.

25. *Sakhtiyaan ki zauf ki shiddat ne itni hijr mein;*
    Saans lene se bhi aajiz hai kaleja dil ke paas.

The separation from my loved one has inflicted innumerable torments on my heart. The hardships that I have faced due to this are uncountable. They have left me weak and exhausted to even take a breath.

26. *Dekha phir gair ko duzdeeda nazar se usne;*
    Teri taaseer hui aahe sharar baar galat.

    All your moans and agonies had no impact on him. It only led him
    to cast piteous glances on strangers and thereby took him farther away
    from you.

27. *Naaz se chalti hai ruk ruk ke gale par waqt-e-qatl;*
    Tere qatil ko nahin hai chashm-e-bismil ka lihaaz.

    My assassin is an unsympathetic soul. He runs his knife slowly on my
    throat so that I undergo the maximum pain and agony. Even my pleading
    looks and entreaties to be saved are met with cold indifference.

28. *Aaina hangaama aaraaish hai kyun pesh-e-nazar;*
    Hai nigahein shauq ko gar va baatil ka lihaaz.

    For those who are perceptive external make-up is never misleading.
    How much ever one might try to conceal one's true nature, they don't
    fail to catch the attention of a perceptive eye that can easily spot and
    identify such falsehood.

29. *Subah shabe firaq ne yeh loot maar ki;*
    Ujada hua pada hai woh dekho dayaare shamaa.

    The long night of separation from my beloved has destroyed me
    completely. If you need any proofs, just have a look at the lamp that
    has been burning there all night. Like me, it has burnt all night, in
    anticipation of his arrival and symbolizes the ruins of that painful
    night.

30. *Aankhon se khoon rulayega darde nihaan zaroor;*
    Lillaah dekhiye na dil daagdaar shamaa.

    The sorrow concealed in my heart manifests itself in the form of the
    tears of blood that I shed from my eyes. For God's sake, if you really
    want to know the true condition of my heart, please look at the lamp
    that has been burning for a long time. Like my heart, it has been on fire
    for long and shedding silent tears of agony, will get extinguished soon.

31. *Bahaar-e-fasl-e-gul mein gar riha kar de tho behtar hai;*
    Qafas se baad-e-mausam go kiya aazaad kya haasil.

    Addressing the captor as a bird caught in his cage, the poetess says:
    If at all you intend to release me from your clutches, please do so in
    the season of spring so that I could enjoy the beauty of the flowers in
    full bloom. What is the use of releasing me once spring is over?

32. *Teri kismet mein dozakh hai nahin tu laayak-e-jannat;*
    Banaane se tujhe baagh-e-iram shaddaad kya haasil.

    Oh evil man! You do not deserve the gardens of Paradise. Like the
    mythological villainous character of Shaddaad who created his imaginary
    heaven known as baagh-e-iram, you might try hard to create an imaginary
    heaven for yourself. But all your efforts would go in vain as you do
    not deserve to enjoy there.

33. *Kisne behboodi buthon se paai hai;*
    Dil lagaye khaak in patthar se hum.

    To hell with loving idols made of stone (in this case meaning a lover
    whose heart is as hard as stone). Has anyone benefitted ever by reposing
    their trust and love in an idol made of stone?

34. *Aap aaye mujhe sehat hai kuch aazaar nahin;*
    Jisko eesa ki ho khwaish yeh woh beemar nahin.

    My illness doesn't require a Christ to come and cure me; separation
    from you is the cause of my illness. Now that you are here, my ill-
    health has vanished too!

35. *Motariz nazm pe meri na ho arabaabe sakhun;*
    Malka isme saleeka mujhe zinhaar nahin.

    All the eminent litterateurs and poets who are present in this gathering!
    Please do not criticize my verses. I do not know the art of writing
    poetry that suits or pleases others. All I do is pour out the angst of
    my heart through my poems; the technicalities of correct poetry are
    unknown to me.

36. *Lazzate qatl jo hai dil mein mere aei qatil;*
    Haan gale se teri shamsheer laga loon tho kahoon.

    Oh assassin! I have no regrets in getting killed at your hands. But before you kill me, let me touch the sword with which you plan to end my life. Hugging it tightly will make me feel that I am embracing you and that temporary happiness would be sufficient to happily submit myself to the tyranny of your sword.

37. *Dil sad chaak pe aei jaane jahaan furqat mein;*
    Kya guzarti hai zara hosh mein aa loon tho kahoon.

    I have been numbed to a state of unconsciousness by the sorrow of separation from you. I can tell you the state of my heart only when I get back to my senses.

38. *Bahana ishq ka hai rashk se parvaane jalte hain;*
    Jo dekha shamaa ko saabit kadam hai sar kataane mein.

    We often think the fireflies are in love with the fire that they hover around and end their lives for their beloved. But in reality, the ability of the fire to burn itself to death creates jealousy in the fireflies and they too end their lives, by burning themselves not in the fire of love, but that of jealousy.

39. *Nahin maaloom kyun gaarat woh karte hain mere dil ko;*
    Buthon ko fayda kya hai khuda ka ghar giraane mein.

    I do not know what pleasure he gets in breaking my heart this way? What do idols (those with hearts of stone) gain by breaking a heart which is an abode of God?

40. *Kabhi tum ashiqon ko maarte ho, ghar jalaate ho;*
    Buthon tum dakhal dete ho khuda ke kaarkhaane mein.

    Oh idol! Why do you interfere in the workshop of God by killing lovers and burning down their houses? Love is a natural emotion and a handiwork of God, so why does your heartless stone interfere with it?

41. *Abhi dast-e-hinaayi dekhiye kya rang laati hai;*
    Hazaron pis gaye paamaal hai mehendi lagaane mein.

    Having applied mehendi (hennah) on my hands I now wait to see
    how they colour my hand. However to prepare this hennah how many
    leaves had to be ground. I wonder if their sacrifices will bear fruit in
    the golden colour that it would impart to my hands or the sacrifices
    would all go in vain.

42. *Abhi naam-e-khuda aagaaz-e-shauk-e-katl aashiq hai;*
    Hazaaron sar tasadduq ho gaye tegh aazmaane mein.

    The actual sacrifice is yet to begin and the assassin is testing the edge of
    his sword on a stone. But the victim's prayers to the Almighty and his
    submission of himself to the assassin's designs, indicate his willingness
    to be sacrificed.

43. *Chain se soye qayamat tak na kuchh khatka raha;*
    Jab kiya ae maut humne apna bistar khaak mein.

    As long as a person is alive, despite lying down on the most comfortable
    of beds, there are numerous complaints, worries and anxieties. But
    death brings in all the comfort that one craves for when alive. Once a
    person is laid to rest in the grave, despite it being uneven and rough,
    it bestows eternal peace to the one who is laid in it.

44. *Na shahadat ka nishaan paayein farishte baad-e-katl;*
    Dafn kar dena hamare saath khanjar khaak mein.

    Here the poetess shows compassion and forgiveness to her assassin too,
    thereby displaying her true love and magnanimity. She says that once
    she is killed, the dagger that was used by the assassin to end her life,
    be buried with her; so that the Messengers of God who would come
    investigating her death, do not get the proof of the crime.

45. *Noor-e-eemaan se jhuki aankhein farishte chal diye;*
    Yaad thi jo sooraye bal fazr azbar khaak mein.

    After I am laid to rest in my grave, the messengers of God came to
    decide my fate based on my actions when alive. But the minute they

saw the glow of absolute faith in the Maker on my face, they left the place with no further questions. Here the poetess alludes to her firm belief that God Almighty has forgiven her for her sins and her steadfast faith in Him has sailed her through.

46. *Mere hone ne mujhe ruswaa kiya;*
    Main na hota to kuch nahin hota.

Had I not been born at all, I would neither have had to face all the miseries of life nor would I have been disgraced this way. What loss would it be for anyone had I not taken birth at all?

47. *Dil ke lene pe hai aamaada woh buth ae Malka;*
    Koi naala sar-e-baazaar karoon ya na karoon.

Whether I mourn and proclaim in public about the snatching away of my heart by the insensitive lover or not, he is bent upon inflicting misery on me.

48. *Mai hai mashooq hai gulzaar hai saaqi bhi hai;*
    Garajein aise mein jo badal woh mazaa dete hain.

There is alcohol, the beautiful garden and an atmosphere totally conducive for romance. To top it all if thunder strikes and it pours heavily, what an ambience would be created! Wouldn't our union be natural in that case?

49. *Chaunk padte hain, shab-e-wisl adoo kehte hain;*
    Kiske naale hain yeh gustaakh jaga dete hain.

When I spend sleepless nights shedding tears and moaning in the pain of separation from my beloved, my enemies angrily exclaim—who is this mannerless person who is wailing in the middle of the night and ruining our sleep?

50. *Hasrath aalood nigaahon se aseeraane kafas;*
    Do ijaazat to nazar jaanib-e-sayyaad karein.

The captive birds desire to look at the captor with pleading eyes. They hope that this would melt his heart and he would free them from the cage.

51. *Maasiyat ka jo main paaband hua bhool gaye;*
    Aap hain ahl-e-karam apna karam yaad karein.

Seeing me commit sin after sin, mistake after mistake; you have forsaken me. Else, you were always a compassionate soul who was ever forgiving and caring. How I wish you forgive me again and accept me!

52. *Phir kisse hum kahein shab-e-gham dil ka iztaraab;*
    Teer-e-khayale yaar bhi dard aashna nahin.

There is none who would understand the plight of my heart. Even the memories of the past seem to be my enemies as they shoot such arrows on my heart by reminding me of those days. Whom do I confide in about my sorrows?

53. *Woh bazm-e-gair mein ho hai iska kya ilaaj;*
    Waade mere wafa na ho iska gila nahin.

I can bear his treachery and his lack of commitment towards the promises he made to me. But what would break my heart is to see him in the mehfils or gatherings of others. (I can not tolerate his taking interest in some other woman.)

54. *Aei mah-visho na husn pe itaraao is qadar;*
    Bas nisf shab ki chandni samjho shabaab ko.

Oh you young beauties! Don't pride yourselves on your good looks and youth. Youth is after all like moonlight. It fades away in time. So arrogance over something temporary is foolish.

55. *Khat aate ki kalaf sa chadha roo-e-yaar par;*
    Ab mohtaab kehna pada aaftaab ko.

Just as the letter of the beloved arrived, her face was covered with an inexplicable glow. Her moon-like face started shining like the sun as her joy knew no bounds.

56. *Hum bakhoobi yaad hain farhaad ko;*
    Woh nahin bhoola abhi ustaad ko.

Talking about her own expertise in the field of love, the poetess says she is far more skilled and experienced in love than the legendary lover Farhaad who made supreme sacrifices for his lady-love Shirin. So much so that even Farhaad considers the poetess as his ustad or teacher!

57. *Tere kooche se nikalne nahin deti jo jafa;*
    Hazrat-e-khijr bhi aaye mujhe behkaane ko.

My footsteps involuntarily lead me to the streets where you live. This despite me knowing about your treacherous nature and the advice of well-wishers to avoid going there.

58. *Katl par woh mere khanjar na uthayenge kabhi;*
    Kuchh murawwat bhi hai kuchh paas-e-nazaakat bhi hai.

My beloved is not so hard-hearted to make plans of assassinating me. After all there is some compassion and emotion in his heart too!

59. *Ashkon se taaza rakhte hain daagon ka gulsitaan;*
    Mohtaaj hum kabhi nahin abr-e-bahaar ke.

I am not sad about the absence of the cool breeze of spring in my life or the barrenness of my heart. The troubles I have faced in life have become indelible marks on my heart. These stains are the gardens of my heart which are not dependent on the breeze of spring. (I have accepted my destiny and instead of complaining, I feel happy with whatever circumstance I am in.)

60. *Ab jeetejee to uthate nahin unke dar se hum;*
    Aei charkh mar ke nikalenge hum kooche se yaar ke.

Oh heavens! Let it be known to you that I am going to languish in the streets of my beloved till my last breath. It is only death that can take me away from his vicinity.

61. *Pehloo se mere darr ke woh uthakar chale gaye;*
    Kurbaan apne naalaye beikhtiyaar ke.

The unfaithful beloved heard the involuntary moans of my heart for him. Instead of consoling me, he just walked away in fright. I am grateful to those moans for helping me distinguish the faithful from the treacherous.

62. *Tha zafaakaar koi tum se na badhkar koi;*
    Par giraanbare wafa tha koi hum se pehle.

None in the world could be as treacherous and unfaithful as you are!
None in the world could also bear the burden of treachery in the manner as I have.

63. *Haaye aei umr jawaani mein dikhaayi peeri;*
    Wisl ki raat kati subh-e-aalam se pehle.

I pity my youth! It has transformed into old age waiting endlessly for the beloved to come. This painful night of separation has no hope at day-break as it brings no message of his return.

64. *Malka ab aata hai tauba ka zamaana nazdeek;*
    Wisl ke lutf uda leejiye apni kasam se pehle.

Oh! Malka! Your days are numbered and your end is nearing. Enjoy the indulgences of the world soon so that you can take an oath to abstain from sin thereafter and atone for the acts of omission committed by you all your life.

65. *Us jangajon ka dil na paseeja yeh kahar hai;*
    Afsaane soz-e-hijr ke laakhon sunaa chuke.

I narrated to him the tale of my entire life, its agonies and miseries. I thought he would understand and comfort me. But he was as insensitive as the rest and like an able warrior shot further arrows on my wounded heart and hurt me all the more.

66. *Zumbishe paa ko hawas koochaye sayyaad ki hai;*
    Yeh bhi yak taaza dil-e-naashaad ki hai.

Unwittingly my steps lead me to the streets of the captor. My agony ridden heart seems to lead me to union with the same person who has inflicted the greatest tortures on me.

67. *Jo raazdaaron ke muh khul gaye ghazab hoga;*
    Zabaan ko rok le aei badzabaan khuda ke liye.

    Having heard the entire story of my life, keep silent oh! Loose-tongued souls! If you narrate my tale to others, I will be ruined totally. So let it all remain a secret!

68. *Bhoole bhatke jo meri kabr pe aa nikle ho;*
    Naaz ki kehti to do haath uthaate jaate.

    Oh stranger who has sauntered around to my grave by mistake, do realise that in the grave no one is big or small and the one inside needs your prayers. So why don't you just pray for my soul at my grave, though you did not come there looking for me?

References and Bibliography

English

1. Bakhle, Janaki, 2005, *Two Men and Music: Nationalism in the Making of an Indian Classical Tradition*, Permanent Black, New Delhi.
2. Bor, Joep and Kai Reschke, 1992, *Masters of Raga*, Haus der Kulturen der Welt, Berlin.
3. Chakravorty, Pallabi, 2008, *Bells of Change: Kathak Dance, Women and Modernity in India*, Seagull books, Calcutta.
4. Chaudhuri, Sukanta, 1990, *Calcutta: The Living City: Vol I: The Past*, Oxford University Press, New Delhi.
5. Dasgupta, Amlan (edited), 2007, *Music and Modernity – North Indian Classical Music in an Age of Mechanical Reproduction*, Thema, Kolkata.
6. ———.2005, *Women of India: Colonial and Post Colonial Periods and Colonial Politics*, Edited by Bharati Ray, Sage Publications.
7. Devi, Savita and Vibha. S. Chauhan, 2000, *Maa Siddheshwari*, Roli books, New Delhi.
8. Eck, Diana, 1998, *Benares: City of Light*, Columbia University Press.
9. Farrell, Gerry, 1997, reprinted 2004, *Indian Music and the West*, published in the US by Oxford University Press Inc, New York.
10. Fox-Strangways, 1914, *The Music of Hindustan*, South Asia Books.
11. Gaisberg, Frederick William, 1947, *Music on Record*, Northumberland Press, London
12. ———.1943, *Music Goes Round*, Arno Press, New York
13. Ganguly, Rita, 1995, *Banaras and Bismillah Khan*, Siddhi Books.
14. ———. Ganguly, Rita, 2008, *Ae Muhabbat: Reminiscing Begum Akhtar*, Stellar Publishers, New Delhi.

15. Gayathri, J.V. and R.K. Raju, 1993, *Selections from the Records of the Mysore Palace: Vol I: Musicians, Actors and Artists*, Divisional Archives Office Publication, Mysore.

16. Gangopadhyay, Sunil, 2000, *Those Days*, Penguin Books India, New Delhi.

17. Gupta, Charu, 2005, *Sexuality, Obscenity, Community: Women, Muslims, and the Hindu Public in Colonial India*, Permanent Black, New Delhi.

18. Kersenboom, Saskia C., 1987, *Nityasumangali – Devadasi Tradition in South India*, Motilal Banarsidas Publishers Private Limited, New Delhi.

19. Kidwai, Saleem, 2002, *Song Sung True: A Memoir*, Zubaan, New Delhi.

20. Kinnear, Michael S., 1994, *The Gramophone Company's First Indian Recordings, 1899-1908*, Popular Prakashan, Bombay.

21. Manuel, Peter, 1989, *Thumri in Historical and Stylistic Perspectives*, Motilal Banarsidas Publishers Private Limited, New Delhi.

22. McMunn, G. 1931, *The Underworld of India*, Jarrolds, London.

23. Mehta, R.C, 2007, *Eminent Musicians of Yesteryears: Short Bios of 766 Hindustani Musicians*, SRM and SHIKM Trust, Baroda.

24. Menon, Indira, *The Madras Quartet*, Roli books, New Delhi.

25. Misra, Susheela, 1990, *Some Immortals of Hindustani Music*, Harman Publishing House, New Delhi.

26. Moore, J.N., 1976. *A Voice in Time: The Gramophone of Fred Gaisberg 1873-1951*, Hamilton, London.

27. Moorhouse, Geoffery, 1994, *Calcutta: The City Revealed*, Penguin Books Ltd., New Delhi.

28. Narasimhan, Sakuntala, 2006, *The Splendour of Rampur-Sahaswan Gharana*, Veenapani Centre for Arts, Bangalore.

29. Neuman, Daniel, 1990, *The Life of Music in North India: The Organization of an Artistic Tradition*, University of Chicago Press, Chicago.

30. Nevile, Pran, 2009, *Nautch Girls of the Raj*, Penguin books, New Delhi

31. ———. 2004, *Stories from the Raj: Sahibs, Memsahibs and Others*, Indialog Publications, New Delhi.

32. Oldenburg, Veena Talwar, 1990, *The Making of Colonial Lucknow: 1856-77*, Oxford University Press.

33. Ruswa, Mirza Muhammad Hadi, translated by David Matthews, *Umrao Jan Ada*, Rupa & Co, New Delhi.

34. Sharer, Abdul Halim, 1896, *Lucknow: The Last Phase of an Oriental Culture*, Oxford University Press.

35. Sampath, Vikram, 2008, *Splendours of Royal Mysore: The Untold Story of the Wodeyars*, Rupa & Co, New Delhi.

36. Vedavalli, M.B., 1992, *Mysore as a Seat of Music*, CBH Publications, Trivandrum.

Hindi

36. Garg, Lakshminarayan, 1957, *Hamare Sangeet Ratna – Part I*, Sangeet Karyalaya, Hathras.

37. Habibullah, Jahan Ara, *Zindagi ki Yaadein: Riyasat Rampur ka Nawabi Daur*, Oxford University Press, Karachi.

38. Nagar, Amritlal, 2001, *Yeh Kothewaliyaan*, Lokbharati Prakashan, Allahabad.

39. Rani, 2005, Dr. Sandhya, *Uttar Pradesh ke Rohilkhand Kshetra ki Sangeeth Parampara – Ek Vivechanatmak Adhyayan*, Rampur Raza Library.

40. Shukla, Shatrughna, 1983, *Thumri ki Utpatti, Vikas aur Shailiyan*, Delhi University, Delhi.

Bengali

41. Bandopadhyay, Debojit, *Beshya Shongeeth, Baiji Shongeeth*, Subornorekha Publications, Calcutta.

42. Chakrobarthy, Somnath, *Kolkata Baiji Bilas*, Bookland Private limited, Calcutta.

43. Chitragupta, 1994, *Gauhar Jaan*, Sashadhar Prakashani, Calcutta.

44. Gangopadhyay, Arddhendra Kumar, 1969, *Bharater Shilpo-o-amar Katha*, A. Mukherjee and Co. Private Ltd., Calcutta.

45. Sanyal, Amiyanath, *Smritir Atalay.*

46. Sengupta, Dr. Bandhan, *Indubala*, Mousumi Prakashani, Calcutta.

47. Simha, Umanath, 1983, *Gandharva Kanya Gaohar Jaan.*

Urdu

48. Jaan, Badi Malka, 1886, *Makhzan-e-Ulfat-e-Mallika*, published by Mahommed Wazeer for Ripon Press, Calcutta.
49. Shadani, Asghar Ali, *Ahwal-e-riyasat-e-Rampur*, Rampur Raza Library.

Kannada

50. Kavale, Vasanta, 1976, *Nadayatra,* Karnataka Sahitya Parishat, Bangalore.

Tamil

51. *Gandharva Kalpavalli*, published in 1912.

Marathi

52. Chandvankar, Dr. Suresh, 2007, *Poorvasureenche Soor,* Swanandi Prakashan, Pune.
53. Tembe, Govinda Sadashiva, *Majha Sangeeth Vyasanga*, Kirloskarwadi, Kirloskar Press.

Journals

54. 'Thumri as Feminine Voice' in the *Economic and Political Weekly*, 28 April 1990, Dr. Vidya Rao.
55. ISTAR Newsletter, April to June 1984, Joep Bor's quotes from Mr F.W. Gaisberg and from Indian Music Journal, Mysore. (1912)
56. Prof D.P.Mukherjee's AIR Talk dated 7 September 1952, published in the Indian Listener, entitled 'Music and musicians'.
57. Newsletters of the Society of Indian Records Collectors. Specifically Volume 9 of *The Record News*, January 1993, for 'The discography of Late Miss Gauhar Jaan of Calcutta', pg 21. Edited by Dr. Suresh Chandvankar.
58. Joshi, G N, 1988, 'A Concise History of the Phonograph Industry in India', 'Popular music', 7:147-56.
59. 'Sangeet Sanga-o-prasanga' by Kumar Deba Prasad Garg of Mahishadal, *Desh* Magazine Binodon Sankhya, (1388 Bengali Year) – passages related to Gauhar Jaan and her photo-sketch by author.

60. *Kheyali* Bengali journal dated 17 January 1931 – satirical verse on the case in Mysore post-Gauhar Jaan's death; another satire titled 'Chief-Gauhar Jaan Samvaad'.

Newspaper reports/articles

61. 'The Darling songstress' by Batuk Diwan, *The Independent*, 18 January 1993

62. 'My name is Gauhar Jaan' by Suresh Chandvankar, 15 December 2002, *Loksatta*.

63. 'First dancing girl, Calcutta' by Suresh Chandvankar, 15 November 2002, *Indian Express*.

64. 'My name is Gauhar Jaan' by Shanta Serbjeet Singh, 10 July 1995, *The Hindustan Times*.

65. 'Dancing into Oblivion' by Meenakshi Subramanian, 11 January 1998, *The Telegraph*.

66. 'The tale of Gauhar Jaan' by Shalini Sharma, 13 August 1997, *Evening News*.

67. 'The Mallika-i-tarannum of the 19th Century' by Sahil Brelvi, 26 May 1996, *The Statesman*.

68. 'Thumri ke Mahan Kalakar' by Sri Bhairav Prasad Misra in AJ dated 15 August 1958.

69. 'Thumri Braj ki Makhan Mishri' by Dr. Trilokinath Brajwal, 12 June 1988, *Dharmayug*.

70. 'The Importance of being Gauhar Jaan' by Pran Nevile, 26 May 2002, *The Tribune*.

71. 'Gauhar Jan in Madras' by S. Muthiah, 14 January 2008, *The Hindu*.

72. 'Making musical waves' by Deepa Ganesh, 3 February 2003, *The Hindu*.

73. 'Melodies on Record' by Pran Nevile, 13 April 2008, *The Tribune*.

74. 'Rebuilding a 100 years of priceless recordings' 17 September 2006, *The Indian Express*.

75. 'Our Masters' Voices' – Album lined up to mark 100 years of recording by Subhro Saha, 1 November 2002, *The Telegraph*.

76. Paper on 'Amrit Keshav Nayak: Actor (1877-1907)' by Harish Trivedi, 2007.

Original documents/unpublished sources

77. Divisional Archives of Mysore, Box No 16, Avasarada Hobli, 1930-34, file no 9 of 1930-34, Sl. 296.
78. Divisional Archives of Mysore, AH 1930, Sl. 297, file no 10 of 1930-40.
79. National Archives of India, New Delhi – Newspaper reports of the United Provinces from 1910-12—for the United Provinces Exhibition and the protest letters thereafter.
80. Statesman Archives, Kolkata, for the Obituary column of Madam Gauhar Jaan, dated 28th January 1930.
81. Documents of the High Court of Calcutta:
    a. Suit No 92 of 1910: Shaik Bhagloo of 49, Lower Chitpore Road, Calcutta by G.N. Dutta & Co. – vs. – Gauhar Jan of 49, Lower Chitpore Road, Calcutta by G.C.Chunder & Co.
    b. Suit No 946 of 1911: Gauhar Jaan Vs Sheikh Bhagloo
    c. Suit No 678 of 1916, Gauhar Jan of 46, Free School Street, at present residing at Rowalpindi in Punjab; by O.C. Ganguly vs. Syed Gholam Abbas Sabzwari, lately residing at 46, Free School Street, but at present at 49, Lower Chitpore Road by C.C. Bosu.
82. Document of the Court of the Munsiff in Benares:
    a. Suit No 545 of 1889: Makhan Lall Vs. Gowhar Jan
83. EMI Music Archives, Hayes, England. Correspondence on India 1902-7 and publicity catalogues 1902-10.

Index

Song list on CD

1. *Hai Gokul ghar ke chora – Khayal*—Raag Multani
2. *Itna joban da maan na kariye* – Khayal—Raag Bhupali
3. *Krishna madho ram niranjan* – Khyal—Raag Malkauns
4. *Aan baan jiya mein laagi* – Dadra—Raag Ghara
5. *Piya kar ghar dekho dhadkat*—Raag Desh
6. *Mere dard-e-jigar ki khabar na li*—Dadra, Raag Jhinjhoti
7. *Maika piya bina kachu na suhaave*—Sohini Thumri
8. *Alwar ke kanhaiya holi khele* – Hori—Raag Sindh kafi
9. *Aayi kaari badariya* – Kajri—Raag Tilak Kamod
10. *Pyaari pyaari mori jiya mein basi*—Raag Kedar
11. *Tan man ki bisar gayi* – Thumri—Raag Pahadi Jhinjhith
12. *Jaao sakhi piya ko le aao*—Raag Sindh Kaafi
13. *Shyam re mori baiyyan gaho naa*—Raag Soruth
14. *Gaari doongi chhaila*—Raag Dhani
15. *Ambuwaki daali thale* – Dadra—Raag Sarang
16. *Pardesi saiyyan neha lagake* – Dadra—Raag Pahadi
17. *Khelan ko hari radhe sang holi* – Holi charchar—Raag Desh
18. *Shyam sundar ki–thumri–titala*—Raag Khamach
19. *Kaisi yeh dhoom machayi* – Holi kaafi jat—Raag Kafi
20. *Jaao jaao mose na bolo* – Dadra—Raag Pahadi Jhinjhit
21. *Mere hazrat ne madeene mein manaayi holi*—Ghazal
22. *Jo piya aaye naa, mose saha jaaye na*—Raag Khambag Jogia.
23. *Rasule khuda bansiwala hai*—Raag Bhairavi
24. *Raske bhare tore nain* – Thumri—Raag Bhairavi
25. *Rasili matwaliyon me jaadoo dala*—Raag Bhairavi